I0846842

Contents

VOLUME 1
SECOND TO THE RIGHT

Wendybird

JOY M WILDAY

Copyright © 2025 by Joy M. Wilday

ISBN: 979-8-218-83251-3

All rights reserved.

No part of this publication may be reproduced, distributed, or transmitted in any form or by any means, including photocopying, recording, or other electronic or mechanical methods, without the prior written permission of the publisher, except as permitted by U.S. copyright law.

The story, all names, characters, and incidents portrayed in this production are fictitious. No identification with actual persons (living or deceased), places, buildings, and products is intended or should be inferred.

Series: Second to the Right

Book Cover and illustrations created with Canva Pro by Joy M. Wilday

Title Page: Wendy character art by Dave – Instagram @davecantchoosename

1st edition 2025

VOLUME 1
SECOND TO THE RIGHT

Wendybird

JOY M WILDAY

Copyright © 2025 by Joy M. Wilday

ISBN: 979-8-218-83251-3

All rights reserved.

No part of this publication may be reproduced, distributed, or transmitted in any form or by any means, including photocopying, recording, or other electronic or mechanical methods, without the prior written permission of the publisher, except as permitted by U.S. copyright law.

The story, all names, characters, and incidents portrayed in this production are fictitious. No identification with actual persons (living or deceased), places, buildings, and products is intended or should be inferred.

Series: Second to the Right

Book Cover and illustrations created with Canva Pro by Joy M. Wilday

Title Page: Wendy character art by Dave – Instagram @davecantchoosename

1st edition 2025

To the storytellers
who see color in the
grey, hear music in
the silence, and
create light for those
in darkness.

"Your life is an occasion. Rise to it."
-Mr. Edward Magorium

"To live will be an awfully big adventure."
-J. M. Barrie

N
W E
S
Neverland
Moat Brae
Neverpeak Mountains
Winter Woods
Neverwood
Kidd Creek
Silvermist
Kirriemuir

Prologue

"*Neverland, a place where dreams are born, time never planned, and one can leap onto the wind's back and away you go.*"

I'm told this phrase embodies the enchantment that once colored our world. However, those days have long since passed, and I hold no recollection of them. Five years ago, I awoke to an eerie silence. My mind was empty—no memories to ground me, everything cleared away. Only one thing remains, and it was given to me. *My name is Wendy.*

Part One

The Fragmented

Chapter 1

everland 1936

N A hush fills the home as darkness paints the sky. I settle in, darning a faded lavender dress—torn at the waist, with frayed lacing along the hem. A silver thread in hand, I loop the needle in and out of the soft fabric, bringing it back to life. Once finished, it will look fresh as a flower blossom on one of the sweet young girls in our neighborhood. In the background, Al Bowlly's voice drifts through the record player, and I hum along, pausing for a sip of steamy black tea, the toasty warmth spreading through my chilled fingers.

Peter is seated across from me in the dining room, at one of the twin mahogany tables set end to end across the floral maroon carpet. Above us, two golden chandeliers dangle, their tulip-shaped shades casting a soft glow over the room. It's an oddly quiet night in the Children's Home, with the others tucked away, lost in the stack of new books. Morgan was like Father Christmas as she and her friend Rose carried the boxes in and unloaded the colorful novels.

A blast of wind slams against the windows, cutting into my calm, and I glance over as a sheet of snow pelts the front of the house. During the first year, such a sight would have mesmerized me, but now it only irritates, as it drowns out the song. When the wind eventually dies down, I breathe easier and return to work.

Clink. Clink. Clink.

I release a silent growl. Peter's lost in thought, pen tapping mindlessly against the table.

Well, it *was* a peaceful night.

I glance his way, and soften. His head bobs, shoulders shimmying as he croons along with Al Bowlly, singing about being happy as a king. That's Peter. Though we're around the same age and bear the same curse that stole our past, we couldn't be more different. He's a hopeful optimist, content in a world I find unbearably constraining.

"What are you working on?" I ask.

"A letter," he says, not looking up.

I press forward, squinting at the paper. "And why would you need to write to someone?"

"Job application."

"Really? Outside Winter Woods?"

"Of course not." He drops his pen, and gazes up, a sparkle in his sea-green eyes. "How would I ever get a job outside of this town?"

"I don't know." My shoulders lift. "But you'll never know unless you try."

He gives me a long stare. "You're losing it, Bird. Only one of us has a handsome boyfriend ready to swoop in and carrying her out."

I giggle, leaning back to take a sip of tea. "Are you jealous, Peter? Perhaps James would help you find work elsewhere, if you asked nicely."

"Go begging to James? No thanks."

"So then what?" I carefully add the final stitches to the base of the dress. "You'll live here forever? Grow old with Slightly and Tootles."

"Wouldn't that be the dream." He taps the pen again. "No, I'll get a job in town, and make the most of things. Maybe meet a nice girl, one who's not so judgy, and settle down to a happy, cold life."

"You're peculiar. I can't imagine giving up. There's a whole world beyond the gate."

The radio hums with a new song, the melody matching my melancholy mood.

"Look Wendy, I get it. You've never truly felt at home here. But I'm different. This place, it's not only a cage, you know? It's family. Even if I found a way out, I'd be leaving you all behind."

"How touching." I press a hand to my heart in an exaggerated gesture. "And also a little idiotic."

The wind rattles the windows, and he gazes toward the darkened glass. "No, what's idiotic is prioritizing escape over integrity."

"Am I supposed to understand what that means?" I snip the silver thread, and examine my work.

"It means you're nearly nineteen, ready to fly—but at what cost?"

"Name the price and I'll pay it," I offer cheekily.

He runs a hand through his honey-colored hair. "Trust me, I already knew that."

Rising, he tucks the pen behind his ear muttering to himself, "*Then, we'll be nothing more than shadows...*"

He looks back at me, sliding the letter into his pocket. "Well, I'm off to cards with John and Michael." He tips an invisible hat to me and heads to the parlor.

"Wait a tick." I straighten. "What did you just say?"

"I'll be in the parlour with the boys?" He glances over his shoulder. "Join us when you're done."

Once alone, I replay what I heard: '*nothing more than shadows.*' A knot forms in my stomach. Those words are eerily similar to ones I penned in my journal, the reason still fresh in my mind.

It was a year ago. I was at Mullin's General Store when two girls from Neverpeak Hills caught my attention. One had a sun-kissed face, a true rarity in this place. She recounted a recent trip while trying on jewelry. I lingered at the counter, waiting for a restock of dry goods, while she boasted of her month-long escape to a place called Moat Brae. She swam in clear waters and basked in warm sunlight on sandy beaches, free of the cold for a blissful thirty days.

I stood there, mesmerized, as she explained how her father was being promoted out of Winter Woods, and soon, she'd be gone for good. In Winter Woods, the social divide is stark: those from the glorious Neverpeak Hills versus the weary sprawl of Neverwood Valley. Escaping this blasted safe haven? That's rare, even for the pampered lot from the Hills. Vacations? For the wealthiest, sure. But no one steps beyond the gates without written permission. It's a privilege granted for only a few and for reasons most will never have.

Where I live, the Children's Home sits somewhere in the middle. Not scraping the bottom of the can for supper, but also not being served dinner by a horde of bow-tied staff. And the truth we've all known since the beginning is there will never be a reason for any of us to leave this town. Peter is unfortunately correct, we might as well settle in and get comfy.

Leaving the store that afternoon, I walked home with the girls' conversation lingering. It stirred the question I couldn't shake since I first woke in the town: *Will I ever escape this place?* My only hope appeared mere minutes later, in the form of James' sleek black sedan, crawling to a stop beside me.

James was our savior—the one who found us, fourteen children and Nibs, unconscious in the burning wreck of Dumfries. Why were we there? Were our parents among the slain? No one ever knew.

James told me the only other survivor lived just long enough to provide our names, but died of smoke inhalation before she could say anything more.

I awoke in the Home to chaos. Screams and cries. No one able to make sense of things with our memories stripped away. Morgan and Llewelyn, our first Keepers, did their best to calm us, but it was useless. A fear beyond understanding settled deep inside each of us. Even now, the memory leaves me uneasy.

Our haven, Winter Woods, remains the safest of them all, pressed against the impassable Neverpeak Mountains. There's soldiers, lofty fences, and a gate guarding us. Yet with the attackers still at large, we are trapped here. Indefinitely.

How lucky for us...

That day, when the car window rolled down and James glanced out at me, a spark lit in my spirit. He's the son of Neverland's Lord Regent, Thomas. From the beginning, he was my first glimmer of light, not distant, but close enough to touch. That evening, with determination seeping through every stroke of the pen, I wrote—perhaps a bit melo-dramatically: *"James will be my savior once more, I will ensure it at all costs. Then, this place, will fade away, like the shadows at the start of my life."*

Could Peter have read what I wrote that night?

I misplaced my journal yesterday, so it's certainly possible. Blast. I swear if he took it... My gaze wanders to the sideboard—his brown bag still sits there. I have to check. Pressing back from the table, I mosey over, and double-checking that I'm alone, lift the bag, humming under my breath as I walk it back.

What if I'm wrong and I'm rummaging through his personal stuff?

I fold my hands beneath my chin, focused on the bag, torn between need-to-know and conscience. Should I put it back? Mind my own business? But the thought that he might have stolen my diary, and read my private musings...

I have no choice.

I pull back the flap—*blast*. My ruby-red journal rests beneath his pan flute. Call me Nancy Drew, because this mystery is regrettably solved. Fingers trembling, I lift the thick, leather-bound book and open to the first page:

They say my name is Wendy, though I wouldn't know if this were true.

It seems only yesterday I wrote these words—yet not only these. Thousands more, day by day, year by year, each page weaving together a story, and that story is me.

The melodious record goes fuzzy in my ears, and I grip the chair for balance as his green socks appear. Peter's wide eyes dart between me and the book.

"Forgot my bag," he says, cheeks glowing red—like the baked apples from dessert. "I see you found it."

My words are slow and measured. "How much did you read?"

"Just one entry."

A swell of emotion roars to the surface. I steady myself, soft breaths to maintain composure.

"It was on the table, and I flipped it open to see what it was," he continues. "I was going to return it, but I figured you'd assume the worst. So, thought I'd return it without you knowing."

My vision blurs as I clutch the chair tighter. "Which entry?"

He sighs. "What does it matter?"

"It matters to me." My voice tightens as our eyes lock. "Tell me, which entry?"

"You already know. Why do you think I said what I did about integrity?" He steps closer, too close. "You can't be thinking this way. When Margaret died, she begged me to keep you from doing this exact thing."

My calm rapidly vanishes. How dare he bring Margaret into this. I swallow hard and glare into his resolute face. "And what thing is that?"

He lets out a breathy laugh. "I think you know, Bird. Selling yourself to the highest bidder."

His words settle deep in my chest, like poison. Insults, implications, and worst of all, betrayal.

Something in me breaks.

It happens so fast—I'm barely aware of myself as the journal strikes his face, his head snapping sideways. He staggers back, body arcing with the blow.

I lift the book again, emotion surging hot through me, but he catches himself, fingers clamping around my wrist, halting me mid-strike.

"Let me go!" I cry.

"You're funny." He wipes the back of his hand across his bleeding lip. "Now, drop the book, and we'll call a truce."

Try as I might to yank free, his grip holds firm, the pressure burning against my skin with each tug.

"Alright, have it your way!" I fling the book down.

He howls, releasing me and hopping back, clutching his toes.

"Dammit, Bird." He scowls. "That's not what I meant."

"I'm not too interested in what you meant."

From the hallway, footsteps echo along the stairwell until JaneAnn appears, dark hair flying as she sprints in, stopping short at the sight of us. "Well, hello. What sweet moment am I interrupting?"

"Just a friendly chat, Jan," Peter says, gently touching his face.

"What he said." I lift the journal and sweep auburn hair from my face.

"Is that so?" She folds her arms, not attempting to hide her amusement. "Well, remind me to avoid friendly chats with either of you. Wendy, not to disturb this chummy moment, but James' car pulled up. Thought you might want to know."

"You're kidding me!" I deflate, not wanting to explain what's happened to James. "Can you please gather my stuff? I should change."

"Sure, but you owe me."

"Clean up the dummy while you're at it," I call as I hurry to the stairs.

Racing to the second floor, I spot Llewelyn, dressed in work overalls, spreading white paint smoothly across the wooden door frame of the girls' room. There's no avoiding him, so I take a deep breath as I draw near.

"*Good evening, my girl,*" he signs, setting the brush aside.

Out of our four Keepers, who act as caretakers in the home, he's the most fatherly. And though he's unable to speak, he communicates through sign language and taught us to understand it.

"Good evening." I step into his line of sight, shoulders sagging.

"*What's wrong?*" he signs, brows furrowed.

There's no sense in lying to him, he's seen worse. "I hit Peter." My grip tightens around the worn book. "He read my journal."

He nods and leans against the wall, wiping his paint-smeared hands on a work rag. "*And did it help?*"

"Of course not." I run my thumb along the crinkling pages. "Just an impulse."

He gives me a knowing look and signs, "*Come here.*"

I fold into him—no words needed. Even if I wanted to avoid him, I couldn't because my heart wouldn't let me; he's my refuge in this confusing world.

The front door creaks open below, and I pull away, reluctant to let go, but also delighted for James' return.

"I have to go; James is here!"

He pats my shoulder and gestures me forward. Rising onto my toes, I kiss his bearded cheek. "I love you."

His lips lift, the corners of his eyes crinkling. "*And I love you.*"

James wears a striking knee-length crimson coat over his tall, broad-shouldered frame. He stands near the parlour fire, hands outstretched towards its golden flame, snowflakes melting into the fabric as the heat wraps around him. I descend the last few stairs, the soft tap of my heels giving me away, and he turns, lifting his calming periwinkle blue eyes to mine. My breath catches, his gaze sends a shiver straight through me.

"Hello again," he says, the distance closing between us.

"Hello," I say, tone silvery.

He wraps his arms around me, and my fingers glide into his thick, wavy black hair.

"It's grown so long," I say.

"Do you approve? Because your opinion is the only one I value."

"Completely. You are *very* handsome. Though you already knew my opinion."

The door flings open, and a cold burst of wind sweeps through the room as Nibs enters, forcing it shut behind him. He turns to us, pressing a hand to his chest.

"James, I didn't expect you till morning."

"My apologies. The second my ship docked, I escaped." He looks at me, a soft smile touching his mouth. "I couldn't stay away a second longer. Though I'm bound for a verbal lashing from Mother, because she expected me for dinner."

"Of course." Nibs nods, tossing his coat onto the hook. "Well, since you're here, shall I retrieve the receipts so you can ensure everything's in order, or wait till morning?"

"Better do it tonight. Bring Morgan along, too."

"Certainly. I'll be back in a moment," Nibs says, disappearing up the stairs.

Gliding to the door beside the stairwell, James unlocks it, ushering us into his two-room apartment. He doesn't live with us, but as the proprietor of the home, he sometimes stays here, with the apartment arranged for such visits.

I settle on the satin chaise while he kneels beside the marble fireplace, arranging the wood. The room holds the scent of the leatherbound books lining one wall of his rich mahogany shelves. Books have always been a kind of transport for me, out of this town and into lush, flowering meadows; or swimming in cool, crystal water beneath a blazing sun. It's a momentary reprieve, but still not the real thing.

James strikes a match, an orange flame flickering to life. He's been the morning sun in my midnight world ever since I awoke that fateful day. I was fourteen; he, sixteen.

"Good evening," James greets Morgan and Nibs as they enter.

Nibs strolls my way, brown hair slicked back, a grin spread wide. He's the only Keeper touched by the curse. Some days, he's all easy charm, confidently debonair; on others, a shadow I know too well clings to him. He and Morgan, both only in their early twenties, shoulder the impossible task of guiding us hollow orphans, toward some semblance of self, despite having nothing to ground us.

"Hey, kid, that's quite the dress," he says.

"What, this old thing?" I wink.

He snickers and meanders past, surveying the fire crackling in the hearth. "I think you're quicker than I am now."

"I *was* your teacher." James chuckles. "It didn't do for me to be the slower one." He glances at Morgan. "A pleasure to see you, Morgan."

"Hello, James," she says warmly.

Her silky black hair is pinned back neatly, a few loose strands framing her pale face. There were times early on, I feared competition over James, but soon understood her heart was only for Nibs. But, alas, with Nibs also irreparably broken, I wonder if he's comprehended the extent of her feelings.

"Forgive me," James says, hand to his heart, "It's been a long day. Would you please make me that drink you did last visit. I've tried conjuring it up myself, but it was never quite right."

"This is why you pulled me away from grading papers?" She strides to the wall-mounted bar and lifts an empty glass. "Cherry and all?"

"Yes, please." He rubs his hands together.

She offers him a mischievous grin. "You bet." Uncorking a bottle of whiskey, she tips it into the glass.

"Thank you, thank you." He looks at me. "Will you be alright for a few minutes?"

"I've got nowhere to be. Take your time."

"Wonderful. Nibs, come along. This'll only take a moment."

The men disappear into the adjoining room while Morgan finishes the drink. "Want something too?" She peers over her shoulder.

"Oh no." I pat my stomach. "I had double portions of dessert, I'm stuffed. But, hey, I saw your painting, it's incredible!"

"Not sure why I hadn't painted it sooner. It's about time we had some scenery in the classroom."

"A picture of the sea is a welcome sight. Helps imagine it."

"It's from memory. The town I grew up in." She wipes her hands on her skirt, her piercing sapphire eyes analyzing me.

As the home's only female Keeper and teacher, she watches over us like a mother hen guarding her chicks. "Well, don't stay up too late." She wags a finger at me. "I recall laughter echoing out of here way past midnight last visit."

"I don't know what you're talking about." I hold out my hand, examining my nails.

"Of course you don't. I'll see you in the morning."

"Night." I giggle and lean back, gaze wandering the intricate stenciling weaving around the crystal chandelier. This space belongs to James. But he's often told me it's ours—a safe place within my small world.

He's not an exceptionally social person and often prefers hiding away together. But I don't mind. I'm starting to see it's not this room that's safe; it's me.

"Next visit, I'll bring you a box of these cigars," James says as the men return, heading for the door.

"Please do." Nibs releases a puff of smoke, a thick cigar between his fingers.

"Goodnight, Nibs." I wave.

"Night, kid."

James closes the door, retrieves his drink from the bar, and sits beside me, one arm extending along the top of the chaise.

"That guy is something else," he says, taking a sip. "Did I mention you look enchanting tonight?" His head inclines toward me.

I tap my chin, inching closer. "No, I don't think so."

"Well, you do. I've been gone a long time, during which, I've had a lot of time to think."

"And what did you think about?"

"You. Me. The future." He stares into the golden liquid in his glass.

"And am I a part of that future..." I glide my fingers along his arm, settling them against the rise of his muscle.

"Do you want to be?" He looks at me.

"Yes. I do."

"Good."

I have to suppress a squeal as I say, "Now, tell me, where did the great Captain James sail away to?"

Breathing out, he recounts his three-month voyage aboard the *Jolly Roger*, his beloved ship. This expedition was unlike any before it—sailing far beyond Neverland. His tale appears like a story in my mind, as I imagine what such worlds must be like.

"I wish I could go with you," I say, as he concludes, the desire like a constant itch I fear I'll never scratch.

"And you will. I swear it. Someday soon, too. You'll stand at the bow of my ship, sea mist spraying your face, wind caressing your hair." He lifts a strand of my auburn locks, twirling it lightly. "And it'll be a journey we'll never forget."

"As always, I'll hold you to that promise," I say, wishing he'd carry me off right now. But no—propriety and safety, he insists. And after years of *someday* soon, I can't help but wonder: are they reasons or excuses? Will someday ever arrive?

"For now, I'd like to take you out for your birthday."

"What kind of *out* are we talking about?"

"Well..." He rubs the back of his neck. "Out on the town. A date, to be exact. It's about time, don't you think."

"A date?" I'm seeing stars. "With me?"

"Who else? Yes, you. What do you say?"

My spirit lifts. "I say yes."

He lifts my hand toward his mouth, but stops short, brows drawing together.

"What's the matter?" I ask.

He gently turns my wrist, revealing faint marks left by Peter's grip. "What happened?"

Of course...

"Peter and I had a spat," I explain. "It was nothing. Childish, really."

"Childish?" A muscle twitches in his jaw. "Nothing about this is child-ish."

"Look, he was just defending himself." I draw back, tension gripping my chest. "Just drop it, please."

Running a hand across his face, he rises, walking to the bar to set his cup down. "I'll talk with Juke..."

"No, you're not!" I stand and stride to his side. Juke is our fourth and final Keeper. Close in age to Morgan and Nibs, but opposite in spirit. His role is to protect—what a joke. The only thing he protects is his own nerves. "Look, I hit Peter, okay? He grabbed me to protect himself, that's all. It's over now."

"Relax." His fingers wrap around mine. "A quick talk, ensure it doesn't happen again. I don't like returning to find you bruised."

He guides me to the door, and as I open my mouth to protest, he presses a finger to my lips. "Appease me, okay?"

I let out a low, strangled groan and swing open the door, marching to the stairwell. The house is quiet, everyone off to bed. He races after me.

"Don't be mad." He tugs me into his arms and offers a pathetic smile.

"You're not being fair. This isn't what it looks like."

"Or you're just too kind to cast blame." He runs a finger across my cheek.

"You're impossible." My foot stomps.

"For you, gladly." His eyes darken with something unspoken.

I hesitate, ready to pull away, but something in his gaze holds me. "What are you staring at?"

"My future." His voice is thick as honey.

For a second, I see myself standing at the gate, watching it rise.

The room fades as the distance between us closes. I'm not quite sure what's happening, but it's overdue, whatever it is. His expression softens, hesitant, and his fingers lift to my neck.

Then our mouths meet.

Unexpected emotions rises in me. His lips are warm and taste of whiskey and cherries. I've never done this before, and I imagine I'm shrinking in size as he grabs me around the back, holding tight.

Are we in love? Is that what this is? Nails digging clumsily into the skin around his neck, I kiss back.

Then—an abrupt bang pierces the air, shattering the moment.

My eyes close for a breath. I don't want to leave this moment. Whatever it is. My hands remain at his neck, heat rushing through me, something like power budding within.

It's James who pulls back first. "What was that?"

"No clue." I murmur. "Bad timing, though, huh?"

"Indeed." He rubs his face, exhaling slowly.

"Well then." I suppress a laugh and press a hand to my chest, attempting to dampen the wildfire. "How shall I sleep now?"

"With dreams of us." He guides me to the stairwell, nudging me up. "Join me for breakfast in the morning, okay?"

"*Okay*." I take a step, then pause, he's frowning. "What's wrong?"

He shakes his head and plants one final kiss on my hand before letting go. "You've got me dizzy, that's all."

"And I hope to again. Goodnight, James."

Ascending the stairs, my mind spins as I touch my mouth, recalling the sensation of his moments ago. At the top, I'm ready to curl into bed with passionate dreams of him and me—until a voice cuts through the darkness.

"Well, that was nauseating."

Chapter 2

I step off the stairwell, gripped by a dark silhouette leaning against the balcony, overlooking where James and I shared our unexpected embrace.

"Who is that?" Heat prickles up my neck.

"It's your punching bag." Peter steps out of the shadows, an ice pack pressed to his cheek. "What's wrong, sweetheart? You seem a little uneasy."

"You're unbelievable." My fists clench. "That was private!"

"Was it?" His brows rise. "Because I could swear you two left his office while I was here icing my face."

He glances at my hands and chuckles. "You ready for round two, Bird? If you don't mind, could you aim for the other side? Even it out a bit?"

"You're not worth my energy."

"No, I suppose not." He rests against the railing again. "The codfish probably depleted it. Boy...that was some kiss. So, does he know your nickname for him?"

I huff and press into the railing, mortified by his bird's-eye view of the hallway.

"Oh, come on. What is it? My *way?*" He points at me. "*Out.* The correct answer is *out.* Poor guy's being conned, and he doesn't even know it."

"We're finished here." I turn toward the girls' room, the scent of Llewelyn's fresh paint still lingering in the air.

"I understand self-interest," he says, "but this is low, even for you."

"I'm not conning him." I whirl around, ready to fulfill his wish of bruising the other cheek. "I'm pursuing what's best for me. And someday, when it's too late, you'll realize you should have done the same."

"Have you considered that some things aren't worth losing yourself over?" He hisses the words.

"Where's this *self* you speak of?" I step closer, nostrils flaring. "Don't you understand? We're not real."

My voice drops low, meeting his gaze head-on, our intensity matched. "We woke one day and were given names. How do you know you're really Peter and I'm really Wendy? Cause a piece of paper said so? I was cheated out of my life once, and I won't be again."

"I wasn't wrong, was I? You really are determined to sell yourself to the highest bidder."

My rage bursts and I shove him backward. "You have no idea what you're talking about!"

He shakes his head, a bitter curve to his lips. "Hit me all you want. I just happen to think you're worth more than hitching yourself to the first man who can open the gate for you."

Without another word, he turns and strides to the boys' room, the door thudding shut behind.

I glare after him, every muscle coiled with fury. I'm glad he's getting a job and I hope he leaves with it. Entering my room, I force thoughts of James back in. His kiss, his promises, anything to shove Peter out of my mind where I hope he disappears.

When morning dawns, the familiar tune of our local songbird wakes me. Propping onto my elbows, I admire his beauty. He shakes away the snow clinging to his rich scarlet feathers and leaps gracefully into the air—flying out of sight.

"Good morning!" Hannah bounces onto the end of my bed.

"Morning." I cover my mouth, yawning. "You're certainly cheerful today."

"Can't say the same about you." Elizabeth smirks, deftly twisting her golden locks into a braid by the wardrobe mirror.

"I could use another hour." I blink in the sunshine streaming through the windows, spilling onto the row of neat white beds with their soft blue blankets. On the mantel, a vase of red roses catches the light, a small card propped against its glass.

"How about I prepare your hair?" Hannah offers, scooting closer.

"Sure, why not? Where did the flowers come from?" I nod toward the mantel.

Agnes lifts the card and walks it over. "These were left for you at the door." She holds out the note.

"Oh?" I take the envelope and, while Hannah begins work on my hair, unfold the note, and read:

Wendy,

I expected to enjoy a day together, but Mother called, insisting I return home. She was livid I missed last night as she had someone for me to meet. Unable to avoid this obligation, I must go. You have my word, I'll be back for your birthday outing.

Till we meet again,

—James

"Everything okay?" Agnes asks, watching me.

"Yeah." I fold the note. "James had to leave unexpectedly. He was letting me know."

My thumb smooths the paper, and I reread the line, *'unable to avoid this obligation'*. Was that really all it was? Or had something shifted in him after our embrace?

"I'm sorry," Elizabeth says, pushing my thoughts aside. "I know you were excited to see him."

"He says he'll be back," Hannah chimes in.

"Hannah!" I turn to her. "Did you read over my shoulder?"

Her cheeks blaze scarlet. "A little... I'm sorry!"

"Well, in the future, I'd appreciate it if you didn't. These letters are private."

Her eyes dart around, and she whispers, "*They* made me do it."

I shoot a look at Agnes. "Oh, they did, did they? That's the *real* reason you offered to do my hair, isn't it?" I slip off the bed and meander to my wardrobe. "Gave you the perfect view for when Agnes handed me the note."

"Can't blame us for wondering," Elizabeth says, applying a red tint to her lips.

"Sure can't." I sift through a line of dresses. "But now I know better than to read around you three in the future."

I pull out a yellow day dress and change into it. Despite James' departure, our kiss has me walking on sunshine.

We saunter to the stairwell, and Agnes presses a hand to her stomach. "Gee—you know it's Mam's day for cooking when it smells like this."

"Indeed, you do," John exclaims, rushing past with Michael on his heels.

"Good morning!" Michael waves, bounding down the stairs two at a time.

"Morning." I press against the railing, "Hey, leave some for the rest of us, will you?"

"I apologize, but I'll make no guarantees at this time," John shouts over his shoulder.

The dining room bustles with morning energy as we cross to our table. And out of the corner of my eye, I catch subtle glances exchanged between the Twins: Jack and Alexander, and Agnes and Elizabeth. Not long ago, these boys were yanking our braids and chasing us with tear-inducing insects. Now, that mischievous spirit has vanished into the past, replaced with slicked-back hair and confident grins.

At least, for them, it has. Slightly and Tootles will still gladly slip a bug into our tea when we're not looking.

While the girls settle in for breakfast, I wander into the cozy, cream-colored kitchen, suppressing a giggle. The sink overflows with dishes, and the table is buried beneath a layer of flour, sugar, and who knows what else. Huddled by the cast-iron stove, JaneAnn and Maimie are deep in conversation, flipping flapjacks and dodging sprays of bacon grease.

"Good morning," I greet, walking to the table.

JaneAnn twists around and points a finger at me. "You have some explaining to do."

"What are you talking about?" I ask, startled by her tone.

"Juke and Peter disappeared last night!" Maimie blurts.

"Will you *be quiet*?" JaneAnn prods her side.

I grip the back of the chair. "How do you know this?"

"I overheard Nibs this morning," Maimie says. "He said Peter wasn't acting right."

"Like he was slipped a dose." JaneAnn raises a brow.

"Poisoned?" I clutch the golden chain around my wrist, a source of comfort since the beginning of this brief life. "But why?"

"That's something I assumed you would know," JaneAnn says. "Nibs took a fist to the face when he tried to intervene. And after Juke and Peter left, James told him not to worry about it."

The world tilts, and I collapse into the chair.

"*Wendy?*" JaneAnn's grey eyes zero in on me. "Tell us."

"It's my fault." I cover my face.

They sit beside me, elbows on the table as I tell them about the journal and James' reaction. "He swore it would only be a talk." I shake my head.

"Yeah, well, if Juke's involved, we know his fists do all the talking for him," JaneAnn mutters.

The frosted windows glisten with sunlight, but the cheer is gone. Despair rolls in like a thick shadow at dusk.

There's no way this is going to end well.

Exhaustion washes over me as heavy as the guilt curling within. I've tried to distract myself, pretend it wasn't my fault, but I couldn't convince myself for even a moment.

I carry a basket of folded laundry up the stairwell, the house eerily silent. No one feels up to late-night cards or talking, not since Peter disappeared three days ago. Juke never aligned with his Keeper role, but his behavior was, at the very least, predictable. After a night of cards, you avoid him unless he's whistling. If he sleeps late, he's often hungover. If he's flexing his fingers, he's hungry.

This is new. Unexpected. And terrifying.

I pause at the landing, Peter's accusations springing to mind. Despite my anger, I never meant for this to happen. And of course, James left before I could demand Peter's return, leaving us with no answers.

Nibs searches for him daily, yet always returns distraught. He doesn't say it, but I know he fears the worst, same as me. This is my fault, and that thought leaves a lingering tension in my chest.

I tread softly into my room, settling the basket by the wardrobes before changing into my nightgown. It's late, and moonlight streams across my bed as I slip under the covers. Every night is a long, restless night.

Shadows float overhead, a passing car on the road. The soft crunch of tires vanish as quick as it came. I sigh, fingers drumming against my chest. A door creaks, and floorboards shift as someone moves in the hall. Likely a boy using the bathroom. Oh well...

This is normal, sleep evading me as I toss and turn, trying to think of anything other than Peter, dead somewhere out there.

An hour passes. I exhale for the umpteenth time, role onto my side, and fluff my pillow.

Why is it so scratchy?

"You have to settle down," JaneAnn whispers from the bed beside mine.

"I'm trying." I slam onto the pillow.

"Look." She leans closer. "I get it, you're worried, guilty, whatever. But since Tuesday, you've been driving me up the wall, tossing, turning, groaning like an animal. There's nothing you can do right now, so please, for Pete's sake, go to sleep. I promise, tomorrow, we'll come up with a plan."

"Yeah, whatever. Sorry."

"Don't be sorry, just relax. You didn't do this to him. There's no need to beat yourself up every night."

I grip the sheets, twisting them between my fingers. "It's easy to say, harder to believe. Especially with his bed empty another night."

"He's resilient. Have a little faith. Now, get some sleep."

I flip onto my back, a wave of exhaustion washing over me as I tilt my head, watching the flames dance wildly in the hearth. Thoughts drift to the story I read today. Lancelot locked away in Maleagant's castle. My lids grow heavy, images beginning to take shape: Juke as Maleagant and Peter as Lancelot. As my eyes close, I become the fair maiden, slipping into the tower and rescuing him.

Sleep begins to press in, but before it takes over, something sharp and powerful yanks me from the edge of dreaming.

I'm flying, the sensation exhilarating.

Enormous snowflakes drift lazily past, the icy air biting at my skin. Below lies a charming village square, an evergreen erected proudly at its center, adorned with hundreds of twinkling lights. Sounds of merriment fill the night air as crowds bustle between shops, their faces lit by the golden warmth spilling onto the streets.

I drift toward a quaint Avenue marked sixth. The lively hum of village life fades as rows of unassuming cottages emerge. Smoke wafts softly from the chimneys into the starlit sky, and beyond the homes looms a deteriorating warehouse, rising from the shadows. Its shingles dangle precariously, with multiple windows boarded over.

Gliding around the building, I squint through the darkness until I see it and lower onto a windowsill. A brief glimpse at my reflection and it all makes sense. I'm a Faerie! I lean in closer, yet something beyond the glass catches my attention.

A body—stretched out and bloody.

I lift off the sill and fly into the room, expanding as I settle onto the icy floor. Body trembling, I crouch beside the empty hearth, tossing in a golden powder, igniting a blazing fire that lights up the room. I crave the heat, but a groan has me on my feet. It's a young man, badly wounded. I kneel and carefully roll him onto his back, another moan escapes him. Guiding his shirt up, I shudder at the blue and red bruising running along the length of his chest. His face is barely recognizable, with crimson blood painting his features, yet I know it's him. And that means, it's time!

I crack my neck and wrap my hands around his forehead, a golden light creeping out of my palms. His body twitches—eyes flash open, and a scream rips from his throat, deep and guttural.

I don't have time to react as I bolt upright, muscles tight, sweat pouring down my face.

Peter!

This isn't a dream. And I know exactly where he is.

Without delay, I slip from the bed, shivering as my feet hit the cold floor. I kneel at the laundry basket and lift out a pair of pants and a heavy sweater. I'm going to need them for what I'm about to do.

I creep to the stairwell and tiptoe up to the third floor. Approaching Nibs' door, I lift my hand but hesitate.

This is a terrible idea.

Yet I can't do it alone, can I? Peter needs us. Flexing my fingers, I knock.

Please wake up, Nibs.

Thump. Thump. Thump.

I whirl around. Someone's on the stairwell, and only one person makes such a clamor. Juke.

Nibs hasn't answered and if I knock again it'll alert Juke to my presence.

Blast.

Juke's drunken humming echoes through the hall.

With time running out, I grab the doorknob, turn it, and slip inside. The door clicks shut as his footsteps draw near. I slowly step away, holding my breath.

"Um, hello? Can I help you?" Nibs asks from behind.

I turn, body stiff. He's tying a robe around himself, face shadowed by the fire in the hearth.

"Wendy? What are you doing here, kid?"

Raising a trembling finger to my lips, I point toward the door. Juke has arrived. We listen as something clatters to the floor, and he curses. A knob jiggles and finally, slam—his door shuts, floorboards quivering beneath us.

I collapse onto the couch, drained. "That was too close."

"What's going on? If he had caught you... Do you need Morgan? She's just down the hall."

"I don't need Morgan." I rock forward, vibrating. "I came because I know where Peter is."

"Seriously?" He bends beside me. "And how could you possibly know this?"

"Might sound crazy, but, I saw him."

I tell him about the vision, and he listens intently, rubbing his jaw.

"I wouldn't usually put much stock in a dream," he finally says. "But under the circumstances. We'll go at first light."

"No! We have to go now. He's in bad shape."

"You don't understand what you're asking." He paces to the fireplace, warming his hands. "We'll freeze out there. And for what? This could be nothing more than a dream."

"Nibs." I glide to his side. "James was angry at Peter because of me. I need to make things right."

The window quakes as a harsh wind rattles the glass. I wrap my arms around myself.

"Please, come with me." My voice drops low. "I don't want to go alone."

He groans, raking his fingers through his hair, messing it. "Are you determined to go with or without me?"

"I have no choice."

"Of course you don't." He glances toward the pitch-black window. "Then neither do I. Let's go."

"You're an angel!" I throw my arms around his neck, kissing his cheek. "You won't regret this."

"I think I already do."

The home is quiet as we step into the dimly lit hall. He guides us forward, my heart drumming loudly in my chest. Every moan of the floorboards sends a jolt through me, but all remains calm. We creep along the stairs to the second floor, cautious as we tread past the boys dormitory, then the girls, and finally reach the last set of stairs.

On the first floor, he switches on the light, and we gather our gear from the hallway closet. Just as I'm about to pull on my coat, he holds another to me, far larger.

"Wear this," he says, extending it.

"Whose is that? Llewelyn's?"

"Probably, but it's thicker. It'll keep you warmer."

"And I'll look ridiculous," I say, handing him mine and taking the new one.

"Well?" I spin, arms spread wide once it's on. "How do I look?"

He grins. "Like Llewelyn junior."

I smack his arm and fling open the door. The world beyond causes me to pause. It's incredible. Silent, still, and deceptively beautiful.

An icy blast hits me full in the face and my body screams for the safety of home, but for Peter's sake, I continue into the winter wonderland.

I glide down the snow-covered stairs, a soft crunch underfoot. Passing through the creaky gate, the snow shimmers under the golden glow of the streetlamps, the night perfectly still. If not for the bitter cold nipping at our cheeks, I might wrap myself in one of these blankets of snow and savor the view.

"My, my," Nibs says, breaking the silence. "This is something, isn't it?"

"It certainly is." I lift the scarf higher, lips trembling.

"To the warehouse, correct?"

"You know the way. Let's go."

I survey the homes of our neighbors as we pass, each one dark, everyone likely warm in bed, dreaming of a life beyond the gates.

"So, tell me," Nibs says. "What caused all this mess? Why would James and Juke target Peter?"

I explain about my stolen journal and how it ended up against Peter's face. Then, how James saw the marks Peter left on my wrist and brought the matter to Juke.

"I should've fought back." Nibs growls under his breath. "I'm an idiot."

"No, you're not." I grab his arm. "You tried, and that's worth something. I shouldn't have mentioned what happened to James. I never imagined he'd respond the way he did. Gosh. Peter and I have quibbled over the years, just never had this happen on account of it."

"James is protective of you. We all know that."

My ears warm. "He asked me out for my birthday."

"Out as a friend?"

"No—" I bite back a smile. "Out on a date."

He dips his head against the wind. "Not sure I want my kid courting just yet."

I grin and press into his arms. "I'm afraid you have no choice in the matter."

His arm tightens around me, reassuring. I cloak my face with my gloves, a temporary relief from the relentless chill. Battling the elements is challenging on a normal day. But now, without the sun, it's unbearable. Yet images of Peter, wounded on the ground, spur me to overlook this momentary discomfort.

The sign for Sixth Avenue soon appears, and beyond it, the warehouse looms, shadowy like a grave.

"There it is." I gesture.

"Not very welcoming, is it?"

"Not at all. Suppose it's time to see if I've lost my marbles."

"I could have told you that without the journey," he says, and I elbow him in the side, nearly knocking him into a snowbank.

"Just keeping up our spirits." He chuckles.

We move ahead, snow swirling around like a wintery dance. A blast of wind hits my face, and when I wipe it away, the broken window comes into view. "There it is. Straight ahead."

"Alright, you ready?" He cracks his knuckles.

"No, but no turning back now. You'll have to give me a boost."

"Of course. But first, let's find something to break the remaining glass."

I spot a fist-sized rock and lift it into my palm, sensing its weight. "This'll do."

"Sure will. Now." He bends. "Hop on, and let's try to be quick and quiet."

"Got it."

I wrap my legs around his neck, and he lifts, elevating me with the window.

"Give it a nice hit." He directs. "It shouldn't take much."

I hesitate, staring at the pane of glass where I'd seen the Faerie's reflection. I sure hope this wasn't for nothing.

"What's the hold-up?" He grips my legs firmly.

"Sorry. Here goes nothing."

Taking a deep breath, I draw back and hurl the rock through the glass. The noise cuts through the air, and I freeze, expectant.

Nothing. I exhale slowly.

"Go on and pull through." He motions. "Best hurry, though, there's sure to be some bobbies patrolling the streets. And I for one don't want to explain what we're doing."

I elbow the remaining shards aside, grab the frame, and muscle through, landing hard. My boots crunch against the shattered glass as I take a hesitant step forward. The room is dark, lit only by the scant glow from the fireplace.

It's exactly as I saw in my vision. "Peter, are you here?"

Silence.

"Come on, Peter." I tap my hand against my side, squinting into the dark.

Still nothing.

Dread twists in my gut. Flickers of Peter's lifeless body, filling my thoughts.

"We're too late," I choke out, pressing a fist to my mouth.

"Over here," a weak voice whispers behind me.

"Peter!"

I spot him sprawled on the ground beside the fireplace, cloaked in shadow, half-resting against the wall. Relief surges through me as I sprint to his side and kneel, my gloved hands gripping his bare arms.

"What happened?" I survey his body. A bandage wraps his forehead and waist. He's wearing pants and boots, but nothing else. "Where's your clothes?"

"It got a little hot in here," he says.

"Hilarious," I mutter, slipping off my gloves, and tilting his head up-ward—his skin like ice. "This is awful."

His lashes flutter. "Wendy... am I dreaming?"

"I wish you were. But no, this is very real."

"How did you find me?" His words are slow, barely a whisper.

"It's a long story."

I take his hands in mine, struggling to warm them. They're stiff, unresponsive. He watches me, lids heavy.

"I'm sorry about this whole mess." I whisper. "It's my fault."

"Don't go being selfless on me now." He attempts a smile.

His fingers remain frozen, and of course they do, his whole chest is exposed.

"You're going to hate me for this," I say, undoing the top button. "But I need to warm you up. Fast."

His eyes sharpen. "Don't you dare take that off."

"I'm not entirely." I unhook the final button and hesitate as I take him in. Gone are the smiles and confidence, the intensity and fight. It's not only the lack of clothing, he's just... different. Emotion swells, unexpected, and I shift closer. Slow and cautious, I guide my legs around him, resting into his lap, and press myself to him. "Please don't tell James about this... or anyone else, for that matter."

He stiffens as I wrap my arms around him, grateful Nibs forced me into Llewelyn's oversized jacket. The material covers him, and I exhale, his heartbeat drumming against my own.

Then, with a jolt, violent trembling overtakes him.

"You okay?" I tighten my hold.

"Ye-ye-yes," he slurs through chattering teeth.

I nod. We weren't just on time, we arrived at the last possible moment. He wouldn't have made it till morning.

We sit together, and over the next few minutes, my body slowly, but steadily warms his. We're silent, an understanding between us.

As the shivering settles and his breathing slows, Nibs' voice drifts through the window. "Psst—Wendy."

Peter straightens. "Who's that?"

"Nibs. He's waiting outside."

Another minute passes, and he calls again.

"I'd best go to him," I say, unsure how to pull away without losing his progress. "Let's make this quick, okay?"

He murmurs agreement but slumps as I pull back. In one swift motion, I toss the coat around him, rip off my hat and tuck it over his head. The only thing left is a scarf, which I wrap around his neck. His eyes are closed, and I don't know if he's asleep or unconscious.

I sprint to the window, cold air cutting through me as I lean out. "Sorry, I couldn't break away."

"What's going on in there?" he scans the street.

"He's alive, but just. I had to warm his first."

He wraps his fingers behind his neck. "Thank God. Well, what do you need from me?"

"If I can get him to the window, you need to get him down."

"Will do. Just hurry. I can't stand this cold much longer."

"Understood."

I turn, kicking glass aside with my boot. "Time to wake up, Peter."

No response.

I crouch beside him and press a hand to his cheek. "Hey? Can you hear me?"

He stirs, nodding weakly.

"We need to get you to the window. Nibs can help from there."

Nothing.

"Okay... let's get you up real quick then."

I tug and his head jerks upright, pain flashing across his face.

"What the hell!" he growls.

"I'm sorry." I pull back. "What did I do?"

"It's my side," he mumbles. "Bloody painful."

"Okay. What do you want me to do?"

"I don't know. Just... try again. I'll have to push through it."

I guide his arms into the jacket, one at a time, a wince with every movement.

"If Juke were here, I'd kill him," I mutter, fastening the buttons and adjusting the scarf. "Let's do this."

I reach under his arm, bracing as I heave him onto his feet. He cries out, body shuddering, then slowly steadies, his features pinched as he clutches his side.

"Okay."

It feels wrong, but with slow steps, I guide him to the window. His cheeks are flushed as we arrive. Outside, Nibs bounces on his heels.

I poke my head through the window. "We're here, you ready?"

"I'm am!" He rubs his hands together.

"Excellent." I turn to Peter, a crease forms between his brows. "What is it?"

"I said don't you dare."

A small smile touches my lips. "You'll just have to get over it." I take his hand. "Nibs will help you down."

"No." He pulls away, jaw tight. "Not until you take your coat back."

After everything he's gone through, is this pride or me?

He tries to remove it, but stops short, grimacing.

I exhale once. "You're being ridiculous."

"But—."

"Shh." My finger silences him. "I just pulled you back from death's door. Wear the bloody jacket and be grateful."

"...Fine."

"Good. Consider yourself Lancelot to Juke's Maleagant."

A subtle curve touches his mouth. "Yes, fair maiden."

I suppress a smile. "Now, can you get through the window?"

"We'll see. You might just have to push me out." He steadies himself on the sill. "Hey, Nibs."

"Peter!" Nibs looks up, visibly surprised. "It's good to see you."

"Same to you. You taking a stroll?"

"It was Wendy's idea." He shakes his head. "Who can say no to her?"

"I've yet to find the strength," Peter says, glancing at me. "Right. Let's do this."

He flexes his fingers and grips the sill, then, leaning through, he drops to the ground while Nibs attempts to cushion the fall. His groan leaves an ache in my chest as he hunches against the wall, head down.

I climb through after him. Nibs catches me and sets me on my feet.

"Dash it, Wendy," he whispers, looking at Peter. "There's no way he's capable of getting home like this."

"I know." I watch Peter for a moment, then square my shoulders. "But, we have no choice. One way or another, we're getting him home again."

Chapter 3

"You did good, kid." Nibs pats my back. "Where's all your gear, though?"

I gesture towards Peter, my teeth chattering. "His was missing, Juke likely took everything. I didn't have a choice."

"Understood." He starts unbuttoning his coat.

"Wait, no." I press a hand over his. "You need it for yourself."

"I also need a beer, but I'm not going to Noodler's anytime soon, am I?" He lifts my hand and places his coat into my arms. "Now go ahead and put it on."

"No." I cross my arms, defiant, though the blasted cold has me quaking like a candle in the wind.

"Kid, every second you argue, he's the one suffering. So, put it on, because I'm not asking."

"Fine." I concede. "But I'm not happy about it."

"And you think I care?" He chuckles. "Now, Plan A: we get under his arms and guide him."

"And Plan B?" I ask, fastening the buttons, heat washing over me.

"Drag him."

We haul Peter to his feet, arms hooked beneath his, as he sucks in a breath, jaw clenched. Nibs gives me a long look, then nods, and we move. We manage a few steps before Peter's face burns crimson, teeth grinding, groan intensifying.

"We need to stop!" I cry.

"What choice do we have?" Nibs snaps, anger rising. "We're not returning him to the warehouse. Let's go!"

"No." I stomp my foot, ready to fight him. "We won't torture him."

"Just do it," Peter cuts in.

"But Peter—"

"It's okay, Bird." He manages a weak smile. "There's no other way. I'll manage. Just get me home and out of this blasted cold."

"You heard the man, let's go," Nibs mutters, avoiding my eyes.

We start again. I watch Peter's face, forced calm as he catches my gaze, an attempt to convince me he's fine, but I know he's not, so I halt.

"Do not stop walking!" Nibs' voice cracks. "For his sake, we keep moving."

I step in front of Peter, emotion swelling. "Are you sure?"

He's attempting to mask the pain, but very badly. "You and I both know I can't stay in the warehouse. So stop being selfless, ignore my moans, and let's go."

I hesitate, then step back into place. He does his best, but each step is agony. His body shudders. He doesn't scream, but his eyes clench shut, his footsteps faltering.

"What are you feeling?" I whisper.

"Like there's a knife in my side," he pushes out.

"Oh, Peter..."

We continue, half-dragging him. Every tremble of his body leaves me numb. Then, without thought, I do what Margaret would do for us girls. When the pain was too real, too raw.

I sing.

"Beautiful dreamer, wake unto me.
Starlight and dewdrops are waiting for thee.
Sounds of the rude world heard in the day.
Lull'd by the moonlight have all pass'd away..."

It's working, and his body gradually calms.

"Beautiful dreamer, queen of my song.
List while I woo thee with soft melody;
Gone are the cares of life's busy throng.
Beautiful dreamer, awake unto me.
Beautiful dreamer, awake unto me...."

Then he falls silent.

"Beautiful dreamer, out on the sea
Mermaids are chaunting the wild lorelie;
Over the streamlet vapors are borne
Waiting to fade at the bright coming morn..."

We press on, the only noise our panting. The walk back takes twice as long, but I barely notice, I'm too focused on Peter.

Then the house comes into view, and my heart leaps. "We made it! I see home!"

His body suddenly goes slack, burdening us under his full weight.

"Let's get him to my room fast." Nibs grunts.

"How are we going to get him up the stairs?"

"No idea."

The wind whistles in my ears, faith in my own strength running dry. Barely upright, I stumble forward in small steps, dragging Peter with me, chest screaming for air.

"Someone's coming," Nibs calls.

He's right. A figure runs down the front steps—it's Llewelyn.

Halting in front of us, he signs, "*I was in the kitchen when you left.*"

He lifts Peter into his arms, relief washing over me, but my legs give out, and I collapse into the snow.

"Are you okay?" Nibs hurries to my side.

"I'm sorry... I can't move."

"Don't be sorry, we did it. He's home. Now put your arm around me. I got you."

I lean into him and he lifts me. Despite his exhaustion, he presses on, one step at a time—through the gate and up the stairs. Llewelyn reappears as we reach the door and scoops me into his arms.

Free of all burdens, Nibs closes the door behind us and sinks to his knees, deflated. "Take her to bed," he says, dazed. "I'll meet you in my room."

Llewelyn nods and carries me up the stairs, entering the girl's room.

"It's the last bed on the right," I whisper.

He moves quietly between the rows, three beds on each side, then lays me down, pulling the blankets to my chin. I don't say anything or notice when he's gone, as within moments, I'm asleep, completely drained of energy.

❄ ❄ ❄

The sound of clicking heels stirs my mind, a heavy haze, wrapping around me.

"Are you going to stay here all day?"

I squint against the sunlight. Morgan stands by my bed, hand on her hip, a floral blue dress clinging to her thin frame.

"I'm sick," I mumble, pulling the comforter higher.

"Are you? Because the doctor's upstairs with Peter. I can fetch him."

My eyes flash open, memories of our overnight escapade returning. "How's Peter?" I press up.

"Not sure, but he was pretty exhausted when I saw him." She gathers a handful of dresses strewn across the girls' beds and glides to the pastel-blue wardrobes beside the fireplace. "He said you saved his life. How did that come about?"

"Oh, it's an odd story." I watch as she hangs the dresses neatly. "I had a vision, he was hurt in the warehouse. Turns out it was true."

She turns back to me. "A vision? Like what Reverend Andrew talked about on Sunday? A dream showing the future?"

"Not exactly, though it held similar value. This wasn't the future, it was the past. I saw Peter after Juke hurt him. He left him to die."

"That's incredible, the vision I mean." She exhales, picking at her nails. "James isn't a bad person, but there's no way around what he's done to Peter."

"I know." I sit with an achy moan, massaging the tension from my neck. "I can only hope he wasn't aware of Juke's brutality."

She sits beside me, her hand resting over mine. "Don't give it anymore thought. Let's just wait till he returns and we can find out what happened."

My gaze drifts to the pale blue curtains framing the sunlit window—blue everywhere, an uneasy reminder of Peter's lips, half-frozen. I know she's right, we can't know what happened without asking James, but still, I'm torn by the matter.

"Well, I'm glad we at least found Peter," I say. "I can't imagine what Nibs would've done had I dragged him outside for nothing."

"Nonsense. He's proud of you." She lifts the brush off my bedside table and glides it through my hair, smoothing untidy strands. "Last night helped him face something he's battled for a long time."

"Oh? And what's that?"

"Margaret's death." Her voice softens. "He's carried it like a personal failure."

"But why?" I turn to her. "What could he have done? There's fourteen of us. No one could have foreseen what happened that day."

"You're right, but it's natural to beat yourself up when things go wrong. Overanalyze what you could have done different."

"Yeah... I get it. What happened was because I told James about a spat Peter and I had. It's hard not to feel like this is on me."

"Accidents happen. And people respond in ways we can't predict." She sets the brush down and rises. "But regardless, it's how we respond that matters most. You and Nibs did the right thing. Let's just hope it's enough to get Juke out for good."

"If I hold any sway over James, Juke *will* be out." I swing my legs off the bed. "Now, let me dress and go check on Peter."

"I'll leave you to it." She hugs me and clicks back to the door, disappearing through it.

Morning prep is quiet today without the usual chatter. I vaguely recall waving the others away after their failed attempts to wake me.

I dress, twist my hair into a bun, and head upstairs.

On the third floor, I pass Morgan's room, then Llewelyn's, and stop in front of Juke's. I could kick this blasted thing in and take a stick to that idiot.

The door behind swings open, and Nibs peeks through. "What in the world?" He grabs my wrist and yanks me inside. "After everything we just went through, you're going to stand outside his door?"

"And what do you suggest? Act like nothing ever happened?" I shove him lightly and slump onto the couch, glancing towards Peter, asleep. His chest rises and falls gently beneath the sunlight streaming through the bay window above the bed. "Together we could do something."

"I understand. I, too, wish he were out. For now, though, let's act normal."

He strides to a wooden table nestled in the corner of the room. "Juke's violent, as witnessed with Peter, and we can't risk a confrontation."

Sitting on one of the plush chairs, he lifts a steaming mug. "When James returns, we'll deal with him. For now, please don't try to be a hero."

"Okay. Fine. No heroism." I stare at the ceiling, wishing Nibs was the confrontational type.

"Good. Now, are you hungry?" He holds out a plate of golden-brown muffins. "Morgan dropped these earlier with a pot of coffee."

"Yeah." I join him, inhaling the sweet aroma of cinnamon and apple muffins. "So, how is he? What did the doctor say?"

"Doc just left. Said he fractured a rib and has signs of a concussion. He'll recover, but it'll take time."

"Did he wake up after we got back?" I plop down, eyes drifting to Peter. Wishing I could undo this whole mess.

"Yeah." He leans back. "We had to tend to his wounds, unfortunately, the bathing area's right next to Juke's room. Thankfully, he's a good sport and kept quiet despite the pain. We cleaned and wrapped him, and Doc said we did a fine job. He's concerned about Peter's emotional state, though."

"And all over a stupid journal."

"Don't." He squeezes my wrist. "Juke did this, not you."

"You say that." I lift the coffee pot, and fill a mug. We settle in silence for a few minutes, both sipping contentedly. "Tell me... do you ever think about Margaret?"

"Sometimes." He scratches his chin. "But it's been a while since she died. Why?"

"Peter brought her up. Implied she was concerned about the choices I was bound to make."

"Why would that be the case?"

I fix him with a hard stare. "Peter read a very specific entry in my journal. It expressed some of my more, desperate emotions. It was a bad day."

"We all have those days." He folds his hands beneath his chin.

"This one was worse. A year ago, I decided James was my way out. His power as the son of the Lord Regent is all I need. Peter read about my willingness to use that. I may have said I was willing to do whatever it took to get out of here."

"Whatever?" he repeats.

"Whatever," I echo. "It was a *really* bad day. Think, *Susan Lenox* bad."

"Oh." His ears redden. "You didn't actually?"

"No. Of course not." I stare into my cup. "Trust me, my goal isn't to become his mistress."

"But you considered it?"

"I spoke of it, and then Margaret talked me off the ledge. James isn't that type anyways, so it was all nonsense."

"Gee, Wendy, is it really so bad here?"

"In some ways no, and in others, yes. The fatigue is constant in this frozen land. Somehow, I've got to find a way out."

"Okay." He nods slowly. "Well, just know, if you ever attempt to go full *Susan Lenox*, I'm locking you in your room."

A chuckle escapes me. "Fair enough. I'm a bit mad, I know. But so are you, so are all of us."

"Speak for yourself." He meanders to the couch, stretching out and resting back on a pillow. "I for one like to think I'm perfectly normal."

I sip the bitter coffee and wander to his bookshelf, a colorful display of novels spanning from floor to ceiling. "I won't comment."

"I'll take that as agreement," he says through a yawn. "Keep an eye on him, yeah?"

"Of course. Oh, and Nibs." I glance at him over my shoulder.

"Yeah?" He pops one eye open.

"I'd really appreciate it if you kept what I shared between us."

"You don't even have to ask."

I exhale, oddly lighter. Margaret was the only person I ever felt safe opening up to this way. The thought surfaced from a scandalous book our friend Henley had snuck from his mother called *Susan Lenox*.

Like me, Susan had no parents and was always on the outside, never truly fitting in. Though raised with love, it couldn't fill the void. Reading her story planted an idea in my head: that a girl in my position could take control of her life through unconventional means, even if society condemned it—and maybe, just maybe, get what she wanted.

I never outright said I'd follow her blueprint, but that day, without Margaret to ground me, I let myself imagine the possibilities in my journal. The same pages Peter took it upon himself to read. I'm still a bit angry with him, but I won't deny the whole experience last night really dampened that emotion.

I peruse the various book titles until one captures my interest and tuck it under my arm. An easy chair waits between the bed and the window, sunlight spilling warmly across its lush fabric. Settling, I nestle in and focus on the little black words:

"Youth was fleeing, as she became his world. The touch of her skin was like heaven's embrace..."

❄ ❄ ❄

My lids flutter open; the book pressed against my chest. I straighten, but hesitate, Peter's staring at me.

"You're awake," I say.

"As are you." His voice is raspy. "I didn't want to wake you. You seemed peaceful."

I breathe out. He's staring, unapologetically. The memory of our...close proximity last night springs to mind, my body against his, restoring the heat Juke stole. Warmth creeps up my neck.

"Well, thanks." I run a hand through my hair. "Uh, are you hungry?" I gesture to the table. "Morgan brought muffins, and there's coffee."

"No." There's no trace of a smile, only an unreadable stiffness. "I'm not very hungry."

"How are you feeling?"

"I'm fine. Look, if you're here to keep an eye on me, don't. I can manage."

"Oh." Any thought that he'd be pleased to see me dissolves. "Well, I'm okay for a bit." I pick at my nails, willing myself not to ask the one question gnawing at me.

"I should probably thank you," he says, "because lying in this bed is far better than the warehouse. That took some pluck and it means a lot that you did it."

"I was glad to." My smile stretches a little too wide.

He looks away. Silence settles between us until he murmurs, "The last time we talked, I said some things I shouldn't have. I'm sorry."

I lean forward, arms wrapped around my vibrating knees. "It's okay. What you read... I was confused. But what you saw, with James, it's real."

"Understood." His gaze wanders around the room, anywhere but me.

"I'm also sorry. I was angry about the journal and about what you said. I could have handled myself better. My behavior was appalling, and I've regretted it since."

He dips his chin. "Then it seems all is well."

Another long silence stretches.

I glance at Nibs, softly snoring, one arm dangling off the couch. There's more I want to say, but under the circumstances, none of it feels right. "I should go." I rise. "You probably want some privacy."

"If you say so."

I step toward the couch, the air stifling, then pause as the question spills out. "What happened that night?"

"Took you long enough, huh?" His mouth quirks.

"You're teasing me." I drift back to the chair. "I feel responsible. What Juke did, it was my fault. I told James what happened between us."

He studies me, then gestures to the bed. I hesitate, a twist in my gut, before moving to his side. His leg is warm against mine, and oddly comforting after the memory of his body turned to ice.

"I don't blame you for this, Wendy. What happened wasn't your fault."

"But it was! I told James you grabbed me, and that's why Juke hurt you."

He exhales heavily. "Your boyfriend was angry. Maybe rightly so. But Juke did what he wanted. That's not on you, okay?"

"Okay…" I clear my throat. "So, what did he do? Jan said you were poisoned."

"Yeah. Juke handed me a drink. I should've known better, but I didn't. Didn't take long before I couldn't think straight."

"So, he dragged you out of here and… you know?"

"Yes. He uh, took a belt to my back, a few kicks to my side, and a final boot to the head. Knocked me out cold."

I clutch his arm, fingers tightening. "How could James have let this happen?"

"Who's to say he did? I don't recall James doing anything besides talking. There's a chance Juke acted on his own."

"Maybe. But, how did you survive all this time?"

"I don't know. When I first woke, I was bandaged. Figured Juke must've tried fixing what he broke. Even if James wanted me 'taught a lesson,' I doubt he meant it to go so far. But what do I know? There was food, water, and the fire was always going."

"Interesting."

He believes Juke helped him. Yet what about the faerie from my vision?

We've heard the stories. A pirate and a pixie led the attacks on Neverland years ago—Captain Worley and Prince Tahreek. They struck Silver Mist, killed the king, burned towns, and then vanished when Thomas and James rallied soldiers. No one's seen them since.

"Wendy?"

"Huh." I blink, refocusing. "Sorry. So, what do you plan to do now?"

"I'd already planned to leave soon, and James made it pretty clear my welcome's expired—" He massages his temple, eyes spasming.

"What's wrong?"

"Hard to explain. I-it's. I'm fine." His eyes shut.

I straighten, unsure what to do when his face goes slack and his hand drops.

"Peter?"

I lift his hand; it's limp. He's unconscious.

A stirring behind pulls my attention to Nibs, stretching on the couch.

"Good morning." He yawns, hair messed. "How long was I asleep?"

I stare, unable to answer.

"Everything okay?" He hops up, slipping to my side. "What's wrong?"

"Peter passed out..."

"Oh. I see. Doc said this could happen with his head injury. How did he seem, though?"

"Under the circumstances? He was okay." Images from his story plague me. "He told me what happened."

He perches on the arm of the chair. "It's okay, he's okay. But you understand now why we have to be cautious around Juke?"

"I have no intentions of spending quality time with the monster, if that's what's concerning you."

"Of course not. Still, he's unpredictable. If there's any cause for concern, you get me right away."

"Got it." My chest tightens, unease curling through me.

"Hey." He tilts my chin up. "It's going to be okay."

I wrap my arms around him, his cozy flannel warming. "I know... It's just that things were already confusing enough without this adding to it."

"Agreed. But we'll get him out and then things will return to whatever we call normal."

"Yeah... let's hope so."

✳ ✳ ✳

For the remainder of the day, I can't shake the discomfort Peter's story left behind.

After supper, craving solitude, I head to the parlor. Settling in a corner chair, nose in a book, I glance up as JaneAnn enters, followed by Michael, Maimie, and John.

John closes the double doors. "That should offer some privacy."

The girls take to the couch, the boys the chairs. They all look at me expectantly. No one speaks. The fire crackles, snow pattering softly against the windows, the atmosphere too peaceful for the disquiet in me.

"What is it?" I look between them. "Why are you all staring at me?"

"We're just waiting." JaneAnn leans back, hands folded.

"For what?"

"For you to expound upon the situation," John says.

"And what situation is that?" I close my book.

"Oh, get on with it!" JaneAnn bursts out. "I know something happened last night. I saw Llewelyn bringing you to bed, and after he left, you were out like a light. Something exhausted you, and I have a pretty good hunch what it was."

"Oh? Well, do tell." I lean on my elbow.

"You found Peter, didn't you?"

"You're good," I admit, and they sit a little straighter. "Yes, Nibs and I found him. He's recovering in Nibs' room. Juke can't find out. Do you understand? For Peter's sake, this information doesn't leave this room."

"Peter's our man." John adjusts his spectacles. "Everything you share remains between us, in good faith."

The others nod in agreement.

"Well, go on." Maimie urges. "Where was he? What happened?"

I share what I know, and of course, Juke's actions surprise no one. When his anger flares, woe to the kid who's within reach of his backhand.

"So, you understand why we can't let Juke know Peter's here," I conclude. "The guy's insane."

"Don't worry. Not a word to anyone," JaneAnn reassures.

"I wish I could fight him," Michael says quietly.

"Fight Juke?" Maimie chuckles. "You've lost your mind."

"I'm well aware I can't." He crosses his arms. "But I wish I could. Everything would be perfect without him."

I'm comforted by his belief that this place could ever be perfect. Due to their younger age, the curse affected Maimie, Hannah, and Michael less. At only fifteen now, his perspective is that our life is good. Without Juke—even perfect. Part of me wants to shake him, say no; freedom would be perfect. But what good would that do? If he can be happy, even in a cage... let him be.

The truth is, if I ever escape Winter Woods, it'll be one less person I'll feel guilty about leaving behind.

Chapter 4

It's Sunday morning, and our group walks alongside our neighbors toward the stone chapel, where we gather for prayers and praises. Many in our community have little, but their hearts are all remarkably full. It's hard for me to make sense of their determination. But here they are, week after week, returning, joy renewed. I can't deny it's contagious, and while together, I often feel their hope... just for a while.

As we enter the building, a few of the older women gather around us, offering warm hugs and pinched cheeks. Their voices resound like the chirping of birds in the morning.

Making our way to our usual pew, we sit, and the minister, Reverend Andrew, steps up. He is a kindly gentleman with thick brown hair streaked with grey and a gentle disposition. Over the years, he and his wife, Beatrice, have generously opened their home to us, offering evenings of acceptance and comfort in their parlor.

He offers a brief welcome, and then the choir leads us through a few songs. The hymns often reflect our quest for freedom and the longing to experience it again.

Once the choir finishes, Bea sits beside me as she usually does. "Good morning, darling," she whispers. "Join us for lunch after service?"

"Oh sure, that sounds wonderful."

"Good." She presses my hand gently, and the Reverend steps up to the wooden pulpit, clears his throat, and reads:

"*Three things will remain forever, faith, hope, and love—and the greatest of these is love.*"

I survey the row beside me. Five years ago, we were comparable to chalkboards—wiped clean, with only the faintest smudge remaining. Is it possible that while everything about us vanished, some things are impossible to erase?

Faith and hope may just be rooted deep within, lingering beyond the curse. But love? I'm not sure I believe in it. Attraction and affection, sure... but love? I use the term as anyone does, but not in the way the reverend describes it. True love is a wild thing. I can't imagine many are capable of it.

When the service ends, our group heads toward the chilly entrance, pausing to greet Reverend Andrew as we pass.

"Morning, Wendy." a young man says, stepping in line beside me.

"Hey Henley. How are you? Did you start the job this week?"

"Yeah, I did." He shoves his hands into his pockets. "Pays well, that's about all. What about you? It's almost the big day. Nineteen. You still hoping to move out?"

"Depends where I'm going. Out of town, absolutely. Out of the home, depends. Can't stay there forever though, can I?"

"Something will come up, give it time. So, thought I'd see you yesterday."

I tilt my head. "Did I forget something?"

He meets my gaze, the silence telling.

"Oh no... the anniversary." I step out of line and sink into a pew. "I am *so* sorry. I feel terrible, and can't believe I forgot."

"It's okay, old girl." He grips the edge of the pew. "It means you're moving on, and she'd approve of that."

I wrap my hand over his and squeeze. "Margaret is always with me. Things have been chaotic at home, and I got distracted... are you okay?"

"No." His face falters, a hollow expression creeping in. "I miss her all the time, and it just seems like moving on isn't an option." He lets out a soft laugh. "She'd scold me for even saying that."

"She would." I offer a small smile. "What can we do about it? I need to see you happy again."

"I'm hopeless." He stares at the stained-glass window. "You know, I told her I was going to marry her. Guess what she said?"

"Knowing Margaret, I can imagine."

"She said, *I expect you will*, and kissed me." A shadow passes over his face, his eyes glistening. "That was the last time I saw her. A few days later, you came with the news. We had so much left to do, and I'm still waiting for her to come back so we can."

"Wendy," Morgan calls, waving me over. "We're walking home."

"Okay, one moment." I wipe away a tear. "It's not fair. There's no way around it. I know she'd be mad at us for fussing. But maybe if we do it enough, she'll come down and yell at us."

"That's an idea." He chuckles and takes my hand, helping me to my feet. "Thanks. I *was* mad at you, but this helped."

I lean forward and hug him. "Don't be a stranger. You know John's always eager to rope you into a board game."

"Once the fog lifts, I'll be by. See you around, Wendy."

"Be well, Henley."

My heart aches as I turn into the aisle, swallowing the well of emotions rising in me. I approach Reverend Andrew, forcing the mask back into place.

"Hello, dear," he greets. "Many thanks for the clothes you mended for my wife. Bea blessed a needy family, and they were overwhelmed by the generosity. A professional couldn't have done a finer job."

"You're welcome. I'll have a few more finished this week."

"Perfect. I'll be by on Wednesday for my usual visit with Llewelyn, and can take whatever's ready then. I'm very proud of you, dear." He pats my shoulder. "Good Sabbath to you."

My face warms. "Bea actually invited me for lunch."

"Did she now? Well, wonderful, then I shall see you soon."

I step into the open air and spot Bea chatting with Morgan. When she sees me, she waves me over.

"I was just telling Morgan here that I snagged you for the afternoon, so if you're ready, we'll go. Andrew will be along shortly."

"Fine by me."

I say goodbye to Morgan, and Bea links her arm through mine, chattering gaily as she walks me to her home just a short stroll from the chapel. Inside, the familiar coziness wraps around me. Mismatched couches draped in crocheted throws; a coffee table dressed with a handmade lace runner where we so often play cards as a group, and shelves Llewelyn carved himself, crowded with books, trinkets, photographs, and a glass vase of potpourri sending its soft orange-and-clove scent drifting through the room.

"Come, let's get the table set; the roasted lamb should be ready," she says, her blonde curls bouncing as she moves through the dining room and into the kitchen. The rich, meaty aroma greets us the moment we step into the warm blue space.

"I'm very glad you invited me," I say. "It smells delicious."

"You've been on my mind. So how are things?" She opens the oven door, bending to peer inside.

"Um... things are okay." *No, they're not.*

"And Peter? He sick or something?"

"He's not sick." I lift plates from the cabinet and set them on the counter.

"Well then, where is he?" she asks, slipping on oven mitts and carefully lifting the steaming meat out and onto the kitchen table. "He rarely misses a service."

I hesitate too long, and she tilts her head at me. "I see." She plants a hand on her hip. "Well then, out with it. Where's the boy?"

While she slices the meat and I mash the potatoes, I walk her through everything that's happened this week. She listens with little shakes of her head and soft mutters under her breath, urging me to go on. By the time I finish, her frown has deepened into a scowl.

"That man... I knew he was a son of the devil. I told Andrew to get him out. But he didn't feel it was his place. Said we shouldn't be busybodies. And now look what's happened. Poor, poor Peter." She sighs. "I'll send some vittles back with you. Oh, and my good cookies, I just made a batch."

The front door slams open, and she wipes her hands on the apron. "Don't say a word of this to Andrew. I'll tell him later. He might say something he'd regret in front of you, and we won't tempt him that way." She winks.

The walk home is slow, weighed down with a bag of cookies, a thermos of hot cider, and a tin of lunch, all for Peter. Reverend Andrew insisted on carrying it, but I said no, I could manage. Not entirely true, but oh well.

At the house, I wander to Nibs' room and knock. The door clicks open, and he motions me in before closing it behind us.

"I wondered if you might come by."

As he steps aside, my attention shifts to Peter—shirtless, seated in an easy chair by the fire. His olive skin glows in the flickering light, and when he turns, his green eyes meet mine beneath a tousled lock of golden hair.

I was wholly unprepared for this and suddenly find it hard to breathe. Nibs speak, but I don't hear him.

"Wendy?" He snaps a finger in my face.

"Huh? What did you say?"

"Nothing important, obviously." He scowls. "I said, since you're here, I'll take a break."

"Oh, sure. Go enjoy yourself."

He glares between Peter and me, then heads for the door. "Hmm. Well okay. I'll be back later. See you, kids."

The door clicks shut.

"So, you came back," Peter says. "Thought I scared you off."

"Not at all." I perch on the edge of the couch. "Was that your goal?"

"Maybe. Seems we're one wrong step from total tragedy—you and I." He winces, gliding his fingers over his chest. The firelight reflects off each ridge and curve.

Catching my glance, he frowns. "Sorry. I get these jolts of pain." He lifts a shirt from the side table and pulls it on with care.

I avert my gaze, cheeks burning, unsettled by my own reaction.

Get it together.

"So why did you come back?" he asks.

"Bea had this bag for you." I lift it onto his lap. "Just needed to drop it off."

"Oh, so that's the only reason?" He sifts through it.

"No." I fidget with the hem of my skirt. "Guess it seemed like the right thing to do."

"The right thing?" He lets out a low chuckle. "Well, damn. You've outdone yourself, haven't you?"

I sigh, rolling my eyes as he continues.

"Poor thing, braving the stairwell to check on the sorry bastard who went and got himself beaten. But please, you've done your good deed for the day. Go on and get some rest."

"I worded that badly." I fold my hands beneath my chin. "Despite what you assume, I do care."

"*Do you?*" He narrows his eyes. "Look, jokes aside, you don't get it. What happened changed me. It's kind of you to be here, but I'm not much for company. Save your sweet smile for someone else."

Why does he have to be so difficult? Maybe I should leave... but something roots me to the couch. My gaze drifts to the book on his side table.

"Is that *Gulliver's Travels*?" I ask.

He glances at it. "Yeah. John and Michael came by yesterday. A little bird told them about my woes, and John insisted this would ease what's ailing me."

"May I?" I hold out my hand.

"Sure." He leans forward, passing it over.

"I was soundly scolded for neglecting to read it a few months ago." I flip open to the first chapter and glide my finger along the text, reading aloud, "*The publisher, to the reader, the author of these Travels, Mr. Lemuel Gulliver, is my ancient and intimate friend...*"

"What are you doing?" he interrupts.

"Reading. And you're disrupting me. May I continue?"

"Fine. What's it to me?" He leans back and waves me on. "Read away."

I suppress a grin, and curl my feet beneath me as I lift the book.

"About three years ago, Mr. Gulliver growing weary of the concourse of curious people coming to him at his house in Redriff, made a small purchase of land..."

✳ ✳ ✳

It's Monday morning. Normally, I'd be lounging with my nose buried in a book, but today finds me in the classroom, helping Morgan instead. Peter usually tutors the younger kids several times a week, but with him unavailable, I've offered to assist.

Michael scribbles answers while I tap my fingers against the desk, observing the wall clock, the hands seemingly frozen in place.

"Wendy," Morgan calls from her desk, "could I speak with you for a moment?"

"Certainly." I tousle Michael's hair. "I'll be back."

"Sure thing, teach." He beams at me.

I stroll to Morgan's desk and lean casually against the edge. "What's up?"

"You should take a break; you're about to fall asleep."

"What? No. I'm a little bored, that's all. I like helping."

"I'll check his work when he's done. Go on."

She opens her drawer, rummages through it, and hands me a black folder. "Here—a certain someone asked for this. Would you mind dropping it off for me?"

"What is it?" I take the folder.

"Something to pass the time."

"Okay, sure. I'll go now."

I slip out of the classroom, the door clicking shut behind me. But as I glance up, I halt at the sight of Juke lounging at the table. Pressing back, my heart catches in my throat. He's reading a magazine, feet propped, chewing on a sandwich. In appearance, totally innocent.

"Whatcha got there, missy?" He gestures at the folder in my hand.

"Something from Morgan." I grip it tighter.

"I see." He takes another bite. "Well, what are you standin' there for? Go on, unless you'd rather join me."

"Of course." I shove my hair behind my ear, forcing myself to walk, slow and steady, until I'm past him. At the stairwell, I take the steps, two at a time, eager to put distance between us. On the third floor, I knock at Nibs' door, and after a minute, it creaks open.

"Hello?" I peek in.

"Come on in," Peter says from behind the door.

I slip inside, and he steps into view. "Sorry... Nibs had to go, and I didn't want to show myself, just in case."

"You're walking!" I gesture to the wooden crutches under his arms.

"Yeah, Llewelyn made these." He holds them up. "Nifty things, aren't they? Been getting around a whole lot easier."

"Well, that's smashing." I settle on the couch, smoothing my dress. "So, how goes it?"

"Would be better if I could leave this bloody room." He slumps into the easy chair. "Nibs said he heard tell your boyfriend would be in town for your birthday. Hopefully that'll put an end to this nonsense."

"It will. I'll make sure of it."

"You are rather persuasive," he muses, "especially when perturbed."

"Funny…" I hand him the folder. "Morgan asked me to drop this off."

"Oh, yeah. Thanks." He takes it and flips through the contents.

I spot *Gulliver's Travels* on the side table. "Did you read any more?"

"Course not." He tilts his head. "I mean, I could have, but we're reading it together, aren't we?"

"We are." I smile. "And I have some time now."

"And I happen to be going absolutely nowhere." He slaps the folder shut.

The afternoon passes, and we take turns reading aloud, both of us fully absorbed in the story. By the time we finish, we're sprawled side by side across the carpet in front of the fire, Peter holding the book above our heads as he reads.

As the clock strikes four, I help him back into the chair and reluctantly say goodbye. I hurry to the kitchen, where JaneAnn and I whip together a hearty lamb stew and bake a loaf of sourdough.

Over dinner, she attempts small talk, but my mind drifts back to the story—back to Peter and the unexpected reprieve found with him. If possible, I'll return later.

When the meal ends, we clear the tables and head to the kitchen, where I take my place at the sink, scrubbing dirty dishes while she dries. We chat about which job we'd rather have once out of the house, and she mentions a conversation she had with Canary at the Diner. Me though, I haven't begun to consider what's next, because I can't bear to imagine a future where I'm still here after my nineteenth birthday.

As we're wrapping up, Morgan leans through the door. "Hey, just wanted to let you know—Nibs and I have to run an errand. I don't know when we'll be back, so if you need anything, Llewelyn's out back."

"Yes, ma'am," I say, glancing over my shoulder.

"What are you two up to this late?" JaneAnn asks, folding her arms and leaning against the counter.

"Nothing important," Morgan shrugs. "See you."

"Yeah, yeah." JaneAnn turns around. "What do you suppose that was about? You don't think they're going on a date, do you?"

"Wouldn't surprise me."

"Well." Her tongue clicks. "I'll have some questions for them tomorrow."

"Of course you will." I wipe the counter and wring the cloth, hanging it to dry. "All done, let's go."

Flipping off the light, the glow from Llewelyn's shed cuts through the icy window, plumes of smoke curling gently from the chimney. Perhaps I should visit him instead. He's a wonder with wood, and I often enjoy evenings watching him carve some trinket while I chatter away. But the pull of the story is stronger tonight, so I toss my apron across the chair and leave the kitchen.

"Want to join me and the boys for a card game?" JaneAnn asks as we reach the stairwell.

"Nah, I'm heading up. Enjoy yourself, and try not to fight with John this time."

"He asks for it." She cracks her knuckles. "See you in a bit." Disappearing into the parlor, the boys greet her loudly.

I continue up the stairs, humming, then pause at the door and knock. A memory stirs, Peter pulling all sorts of voices for the characters. I smile, eager for the rest. Drumming my fingers against my side, my hum turns to song: "*All is calm, all is bri—*"

Like a burst of icy water, a beefy hand clamps over my mouth, cutting me off. Panic shoots through me. I claw at the door, desperate to slam my fists against it, but I'm dragged backward, overpowered.

Lashing at the unseen figure, I scratch blindly like a wild animal, and the attacker grunts as I make contact, nails digging into flesh. Then, a flash of white explodes across my vision as a fist meets my face, pain radiating through my skull.

My arm twists behind me. A hot palm slaps over my lips, and the door to Juke's room shuts with a chilling thud.

Darkness swallows me, save for the sliver of light beneath the door. *I should have gone to Llewelyn's shed!* He releases me, and I fall to the floor, body trembling as a blinding light flickers on.

"Stand up." Juke says.

A sharp ache pulses across my forehead, the blow threatening to pull me under. I can't breathe, but I make myself with small, ragged gasps.

"I said get up!"

I force my legs to steady. The room spins. Vomit crawls up my throat as I grip the bedpost, aware if I'm not careful, I'll be kissing the emerald carpet.

"Wonderful." He nods, rubbing his neck where my nails left their mark. "Now we can talk eye to eye."

Nothing about the room feels right, from the frosted chandelier, to the curved velvet headboard above the emerald bed, or the half-naked woman staring at me from the painting over the fireplace.

This is disgustingly lavish for a snake.

"What do you want?" I mutter.

"Now look." He leans against the door, arms folded. "I never meant to hit you, but you forced my hand. Just remember that."

"What are you talking about? You grabbed me! Did you expect I'd go willingly?"

"I did what I had to. Now, we've got some things to discuss—like why you're spending hours in Nibs' bedroom."

"I can spend time with whomever I please."

"Oh, I see. So, you were going to see him just now?"

"Yes."

"Yet Morgan just told you they were leaving. So... why would you go straight to his room then? Unless, you weren't going to see Nibs, but someone else."

I swallow, sensing the trap. "I'd like to go now. You've done enough damage, don't you think?"

"Hardly. See, James trusts me. He has me watching over things here. But someone interrupted my work, and I know it was you and Nibs."

"He only gave you that task to protect me." I step closer. "What do you think he'll say when he sees what you did to me. A few marks on my wrist are nothing compared to this." I touch my forehead gently.

He raises an eyebrow, lips curling into a grin. "You might have a point there, girlie. One I hadn't considered."

My pulse quickens. "And what's that?"

"You and I, we're not so different. We've been locked away in this blasted town with little hope of escape. But I just thought of a brilliant solution to my problem."

Pushing off the door, he strides to me, grabbing me by the back of the neck. "Peter's probably lonely in there, don't you think?"

He leads me into the hallway and knocks on Nibs' door. "Let's surprise him. When he asks who's there, you offer the ole charm. Got it?"

"Never." I glare ahead, my mouth dry. "Whatever your brilliant idea is, it won't include me baiting Peter for some twisted game."

"Wendy?" Peter's voice comes from within. "Is that you?"

I'm silent, willing him away.

"Hello?" Peter repeats.

"Time for some fun." Juke's fingers dig in. "Peter, if you'd be so kind, sweet little Wendy's out here with me and—"

The door swings open. Peter's expression hardens. "Blast it, Juke. Release her."

"Oh, no, no. She's about to help me get the hell out of this town." Juke pushes past, dragging me behind him. "Close the door."

"I'm not going to do that," Peter says, voice dangerously low. "Last time you and I were alone, things didn't go so well."

"Then it's your lucky day. Because I'm no longer interested in you." Juke's grip tightens, drawing a cry from me. "Now close the door."

Peter looks at me, a crease forming between his brows, then slams the door, floorboards quivering.

"Good. Now you and I have some unfinished business. Out of curiosity, how did you get here?"

"I walked myself home."

Juke barks a laugh. "Clearly, with the crutches."

"Are you willing to risk your neck over her?" Peter asks.

"That's exactly what I'm about to do." He presses his lips to my neck, breathing in as though I were a flower in bloom. "Now, I had intended to mess with you, you cocky bastard—but she's far more desirable. I'm sure you can agree."

Peter grips his crutch, knuckles white. "And if I refuse to play along?"

"You'll be dragged out of here, headfirst, both legs snapped like twigs," Juke says calmly. "Trust me, it makes no difference how this plays out. But I assure you, it will."

I expect Peter to snarl, explode like a volcano, but instead his shoulders sag. "When I leave... what happens to her?"

"No!" I cry.

"Hush now." Juke pats my shoulder. "That's none of your concern, but—" he lifts a hand. "On my word as a gentleman, she'll be treated like a lady. If you catch my drift."

Peter dips his chin. "Okay. Look Wendy. What choice do I have?" He spreads his arms. "You said yourself this wouldn't have happened if you hadn't told James about us."

"Smart boy." Juke's grip tightens around my waist, his breath reeking of alcohol. "Go on now Pete. Take a seat in my room. If you're lucky, you might get it once I'm gone."

I glance at Peter, but he avoids my eyes. A hot tear escapes. I don't want to consider what's about to happen.

"I just need my other crutch." Peter mumbles.

"Of course," Juke motions around. "Take whatever you need."

I focus on the floral carpet as Peter limps to the bed, each thud echoes loudly, rattling something inside me.

"There's a book on my coffee table you might enjoy," Juke offers. "Gift from my good buddy Noodler."

"Alright." Peter reaches for his crutch, crooning under his breath, *"Beautiful dreamer, wake unto me..."*

He's mocking me with the same song I used to comfort him?

My neck burns, tears slipping down my cheeks as Juke's fingers glide around my body rising toward my chest. *I hate him.* And yet, he's right about one thing. Peter *is* a bloody bastard!

"Okay, okay." Juke waves a hand, "Don't take all night."

"Sure thing." Peter tosses the crutch and catches it in his palm. "Better duck, Wendy."

I barely register the words when the crack of wood hitting skull echoes in my ears, and Juke crumples to the ground.

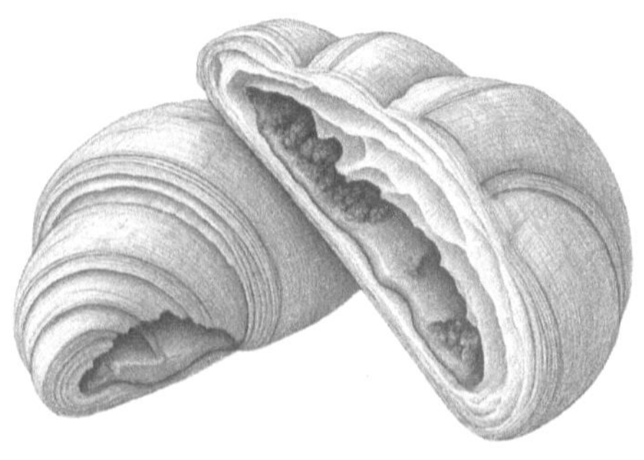

Chapter 5

My feet are glued to the floor, unwilling to move. *What just happened?* My breath is short, unsteady, as though I've forgotten how to draw air. Juke lies unconscious beside me, and Peter stands gripping his crutch.

"What—" I whisper, trembling. "I don't understand."

"Are you okay?" He gazes at me. "You're white as a sheet."

"I don't know."

The room spins as he takes my arm, guiding me to the couch, where I collapse.

"Did he do this?" His fingers graze the side of my face.

"Yes." My throat tightens.

"*Okay,*" is all he says as he turns and takes one slow, deliberate step after another toward Juke. "Indeed, we have unfinished business."

In an instant, the crutch cracks against Juke's nose, and I gasp as blood trickles out.

"Disgusting piece of trash," Peter says, eyes dark.

I watch, caught between terror and relief as he kicks Juke again and again. But something in his expression unnerves me, so I say, "That's enough."

He doesn't hear me as he continues unleashing all his pent-up rage.

Shaky but determined, I push up and as he rears back for another hit, I step between them, getting kneed in the process.

"What are you doing?" He cries, nearly toppling over.

"I said that's enough!" I rub my aching leg. "You don't need to kill him."

"Don't I?" His eyes are wild.

"No, you don't." I glance at Juke, bloody and broken. "You're just hurting yourself."

"Probably. But I don't care." He maneuvers to the couch and settles in exhaustion, sweat lining his forehead. "I can't believe that just happened. What the hell got into him?"

"He said he wants out." I wander back to the couch and sit. "He claimed he's as stuck in this town as I am and thought this was the solution."

"He's insane. I hope you knew I wasn't going to leave you with him."

I hesitate a moment too long.

"Oh. I see." He presses his head back, jaw set.

"No." I cross my arms, hugging them to my chest. "It's not like that. It just made sense if you wanted to avoid another beating."

"And I'd avoid it by letting him ravish you?" He glares at me.

"If that's what it took." I press my fingers to my temple. "I wasn't thinking clearly, okay?"

"Well, in case you need to hear me say it, I would gladly take the beating."

"I'm sorry! I shouldn't have assumed the worst."

"Yeah, well..." He yanks the blanket off the back of the couch and leans forward, gently draping it over my shoulders. "Maybe that says something about me."

"No, it doesn't. Look, don't give it another thought, *please.*"

"Not sure that's possible. But we need to get you out of here. He's bound to wake any moment."

He holds out a hand, and our fingers intertwine, his skin hot and reassuring. But as we rise, the door bursts open and Nibs storms in, eyes darting from Juke on the floor to us. Morgan follows, hand covering her mouth. And then—the last face I expect appears.

"*James*!"

He's at my side in a flash, pulling me away from Peter and into his arms. "What's happened?"

I blink, unable to find the words, so Peter answers for me. "He told me to go so he could have his way with her."

James stiffens. "He what?"

"You heard me," Peter snaps. "Told me to go relax while he did what he wanted to her. Are you surprised? What did you think would happen, letting a wild animal loose in this place?"

"I—I don't know," James stammers. "He's gone tonight. I swear it."

I pull away, but he catches my arm. "Wendy, I mean it."

His grip doesn't hurt, but it twists something in my stomach, a flicker of unease. "Yeah, I know." My shoulders lift in a weary shrug. "I'm not mad. I just... need some space. That was a lot."

He lets go. "Can I see you tomorrow?"

"Of course." I glance at Peter. "Thank you."

"Anytime."

I walk past Nibs, who watches me. "You won't see him again," he says. "I promise."

I touch his arm, then follow Morgan as she leads me down the hallway into her room. It's soft, bathed in light blue, with sunshine yellow scattered across couch cushions, a wall painting, and the thick carpet beneath my bare feet. It's quietly comforting. Like the Springtime we never get.

"You can stay here tonight," she offers, motioning to the bed.

"Thank you. I'd like that. After everything, I don't think I'd hold it together well, and Jan's sure to notice something's wrong."

"Then don't worry about it. Get some rest. If you need me, I'll be right here." She gestures to the couch.

"No, I'm fine. Goodnight."

I shuffle to the bed and lie down, drawing the comforter to my face, mind swirling with endless emotions. I fear the moment I close my eyes, he'll show up in that world, so I stare at the ceiling, watching the shadows dance across it.

Instead of calm, memories press in, his hands, his breath, the sickly feeling of his lips on my skin.

"Morgan..." I whisper.

"Yeah?" She rises, book in hand, and walks over.

"Could you stay with me?"

"Of course. Scooch over." She props a pillow and slips under the blankets.

"What are you reading?" I turn on my side, facing her.

She tilts the cover toward me. "Somedays more than others, it feels impossibly dark, so I find comfort in this." It's the same Good Book Reverend Andrew preaches from.

"Read a line to me. Maybe it'll take my mind off things."

"Okay, this is one of my favorites... *'Faith is assurance of things hoped for, proof of things not seen.'*"

"And that comforts you?"

"How can I put this into words. Do you remember the story of Joseph, Reverend Andrew told?"

"Of course, his brothers betrayed him and sold him into slavery. Hard to forget that."

"Yet, he found purpose everywhere he went. That inspires me. You know? No matter if it was slavery, prison, or a palace, he rose above the circumstances."

I sit up slightly. "Is that how you feel? Like you're trying to be impactful in our prison?"

"Yes." She nods, a small smile lighting her face. "At the end of his story, he says something that's stuck with me: *'You meant evil against me, but God meant it for good.'*"

"I don't think I have the kind of faith to believe everything bad is actually good." I frown.

"Of course not. But the way Bea put it was—despite the bad, God creates good. While the darkness is suffocating, the light burns brighter."

"And what's the rest of the chapter say?" I rest back.

"It's all about people who kept faith despite their circumstances. Do you want to hear them?"

I nod, and as she reads one story of faith after another, there's a quiet sense of hope that blossoms inside me. Despite full understanding, I cling to her words and the warmth they bring because if I don't, I'm certain I'll be crushed under thoughts of Juke.

The mirror reflects my face, yet I get the sense someone else stares back. I'm not the true Wendy—this I know. She disappeared the day I was born. I often wonder where she went. It's probably a trick of the mind, yet sometimes, I swear I see her screaming through the reflection, slamming her fists against the glass, begging to be set free.

Lifting the brush, I glide it through my hair, sunlight cloaking each strand, wrapping me in a rosy glow. Today feels like a fresh start, a day filled with hope. Juke's dark shadow will no longer haunt this house, though his imprint lingers on my skin in the form of a small, dark purple patch.

I glance at my dress, wrinkled from sleep. I'm in desperate need of a change before seeing James. Slipping back to the girls' room, a flutter of nerves stirs in my stomach as I enter and find JaneAnn waiting, arms folded.

"Well, well, well," she says. "Where were you last night? Seems this is becoming a thing for you."

I glide past her to the wardrobe and throw off my dress. "I have something to tell you."

"Oh? Well." She flops onto her pillow, hands tucked behind her head. "Do tell."

I recount the night's events, weighted but honest, sharing the part where Juke held me close, alcohol on his breath, and expectation in his mind. There's a shift in her demeanor as she listens, a look reminiscent of Peter's before he raged at Juke's unconscious body.

"So, you're telling me good ol' Juke is gone for good?" she asks.

"James and Nibs swore it to me." I straighten my day dress and check it in the mirror. "Yet, I'm torn, because that was his hope. To find a way out of here."

"Out of the house, yes, but out of the town? I'd hope not." She walks to the window, leaning against the sill. "It would be an absolute pleasure to run into him in town someday."

"No!" My voice cracks. "Do not go near the guy, ever."

Her eyes flick toward me, a crease forming between them. "I'm only having a laugh. Calm down."

"Yeah, well..." I slam the wardrobe door shut and snap a flower hair-clip into place. "I'm sorry if I don't find it funny after last night."

"Hey." She slips to my side, hand on my shoulder. "He's gone, you said so yourself. And three cheers for Peter. I hope you rewarded him richly for that?"

I frown. "I thanked him. Yes."

A sly smile curves her lips. "Oh, you could have done better than that."

"Really, Jan?" I nudge her lightly and walk to the door. "Juke's lips on my neck one minute, and you expect I'd kiss Peter's the next? Let's go."

We meander downstairs, and as she heads into the dining area, a voice from the parlour stops me.

"Good morning," James greets, leaning against the doorframe.

"Good morning." I step closer. "Why are you out here?"

"I thought we might go into town for breakfast." He lifts my coat. "Would you like that?"

"I suppose."

He holds the coat open, and I slide my arms through, his hands reaching around, guiding each button into place. My eyes drift shut, welcoming his nearness, yet the memory of Juke rises like a sharp chill, and I step away.

"Where are we going?" I clear my throat.

He shoves his hands into his pockets. "He's gone, you know? Nibs and I dealt with him last night. He won't bother you again."

"I'm relieved to hear this." My tone is stiff.

"Yet you're still angry with me, aren't you?"

"It's Peter who has every right to be."

"I know, you're right." He exhales, resting against the wall. "I've invited him along too, is that alright?"

"It is. But why?"

"Morgan laid into me this morning. I acted rashly and told Juke to teach him a lesson. I don't know what I thought would happen. But when I saw the marks on your wrist, it enraged me. The idea that anyone would hurt you. I expected a punch, not a broken rib, and certainly not leaving him to freeze to death. I've made a mess of things and I'm sorry."

I stare a moment, then reach for his hand. "You did mess things, badly. And it could have cost Peter his life. But what's done is done, and I forgive your rashness. Heaven knows I've acted as badly."

"Yes, but..." He lifts a hand to my face, gliding a finger along the bruise. "It wasn't only Peter hurt, was it? And had he not stopped him..." His eyes darken. "Juke would have done far worse to you than even Peter. And it would have been my fault. So yeah, he's coming, because I don't know how to begin repaying him for protecting you."

The soft thud of crutches turns us to the stairwell, where Nibs and Peter descend. James sneaks a kiss, then strides to them. "Good morning, gentlemen."

"Good morning," Nibs says, guiding Peter by the arm, who glances between James and me. "Do you have time for a quick word in private?"

"Of course. Let's go to the office."

Situating Peter at the bottom, Nibs pats him on the back and slips away with James.

"Well." I sway gently on my feet. "You're free. How's it feel?"

"Like everything's changed." His gaze sweeps the hallway.

A beam of sunlight streams onto his forehead, and I take in Juke's handiwork, similar to my own—purple and gold bruising. I step closer and, as James did to me, brush my fingers along it. "I'm sorry I hit you."

"That was Juke's boot, but regardless, what you did was well deserved. I acted like an idiot, and had I not invaded your privacy, you wouldn't have felt compelled to lash out."

"All right," James says, returning, and I step away as he presses a hand to my back. "Breakfast awaits."

Propping the crutches, Peter walks ahead and swings open the door. "Ladies first." He gestures.

James and I stroll through, but I pause as Peter approaches the icy stairwell, hesitant at the incline. We watch as he tries to figure out how to get himself down, and when I've had enough, I step beside him.

"Follow my lead." I loop my arm through his. "One foot in front of the other."

"If I go down, you're coming with me. You sure?"

"Completely."

We step out, inching forward, cautious until we're safely on the ground.

"Thanks," he says, winded.

"I could have assisted him." James wraps an arm around me and tugs me ahead.

"No need." I wriggle out of his grip. "I'm quite capable, as you saw."

"Good morning," a young man in a black cap and suit greets us. He's positioned beside James' sedan and offers a low bow. "My name's Kit. I'm Cap's driver."

"Hello, Kit. It's lovely to meet you." I peek past him to the luxurious sedan with its maroon seating.

"Allow me." He takes my hand, and a flicker of memory sur-faces—stepping in a year ago, with all the optimism of what might lie ahead.

James follows me in, and once we're seated, he pulls me close. "I regret inviting company."

"Oh, stop it. You just finished saying you felt terrible for what hap-pened to him."

"Yeah, well." He leans his head against mine. "I want your attention. *All of it.*"

"You'll have it on Friday. Just don't go inviting anyone else to our date."

"Yes, ma'am."

He kisses me as the front doors open, and Kit and Peter climb in. I settle against James while Peter maneuvers the crutches into place between the seats, a pained expression across his face. Kit puts the car in gear and we pull away from the home, a wave of childish enthusiasm washing over me as we speed through the neighborhoods, the world flashing past.

Downtown appears, along with the two-story restaurant, Will's Bake-house, its name above the entrance in cheerful, bold lettering. The car parks, and I step out, admiring the evergreen garland twining along the picture windows in front. Will is brother to Morgan's friend Rose. I've heard of their restaurant, but never had the opportunity to visit.

James wraps a hand around me and leads us inside, where we're greeted by a warm, inviting aroma: hints of cinnamon and buttery dough. My lids lower for a moment, savoring the heavenly scent. When they open, unease grows as I take in Peter and James, their gazes fixed on me.

"Good morning!" a bright voice calls, pulling our attention. "James, how wonderful to see you." It's a young woman with thick chestnut hair and wide grey eyes.

"Rose." James takes her hand warmly. "Lovely as ever. How's your brother?"

"Oh, you know him, busy as ever. After your call, he insisted I snag you the moment you arrived."

"I'm a bit preoccupied at the moment." James gestures to me.

"Yes..." She glances over, studying me. "Hello, Wendy, Peter. I'll get them settled while you pop in. He'll be ever so grateful."

"Go on." I nudge him. "We'll be fine."

"All right." He lifts my hand to his lips. "Order for us, will you?"

"Certainly. See you in a minute."

He turns, but as he does, he bumps into someone. "Excuse me. My apologies." He steps back, flattening his shirt.

"No, my bad." Reverend Andrew and Bea stand there. "Captain James, yes?"

"Yes, it is. Please, remind me of your names?" James asks.

Andrew looks to Bea and grins. "I'm Reverend Andrew, and this is my wife, Bea."

They glance at Rose, who's watching the exchange. "Hello there, Rose," Bea greets. "You're radiant today, my dear. Oh, and Wendy and Peter, too! Hello, dears."

"Hello, Bea," I wave. "Do you come here often?"

"Oh yes." She clutches her husband's arm affectionately. "We've been friends with Rose and William for years. Tried to get them over to our little chapel, too, but maybe someday."

"You know if it were up to me, we'd have gone long ago," Rose says, lifting a stack of menus into her arms. "I far prefer you to Bishop Gehry."

"Well," James interjects. "Hate to break up the reunion, but I'd best go and talk with Will before Wendy starves. It's good to see you, Andrew, Bea."

"The pleasure's ours." Reverend Andrew shakes his hand, and James slips behind the counter and through the door.

"Cap'n!" A cheerful voice rings out. "Come on in, sir, and do take a load off."

"Smee, you've got five minutes, friend." James disappears inside.

Rose stares after him, then clasps the menus to her chest and motions us forward. "Let's get you all seated, shall we?"

We follow her through the dining room, and I take it all in. Elegant round tables are draped in silk cloth, decked with flower-filled vases. Stained-glass lamps dangle from the ceiling, their colored panes catching sunlight and casting a golden sheen across the room. Along the back wall, I'm drawn to the enormous windows showcasing the magnificent Neverpeak Mountains beyond.

It's breathtaking.

Rose seats Peter and me near the back and hands us our menus. "I'll have the waiter bring you our special, *Pain au Chocolat*, as an appetizer on the house. And what can I get you to drink?"

"Coffee would be lovely," I say. "Thank you."

"Same as the lady," Peter adds.

"Wonderful. Your waiter, Mr. Greyson, will bring those right out."

She glides away as Reverend Andrew and Bea wave goodbye, and settles them a few tables over with another couple. I lift the menu and blink at the endless array of choices. "How about you pick for us?"

"If that's what you need." He raises the menu and scans.

A minute later, the waiter appears, placing a basket of chocolate croissants, three coffees, cream, and sugar in the center. "Good morning, I'm Leonard. Have you had a chance to look over the menu?"

"We have, Leonard," Peter answers. "We'll get a pile of flapjacks for three."

"Certainly." Leonard jots it down. "With all the sides?"

"I'd say so. Wendy, anything else?" He glances at me, and I shake my head. "Then it seems that'll be all."

"Of course. I'll be back with your order." He strolls away, disappearing through a pair of double doors on the far side of the room.

I add a bit of cream and sugar to my coffee and stir, my gaze drifting out the window.

"So... did you sleep well?" Peter asks, reclining.

"Fitfully, but I managed. I told JaneAnn what happened."

"Really." He raises an eyebrow. "And what did she say?"

"She said she'd like to meet him in town." I warm my hands around the mug.

"Relatable." He lifts his coffee and sips.

"She also thought you were grand, as do I."

"Even as you nearly fainted, thinking I was about to abandon you? Surely, not."

I laugh softly. "I *was* furious when you started singing. Assumed you were mocking me."

"No." His fingers drum the table. "It was meant as a message, one he wouldn't understand."

"I should've known."

"Well, now you do." He extends his hand, offering me a croissant. "In the future, Madam Bird, you can count on me and my trusty crutch to fight off all those nasty ogre Jukes."

"What a hero." I wrap my hand over his, grinning.

I bite into the croissant, buttery layers mingling with warm chocolate, and release a moan, "Ooh. This is divine, you have to try it."

Pressing it to him, he tilts his head. "You know it's my ribs that broke, right? Not my hands."

"I know what's broken, silly. Now take a bite." He relents and takes one. "Good, huh?"

"Delightful." He pats his mouth with a napkin.

"So, tell me. The day we started our book, you said what happened changed you. Are you truly altered beyond repair?"

"Altered, yes..." He runs a hand through his hair. "But not beyond repair. Your insistent sweetness didn't let me stay broken for long. Did it?"

My cheeks warm, and we continue talking until Leonard returns, setting down steaming plates piled with flapjacks, eggs, bacon, and fried potatoes. James reappears, patting him on the back. "Leonard, good to see you."

James slips beside me and looks between us. "Sorry about that. Oh, this looks great."

"What did your friend want?" I ask.

"He had a request for me." He pops a piece of bacon into his mouth. "Nothing urgent. So, what do you think of the place?"

"It's beautiful, thank you." I kiss him and catch Peter's stare as I pull away, but he quickly averts his gaze.

"So, Peter, any future plans?" James asks.

"Yeah." Peter stabs a potato with his fork. "I've got a job interview with Starkey Manufacturing. They're looking for a new bookkeeper, so, we'll see."

"Because of the letter you wrote?" I ask.

"It is, yes."

"I didn't know you were a numbers guy," James says, biting into a croissant.

"He is. Even helps Morgan with tutoring the younger kids."

"Well, I'm good friends with Gentleman Starkey," James says. "I could offer a personal recommendation. Ensure you get the job."

"No, thank you," Peter replies. "I've got it."

"Suit yourself." James slips an arm around me.

"What about you?" Peter leans back. "Planning to stay in the family business?"

"You mean my father's job as Lord Regent?"

"Sure. Will you join ole dad in the capital?"

"Well, this isn't exactly how I planned to share it, but..." He turns to me. "You know Thomas was Chancellor before becoming Lord Regent?"

"Yes." My voice wavers.

"What you don't know is the reason he's not king." He exhales. "There was an agreement. He would rule as Regent until I turn twenty-two, at which point... I will be crowned King over Neverland."

"I'm sorry. What?" The fork slips through my fingers, clattering onto the plate. "You're—" I swallow hard. "You're becoming king?"

Chapter 6

"I'm sorry I never told you," James says.

"Heaven's sake!" My voice is unpleasantly shrill. "Why would you keep this to yourself?"

"You couldn't understand." He clenches his fork, pressing around the eggs. "I don't do this for myself; it's for my family. I'm duty-bound."

"Don't let duty bind you to a life you don't want," Peter says flatly. "No one will thank you for it."

"And what do you know about this?" James retorts. "Your big decision is whether to be a bookkeeper or not. Mine is about whether to become king of Neverland."

"*James...*" I whisper.

"Sorry. I only mean there's a world of difference between our lives, and it's not as simple as he implies."

Pressing back from the table, Peter stands. "You're right. But I guarantee prison isn't only chains and bars. For someone like you, it might look a hell of a lot like a crown. Excuse me."

He limps away, crutches tucked under his arms.

"I'm sorry." James takes my hands. "I've wanted to tell you, but I don't like how people act when they find out. Can you understand?"

"I do." I run a finger along his chin. "But I'm not them, and it's an insult if you think I am. Dash it, James! I have half a life, yet you still care for me. This doesn't change us. Titles, crowns, they mean nothing."

He stares, intensity in his gaze, then wraps a hand around my neck, pulling me close until our lips meet. Soft, but insistent.

"I love you, Wendy."

I don't move, only blink. "You what?"

He searches my face, releasing a laugh. "I didn't plan that. But you're my future and I'm not going to let anything ruin that."

I should say something, yet words fail me. He presses his forehead to mine, reading my silence.

"Don't overthink it. You don't have to say anything. I've been thinking about us for a long time. Take as long as you need, okay?"

"Thank you. You caught me off guard, that's all." I wrap my arms around him, holding tight. "I assure you, your words mean the world to me. And you're not the only one who's been thinking about us."

"I'm relieved to hear that." He pulls back smiling. "I'm eager for your birthday, as I'm confident my gift shall leave you far more speechless than I've made you now."

"Oh really. And do I get any hints?"

"None." He taps my nose. "You, my dear, must wait a miserable two days."

"Well, aren't you cruel?" I purse my lips. "Speaking of my birthday, I never asked what you were doing in town last night? You were early."

"Morgan reached out and said I was needed back. She and Nibs explained everything and said he needed to go. I was going to talk with Peter when we found you. I'm really grateful Morgan stepped up... but sorry it came to that."

"I see, well, I'm grateful too. But now that it's over, let's put it in the past where it belongs. Today is a new day, and I for one want to think about the future and perhaps, this gift you mentioned."

He chuckles and pulls me close. "Think away, but you get no hints."

"It was worth a try." I kiss his cheek.

* * *

A gentle breeze sweeps along the glistening pathway, lifting delicate snow flurries into the air. White flakes dance and sparkle in the golden sunlight, landing onto my gloved hand where they vanish. Above us, the sky is painted a deep cerulean blue, with not a single cloud in sight to mar the canvas. We stroll as a group toward Solomon Caw's Pond, ice skates slung over our shoulders and enthusiasm brimming in our spirits.

Today is my nineteenth birthday.

"So, enlighten me." John nudges my shoulder. "When can we anticipate additional provisions at dinner?"

"Oh, I think you're getting more than enough at mealtime, Johnny." I pinch his stomach, and he hops to the side, chuckling.

"Are you leaving so soon?" Maimie asks, arms wrapping around herself.

"Not sure, Mam. I'm getting a little old for the home, so Morgan offered to help me figure things out. Who knows what'll turn up."

"I heard Mrs. Brewster at church has generously opened her home to any of us poor orphans in need," JaneAnn says.

"Oh yeah?" I roll my eyes. "And what's the catch?"

"The usual stuff. Clean the house, make the meals, fetch the groceries, and of course, keep a job to pay a hefty rent. She's got such a big heart, though, so who could turn down such an opportunity?"

"And here I thought living with Juke was bad." I shiver.

Chuckling, she and Maimie move ahead.

"So," John says, "what do you aspire to, then?"

"Oh, I don't know. Guess I haven't aspired much. You probably have it all figured out, don't you?"

"Sure do." He leans close. "Stu Foggerty assured me of a position at the newspaper for the coming year. And between us, he's already compensating me for editorial work on his behalf."

"You have a job at seventeen?"

He holds a finger to his lips and nods. "However, that remains confidential. I haven't mentioned this to Nibs yet."

Michael tugs on his arm as the pond comes into view. "Well, I'll see you on the ice."

The two dash ahead.

It's official. I'm the only one with absolutely no plans. Probably because all of mine exist beyond this town, which I'm stuck in. Still, there's something about their readiness to settle. Create a life for themselves without the help of anyone else. Something I'm incapable of doing, it seems.

Resting on the pond's edge, the girls leisurely change into their skates while the boys hop about, tugging off boots. Slightly and Tootles are already on the ice, balancing unsteadily, tying their laces.

Llewelyn reclines nearby, so I meander over. "Mind if I join you?"

He glances up. "*Sit, sit,*" he signs, then pats the ground beside him.

"Thanks." I sit and loosen my boots. "So, James is taking me on a date tonight."

"*Really?*" He looks at me with an air of surprise. "*Perhaps you wear this then.*" He holds up a finger, reaches into his pocket, and lifts out an elegant blue box.

"For me?"

"*For you.*" He flips it open to unveil a golden necklace, the charm a delicate bird caught in flight.

"It's beautiful!" My breath catches. "Thank you…"

He lifts the necklace, fastening it around my neck. "*Perfect.*"

"I'll never take it off. And look." I tug back my sleeve, revealing the golden chain. "They match. Almost like they were made for each other."

"*You look like royalty.*"

Thoughts of royalty lead me to consider James' future as king. He'll be twenty-two in a year. Love or not, duty will surely outweigh any affection he has. This new information seems like a wrench in all my plans. We finish lacing our skates and glide onto the ice, my arm looped through his. One step after the next, and we coast effortlessly, the wind caressing our cheeks.

"*Remember.*" He points at me, then closes his fist, pressing his palm over it, and sliding it forward twice. "*You're enough.*" He tilts his head. "*Do you know this?*"

"I'm not so sure." I lean into him. "I'll always be halved. You know? Halfway to whole. Almost there, but never arriving."

"*No one ever arrives; it's all about the aim.*"

"I adore you, you know that?"

He beams and kisses my forehead. "*I love you, little one.*"

"Not so little anymore."

A shout breaks the moment: Michael calling his name.

"Sounds like someone needs you." I gesture to Michael, taunting him, arms flailing wildly.

He shakes his head. "*Of course, I'll see you.*"

Then he's off, racing full speed across the pond. Michael yelps as he draws near, but it's too late. Llewelyn scoops him up and tosses him into a snowbank, flurries of snow exploding everywhere. He pumps his fists in triumph as the group breaks into laughter and applause.

I giggle and glide away from the noise, seeking solace on the far side of the pond where it's quiet. As I skate, I gaze toward a nest perched on a thick tree branch, chicks chirping hungrily within. As the mother flutters past, breakfast in her beak, a memory stirs—Margaret and I, our final skate. Her final hours.

"*Come on, Wendy, you've been in a sulk all day,*" she said.

"*Just one of those days,*" I said. "*The stupid cycle's getting to me. It's three years now, and I'm just tired. Give me a reason to smile, and I will.*"

"It's time you make your own magic, sis." She flipped around, skating backward, eyes on the sky. "Take a deep breath and make the most of what you've got. Things aren't so bad, really. We're better off than most folks in Neverwood Valley, that's for sure."

"It's not just our station; it's what we represent. Yesterday, Levi Gilmour stopped in the street, shouting, 'Crikey! It's the cursed orphans! Don't look them in the eyes lest you catch it.' Jan kicked him straight between the legs, so that shut him up, but still. I know wherever we go, no one's going to understand us."

She twirled, balancing unsteadily on one leg, arms spread wide like wings.

"Are you really going to let Levi get to you? He'd make his own mother cry."

A chirping caught our attention and she gestured to a cluster of spruce, where a cardinal flitted between the branches, his coat a glorious red.

"That's my bird," she said with pride. "See the pale feathers? That's his necklace. I named him Robin. On our first day here, he came to Peter and I while we sat on the stairwell."

To my surprise, Robin flew over, landing on Margaret's shoulder. Her eyes widened with delight and she gave me an exuberant grin.

Then as quick as he came, Robin flapped his wings and vanished into the woods. "Let's follow him," she said. "I bet there's all sorts of stuff in there to get your mind off these woes."

"No, not today," I observed the shadowy woods. "I'm hungry and cold. Let's skate a little longer and head home for lunch."

"Come on, please." She puckered her bottom lip.

"Another day."

"Fine... You're no fun today."

If only she'd grabbed my hand—told me she didn't have another day to spare. Instead, she let go, and we kept skating until the fateful moment.

A crack echoed, the ice giving way beneath her. She plunged into the freezing water, and instantly, I slammed onto my stomach, grabbing her hand as she submerged beneath the surface. My grip was the only thing *that kept her from going under the ice, but it wasn't enough to get her out.*

I screamed for help till my throat was raw, but we had come alone, so she flailed, gasping, as my strength waned. I didn't stop trying, and suddenly drawn to my screams, Peter burst through the trees, breathless. He was by my side in an instant, and together, we pulled her out and onto her back. But she had been submerged for too long, her skin blue, and breath shallow. Wrapping her in his coat, Peter tried desperately to warm her, to no avail. We began the arduous journey home; fully aware things were grim.

The moment we stepped through the door, Nibs whisked her away, and Morgan ran for the doctor. I slumped by the parlour fire, numb from exhaustion. Peter sat with me, rubbing my arms, attempting to restore some warmth to my half-frozen body. He wrapped me in a blanket and stayed close, but my mind had shut down, and at some point, he disappeared.

Eventually, Morgan came and guided me to Margaret, speaking calmly into my ear. The moment we entered, I dissolved into tears, everything she said flooding back. Margaret was dying, and it was time to say goodbye. I drifted to the bed, sinking to my knees, holding onto her, praying desperately for my life to somehow extend hers.

"I'm so sorry!" I choked out. "This is my fault. I should have listened to you."

"Oh, stop it. This wasn't your fault," she said, voice barely a whisper. "I do what I want." She paused, catching her breath. "Henley says there's a dozen ways we could die every day, but also a dozen ways we can live. On Sunday, he and I imagined what heaven would be like, little did we know..."

Her gaze wandered to the window, snow falling softly beyond the glass. "I know you're feeling stuck. But be patient. You'll get out of here someday. I'm sure of it."

"But how can you be?"

A calm passed over her features. "Because I saw it. We were in pink... and oh, how he soared."

She gripped my hand, eyes closing.

"Margaret?"

Her lids fluttered, but remained shut. I buried my face into her shoulder, aching for more, but time was short. "I love you," is all I managed.

It took a moment, but her eyes opened a fraction and she whispered, "And I you..." She squeezed my fingers. "Tell Henley... I meant what I said."

And for the final time, her lids lowered, and she surrendered to a deep sleep she never woke from.

Her death was a painful blow to my already fragile heart. For a long time, the light within was extinguished. But I wasn't alone.

A year later, Henley and I walked to the pond, and Margaret's redbird came to me. I released my sorrow there. And nearly every day since, Robin appeared on my windowsill.

I glide along the pond's edge until I spot my boots and settle, loosening the skates and pulling them off.

"Finished already?"

I glance over my shoulder. Peter stands nearby, leaning on his crutch.

"When did you get here?"

"A few minutes ago. Wasn't sure I'd come at all, but thought I might as well get some air."

I nod to the woods. "I'm going to take a walk. Want to join me?"

"I'm honored, but I should warn you, I'm slower than Nibs in the morning with these things."

I stand and face him. "Then we'll inch through it together." I tug on his arm. "Come on."

"You've been warned. But lead on, birthday girl."

We head toward an opening in the stand of spruce hedging the pond, but pause when Nibs calls out. "Where exactly are you two sneaking off to?"

"Just taking a hike," I say as he and Morgan stroll up. "Want to join us?"

"I'd say so." He motions between us. "You two need a chaperone."

"He's in denial that you're leaving us," Morgan says.

"Oh, please do save the tears till I'm gone."

"So cruel." Nibs presses a hand to his heart.

"Come on, Peter."

We enter the misty woods, the merriment behind us fading beneath the howl of wind and the crunch of snow beneath our boots. As I gaze around, it's as though we've entered a new world, trees painted silver, their branches intertwining like delicate braids.

"So, nineteen years. How's it feel?" Morgan asks, stepping beside me.

"Like I've only been alive for five of them."

"Tell us what you really think," Nibs says.

"Sorry... It's just hard to say I feel nineteen when most of it's non-existent. Wouldn't you agree, Peter?" I glance at him, slogging through the deep snow.

"Not sure I even have the maturity of a five-year-old," Peter says, lifting a crutch, "maybe a three-year-old?"

"Even that's being gracious, bud," Nibs adds.

"You know what, never mind." Morgan shakes her head. "I was just trying to make polite conversation."

"You must know that's a hopeless cause with us." I laugh.

"Clearly." She chuckles.

"So..." Nibs spins, walking backward in front of me. "What Morgan meant to ask was, how's it feel to be five now?"

Peter looks at me, eyebrow raised, likely wondering if I'll dare be honest.

"I'll never feel my age or like I belong anywhere," I say. "But can't say it's all been bad. There's lots to be thankful for too. Like you three."

Peter offers something like a smile, tinged with a sadness I understand.

Silence settles, not heavy but safe and we walk along, breathing hard as we push through the heavy snow. Up ahead, birdsong rings out, and then a flash of red catches my eye.

It's Robin.

I watch him. He perches on a branch ahead, but takes flight as we draw near. Peter studies him, and says quietly, "That looks like the bird Margaret was so fond of."

"It is." I nod. "Come on."

I lead the way, following as he flies ahead.

"Remember your first blueberry pie?" Nibs pipes up.

I groan. "Why in the world is that on your mind?"

"Because it's such a *you* story."

He launches into the sugar-to-salt fiasco that sent Elizabeth sprinting to the bathroom sick. Everyone laughs while I soldier through, allowing them this moment. Morgan follows with a kindlier story: my first sewing attempts. She taught me the basics, and I took the initiative to resize spare hand-me-down dresses for a local family in need. I can't deny the memory is warming, unlike Nibs'.

"Go on, Peter," Nibs says. "Share an embarrassing tale of the birthday girl, it's customary."

"It's really not," I mutter.

Peter looks at me, amused. "I was thinking of our first Christmas the other day."

"I don't know if I remember that," I say.

"Well, I do. You were determined to make it perfect. Ornaments, decorations, a homemade wreath. Then you came down with a fever on Christmas Eve."

"Oh, yes. It was horrible. The first time I got sick and it ruined everything."

"You may not have realized it," Peter continues, "but that was the first time we all came together. When you went down, JaneAnn stepped up and rallied us. We got a tree, decorated it, and bought gifts. Your reaction the next morning was perfect."

"I didn't know JaneAnn took charge," I say.

"She sure did," Nibs grumbles. "Hadn't realized till then how bossy she was."

"Perhaps you'd be surprised what others would do for your happiness," Morgan says softly.

"Perhaps I would. I certainly didn't—" I pause.

Robin takes a sharp turn and enters a shadowy cleft in the nearby hillside.

"What's wrong?" Morgan asks, hopping aside as a gray-haired squirrel darts past.

"Look over there." I gesture to the hill. "Come on."

I march toward the cleft, where a large opening splits the rock, and a crescent-shaped etching is carved into the stone.

"Interesting." I lean closer. "What do you think this is?"

"Looks like some sort of marker." Peter traces the curve.

"A marker usually means there's something inside," Nibs says.

"Then let's check it out." Morgan grabs him by the sleeve, and the two vanish out of sight. I look at Peter, and we follow.

The world grows dim as we enter. Too dim. I brush away a cobweb. "Well, this is a bummer. Can't see anything."

"Nah, just got to feel your way," Nibs says, shuffling.

"Hey!" Morgan yelps. "Hands off, pal."

"Sorry," he mumbles sheepishly.

I giggle and glance around, eyes catching a faint flicker ahead. Leaning forward, I stare at whatever it is. It's not steady, but surely something's there. "There's a light in the passageway."

"Where?" Morgan walks closer.

"Straight ahead. It comes and goes."

"Whatcha got for us, birthday girl?" Nibs places a firm hand on my shoulder.

"If you focus, you'll see it."

We stare, the world around us silent, save for the soft drip of water echoing from somewhere deep within. I dig the heel of my boot into the ground, watching... waiting, the rich scent of damp earth filling my nostrils.

"I can't see anything." Morgan eventually groans. "And let's be honest, if we wander off, we'll never get out again."

"She's got a point," Nibs says. "There's a lot of darkness, and that's about all. It was a fun idea, but we should go back."

"Not yet," I protest. "Wait a little longer."

"Sorry." Morgan squeezes my arm. "We'll get a flashlight and return another day. I promise."

"Cheer up." Nibs nudges me. "There's cake and presents at the house. Come on."

Neither wait for a response, and saunter to the exit, disappearing into the light.

"You coming?" Peter asks.

Resigned, I turn to go, but a chirp deeper in the cave holds me.

"No," I say. "You go on, and save me a piece."

"*Okay*." He breathes out. "Let's have it. Why are we here?"

"She wanted to go exploring that day," I say. "Per usual, I was being stubborn and said no. What would have happened had I just gone?"

"So, you're off on some adventure into the unknown for Margaret, is that it?"

I exhale, staring into the darkness. "I owe it to her."

"Do you?" His crutches scuffle closer.

"I know it's silly, but I can't shake the feeling."

"As crazy as it is, I actually do understand. Okay. Take my arm."

"Really?" I wrap my hand around his forearm, heart swelling.

"It's your birthday." He pats my shoulder. "What kind of friend would I be to deny you today of all days?"

"You're being nice, but you don't have to do this."

"I don't?" He guides us forward. "How generous of you. I feared another beating otherwise."

"Well... thank you." I lean forward and kiss his cheek.

His crutches catch on a rock, and he stumbles forward. I throw myself around him, holding fast while he steadies.

"Thanks..." he says, voice soft in my ear.

"You okay?" I pull away, a flutter in my chest.

"I'm peachy."

My fingers slide back around his arm, and we continue, inching into the darkness, with only a glimmer of light in the distance beckoning.

We continue on, the chirps fading, leaving only silence.

"What if it never arrives?" I glance behind, the shadows consuming us on all sides. "Like those nightmares that just keep going endlessly."

"We're nearly there," he says, the exertion hitting him.

And he's right; another minute passes, and we arrive. The light, though dim, gathers like bubbles floating gently within a wooden archway.

"Jeepers..." I breathe out.

"Yes indeed, but don't get anxious on me now."

"What *is* this stuff?" I step through the archway, the bubbles expanding into warmth. A glowing mist surrounds us, dancing on our fingers like paint droplets.

"Not sure." He flexes his hand, vapors swirling around it.

With each step, a strange energy coats my skin, clinging and raising goose bumps.

"Don't let go." I press closer to his side, taking his crutch so he can balance against me.

"I wouldn't dare."

A quiver rushes through me as I dart a look around the tunnel of light, an overwhelming sense of being swallowed alive. Mist washes over us in waves, over and over, until it gradually dissolves. Then, at last, we step into open air, onto a rocky incline overlooking a vibrant village in the depths below.

"I must be dreaming..." I mumble.

"Me too." He lifts his other crutch and tilts his head, staring at it before throwing it aside.

"Why did you do that?"

"Because." A grin fills his face. "The pain is gone."

Chapter 7

"The pain is gone? But how's that possible?" A knot expands in my chest. "The mist?"

"Maybe." He turns his head to the side. "How's my face look?"

I lean in, examining the edge of his forehead, the bruising gone. "It's perfect."

"Oh?" His eyebrows lift. "Well, thank you."

"Vanity at a time like this?" I turn toward the open expanse. "Where in Neverland are we..."

I gaze out at the quaint village nestled in the immense cavern below. My whole world is shifting, and I know there's no returning from what we've unearthed here. For five long years, we've known only cold and snow, with the occasional warm day when the icicles melt. Here, in this strange world far from the luminous sparkle of snow, the air itself seems to buzz with the promise of something more.

From up here, I can see the circular patterns of the neighborhoods stretching out from the town's center, where a bell tower rises into the black sky. The homes are honey-colored stone cottages with thatched roofs and bright red and yellow flower blossoms beneath the windows. It's like a storybook come to life.

"Where's all the people?" Peter asks.

"You're right." I scan the village. "There must be someone home. How else are the lights on? Or the fountains still flowing?"

"I agree. But there's one way to find out." He glances at me, shoulders lifted.

Between us and the village lies a steep hillside, something Peter couldn't have managed ten minutes ago. "You sure about this?"

"I've never felt better." He takes my hand. "Come on!"

I follow him to the edge, and we begin our descent, zig-zagging carefully, avoiding sharp ledges and prickly bushes, until we reach the bottom, climbing down the remainder of the way. Once on solid ground, we brush off our clothes and face a cobblestone path, with a wooden arch at the entrance bearing the words '*Winter Woods*' etched across.

"Interesting," Peter muses. "So... which came first? The town above or the town below?"

"Let's find out."

We stroll beneath the arch, passing into the village, the air balmy—infused with the intoxicating scent of sweet jasmine trailing along the cottage walls.

"You may have to drag me out of this place," I say, spinning to take it all in.

"I don't know about that. If it's so wonderful, where is everyone?"

"Oh, come on. When was the last time we were warm without a fire? The cold doesn't faze this place. It's like magic."

"Enchanting as it is, something's wrong. I can sense it."

We follow the cobblestone path to the village center. In the middle a majestic marble statue stands, depicting a winged man beside an oversized owl.

"Lord Malori and his faithful Foxmoon," Peter reads from the statue's base. "I'd say he's a Faerie, judging by the size difference."

"A Faerie?"

"Yeah, but it's just a statue."

"Perhaps it's not. Peter, I never told you how I found you that night in the warehouse. I had a vision. It was as though I saw the world through the eyes of a Faerie. I knew where you were and came to you, made a fire, and saw you…" I pause, the memory unsettling. "You were bruised and bloody, unconscious. But when I touched you, you woke screaming. Maybe it was real, and maybe the faerie came from this town!"

His eyes narrow. "You saw me that night?"

I step closer and reach for his shirt, lifting it, his skin smooth and untouched. "There was a bruise stretching along this area."

"Why are you telling me this now?"

"It seemed too fantastic to be true." I step back.

"*Wendy! Peter*!" a voice calls out in the distance. It's Morgan.

"We're over here!" I call back.

She and Nibs round the corner, red-faced. "What's going on?" Nibs demands. "Where *are* we?"

"We were waiting for you," Morgan says, "but you never showed. And what the heck was that light tunnel we passed through?"

"I have no idea, but look!" I gesture around. "Isn't this amazing."

"So, I ask again." Nibs inclines his head up. "Where *are* we?"

"Winter Woods," Peter answers. "Pretty little town that's been abandoned. Unless everyone's just… asleep? Still figuring it out."

"Yes, we are, so let's go and do that." I tug on his arm. "We'll check this direction, and you two go that way."

"Fine, but shout if you find anything important," Nibs calls.

We pass a row of shuttered shops with "Closed" signs on the windows, the sight a bit depressing.

"Look at the vines," I say. "They're everywhere."

"Yeah… no one's maintained this place for a long time, it would appear."

In the distance, a faint squeak catches my attention. I pause, listening. The sound weighs on me, as though something deep inside is trying to claw its way up.

Without thinking, I sprint towards the sound.

"Hey!" Peter jogs after me. "Where are you going?"

I stop short as they come into view. "It's a swing set."

"And how do you know this?"

"I'm not sure." I stare, drawn to them. "Come on!"

I push open the creaky gate, gliding through the overgrown grass till my fingers grip the swing's chain, cool to touch. Sitting, I let my body take over—kicking forward, then back, momentum lifting me higher and higher. Peter stands at the edge of the park, watching.

"Come here!" I beckon to him.

He approaches, sits beside me, and studies my movements. Then, gripping the chains, he kicks off, slow at first, but soon gains speed until we're side by side. The moment sparks something to life in my chest, and then the world flickers like a candle in the wind, and everything disappears.

I'm blinking in bright sunshine, fingers trembling at my sides, standing at the edge of a cliff. Below, emerald waters stretch into the horizon.

"You ready?" Peter asks, determination in his tone.

"Not in the least," I say, breathing in the salty air, a warm breeze brushing my skin, calming my quivering body. "But this is what we're here for. So, let's do it before I faint."

Our hands join together, our feet moving to the edge.

"Alright," he says. "Three, two—deep breath—ONE!"

We run, leaping off the edge and into the open air. Wind rushes past, weightlessness taking hold, and a scream rises in my throat. And then... cool water meets us like an embrace, folding around our bodies as we plunge deep beneath the surface. All is silent, the world far away. Sunlight flickers through the water, illuminating a school of rainbow fish, their dazzling colors drawing me to them.

"Wendy?" Peter's beside me. "What's happening?"

The sea and sunlight flicker and vanish. I'm back in the swing, fingers gripping the chains.

Peter stares at me. "Hey. Talk to me. What's wrong?"

"I'm okay." I blink and look around. "I think I... I just had a memory."

"You what?" His mouth falls open.

"I know."

"But how? We don't get memories!"

"Yet I did." I press my hands to my cheeks, laughing. "And it was as clear as you are to me now."

"Okay..." He wraps a hand over my wrist. "Tell me."

"It was brief... and we were together." I look at him, seeing him in a new way. "Peter, we were close before all of this."

A quiet ache surfaces in his eyes before he looks away. "What were we doing?"

"We were high above the sea, and we jumped. It felt real. Every second of it. The sunshine... the warmth."

"Well, that's incredible... an actual memory. But how?"

"I don't know, but it's time we check the homes for clues. We're bound to find some answers."

We leave the park, approaching the nearest house, and knock. No answer. We try the next, still nothing. After six more, he opens the door, and we enter a musty room with cobwebs clinging to the corners.

"As presumed, no one's home," I say.

"Clearly." He lifts a pamphlet from the table. "What do we have here?"

He holds it under a stream of light pouring through the window from an outside street lamp. We lean close to read.

To: The Esteemed Heads of Households in Sector B,
Honoured Sir or Madam,
By decree of Lord Malori, and in keeping with accords set forth for the preservation of our Village, you are hereby informed of imminent relocation measures concerning your residence within the bounds of Evacuation Sector B.

In accordance with the protocols of safe passage, all affected households shall present themselves for registration at Skyway Avenue, precisely at the fifth hour past midday.

This course of action has been enacted with solemn intent: to safeguard the well-being of our people. Your composed cooperation in this matter is both expected and deeply valued.

Further instruction and particulars shall be conveyed in Malori Square, at the sounding of the sixth hour.

I am, Madam,

Your obedient servant,

Lympia Griffiths

"Well, that answers it." I press against the table. "They're gone. But why? It doesn't say."

"As I said, something doesn't add up. But let's keep searching."

We head out of the home and back toward the village square. Trekking along a narrow side street, we come upon a notice board positioned beside a shuttered business called *Figsworth Tavern*. A paper, yellowed with time, is nailed to the wood and reads:

BEWARE BLOOD

The hairs on my arms stand on end. "What does that mean?"

"Not sure." He rubs his neck. "Let's find Nibs and Morgan, though, and show them the pamphlet."

The town is quaint—rockers on storefront porches, white picket fences where neighbors likely conversed once. Windows are cracked open, and I imagine smells of baking bread or pies drifting out. But now, flowerbeds spill over, hedges grow wild, and the windows are dusty. I wonder, was this a sweet place, full of lovely people who cared for one another?

Even empty, it seems full. And yet... something terrible drove the villagers away. But what was it? What does 'blood' refer to?

I enjoy a good mystery as much as anyone, but this is different. Unlike a story, where the worth of each character remains safely within the pages of a book, this involves real people who once roamed these streets. Was the Fae in my vision one of them? Are they now alone? Or were they ever real at all, and my dream merely a coincidence?

We navigate the winding streets until spotting a brightly lit cottage, its door partially ajar.

"Looks like we found them," Peter says, slipping a warm hand into mine and pulling me toward it.

Something in his touch is assuring, despite the confusion around us. Nothing here makes sense. Lights on with no logical explanation, almost like the village is alive, even without the people.

At the cottage, we press open the door and stumble upon an unexpected sight: Morgan weeping into Nibs' arms.

"What's wrong?" I step closer.

They look up, startled. "Uh, well." Nibs looks to Morgan.

"We found this pamphlet." She dabs her face with a hanky. "It upset me, that's all, but I'm fine."

I take the familiar paper. This one's addressed to *Sector A*, but it's otherwise identical to the one we saw earlier. I flip it over and there's a handwritten note on the back:

A decision has been made due to those killed yesterday. Malori instructs us to flee by dawn. Blood is fast approaching, along with fears of Anathema. We did what we could. We can't risk more lives. Get the family and go.

—Marin

I settle on the edge of a chair, and Peter stands behind, gripping the backrest.

"We found the same in another home," Peter says. "But we should mention we've both had some... unexpected changes. Wendy got a memory from the Before. And my body, well, it healed somehow."

Their eyes widen, lips parting in surprise.

"How's that possible?" Morgan asks, forehead creased.

"I don't know." Peter lifts an arm. "I felt the change after going through the mist. It had to be what fixed me up. As for Wendy, I couldn't say."

"I can't believe I didn't notice earlier," Nibs says. "I guess with all of this distracting me, I missed it. I'm happy for you, truly, but I question the safety of being here now."

"He's right." Morgan rises. "We should consider what we're getting ourselves into by being here. Maybe this has been enough for one day."

The two look to Peter and me, waiting for our response.

"I was hoping to come back," I say. "This place, it's incredible. I'd hate to run away after something wonderful happened. Right, Peter?"

His head stays low, but his eyes lift just enough to catch Nibs' gaze. What could he be thinking? I glance at Nibs, his nostrils flare, and he offers the slightest shake of his head, causing Peter to turn away.

"We'll head home, eat cake, and talk it over," Peter says.

I get the sense that's not actually what he wants. But I don't question it, as the others are noticeably on edge.

"Yes," Morgan agrees, taking my hand. "Wendy... tell us about the memory."

"I'll share it on the way back."

We head for the hill, and I recount the vision. I expect wonder, maybe even joy—but the mood stays somber. Heavy. The weight of everything hangs in the air between us. I want to ask them what the blazes I'm missing? But, I don't. I'm not accustomed to feeling kept in the dark, yet it certainly seems to be the case right now.

At the base of the slope, we begin the slow climb, my mind struggling to make sense of everything. As we near the top, my foot slips on a smooth stone and I stumble backward with a yelp. Peter shoots his hand forward, catching my wrist, and pulling me into himself.

"You okay?" His face is inches from my own.

"Yes, thanks." I swallow hard.

"Anytime, sweetheart." He steadies me. "Just watch my feet, one step at a time."

I bump into his shoulder, biting back a smile. He helps me over the final crest. The mist waits ahead, dense and glowing.

"Good riddance," he says, gliding past the crutches and stepping into the fog, Morgan close behind.

"I know you want to stay," Nibs says quietly, facing the light.

"And? We're leaving, so I'll have to get over it."

"You must see, this place may not be safe. Healing and memory seem nice on the surface, but what else is happening to us? I can't help but fear the longer we remain, the more our bodies will react to this world, and who knows if it's all for the good."

"I hear you, don't worry about it. Let's get home."

I glance back at the village, already sure I'll return. The only question is, will I come alone? I'm ready to do so. No amount of fear or worry could keep me away now that I know it's here.

He wraps an arm around me, and we step into the mist, the enchanting village fading into the background.

"**Happy birthday**!" the group exclaims as I enter the dining room.

Maimie reaches for my hand, tugging me toward a chair, where a pile of presents waits for me. "Where have you been?" she scolds. "We started to worry!"

"Wouldn't you know it," Nibs says as we sit, "we went and got ourselves lost exploring the woods."

"Yes, I'm sorry we're so late," I add.

"Oh, well, at least you're here now." She presses a gift into my hands. "This is from us girls. We all chipped in."

"Thank you all so much!" I tear off the wrapping and lift out a pale blue dress with puffed short sleeves, a dark blue sash around the waist, and delicate white lacing along the collar and hem.

"This is lovely." A matching hair bow slips onto my lap, and I hold it up.

"I hoped you'd like it!" Maimie wraps her arms around me.

"I *do*—it's exactly my style." I give her hand a grateful squeeze.

"I'll fix your hair up with the bow when you wear it," Hannah says.

"As long as you come alone." I shoot a look at Agnes and Elizabeth, who giggle.

"Mine's the black bag," Morgan says, settling across from me.

I place the bag on my lap and reach inside. There's an array of luxuries—face cream, a powder box, rouge, eyeshadow, mascara, lipstick, and nail color. I examine each one, dazzled.

"Wow... thank you! These are wonderful."

She bobs her head, eyes still red around the rim from her earlier tears.

"Last one." Maimie puts a final gift on my lap.

I glance around, waiting for someone to claim it, but when no one does, unwrap it. Inside is an elegant leather journal with my name engraved on the cover. A tiny silver key rests within the lock. Aware of who the gift giver is now, I gaze at Peter, inspecting his fingernails with a sly curve on his lips.

"Thank you all." I suppress a laugh. "I'll treasure these always."

Elizabeth and Alexander emerge from the kitchen carrying steaming Quiche Lorraine, followed by Agnes and Jack with bowls of fresh fruit. I push the presents aside and settle in for a late lunch.

My mind's a whirlwind of questions, none of which I can answer. So, I listen instead, leaning on my elbow while Slightly, Tootles, and the Twins discuss a venture they're working on. Llewelyn has been mentoring them in carpentry, and now they intend to start a business together. Their big debate is what to name it. Needless to say, my mind turns to mush as they go back and forth, until JaneAnn announces it's time for dessert. She slips into the kitchen and returns with a chocolate cake, a single candle flickering on top.

"Make a wish!" Michael says, nearly bouncing from his seat.

I stare at the flame, the phrase "*make a wish*" echoing.

The world is vast, and like the flame, I am ready to blaze brightly, lest I be extinguished. This place we've called home; I outgrew it long ago.

I blow out the candle, a wisp of smoke fading—my wish—to see the world beyond this town.

JaneAnn pats my shoulder and begins slicing the cake. "Enjoy! Mams made this herself."

"Thank you." I place a hand over hers. "I don't say it enough."

She reaches around, hugging me, and I grip her firmly.

As John distributes the cake, I take a bite, leaning back to savor the moment. But then an unexpected *bang* pulls me from my thoughts. The front door bursts open. The room falls silent as everyone turns toward the hallway, a striking young woman striding in.

Her skin is radiant, a golden-brown tone, and her long, flowing black hair cascades over her shoulders. She searches the room until she spots me.

"Well, well, Wendy." She inclines her head to me. "We finally meet."

I glance at Nibs, puzzled, and he shrugs.

"I'm sorry," I say. "Do I know you?"

"Of course not."

She snaps her fingers. A man with wavy, coal-black hair and a woman with white-blonde hair step beside her, both dressed entirely in black. The woman holds a dress bag, and the man carries a silver case. The two glare around the room as if we were insects.

"The Captain sent me to prepare you for this evening," the woman continues. "My name is *Tiger Lily*. It's nice to meet you."

Chapter 8

Tiger Lily's vibrant hazel eyes study me, awaiting a response.

"Uh, hi." I glance around at the group watching us. "James hadn't mentioned this, so I apologize, I wasn't expecting you."

"It's no trouble at all. Now that we're here, though, are you ready?"

"Yes, certainly." I stand and flatten my skirts. "Um, the girls' dormitory is up the stairwell."

Noting Maimie's excited expression, Tiger Lily purses her lips. "Somewhere private would be best."

"You can use the office," Nibs offers, pushing back from the table. "I'll unlock it."

"That would be appreciated." Tiger Lily follows him out of the room with the man and woman trailing behind.

"Well, go on now." JaneAnn pokes my side. "You've got a big night ahead of you."

"Oh, I know it." I chew my lip and glance at Peter, pushing the cake around with his fork. "Thank you all for the lovely birthday."

He doesn't look up, and something about that leaves me uneasy.

"Have fun with the captain," Maimie chirps, pulling my attention.

"Yet with a measure of restraint, of course." John wags a finger.

"Thanks, Johnny. I'll be sure to only have a marginally good time. Well, if you'll excuse me, the trio awaits my presence."

A chorus of farewells follows as I exit the room and approach the office, pausing at the door.

The woman beckons. "Come, come!" She's a fascinating creature with a devastatingly tight bun and dark, claw-like nails drumming against her hip.

I obey and step in just as the man kicks the door shut, a knowing grinning tugging at his mouth. He folds his thick arms and circles me slowly, sizing me up like a hungry wolf.

"Boh, we can-a certainly work with this, no?" he says.

"Indeed," Tiger Lily agrees, unzipping the bag. "Would you like to see your gown, Wendy?"

"Oh yes, please!"

She lifts out a floor-length, glittering gold evening gown and holds it under the light. "Picked it myself."

"It's... beautiful!"

"There's also a pair of silk gloves." Tigerlily rests the dress on the chaise. "And Cecco, show her the shoes, let's get her thoughts on those."

"Sì, certo, signora."

He opens the silver container, revealing a pair of shimmering golden heels. My mouth drops open.

"Well then, that's answer enough." Tiger Lily observes me. "We have much to do and little time. Let's get to work."

Over the next couple of hours, I am pulled, pinched, and pressed as my appearance transforms. First, I grit my teeth—my ribs assaulted with every tug of the corset as Jill, the blonde, cinches it tightly around my waist. The effort pays off, though, and the dress slips on like silk, hugging every curve and lifting the uppermost part of my chest. Feelings of girlhood flee; tonight, I am undeniably a woman.

Next, my nails are sculpted and painted a daring red. Then come various kinds of makeup carefully applied. A pair of dangling earrings is added, and my hair is styled into an elaborately braided crown, with a strand loose on each side.

Finally, the shoes are slipped onto my feet, a spritz of jasmine and a hint of musk dust my neck, and I'm led to the full-length mirror for the reveal.

I'm still myself, just enhanced. And judging by their expressions, I'd say that's for the best.

"She's perfection!" Jill fans herself, collapsing onto the chaise.

"Weh coodn't-a done-a better, no?" Cecco says, plopping beside her and wiping his forehead.

Evidently, perfecting me is an exhausting job.

"What do you think?" Tiger Lily asks, resting her hands on my shoulders. "Do you like it?"

I can't deny I'm striking. Red lipstick to match my nails, bold black eyeliner sharpening my gaze, and my body wrapped tightly in glorious gold fabric.

"It's perfect!"

"He's here!" Morgan peeks through the door. "Well goodness, look at you."

"You like it?" I pose.

"Oh yes, and he's going to love it."

"Okay, well, tell him she's coming," Tiger Lily says.

"Will do."

Morgan disappears, and Tiger Lily nudges me to the door. "Time to go."

"Buona fortuna, mademoiselle!" Cecco blows a kiss. "Sei Bellissima!"

"He said good luck, and you look beautiful," Jill says with a yawn. "And he's right. You're going to make him weak in the knees."

"My thanks for all of this." I gesture to myself, hurrying past.

The door opens, and my breath quickens as I enter the hallway, drawn to James, who paces near the entrance. Jill is wrong. I'm the one who's weak in the knees. He looks incredible, his hair neatly slicked back and dressed in a fitted navy-blue suit with a vest and bow tie.

I turn to Tiger Lily, who winks before closing the door, catching James' attention.

"Gracious..." He looks me up and down, lips parting. "You're stunning!"

"This was your three-person crew's doing." I approach, the click of my heels echoing on the hardwood. "I must admit, though, I share your sentiment—but for you, of course."

"You are naturally breathtaking. With or without my three-person crew."

I press a gloved hand to my burning cheek. "You flatter me, sir."

"Good. For I dearly mean to." He hands me a navy-blue gift bag. "This is for you. Happy birthday."

"Thank you." I reach in and lift out a white coat lined with lustrous gold buttons, a fur collar, and cuffs. "You got this for me?" I stroke the silky material, captivated by its softness.

"Absolutely." His face glows. "That's cashmere and wool. The finest coat money can buy. When I saw it, I knew it needed to be wrapped around you."

I place it in his hands and spin. "Help me?"

"My pleasure." He slips it on, one arm at a time, then steps away. "A perfect fit."

"In that case, I believe we're ready to go."

He opens the door, and we step onto the porch, frigid air nipping at our noses. Taking my hand, he guides me down the stairs, his arm secure around my waist as the dazzling heels quickly become impractical against the ice. Ahead, the car waits, engine humming.

"Right here, boss," Kit calls.

We turn to where Kit and Peter lean against the fence. My neck warms under Peter's gaze. He removes a cigarette from his lips, exhaling slowly, one brow raised, surveying me.

"Oh, good, there you are," James says. "What are you doing?"

"Just getting some air. You've been working me like a dog all day." Kit pushes off the fence and takes a final drag. "Good talkin' to you, Peter."

He tosses the cigarette into the snow and strolls to us. "Good evening, Ms. Wendy. My, my, aren't we lovely tonight?"

"Kit," James cuts in, "could you kindly not treat the lawn like your personal ashtray?"

"Sure thing, Cap." A broad grin spreads across his face. "Now let's get this beauty out of the cold and on her way."

James leads me forward, and I glance back at Peter. He holds my gaze then drops the cigarette, crushing it beneath his heel, and disappears into the shadows along the side of the home.

The restaurant sits at the foot of Neverpeak Hills, its brightly lit marquee glowing with the name, *Rêveur Éveillé,* in graceful cursive. Crawling to a stop, Kit parks the sedan behind a line of other cars, edging a double-wide sidewalk. Opulently dressed men and women stream toward the entrance, a blur of dazzling elegance.

No matter how often I've imagined this world, the mind cannot truly create what it doesn't know. As Kit opens the door, I take his hand and step into the luxury firsthand, my heart twirling with delight.

A young man saunters past with some companions and averts my attention as he whistles. "Ooh wee! Got a real hotsy totsy here. How you doing, sweetheart?"

My lip curls as I study him. "No thanks."

"Come on, doll." His arm stretches to me. "I could give you a real good time."

"Hey, watch it, buddy," Kit snaps, stepping toward the boy.

He and his friends erupt with laughter. "Relax grease monkey. Best focus on his lordship's wheels."

Kit doesn't flinch, but steps closer, hovering a full head taller than the boy. "Shall we dance or are you done making a fool of yourself?"

"Everything okay, Kit?" James asks, stepping out of the car.

When the boy sees James, he swallows hard, face paling. "Captain James! Uh…" he gazes around at his friends, all slowly backing away. "No sir, we meant no harm, only sport."

"I see, and what exactly was the sport?" James places an arm around me.

The boy looks between Kit and I, then nods. "My mother's calling me sir, I should go. Excuse me."

As the group runs off, Kit shakes his head. "Bunch of heels."

"But what a gentleman you are," I say.

"What have I missed?" James asks. "Seems that was a simmer about to boil."

"Just defending the lady's honor from a real cad, sir."

"Well then, I'm beholding." James nudges me forward. "Dinners on me tonight."

"Thank you, sir." Kit tips his hat. "Well doll, enjoy your evening. I'll see you when it's over."

He slips into the car, and pulls away.

"And with that." James rubs his hands together. "Let the birthday festivities begin."

He guides me to the frosted glass doors and into the foyer, where an older gentleman in a top hat and suit bows low.

"Good evening, madam, sir," the man says. "May I take your coats?"

Removing his, James hands it over, but I stare, unwilling.

"You'll get it back," James whispers, nudging me with a gentle prod.

I unbutton and begrudgingly pass it over. "Take good care of this."

"It's our job, miss." The man takes it from me. "It'll be good as new when it's returned."

"Of course, it will." James presses his palm to my back, moving us forward.

All around, the area expands, chandeliers shimmer overhead, scattering light across the space. A wrap-around balcony overlooks the room, where luxurious navy-blue booths line an energetic dance floor, accompanied by a multi-tier dinner orchestra performing a lively waltz.

Beside us, there's a mahogany bar with plush velvet couches crowded with patrons enjoying a drink; their conversations boisterous, and their laughter echoing louder than the music.

"So, what do you think?" James asks.

"It's spectacular!" I look around, awestruck.

He takes my hands and draws me close. "I'll never tire of finding the very best for you."

"Well, if it isn't the old high hat himself. Captain James!" A man's voice booms.

"Chas..." James exhales. "A pleasure, old friend."

"Is it?" Chas grabs him into a hug. "Figured you thought yourself too good for us simpletons. How long's it been?"

"You know how it is in my line of work. Very little leisure time. But forgive me for missing your last invitation with Will and Rose."

Chas' gaze locks on me as he steps away. "No, no—forgive *me*. Who is this absolute heartstopper? Say she's your cousin, and I'll snag her for the night."

"Now, now, Chas." James' jaw tightens. "This is Wendy. Wendy, meet Chas Turley, owner of *Rêveur Éveillé* and an absolute scoundrel."

"Hello, Chas." I curtsey.

"Wonderful to make your acquaintance." He bows low and gestures grandly. "I've had my private booth prepared for your evening. So, if you'll follow me."

As we walk, he lifts a goblet off a passing tray and downs it in one gulp before returning it. The waiter offers a curt nod, then turns, likely returning to fetch another for the awaiting guest.

We stroll across the room to a booth tucked away, surrounded by lush greenery and a wall fountain. Pressing onto the half-moon seat, I admire the centerpiece, layers of burning candles and white roses, the scent delicate and creamy.

"Thank you. This is perfect." James settles beside me.

"Anything for such a *good* friend." He offers a tight smile. "The chef has your menu requests. So, relax, enjoy a glass of our finest champagne, and your order will be out shortly."

James shakes his hand, and Chas meanders away, hips swaying to the music.

"Interesting fella," I say, watching him glide into a booth full of giggling young women.

"I'm sorry about him. He's a handful."

One of the girls playfully twirls a finger through Chas' thick hair and leans close, whispering. In response, he grabs her leg with a low growl, and she squeals like a child, slapping him away.

"Yikes…"

"Hey, ignore him." James uncorks the bottle, and a white cloud rises as he tips the champagne into our glasses. "This is our time. Now…" He lifts a goblet and holds the other to me. "Happy Birthday!"

We clink glasses, and I take a sip—delightful citrus flavor flooding my mouth, culminating with a light fizz. A young waiter arrives, balancing a tray of steaming soup bowls and a basket of golden bread.

"Good evening, my name is Luther. Here's your starter course of minestrone soup and sliced baguette."

He places the food in front of us and bows. "Enjoy."

James lifts a slice of bread and slathers it with butter, holding it to me.

"Thank you." I take a delicate bite, aware of his gaze. "What are you staring at?"

"My whole world." He sips his champagne.

"You think too highly of me, Captain."

"I don't believe that's possible." He rests back. "You should see some of the women I've crossed paths with."

"Oh well, do tell." I take a spoonful of the rich soup.

"When word spread about my future endeavors, any lady with ties to the palace found a way to sit at our table. It was unbearable for me, and unfortunate for Mother. I was forced to make small talk with far too many vapid young women."

"You poor thing." I roll my eyes.

"Indeed." He chuckles. "It was quite unpleasant. But made me certain of your qualities. Now, you may laugh, but more than once, I imagined you sitting there, rolling those eyes of yours as you do now. And in my mind, I envisioned you scolding me soundly for wasting a second of my time on those foolhardy young ladies."

"As I said, you think too highly of me." I cup his chin. "Perhaps I, too, am only in it for your crown."

"Then I shall place the crown upon your head and make you ruler, while I sit at your feet, admiring your beauty." He presses his forehead to mine. "How's that sound?"

"Perfect." I lean in and we kiss.

When the main course arrives, I inhale the scent of roast duck à l'orange, its sweet citrus sauce making my mouth water. It's served alongside a crisp sautéed chestnut and apple salad, and for the entirety of the meal, I'm in heaven. By the final bite, I drop my fork in surrender, wishing I could loosen my corset.

"So," James says. "Tell me about your day? I was sorry to miss it, but I was working on another surprise you'll see tomorrow."

Memories from the cave discovery resurface. Is it wise to tell him the outlandish story, regardless of its validity?

"I didn't think such a simple question would stump you," he says.

"It's not that. It's just... a long, strange story."

"Really? Well, stranger the better." He leans onto his elbows. "Now I'm intrigued."

"Okay, well, fair warning, this will sound a bit bizarre, but it's true. During a spur-of-the-moment hike through the woods, a few of us stumbled upon an underground village also called Winter Woods. It's accessed through a cave near Solomon Caw's pond."

A subtle crease forms between his brows, but he remains silent, and it's not till I mention the memory from the Before that he slams his cup down.

"You had a memory?"

"It wasn't much. Just a flash of swimming once. Still… it was amazing, if only for a brief moment."

"I can't believe it." He rubs his chin.

"I feared you wouldn't."

"No, that's not what I meant. I do. It's just shocking. Has anything like this happened before?"

"Not that I'm aware."

Raising the champagne bottle, he pours another glass. "Sounds like you already had quite the birthday without my help."

"And that's not even the half of it. While searching for signs of the townsfolk, we discovered pamphlets—*warnings*. They said blood was fast approaching, and everyone had to evacuate. Isn't that strange?"

"Very." He takes a long sip. "The whole thing sounds unsettling. I sent out teams to map the land, so how they could miss an entire underground village, beats me." Placing the glass down, he takes my hands. "Will you take me there? I'd really like to see it for myself."

"I will. Gladly. How about tomorrow?"

"Tomorrow it is." He sets aside his napkin and rises, offering me a hand. "Shall we take a stroll to the dance floor?"

"Oh, that'd be lovely. The only dancing I've done is impromptu balls at home."

"Then this is long overdue. Come along."

Hand in hand, we approach an enthralling scene, dancers weaving in and out—dainty and graceful, like vibrant threads on a crochet hook. Their gowns, like my own, glitter in the shimmer of the chandeliers, leaving me captivated by each twirl and bend.

As the song ends, it's our turn to join in, and I follow him, breathless with anticipation. The orchestra begins an enchanting melody, the world around us transforming. With James' hand on my shoulder and mine on his, we move together, soft and flowing.

At first, my mind floods with instructions: Step back with the right foot—step to the side with the left. Soon enough, the movements become natural, allowing me to relax.

During a short break, we enjoy martinis at the bar while reminiscing. And when the band starts again, we're off, whirling across the floor, laughter deep and spirits soaring. I can't remember a night like this before. No curse. No Children's Home. No worries. It's hours of pure bliss. When we've had our fill and are ready to collapse, he leads me to a spiral stairwell, where a man stands beside a roped-off area.

"Name?" the attendant asks.

"Captain James."

"Oh, yes, Captain, certainly." The man unhooks the rope and steps aside. "We've reserved the last couch on the left for you."

We step past, my legs aching as we ascend the stairs. Below, smoke rises from a group of gentlemen relaxing on the couches. And I imagine James alongside them, talking business as Captain of the *Jolly Roger*.

On the upper level, multiple couples are appreciating a bit of privacy away from the crowds. Our corner is the largest—red velvet couch set atop a thick white carpet, a roaring fireplace casting warm light, and a coffee table laid with two plates of a decadent dessert.

"Peach Melba." James gestures to the plates. "It's my favorite."

"Delightful." I sit, lifting one onto my lap.

"Allow me." He scoops a spoonful of peach covered in ruby-red sauce and holds it to me. I take a bite. "So, has your birthday been everything you hoped?"

"Absolutely." I cover my mouth with a napkin. "But you spoil me too much."

"Well, that's my goal, you know." He leans back, one arm stretched across the top of the couch. "So... what do you plan to do now that you're nineteen?"

"Not quite sure. Whatever it is, I imagine it'll be out of the home. I've loved many moments there, but it's time to move on."

I place the plate onto the table and sink into the cushions. He takes my feet and lifts them onto his lap. "What are you doing?" I press up.

"Lie back," he directs.

"Well, okay." I prop a pillow beneath my head and recline, lashes lowering. He removes my heels and wraps his fingers around my feet, massaging. I could fall asleep, lulled by the soft melody rising from the orchestra and the gentle touch of his hands.

"You know, I still haven't given you the very special gift I mentioned the other day," he says.

I crack one eye open. "You're telling me the coat wasn't the gift?"

"Oh no, that was a mere trinket."

"Mere trinket? Darling, don't tease me."

He snickers. "I'll word it this way: in comparison, I *hope* the coat feels like a mere trinket."

I push onto my elbows. "Am I to guess what it is? Or will you let me in on the secret? I can hardly imagine a gift lovelier than the coat."

"Trust me, this is." He takes my hand, a noticeable tremor in his fingers.

"You're nervous." I straighten.

"You'll see." He reaches into his vest pocket and lifts out a small black box. My heart is in my throat. This isn't going to be like Llewelyn's gift.

He stares at it for a long moment, then says, "I have some ideas of what you might do this year. Want to hear?"

"I'm all ears."

"Okay, here it goes..." He releases a quivering breath. "Since I was young, I've struggled to know who I am and what my purpose was. I suppose that's what drew me to you. Neither of us could make sense of this maddening life. And even as I've struggled against the chaos, you've been there, a calm in the storm. And well, I think it's about time you and I got out of this town."

He grips the box, slowly opening it to reveal a glistening diamond ring.

"Will you marry me?"

All the noise fades into the background as I take in the ring, the weight of his words settling over me. It's happening. He's actually choosing me.

"Yes," I say without hesitation.

"Yes? You sure? This'll mean leaving Winter Woods."

"Yes!" I giggle, tears sliding down my face. I throw my arms around him and hold tight. "I've dreamt of this for so long."

He pulls back and lifts the ring out of its box and slides it on my finger. "A perfect fit."

"Indeed." I lift my hand to his cheek, wiping away a stray tear, and press my mouth to his.

The ring is beautiful, as are his proclamations—but they're not what matter most to me. James, the future King of Neverland, chose *me*. The one man capable of opening the gates *will*. Soon, the aching, the longing, all of it—will fade like the darkness at sunrise, when he frees me from my bondage and all my dreams come true.

We drive home in a comfortable silence, the many drinks leaving me in a blissful daydream while his fingers idly caress the ring. At home, an odd sensation washes over me: everything is about to change.

"What a perfect night, my darling." He kisses my hand.

"Indeed, it couldn't have been any better." I grin up at him.

"Now, forgive me, but I'm about to fall asleep standing here. So, I'm off to dreams of you. I'll see you in the morning."

"I'll be here."

He kisses me and shuffles to the office, pausing at the door to glance back before disappearing inside.

Alone, I hold my hand beneath the hall light, the ring sparkling in its yellow gleam. I could use a glass of water and a long sleep. Exhausted, I drift through the dining room, music spilling from the kitchen, and push through the swinging door to find Peter sitting at the table.

"Well, hello. You're up late," I say, leaning back, swaying slightly.

"What time is it?" He focuses on his mess of papers spread across the table.

"Past midnight, I imagine." I pull out a chair and collapse into it without grace.

"Oh." He glances up, frowning, "Nibs and I were talking. Guess I lost track of time." He lifts a glass of amber liquid and drains it. "Welcome home."

"Please, don't let me interrupt." I reach up and undo my braided bun, letting my hair fall loose around my shoulders. "I only came in for water, but I'm so tired I could fall asleep right here."

"I'll get it." He rises and heads to the counter, filling his glass to the brim. "Would you care for a nightcap?"

"No." I rest my head in my arms. "I've had far more than I should have."

He opens the cupboard, removes a cup, and fills it with water, carrying both back to the table.

"A water for the lady."

"Thank you." I prop my chin on my hands and nod toward his papers. "So, what's got you up so late?"

"Work." He takes a sip and grimaces.

"Oh? The job you applied for?" I straighten and lift my glass, taking a long swallow.

"I start Monday." His finger taps against the table as he scans a page.

"Well, congratulations!"

"Says the girl who thinks I'm an idiot for getting said job." His gaze drifts from the papers to the ring on my finger. "Well, would you look at that?" He places a cigarette between his lips, flips open a lighter, and raises the flame. "You won a prize. Let's see it."

I extend my hand, reluctant. He brings it to his face. "Bloody hell, this must be from the royal treasury."

"A simple congratulations would suffice." I pull away.

"Who said I'm happy for you?" He offers me the cigarette.

"No, thank you." I sip my water. "It's a nasty habit."

"Suit yourself. So... was tonight everything you hoped for?"

I rise and carry my cup to the counter. "Fancy restaurant, fine food, doting dance partner, and a diamond ring? Heavens, yes."

He glides toward me, pinning my body lightly against the counter as he sets his cup down. "I do believe I was your first dance partner. Remember that?"

My eyes narrow playful. "You're drunk," I whisper in his ear.

"Very." He laughs and steps back, swaying to the music much like Chas earlier. Taking my hand, he lifts it to his shoulder. "How about one more, sweetheart? You know, before he steals you away?"

"Good grief, Peter." I glance at the door. "What if James comes in?"

"Let him."

I shake my head. "He'll knock you into next week, you bloody idiot. A dance with me isn't worth that, now, is it?"

He doesn't answer; only wraps an arm around my waist, pulling me close, fingers trailing over my neck and spine. He moves with me, and my whole-body tingles at his touch.

Oh goodness, please don't come in now, James.

His fingertips graze my skin, heat spreading through me as the radio hums in the background.

Why do I do just as you say?
Why must I just give you your way?
Why do I sigh, why don't I try...to forget?

I lean into him instinctively, warmth pooling in my belly, and his fingers respond, pressing against the small of my back.

It must have been that something lovers call fate
Kept on saying I had to wait...

My arms wrap tighter with each sway. Tears prick at my eyes, though I don't know why.

I saw them all, just couldn't fall...till we met.

He pulls back, wearing that same unreadable look from earlier. I regret drinking so much as a tear breaks free, my emotions unraveling in his arms.

His brows draw together, and he traces a finger along my cheek, a bittersweet smile tugging at his lips. With a gentle spin, he turns me so my back rests against his chest, guiding my hand around his neck, the swift thrum of his pulse beating beneath my fingers. I close my eyes and breathe out.

It had to be you, it had to be you.

He's my friend. I'm safe with him—that's all this is.

I wandered around, and finally found the somebody who...

I'm just overwhelmed from the engagement.

His cheek rests against my forehead, pulling me from the haze. I turn toward him, his hand cupping my face.

Could make me be true, could make me be blue
And even be glad, just to be sad
Thinking of you...

He goes still. A shadow crosses his face as the final line fades.

It had to be you, wonderful you...it had to be you.

As a new song begins, I blink and step away, breaking the spell. "I think I'm a bit tipsy too. Forgive me."

"Yeah... tipsy," he mutters.

I avoid his gaze and after a moment, he turns and flings open the back door. A burst of cool air floods in, and then it slams shut behind him, glass rattling.

He's gone.

I stare for a moment, expecting his return, but when nothing happens, I follow and pull open the door.

"Peter?" I call into the night.

No answer.

The air bites, wind howling, snow swirling around me. I step back inside, shutting it out. *What just happened?*

His papers are strewn across the table, so I gather them with an unsteady hand, carrying the stack to the counter. As I set them down, something catches my eye—a handwritten note in the bottom corner of the page.

The words stop me cold. They make no sense, yet they cut through me like a knife. I grip the ledge for balance and read them again:

Wendy Moira Angela Darling.

Part Two
The Stirring

Chapter 9

"Ladies, let us extend our warmest Finishing School welcome to our newest classmate, Wendy. She'll be joining us for a brief period of three months before her upcoming marriage. I trust each of you will help her feel comfortable and supported during her time here."

A soft greeting rises from a sea of navy blue uniformed young women sitting around the creamy, sun-filled classroom: "*Welcome, Wendy.*"

"Very good." Madam Esme nods approvingly. "Wendy, you may sit by Grace in the back. If you have any questions, she'll assist you."

"Thank you, ma'am." I glide to the last row, where a girl with soft, flowing blonde hair and bright blue eyes regards me with reserved curiosity.

"Good morning," I offer, sitting beside her.

"Hello," she replies. "It's certainly nice to have a seatmate again."

"Where did the last one go?" I cross my legs, adjusting the navy-blue skirt over my knees.

"First tip. Uncross your legs. The Madam has this stick she uses for such occasions, and *trust me*, you don't want to get poked with it."

Uncrossing my legs, I mimic her posture. "Better?"

"Much." She grins. "Anyway, my previous seatmate left six months ago. Her family moved to Moat Brae. Lucky devil."

A flash of memory stirs—a sun-kissed girl boasting about visiting Moat Brae. I tilt my head, studying Grace. *She's the other friend.*

"I think I've seen you before."

"Alright, ladies." Madam Esme raps her ruler against the desk. "Time to open your book on household management. Wendy, if you'll begin with chapter one. We'll read for twenty minutes before moving on to the application."

Papers rustle throughout the room before all falls silent, and I flip open my book titled "Mrs. O'Leary's Book of Household Management" and read.

Welcome, merry mistress.

May it never be said that a young woman who underwent my personal instruction ever failed to properly manage her home as expertly as a ship captain commandeers his vessel. You face a truly monumental task, becoming the shining example for every servant to admire and respect, from the least to the greatest. Your husband shall wear your capability with the greatest pride, fully assured that his estate is in the most proficient hands.

Whenever the doors of your home open, it shall garner the highest praise. And shall another mistress enquire how you exude such grace and competence? You will confidently press Mrs. O'Leary's book of Household Management into her hands.

I glance up from the page, already bored. Nothing about this interests me. Staring out the window, my mind drifts to the weekend.

The morning after James proposed, he and I set out on our planned hike through the woods, tracing my steps from the day before. It was going to be incredible entering that world again, this time with James by my side. But when we eventually stumbled upon the crescent marking, the entrance was nowhere to be found.

"It's gone," I cried.

"How's that possible?" James said. "Let's keep searching. Don't worry, we're bound to find it, a cave can't disappear."

We walked for half an hour in both directions, running our fingers along the stone, but found nothing. It was gone. He led me home, my spirit heavy. There was still so much to explore, maybe even a few clues left to uncover. But now I'd never get the chance, and the whole thing felt disheartening, like reading to the end of a mystery only for the final pages to be ripped out.

At home, a group of men were refurbishing James' quarters—a surprise gift for me. The bedroom was getting a refresh with turquoise curtains, a rich satin comforter, and embroidered cushions scattered atop the bed. Two pieces of furniture were being carried in: a tall wardrobe and a rosewood dressing table, both specially carved by Llewelyn as a wedding gift.

The office was being painted a soft cream, and the old chaise had been replaced by a golden-yellow one, paired alongside a floral blue couch. A holly coffee table stood between them, draped in a cream cloth, and topped with a vase full of bright yellow roses. Resting against the couch were two large paintings, awaiting their places on the wall, both scenes from a world I've never seen.

"What do you think of the paintings?" James' hands rested on my shoulders.

"They're lovely... but where are they from?"

"I commissioned an artist to paint them at our new home."

I turned to him, surprised.

"Yes, my love. A view from our future backyard. In a couple of months, you'll be picking wildflowers there."

I gazed at the painted scene—white sands drifting into deep emerald water. "It's perfect..."

"Time, ladies," Madam Esme calls, pulling me back to the present.

I close the book and rise as she instructs us to line up for the practical application portion. The remainder of our morning is spent on various tasks and tests, each one guided by her ever-watchful eye. If I've learned anything, it's this: I'm woefully unprepared to be mistress of the manor. These girls have trained for their societal roles since childhood, while I've spent the past five years learning what it means to be a person.

The girls are nice enough, though most are somewhat featherbrained. They observe me with quiet wonder, while a few outright glare, their noses wrinkled, as if seeing straight through the fancy clothes to what lies beneath. Grace is the only one who sets formality aside, chatting gaily about the day-to-day goings-on at the academy.

When lunch arrives, she guides me to the dining hall, dressed for the Christmas holiday. An evergreen stands against the far wall, draped with holly, twinkling lights, and delicate glass baubles. Spiced cinnamon drifts from scarlet candles nestled in glass vases along two oak tables, that stretch the length of the room. Each one glistening warmly beneath honeyed sconces.

We settle with our trays of thin sandwiches and slices of fruit—surprisingly meager portions for such an expensive institute. With an air of self-importance, Grace explains, "A young maiden must always appear her best, dressed to the nines." She grins mischievously and leans in to whisper, "—or when not dressed at all."

She continues breezily, "Basically, we aim for a perfectly trim figure, ready whence the man of our dreams swoops in to rescue us from our miserable, lonely lives. Then we become the merry mistress we've all dreamt of becoming." Her eyes roll for emphasis.

I raise an eyebrow and laugh. "Good to know."

Lifting the sandwich, I inspect the inside. "So, how long have you attended Madam Esme's?"

"My mother passed away when I was young. Before living in Winter Woods, I was tutored at home, where my aunt oversaw my studies. After moving here, she enrolled me in the school and became the dance instructor. You'll meet her in your private session."

"She has her work cut out. I'm pretty green."

"Nonsense. Unless you have two left feet, she'll have you dancing like a professional in no time. But I've been meaning to ask you. You said you'd seen me before?"

"At Mullin's General Store about a year ago. You were with a friend, perhaps the one who moved away. She talked about her family's vacation to Moat Brae, and it caught my interest."

"Fascinating." She picks at her apple. "That's Violetta for sure. So, you're not new to town. So why join the academy now? Were you privately tutored before?"

"You could say that."

Revealing my identity could make things uncomfortable. Yet, I like her. She's nice, and perhaps we could be friends.

"Truth is, I'm from the Children's Home."

"I'm sorry?" Her expression twists. "I must have misheard. You're from the asylum?"

"Correct."

"Knock it off!" She grabs me. "You're joking."

"I'm not..." I glance at her hand, wrapped tightly around my arm. "If we could keep this between us, though, that'd be swell."

She removes her hand. "I'm sorry. It's just." She lowers her voice. "I've heard you're all...you know, *cursed.*"

"True. We have no memories from before Winter Woods."

I bite into my sandwich, weighing my words. "That's part of the green. But my fiancé is from a world far different than my own. So, the goal is to join him there."

"And would I know your fiancé? Word of local engagements usually spreads fast; can't say I've heard about yours."

"I'm marrying Captain James. He helped found the Home where I live."

"Great Scott!" Her mouth drops open as though she's seen a ghost. The hushed conversations around us hum, and she leans close, whispering. "You're marrying *thee*, Captain James? As in, next king of Neverland?"

"How do you know about that?"

"Violetta told me in a letter. Their mothers hoped to set him up with her. Things didn't go well. His mother wasn't aware he'd already set his sights on another. And not just another, but you!"

Her head sways side to side. "I can't believe my seatmate is going to be the next queen. Somebody pinch me. But do tell, what's it like being cursed?"

I consider it for a moment. Few ever truly understand our lives, fewer still want anything to do with us once they do.

"Imagine a wall covered with paintings," I say. "But there's something *off* about them. Spread across the canvases are smudges and black spots, the pictures all distorted. You know it's a painting, but it makes you uneasy to look at." I lift my shoulders. "That's us. And our job is to try to fill in what's missing, though we don't know what was there to begin."

Her face grows somber.

"What about you?" I ask, attempting to change the topic. "What was your life like before this place?"

"Me? Large house by the seaside, windows that opened to the ocean."

Her voice trails off as she stares toward the lofty windows draped in garlands of holly and ivy. "There was nothing quite like falling asleep to the sound of the waves. And if I'm honest, it's hard to remember what was lost. Still, I don't envy you for not knowing. I spent those first years praying every night we'd go home. But during a partially drunken stupor, father set me straight. He said his work required him to remain here, and I'd better dry my tears and let it go."

"How awful."

"Perhaps." Her features soften, something wistful lingering in her eyes. "But it helped me refocus, settle in better, and make friends. Now, I've even met a man." She pauses, a blush rising to her cheek. "I wouldn't have been able to do that before, holding myself back as I was, always looking ahead, but never in the present."

"It's like you're reading my heart," I say. "Though I've never found the peace you speak of. So, you and this man are also engaged?"

"Oh no." She chuckles. "Gosh, I wish we were. His name is David, and he works for my father. So many men barely go skin-deep, but he's different. Until last night, we'd only exchanged pleasantries, but Father brought him home for dinner, and we talked for hours. I'd sure love an engagement of my own, though, because I'm dying to plan a wedding."

We continue eating. She peppers me with more questions about the Home, about James, and what's next. I ask a few questions about the school, and what to expect.

As lunch concludes, we lay our empty trays aside, and she leads me to the music room, where she introduces me to Theo Van Lori, a world-renowned pianist.

As an entertainer, he enjoys the privilege of traveling around Neverland, performing in the finest theaters for the wealthiest citizens. He chose Winter Woods for a change of scenery, he says, and has been teaching at the academy for the past three months.

I can't deny the idea that anyone would choose this town baffles me to no end.

"How long have you played?" he asks once I've demonstrated my ability.

"A few years," I say. "There's a piano in our parlor, and I just... took to it. We had a few books lying around, so I taught myself."

I don't mention how it felt as though I'd always known the keys, as if my fingers were recalling a past life, one I sadly hold no memory of.

"Well, you're quite good, almost like you were trained from a young age." His eyes soften. "You play with heart. My job is to strengthen that. And though our time is limited, I'm confident in three months' time, you'll be a new woman."

When class ends and I'm back in the hall, Grace steps beside me, arm looping through mine. "So, how horrid did he say you are?"

"He said I was good. Is that strange?"

"My, my, you truly are one of a kind, aren't you?"

We enter the dance studio—a vast room where hardwood gleams beneath our feet, gold trim wraps around mirrored walls, and chestnut shelves brim with records, neatly folded towels, bins of materials, and a handful of framed photographs.

Ms. Diana meets us at the door, her curly red hair as vibrant as her personality. "Good afternoon, ladies," she chirps. "You must be Wendy, my new student."

"I am. It's a pleasure to meet you, Ma'am."

"Pleasure's all mine. Grace, thank you for bringing her. I'll see you at home, dear."

"Certainly. And be kind to her, Aunty, she's a real newbie."

"Thank you, dear." Ms. Diana's lips press together, motioning her toward the door. "Now shoo."

Grace winks at me and slips into the hall.

"Today will be similar to your music class," Ms. Diana says. "We'll assess your capabilities while you're partnered with my assistant. How does that sound?"

"Fine. Grace is right, though. I haven't had much opportunity to dance."

"No problem. My job is to prepare you for the future, not worry about the past. Ah, here comes my assistant. I'll get the music ready."

She strides to the corner and glides her fingers along the records lining the shelves. I press my hands into my pockets and glance at the assistant approaching.

"*Henley?*" I stare in surprise.

"*Wendy!*" He hurries over, wrapping me in a warm hug. "What in the heck are you doing here?"

"I'm here for class. Joined the academy today! What about you? Is this the job you mentioned?"

"No, this is new. I was fed up with the manufacturing plant when I met Grace. Embarrassed to say she spotted me doing a little dance for the boys, just a gas, really, but she thought it was good. She mentioned that her aunt needed a new assistant and thought I might be the perfect fit."

"He's proven himself perfectly capable," Ms. Diana says from across the room. "Now, if you two are ready, we'll get started."

We take our places under the amber lights, and she sets the needle onto the record. A soft crackle, then a rich, golden sound fills the air, and we're off.

"So," he says, as our feet move in time. "Why are you here?"

"James and I got engaged over the weekend!"

"Oh. Well, congratulations!"

"Thank you…"

He spins me and pulls me close, the moment stirring a memory—Peter's face pressed to my ear, his breath warm and body propelled by liquor. A wave of sadness washes over me, and I'm back in the kitchen, talking with Nibs the following night.

"Where's Peter?" I asked, pulling out a chair.

I was determined to confront him about what I'd seen on the paper. Was that my name scrawled on it? But he was nowhere to be found.

"Yeah, I figured you'd be here soon," Nibs said, shadows lingering beneath his eyes. "He's moved out. And I don't know if he'll be back."

"What? Why would he do that?"

"He was offered housing through his new job and decided to take it. He said goodbye while you were asleep. I told the others not to mention it, as I wanted to be the one to tell you."

I rubbed my neck, the air in the room stifling. "Why wouldn't he say goodbye to me?"

"I'm sorry, kid. But, consider that your fiancé was the one who told him to leave."

"Yeah, but I thought things went back to normal after Juke left. This doesn't make sense." I stood gesturing at the floor. "Last night we were dancing right there, smirk on his face and all."

"You know better than anyone, we're all experts at faking our emotions. I understand you're upset, and honestly, I felt the same way. But maybe we can try to be happy for him. This is what he wants."

But I wasn't happy. I was livid. How could he say goodbye to everyone except me? Back in my room, I poured myself a glass of wine, turned on the record player, and drank, detaching from the world.

The music fades, and I gaze at the mirror, catching the sparkle from my engagement ring under the bright lights.

"Wonderful!" Ms. Diana claps. "The next selection's a bit upbeat—keep up if you can." She runs a finger along the records. "Henley, where's *Fascination?* I don't see it here."

"I put it in the back room, sorry."

"No worries." She waves him off. "Give me a moment to collect it."

"You're a natural," he says, turning to me.

"I doubt it, but I'm glad you took this job, because it's a relief to have you here."

"I feel the same, old girl." He squeezes my hand. "And let me say, I'm grateful for the pep talk the other day. It's what inspired me to quit the job. Father wasn't thrilled with my reasoning, but I know it's the right decision. I've decided to focus on where I *need* to be and what will get me there."

"I can relate. Can't say I'm excited about the academy, but I'm confident it's the path to where I belong."

"Okay," Ms. Diana calls. "Let's begin again."

Dance is the last class of the day, and once it's over, I'm free to leave. Pressing through the front doors, I spot Kit waiting beside the black sedan and descend the stairs toward him, the sky a dull sheet of grey.

"Hey there, doll." He opens the back door. "Looks like you had a fun first day."

I head for the front and toss my bag inside, settling into the seat as he slips in beside me. "It was so-so."

"Wonderful. Now look." Kit stares over at me. "I don't mind you sitting up here. But maybe don't mention it to Cap. He wouldn't approve."

"Geez. I'm already sick of keeping up appearances." I lean back, arms folded.

The car pulls away from the academy and speeds toward home.

"Forgive me if this is rude, but... why marry him if you hate the lifestyle? Aren't you training to be a queen or something?"

"Call it a sacrifice for the relationship. I may be unqualified, but I'm determined. Hopefully that's enough."

"Hopefully. Cause you've got a lifetime of keeping up appearances."

"What about you? How'd you end up in this bleak, lifeless village?"

"I was driving for Thomas, James' father, when I first met him. His previous chauffeur had retired, so he offered me the job, saying it would only be for a few months. I thought, 'Why not?' But I had no idea what I was getting into."

"Cold, dark misery, that's what you were in for."

"Quite an accurate description." He chuckles. "Let's hope the next few months pass quickly so we can both put Winter Woods behind us."

"Yes, please," I agree. "Far, far behind."

Chapter 10

The following days at the Academy unfold much like the first, and by Thursday, Christmas Eve, I'm grateful for the long weekend ahead.

Strolling out of the school with Grace, we stop short at the sight of James stepping out of the sedan, a rogue grin across his face.

"Is that him?" Grace nudges me.

"Yes, that's him. I'd better go. See you Monday!"

I hurry down the stairs and into his awaiting arms. "You told me you were coming in the morning!"

"This is more fun." He twirls me around. "Are you happy to see me?"

"Of course! I expect you'll join us for the candlelight service at the chapel?"

"I had something a little different in mind. Are you up for a change?"

"A change? You mean, miss the Christmas Eve service?"

"I know it's special to you." James' voice is hesitant. "But, I was hoping we could make some new memories tonight."

Christmas Eve is an evening I've always treasured, especially this year, my final one. There's something special about Reverend Andrew's reading of the first Christmas, and the songs Agnes and Elizabeth harmonize. The older ladies bring towers of baked goods and thermoses of creamy hot cocoa, and we always end the night with candlelit carols.

Yet James stands before me now, expectant. How can I say no?

"Okay, we'll do whatever you have in mind," I concede.

"Perfect." He opens the door to the back seat, gesturing me in. "It'll be great, I promise. Now, let's get you home so we can start our night."

The house is full of holiday cheer the moment we enter. Carols drift from the record player and the air—festive with citrus and spice—smells like memories. Elizabeth and Agnes snag me the instant I've kicked the snow from my boots, dragging me to the parlour.

"Isn't it glorious!" Agnes spins, gesturing to the decorations.

"We just finished the tree," Elizabeth says proudly.

"You mean you fixed everything we did to help," Alexander says.

"Of course not." She frowns, stepping behind the tree and motioning. "I left all of this that you did."

"No one can even see those!" Jack laughs.

"Well, I think it looks great in here." James says, shoving his hands into his pockets as he takes it all in. "Glad I'll finally be joining this year."

"Yes, it looks beautiful," I say, moving to the mantel, fingers threading through the ivy lining its edge. Christmas cards from neighbors stand in a neat row. Tall cream candles cast a yellow glow over everything, and at the center sits a small, hand-carved nativity Llewelyn made our first Christmas.

"Who's ready for some eggnog?" Morgan exclaims, sweeping in with Nibs, both balancing trays of the creamy drink. "James!"

She sets the tray down and throws her arms around him, cheeks pink. "I didn't know you were joining us tonight! How wonderful. It's going to be such fun."

He forces a smile. "I'm sorry, Wendy and I were only stopping in while she changes. We've got plans."

The joy on her face falters. "Oh." Her eyes flick to me, as if to confirm, and I nod. "But you'll still join us tomorrow, won't you?"

"Of course." He gives her hand an affectionate squeeze. "Wouldn't miss it."

A sinking feeling settles in my chest. Everything is perfect but because I won't be able to enjoy it as planned, it's becoming almost oppressive.

"Well." James glances at me. "You'd best get ready, our night awaits."

"Okay… Yeah. I'll be back."

I turn toward the hallway, and when I look back, Nibs is handing James a drink. They raise their glasses, clink and take long sips. Nibs mumbles something after and James bursts out laughing.

I exhale and retreat to my room. It's far too quiet. The air holds a chill unlike the warmth of the parlour. I stare at the dress laid out on my bed, waiting for me, and press the door shut.

Facing the mirror, I smooth the forest-green dress I had chosen for the candlelight service. A sigh escapes me. I shouldn't be ungrateful, this is what I signed up for. I run lipstick along my mouth and shape a smile, burying the ache in my chest. Tonight will be different, but that's not necessarily a bad thing.

As I leave the room and stroll past the parlour, JaneAnn collides with me.

"Whoops." She giggles. "So sorry! But look at you, how beautiful. I was just about to go change for service, too. I thought my red dress might be nice."

"Yes, it would. But this isn't for service. James had other plans." My tone carries a hint of apology.

"Oh, I see." Her cheerful demeanor fades. "Off on another adventure, are you?"

"Something like that. He didn't say where we're going. I promise I'll be here tomorrow."

"You're leaving soon anyway, off to bigger and better places. We'd best get used to it. Have a fun night." She hurries away and disappears up the stairs.

"Have you ever looked bad a day in your life?" James strides out from the parlour, chewing on a sugar cookie. "You are lovely, my dear." He kisses my nose. "Are you ready?"

"Do I look ready?" I let my hands glide over the fabric of my dress, lifting the skirt with a slight sway.

"Oh, I'm not sure." His lips curl, and he presses me slowly against the wall. "Maybe you and I should go into your room so I can inspect the dress—ensure it fits just right."

My mouth parts, and I glance around. "You'd best hope Nibs and Llewelyn haven't heard you speaking to me that way, *sir*."

"I care about many things, but not that." He leans in, capturing my lips with his, a sense of hunger in the kiss.

"Gross..." a voice murmurs behind us, and we break apart. Michael stands by the stairwell, nose wrinkled.

"We were just leaving," I say, gripping James' hand and guiding us past Michael to the front door, my neck burning as James' laughter echoes.

Our first stop is *Rêveur Éveillé*, where the dinner orchestra fills the air with festive songs, and gold and silver leaf wreaths line the walls, scented with cinnamon and orange. A massive, brightly lit tree stands beside the orchestra, reaching nearly to the upper level.

We settle in a booth by the dance floor and savor a delicious four-course meal. I share stories of my week at the Academy, while James listens attentively, appearing pleased, especially with my friendship with Grace. Once dinner ends, we take to the dance floor, the lights low, music stirring, and sway together, my lids closing as I rest into him, the wine calming my spirit.

But when I open my eyes again, I draw back, breath catching—Peter is staring at me from across the floor.

"What's wrong?" James tilts his head, blocking my view.

I shift to the side, craning my neck, but the space is empty.

"Excuse me a moment." I squeeze his hand and slip off the dance floor, gazing around, but no one's there.

"*Hey.*" James touches my shoulder. "What's going on? What did you see?"

I scan the booths, only to receive a few odd glances from the diners. "Sorry, it was nothing. The wine hit a bit harder than expected."

"Oh, well, here, let's sit by the fire. You do look pale."

He guides me to a seat near the white stone fireplace, then slips away for drinks. Could I have imagined seeing Peter? Surely not. Yet, he isn't here, is he? I dislike how he lingers in my thoughts, intruding without invite. If not here, though, I wonder where he is? Is he going to spend Christmas alone, instead of with us?

"Here you go." James hands me a mug of cocoa.

"Thank you." I hold it to my lips, the steam curling gently.

"You know, it's been many years since I truly enjoyed the holidays." He pulls me close. "I'm glad to be with you this year. And to think, this is the first of many."

"What's Christmas like at your home?"

"Oh, the usual. Mother cherishes this time of year and insists the entire palace be decorated top to bottom. So, a grand selection of spruces, ivy trailing on every doorframe, and stairwell, and enough twinkling lights to blind a person."

He chuckles thoughtfully. "It makes her happy, so we bear with it. But if I'm honest, my family isn't quite what it used to be. In recent years, something's been missing."

"And what do you think that is?"

"Not to sound overly sentimental, but the holidays are only as good as the people you spend them with. I love my mother, but there are limitations to what she can recreate."

He pauses, staring at the wisps of orange and yellow flames coiling in the hearth. "I never told you this, but I lost a sister when Neverland got attacked. Christmas hasn't been the same since."

"I had no idea. I'm so sorry. Will you tell me about her?"

"She was my best friend. But her selflessness became her downfall. And I lost her."

I grab him into my arms, my fingers finding their place in his hair. "I wish I knew sooner. That's a terrible loss."

"We all lost, though, didn't we?" He kisses my cheek, then presses his nose to mine.

"Grace and I talked about what she lost during the attacks," I say, leaning back. "There's a quiet debate in my mind about which is worse: to lose and remember, or to lose without knowledge. The trouble is there's this ache in me, like whatever was lost is immeasurable and there's nothing I can do to make it go away."

He looks at me, features pinched tight.

"Don't pity me," I say firmly. "If you're to be my husband, I won't tolerate pity. Agreed?"

"Yes, ma'am." He swallows hard.

We finish our cocoa in silence, the mood more somber than festive. Then he guides me to the exit, wrapping me in my cashmere coat before leading me back to the car.

Kit drives us through the snowy streets, shops all shuttered for the holidays. We pass a group of carolers, candles in hand, singing as they wander past the tall, three-story homes lining the road. I rest against the cool glass, their haunting melody tugging at something deep inside me.

As we near the Neverpeak Cathedral, children dart across the street, hurling snowballs at one another, and one hits the car window as we roll past, leaving them bent over, shrieking with laughter.

"Kids these days..." Kit mutters under his breath.

I can't help but smile, recalling my friends and me walking home from the Christmas Eve service. Despite the darkness, the streetlamps shone brighter, leaving a sense of magic in the air. Snowflakes floated softly down, and candles glowed in every window along the road to our home. The whole neighborhood walked together, full bellies, lively conversations and Christmas spirit swelling in our hearts.

I suppose not everything here is bad. Margaret always warned me I'd regret not appreciating what's right around us. And here and now, she's right, and I dearly wish I could be with my friends tonight.

Kit parks the car and opens the door, where we join a crowd of well-dressed men, women, and children strolling up the steps of the church and through its double-wide doorway.

Unlike our modest stone chapel, this has pinnacles reaching toward the heavens, and stained-glass windows spilling rainbow colors onto the snow-dusted ground. In contrast to the kind-eyed Reverend Andrew, who welcomes everyone with a friendly nod, a bishop in ornate robes stands at the door, clutching his curved-topped staff with a permanent scowl across his rigid face.

"Bishop Gehry." James bows low. "This is my fiancée, Wendy."

The bishop's gaze is sharp. "I don't believe I've seen you before. Are you not a God-fearing woman?"

Caught off guard, I stammer, "I, uh, no—it's just—"

I hadn't considered what I'd say in such a situation. Do I tell him the truth and shame James? Or lie and shame myself...

"She's new to town," James interjects smoothly.

A lump rises in my throat and I catch Kit's curious expression.

"Is she now?" The bishop fixes me with a look, lids low and chin tipped upward. "Well, welcome to town. From where have you traveled?"

I look at James. "She's from far, far away," he says. "But we should get in, Merry Christmas Eve to you."

"Of course." The bishop dips his head as we walk on. Perhaps he recognizes me. I've certainly passed the church often enough—waved a time or two, though he's never acknowledged me.

As we enter the nave, I crane my neck, taking in the vaulted ceiling overhead, adorned with lavish chandeliers, and a mural of Old Testament stories. They're majestic, but I can't fathom how anyone could manage to paint so high up.

Following the slow procession through the central aisle, the pews creak as parishioners take a seat, some sitting in respectful silence while others whisper to one another behind gloved hands. Marble statues line either side of the pews—saints, frozen in time, gazing down on us, humble sinners. As we near the front, a rich, earthy scent rises—incense, curling from a brass burner hanging near the stone altar.

Kit pats me on the back and slips away into a row where Tiger Lily awaits him. She offers a slight wave when our gazes meet, and I return it.

Hand on my back, James guides me into a pew, settling beside Rose and her brother William. Rose's eyes widen as they flick from James to me, bright with surprise. James leans forward to shake William's hand before pressing a quick kiss to Rose's cheek.

"James," William says, "you remember Laurie and Clara?" He gestures to a couple sitting beside them. I recognize both faces. Laurence is a friend of Llewelyn's, and Clara to Morgan.

"Hello again," Clara says, studying James, then me.

Laurence takes his wife's hand and clears his throat. "Captain."

Just then an older woman with deep wrinkles carved into her solemn face, positions herself at the massive pipe organ, and plays, the notes filling the space.

I focus on the gleaming silver pipes, and silently mouth the words: *"Silent Night, Holy Night, all is calm, all is...."*

Unwelcome memories spring to mind. My body dragged backward, my screams silenced. Tension floods through me.

"What's wrong?" James whispers.

"Nothing..."

The music plays on, and the congregation joins in, their voices soothing my rattled nerves. After a few more hymns, Bishop Gehry steps forward, eyes sweeping the crowd.

His voice isn't warm, it's stiff, cold, as though he's the only one destined for the pearly gates. He speaks of the babe born in Bethlehem, but not as a savior and friend as Reverend Andrew does, but rather someone wary of us weak-minded sinners.

The collar of my dress is tight, almost suffocating. I want to leave. I've taken the joy in my own community for granted; I see this now. There's no hope here. No love. How do these people endure the bishop's hard stare, week after week?

How dearly I wish for a glimpse of Reverend Andrew's kind smile. The sparkle in his eye as he reads from the yellowed pages of the Good Book. When he gazes across the pews, his voice is full of longing that we might share in his joyful faith. It's never led him to anger or insufferable judgment. No, it moves him to action. I know he believes the words he reads, because he lives them, far beyond the walls of that little stone chapel.

Rose glances over, her expression unreadable, her stare lingering. I offer a polite smile, and she turns away. Why must I think so much? Why can't I behave like all the other girls at Madam Esme's that I see here tonight—lips turned up just so, hair soft and flowing, cheeks pink, and figure trim? Just focus on being a merry little mistress for my husband-to-be and nothing more. My dreams are about to come true, my goodness...

Yet I suppose it's because I'm not one of them. So, we can play house. Dress me pretty, put on a bit of makeup, and teach me manners. But deep down, I know—I don't belong in James' world.

And if I'm honest... I never will.

❋ ❋ ❋

I'm the first to rise when the service ends, eager to leave. But as Clara and Laurence usher Rose and William away, a man steps into our path, blocking us.

"Gentleman! Good to see you." James shakes the man's hand vigorously. "I'd like you to meet my betrothed, Wendy."

The man turns to me and bows. He's attractive, with long, wavy hazel hair and a broad grin. "My daughter Grace speaks fondly of you."

"Oh, you're Mr. Starkey! A pleasure." I curtsey.

"Indeed, and speaking of my feisty daughter, here she comes now."

"Wendy!" Grace nearly knocks me over, wrapping me in a hug. "I saw you arriving and would have invited you to sit with us, but Father insisted I leave you be."

"Wouldn't have been proper, my dear," Mr. Starkey says.

"Of course not." She rolls her eyes. "Oh, but I am terribly sorry you couldn't. David sat with us! It would have been lovely to introduce you both."

"I'm sorry to have missed the chance, next time. Is your aunt here?"

"Oh yes, she's over there, talking with that gaggle of ladies."

I spot Ms. Diana chatting animatedly amongst a group of women, a softness in her smile. Perhaps some here I can relate to—though likely only a few.

"Well, my dear." Mr. Starkey takes Grace's arm. "Let's not keep them any longer. Just wanted to wish you a happy Christmas Eve, Captain."

"And to you, Starkey." James wraps an arm around me and tips his hat to Grace. "Good evening to you both."

I wave goodbye as we follow the procession out of the church. And once inside the car, relief washes over me to be away from the crowd. Gazing out the window while Kit and James converse about the evening, I block out the world, their words a blur as a sense of hopelessness fills me.

Arriving home, the house is empty as we slip to my room and settle on the couch, a record humming in the background, and his fingers gliding up and down my arm. "I'm sorry I lied to Bishop Gehry," he says. "I feel like a heel."

"Nonsense. What other option did you have? Tell him who I am? Explain my past? He would've thrown me onto the street before I dirtied one stone of his precious church."

His grip tightens. "Do you really believe I'd allow such a thing? I assure you, I'd have any man, bishop or not, by the collar and onto the street myself were they to attempt such a thing."

"It's sweet of you to say, but have you considered how ill-matched we are? Even in this town, many would rather cross the street than be near someone cursed. Some even hold the belief that what's happened to us is contagious."

"In that case, it's fortunate we won't be living in Winter Woods once married."

"But what of my past, then? Shall you always create a tale to hide who I am? What kind of life is that? For either of us." I sit forward and shake my head. "I don't know, James. This is all I ever wanted, but the more I attempt to become what you need, the more I see how great the chasm is between us."

"I haven't told anyone this, but I trust you, and this seems the appropriate time to say it." He lets out a deep breath. "Thomas isn't my father."

"What?" I stare, the words not making sense. "If not he, then who?"

"A man I've tried to outrun my whole life—someone who chose privilege and title over family. My mother wasn't always a great lady. She was a stage actress in her youth and attracted many men with her beauty. One in particular pursued her. He was my father. He was a man of... importance. And when the time came to choose between where he came from and where he was going, he denied us. I never saw him again."

"I'm so sorry, James. How despicable. I can't imagine the sorrow your mother must have felt."

"I watched her disguise tears during the day, and muffle sobs in the evening. I vowed I would never do as he had. When I loved, it would be without concern for consequence, and because I could not help myself."

He drops his head, exhaling.

"I know you love me." I stare into my lap, the weight in my chest expanding. "But I'm no good at this. They want me to be a merry mistress, and all I feel like is a failure. You need a woman of strength, beauty, grace, and an ounce of decorum. I fear I fail on all four accounts."

He lifts my hands to his chest. "No, you're wrong. It needs to be *you*. Madam Esme's was Mother's idea, not mine. She insisted you be trained in the way she wasn't. But you fail to see, living as you have, gave you a strength far greater than any of the witless poppets I know."

He pauses, brushing my knuckles. "As for your beauty and grace, you have it and more. You are dignified, Wendy. Not because of tutors or lessons, but because of experience. This will serve Neverland far more than you realize."

"I don't deserve you."

"Tiger Lily is in charge of your schedule. I'll let her know we are done with the academy. From now on, I expect you to put your feet up until the wedding." He tilts his head with a grin. "That would be perfectly rich of you."

"No." I rest into him. "If you can have such faith in me, I can learn for you."

He kisses my forehead. "I leave the choice to you. Just know, you are enough—with or without it."

His kindness overwhelms me. Humbles me. I could never deserve him, not in a hundred years. Shame prickles as I think back to *Susan Lennox*—and the arrogance of believing I could seize what I wanted by using whomever I pleased.

Peter was right. Some things aren't worth losing yourself over. I've been such a fool. It's time to stop thinking only about myself, and I can begin by returning to Madam Esme's. I will change, for James. He trusts me, and I won't let him down.

Not ever.

Chapter 11

The snowball collides with Tootles' cheek, spinning him off his feet and onto his back into an explosion of flurries. Behind a nearby snow hedge, Slightly dives to the ground, snickering. John and Michael seize the moment, pummeling Jack and Alexander, who have rushed in to assist their fallen comrade.

Their victory is short-lived. Reverend Andrew steps in with unexpected precision, pegging them with perfectly formed, perfectly aimed snowballs that sends them sprawling.

Within moments, an all-out war has commenced, snow flying, screams echoing, and the wintery battlefield alive with jubilant pandemonium.

Sipping steaming cocoa beside the parlour window, I snuggle close to James as I watch the boys' spirited gameplay. They have no cares or worry; it's a type of freedom I can appreciate.

"I'm telling you, take it out now or it's going to be dry like last year," Nibs proclaims, trailing close behind Llewellyn into the dining room.

The savory scent of roasting goose wafts in from the kitchen, making my stomach rumble as we wait for our Christmas dinner.

"What are you watching?" James rests his face beside mine.

"Did you ever have fun like that as a kid?" I gesture to the boys.

"Are you asking if I ever had a snowball fight?" A trace of good humour plays on his face.

"Yes, but why does this amuse you?"

"I *was* a child once, wasn't I? Growing up, I had many snowball fights. I was quite good at it, too. Maybe not as good as Andrew there, but not bad."

"Tell me about it." I lean forward. "Where did you grow up?"

"My family lived in a cottage by the sea in Kirriemuir. Our dwelling was near the docks, where the air reeked of fish and seaweed. But I wouldn't have had it any other way. For a young boy, it was heaven and led to my dream of becoming a sea captain."

Morgan sits across from us, reading, but her attention wanders to James as he shares. There's a wistfulness in his voice, as though every word draws us into the memory with him.

"It wasn't cold like here, but it would snow in the winter. It piled high on the roofs and blanketed the streets. And we'd snag tin lids off dustbins and use them as sleds to race down the hills. Chas Turley and I met during one of those snowy escapades."

"You've known him since childhood?"

"Yes, and Smee, William Smee, that is. Chas' father was the mayor, so they were well-to-do. But Smee, Rose, and their mother lived in a pretty, run-down neighborhood. My sister and I would often bring baskets of supplies, and over the years, we became like family.

"When he was old enough, Smee got work on a steam trawler as a deckie. Oh boy, was I jealous. He'd return soaked through, chilled to the bone, and covered in fish guts... but to me, I saw an adventure."

"Did you ever become a deckie?"

"Mother wouldn't hear of it." He chuckles. "She pulled a few strings, though, and got me into a proper upper-class sport fishing company. I became first mate to Captain Clark—he taught me everything I know."

James glances toward Morgan and smiles warmly, but she averts her gaze to the book, flipping the page.

"Thank you for sharing," I say. "Hearing these stories... it's like seeing into your past. And hey, at least one of us has a childhood worth remembering."

He frowns, though I meant it as a light-hearted joke. I suppose it reminds him that I'll never be the reminiscing type. My memories are brief and filled with winter and winter alone.

"Exactly as I said." Nibs stumbles into the dining room, balancing a stack of plates. "The meat was *this close* to being ruined if we left it in a second longer. So, you're all welcome. I'm a regular Saint Nicholas over here."

"And aren't we grateful for it," I call out. "And do you need any help, Saint Nicholas?"

"Not at all, your royal highness." He bows low. "Jan can help me."

Reclining beside the Christmas tree, JaneAnn holds *Murder on the Orient Express* above her head, reading. "No thanks."

"Come, come, Jan." Nibs peeks around the corner.

"Why should I?" She growls, slamming the book shut. "Do they not have four capable hands amongst them?" She nods at James and me.

"Oh, stop your complaining!" Nibs beckons to her.

She rises with a huff and glares in our direction before stomping into the dining room, grabbing the plates, and setting them with a technique destined to leave a crack in each one.

"I should go help her." I press forward.

"Whoa, now, you heard the man." James guides me back. "You, my dear, are royalty."

"Not yet, I'm not." I yank free and follow her into the dining room, lifting the glass goblets from the sideboard.

"I don't need help," she mutters. "Nibs is right. You should be sitting with your feet propped."

"That's nonsense." I place a cup at each setting. "Are you angry with me?"

"Me, angry with you? That's nonsense."

She disappears through the swinging door, and I trail behind, perplexed by this unusual treatment. In the kitchen, Llewelyn stands at the table, carving the goose, each slice glistening with buttery juices.

"You've outdone yourself," I say, as I slip past.

"*He?*" Nibs barks a laugh. "This, my dear, was the work of yours truly. Twas I who labored over the onions, measured the seasonings, made the apple and prune stuffing, and basted it to perfection. Helpful as Llewelyn is, he's only slicing it."

"And that's because you sliced your hand last year," Bea says, chuckling while she washes the dishes.

"I don't want to talk about it." He holds up a hand.

"Not only sliced it, but nearly fainted from the blood." Maimie chimes in as she grabs two bowls of mashed potatoes.

JaneAnn gathers a bowl of parsnips, brussels sprouts, and turnips. And they push through the door, followed by Elizabeth with the bread sauce and gravy, and Agnes carrying the stuffing. I lift the basket of fresh-baked rolls and bowl of butter and step into the dining room, where Morgan lays out the embroidered Christmas tree napkins she made years ago.

"You're going to have to reel Nibs in," I whisper in her ear.

"Oh, am I?" She purses her lips. "A stern talking-to?"

"Or to bed with no supper." I laugh.

Just then, Nibs enters, holding the door for Llewelyn, who carries the roasted goose. He sets it on the table, and the savory, tangy aroma floods the space.

Swinging open the front door, Nibs calls, "Come on in, boys! And Reverend..."

Reverend Andrew enters first, hanging his gear neatly. "They certainly know how to wear a man down," he says, offering me a grin before strolling to the parlour fire to warm his hands.

A blast of cool air whips through the hall as the group of red-faced young men pile in, kicking up snow and tossing their wet coats into a heap.

"No, no, no!" Morgan snaps her fingers. "We are *not* making a habit of leaving our things everywhere. Unless you'd all like a turn at kitchen duty? Do we understand each other?"

"Affirmative, ma'am." John salutes, and the others comply meekly, retrieving their gear and hanging it neatly.

"Good, then you may take your seats."

Everyone gathers close, the two tables pressed together so we can enjoy the feast as one. Llewelyn stands at the head and signs, "*Nothing warms the heart like being together.*"

I lean close to James, whispering the words in his ear, aware he can't follow the signs.

"*We each know loss, hardship, and longing,*" Llewelyn continues. "*The world can often feel dark, even cruel.*" He catches my eye for a moment. "*But look up—never stop looking up. For even in the deepest night, a light still shines. Brighter than the star that guided the shepherds to the babe in the manger. That light is the babe himself, the Saviour of the world.*"

He stills for a moment, a small smile pressing at the corners.

"*Embrace the gift He's given us, and always remember, never let the past dictate your future, or your weaknesses limit your opportunities. The great Author gives you a fresh page to fill each new day. Make the story one worth telling.*"

He lowers his hands and looks around the table one final time, face heavy with emotion, then sits.

I could swear there's a glint in James' eye.

Nibs raises his glass. "To a new year, may we discover who we're truly meant to be!"

We lift our glasses, and exclaim, "To a new year!" And drink.

We eat, savoring the delicious meal, the lively conversations, and a few laughs at Tootles and Slightly's expense. There's a safety in these moments, a belonging I never seem to appreciate enough. I look around the table at my friends caught up in their chatter, Morgan and Bea giggling with their heads pressed together, and Llewelyn and Reverend Andrew deep in discussion, wearing expressions so peaceful I almost envy them. This will never be replaced, no matter how grand the palace.

Once we girls have satisfied our appetites, and the boys have refilled their plates for the third time, Morgan rises and shares a humorous memory from a past Christmas.

It all began when JaneAnn thought adding extra heat to John's hot cocoa would be amusing, thus making it *actual* hot cocoa. *After swallowing a mouthful of the usually creamy liquid, John's face burned bright red, sending her into a fit of giggles. Pride wounded, John vowed to retaliate and did so by placing a newly captured spider onto her back. The spider, obviously in on the joke, crawled over her shoulder, leading to a tear-filled stampede from us girls.*

Thus, the fight continued with one trick after another until Christmas Day. John persuaded the boys to participate in what became the final battle. Using Llewelyn's ladder, they climbed onto the overhang above the front porch and transferred dozens of perfectly formed snowballs into position. Little did they know, Maimie witnessed everything and promptly alerted us.

When Michael came to fetch us, we assured him we'd be there in a moment. But instead, we snuck around the house and removed the ladder. Then, grabbing umbrellas and buckets filled with our own snowballs, we marched out, announcing our arrival.

As soon as we came into view, the boys began battering us with snowballs from above, but we flung open our umbrellas. No matter their aim, they couldn't land a single hit, and before long, ran out. Aware of their defeat, they turned to leave, only to discover the ladder removed. At JaneAnn's signal, we lifted our snowballs and rained them down upon those helpless boys. With nowhere to hide, it was easy work, and once finished, they were half-frozen, shivering, and thoroughly humbled.

Bowing to John, JaneAnn asked in a superior tone, "Do you surrender, or would you like to remain there all day?"

With six snow-coated companions shooting daggers at him, John had no choice but to nod humbly. "You have thoroughly bested me, and as such, I yield to your superiority, ma'am."

Applause broke out at her victory, and Margaret and I carried the ladder over, holding it steady, while one boy after the next climbed down. They muttered and shook their heads, their bodies trembling fiercely from the chill. Only Peter offered a wink as he passed by on the ladder, then stopped to salute JaneAnn.

Oh Peter... where are you?

Shaking with laughter, James whispers, "I had no idea things were like this here."

"Worse than you can possibly imagine," I murmur.

He chuckles and plants a kiss on my cheek.

When gift time arrives, Morgan ushers us into the parlor. Some settle on the couches and chairs, some on the floor, and James and I huddle by the fire.

Gifts are distributed by name, and soon everyone is tearing off wrapping to reveal their presents. Among the gifts are jigsaw puzzles, erector sets, and an electric train set. There are also new jazz records, fountain pens, and books. Each girl receives a new handkerchief embroidered by Morgan, while the boys receive wristwatches from Nibs. Llewelyn carved a beautiful chessboard complete with all the pieces for the boys, and each girl receives an elegant, engraved hair comb.

Pressing a gift into my hand, James says, "Merry Christmas."

"Thank you." I loosen the blue ribbon around the cream cloth, and a stunning pearl necklace falls into my palm. "Oh my! It's beautiful."

"Wow!" Hannah exclaims, pointing at my necklace. "That's the prettiest I've ever seen."

JaneAnn glances over as I hold it up, and perhaps I'm imagining it, but I could swear there's a momentary flash of anger across her face.

"Indeed." I wrap it in the cloth again. "And I'll be sure to wear it soon."

"Oh no, let me put it on you now." James reaches for it, but I pull away.

"No," I whisper. "Not here, later."

He looks around, everyone's busy with gifts. "I'm sorry, did I do something wrong?"

"No. It's just... you've already given me so much. I fear I'll take away from the others' excitement with something so... expensive."

"Oh, I see." His lips press together, constrained. "No worries. You can wear it another time."

I slip the necklace into my pocket.

"I almost prefer not to give you my gift," I say, dropping a package onto his lap. "But, I will. Just know it doesn't compare to yours."

A flicker of surprise crosses his face, quickly melting into warmth. He turns the gift over in his hands, smiling gently. "I didn't expect this, thank you."

He tears off the paper and holds up a thick burgundy scarf and gloves, "Did you?"

"Yes." I shake my head. "Made it myself. I know, I should have bought one, but thought I'd try. Sorry, it's a bit simple."

His smile breaks into a wide grin, and he wraps me in his arms. "It's perfect, I love it. Store-bought can't compare to knowing your beautiful fingers made this."

"I'm relieved!"

"It's often so quiet at my home," James says. "A record player, some whispered gossip between Mother and Father, otherwise, relatively calm. Not like this."

"It *is* a bit overwhelming."

"No, it's not. It's nice and how I imagine every family should be."

His gaze falls on Morgan and Nibs, sitting nearby. Nibs is tying a necklace around her neck, and she looks at him—something unspoken passing between them.

"Are they courting?"

"Not that I'm aware. But they do seem awfully friendly."

"Doesn't seem like a good idea." He clicks his tongue. "They need to focus on the home, not each other."

"Oh, stop it." I elbow him. "Don't you start interfering. If they've found love, let it blossom without blocking the sunshine."

He chuckles. "You make it sound criminal when you put it that way."

"Because it is. We've already discussed how others may disapprove of us. Will you become guilty of the same?"

"No, I suppose I shouldn't. Still, I worry where such things could lead."

"If it's meant to be, it'll lead to something beautiful."

When the excitement settles, the trash is cleared, and gifts stacked aside, Morgan announces, "Time for Charades!"

Games are always a bit chaotic in our house. Even with my fair warning, James watches, brows arched, as several get a little too invested in the theatrics. Still, he seems to enjoy himself and even takes a turn acting out a card of his own.

After a few minutes of comical effort, Morgan discovers James' card, *girl at the ball*, wasn't in the deck at all—Slightly had written it himself. Tootles pats James on the shoulder after. "Good effort, old chap, next time, chin up, chest out, and lashes low, and it'll be just right."

"Thanks for the tip," James replies wearily while I rub his back, consoling.

As the game winds down, we're called into the dining room, where the tables are covered in delicious-looking treats.

"This is your surprise," Morgan says, beaming at James. "Why don't you explain!"

"Certainly. As a thank you for letting me crash your shindig, I ordered some of my favorite Christmas desserts from Will's Bakehouse."

"Maybe we were wrong about this guy," Slightly says.

"Yeah, perhaps all those horrible names we called him weren't true, after all." Tootles sniggers.

"Thanks for the input, nitwits," I say. "Go ahead, though, enjoy his generous contributions."

"Who even invited these guys?" Alexander nudges me. "You want us to deal with them? We've been waiting our whole lives to do that."

"Yeah, all five of them," Jack chimes in, and the group laughs.

Taking the boy's warped sense of humor in stride, James grins, and gestures at the dishes. "We've got my favorite Pecan Pie, and over here, Croquembouche. Then a delightful Bûche de Noël and some Brandy Snaps. Please, enjoy it all, and leave no leftovers."

Enjoy, we do. It doesn't take long for the desserts to be sliced, served, and devoured, and James' recompense is several pats on the back and choruses of, 'Thanks a heap,' or, 'Cheers, *old sport*!'

Carrying a stack of dirty dishes into the kitchen with Bea, we unload them in the sink, where Llewelyn is already washing. Bea slips away but I stay, wrapping my arms around his waist. "Thank you for the lovely gift."

He kisses my cheek, and I grab a towel, lifting a clean dish to dry.

"So, I've been thinking a lot about the wedding," I say. "I wonder, are you pleased for me?"

He dries his hands on the apron and signs, "*Your happiness is my happiness, little one.*"

"I'm learning all about wedding tradition from Tiger Lily. One in particular stood out to me."

He passes another dish, nodding.

"When a young woman marries, it's customary for her father to give her away. Obviously, I don't have that luxury, do I?"

He pats my arm, a look of understanding crossing his face.

"For girls like me, the custom is to ask someone who's acted as a father, and this was something I'm confident I do have. *So...* Llewelyn, will you give me away on my wedding day?"

Turning off the water, he faces me. "*Nothing would please me more.*"

"Really?" I hug him, and he holds me tight.

There's so much I've missed out on in my brief life, yet I'm beginning to understand that it all found me in ways I never fully appreciated. As we pull apart, I wipe away a stray tear, and he guides me out of the kitchen, where I settle at the piano nestled in the corner of the parlor.

Pressing on the black and white keys, the room falls silent as I sing.

Deck the halls with boughs of holly,
Fa la la la la, la la la la...
Tis the season to be jolly,
Fa la la la la, la la la la...
Don we now our gay apparel...

Elizabeth and Agnes step beside me, one on each side, their voices always perfectly harmonious.

Fa la la la la, la la la la...
Troll their ancient Yuletide carol,
Fa la la la la, la la la la...

We sing the remainder of the song together, and then the room breaks into applause.

"Ladies," Alexander says, "grace us simpletons with another, will you?"

The girls blush and look at me. "Of course," I reply and press on the keys as Elizabeth and Agnes begin again.

It's good fun, and soon, everyone gathers around to sing along, and do they ever. This isn't new, we do this every year—but knowing it's my last somehow makes it brighter, *merrier*. There's a festiveness in the air today that I wish I could hold onto, just for a little while longer.

When we've sung our fill, everyone cheers and disperses, with James guiding me into the hallway. "What a charmer you are. Now, before I depart for the night, I have one final gift."

"Another?" I chuckle. "And pray tell, what could it possibly be?"

"Come outside, and you'll see."

He pulls on his gear, helps me into my coat, and then wraps his new scarf snuggly around his neck. We step onto the porch. A horse-drawn sleigh awaits, driven by none other than Kit, with a grinning Tiger Lily by his side.

"Merry Christmas," she calls in a sing-song voice, waving.

I hurry toward them, enchanted. "This is wonderful! I've never been on one before."

"All for you," James says, guiding me onto the sleigh. We sit, and he lifts a fur blanket over our laps, our bodies pressed tight. "We're ready."

"Walk on," Kit calls, snapping the reins. The horses trot forward, harness bells ringing softly.

Dusk settles, the sky transforming into rich hues of purple and blue. Snuggled close to James, I'm captivated by the delicate snowflakes drifting past. The ride is magical, winding through the downtown and into Neverpeak Hills, the homes decorated the same as James described the palace. Enormous wreaths on the windows, lights around marble pillars, and festive celebrations drifting from within.

"Where do the Starkeys live?" I ask.

"Their home is up the hill a way, down a long winding road. I look forward to taking you there when I'm back."

"Me too. So, how long will you be gone this time?"

"Seven weeks. But I swear, no more after this. I told Father I'd like a long break. Enjoy married life."

"Good. Because I don't intend to be a lonely bride."

"Perfect, because I intend to be an adoring husband." He nuzzles his nose against mine, his body heating my own.

It's dark when we return home and he walks me to the door, the porch lamp casting shadows over his face. "I leave you here, though it breaks my heart to do so." He cups my chin and we share a warming kiss. "I love you, Wendy."

"You better," I say wistfully. "I'll be counting the days till you return."

"And I'll think of you every moment we're apart."

"Goodbye beloved," I whisper as his fingers leave my own.

He starts down the stairs—then pauses. "I forgot to mention, Kit's moving in on Monday."

"He's *what*?"

"Yeah, figured he could take Juke's old room. Save some travel time. Remember, he's here for you. Go wherever you wish, whenever you wish. Every establishment in town has you on my credit, so spend away, and make yourself outrageously happy in my absence."

"You're too much. And I thank you."

His face grows serious as he stares, then takes the stairs, tugging me forward, holding tight. "Should I stay?"

"No." I hold my hand to his cheek. "I'll be here when you return. And then, we marry. Don't make me the reason you neglect your work."

"But—"

I press a finger to his mouth. "I won't hear of it. Your ship means a great deal to you. So go and I'll see you soon"

"Okay." He presses his forehead to mine. "Seven weeks and I'm back."

"Seven weeks and you're back."

He breaks away and at the bottom, hesitates, glancing over his shoulder. "Don't forget me, my love."

"Never." I blow a kiss.

He climbs into the sleigh and waves as Kit snaps the reins and the horses clop away.

"See you on Monday!" Kit calls.

"See you..." I wave and watch with a heavy heart as they disappear around the corner, James' eyes never leaving mine.

Chapter 12

The home is quiet as I step inside and hang my gear on the hooks, a low murmur of conversation coming from the parlor. I peek in. Nibs sits beside Morgan, his hands tangled in her hair, their lips pressed together in a passionate embrace. I blink, my mouth falling open. I'm not surprised, but I certainly didn't expect to see this.

Tiptoeing out, I slip into my room and close the door.

"There you are," a voice says.

I swing around, JaneAnn's seated on the couch.

"Hey! What are you doing here?" I approach.

"I have to talk with you."

"Okay... is something the matter?" I sit beside her, uneasy at her tone.

She clears her throat. "Before Margaret passed, you may recall I tried a little too hard to get your attention. I thought if you and I could be like sisters, maybe everything would be okay. There was a lot of envy in me, because I wanted what you two shared."

"Where's this going? You and I *are* like sisters."

"No, you would never have abandoned Margaret the way you're about to abandon me. In my naivety, I believed you and I would leave here together—get work in town, watch each other's backs. But now, I see I'm on my own."

"What would you have me do? Choose between you and James?"

"You've already chosen, and so have I. I don't like pretending I'm okay when I'm not. It's best we separate now, and this way, when you leave for good, my heart breaks a little less."

Words fail me as her determination is clear.

"I-I'm sorry," I stutter. "Please know how deeply I wish things could be different. I don't want our friendship ending like this, though. What can I say to change your mind?"

"There's nothing you can say," she replies, a hardness about her I'm not used to. "Now..." She lifts a wrapped package from beside her and holds it out. "Before I go. Peter asked if I would give this to you."

I take it from her, confused, and shakily remove the wrapping, holding back the emotions welling up inside. The item is a painted canvas, and as I lift it out, it reveals a picture of a group of us, standing in front of an ancient oak, our faces caught mid-laughter. Our expressions are oddly surreal, as are the vibrant leaves flashing under the hot sun. It's the kind of photo one could imagine might come to life at any second.

"What do you make of this?" I hold it to her.

She stares at it, but before speaking, a knock sounds at the door.

"Excuse me." I cross the room and open it to find John on the other side.

"Board game?" He holds up a colorful box with a grin.

"Oh, yeah—"

JaneAnn sprints past, shoving John aside as she races into the hall, disappearing into the parlor.

"What was *that* about?" He steps in, eyebrows quirked.

"I don't know."

He wanders to the couch and picks up the painting. "And what's this?"

"Peter made it. I couldn't tell you why, though."

He carries it under the light, face paling as he stares. "Why in the blazes would he paint this?"

"Beats me."

Pressing a palm to his temple, he squints. "You shouldn't have this."

"John?" I approach him. "What's wrong?"

"Dash it—" His eyes flutter and he crumples to the floor with a thud.

I stare at his unconscious form, my mind unable to make sense of what's just happened. Then, in a flash, I drop to my knees and cradle his head in my lap. "Help!" I cry out. "Somebody please!"

Nibs bursts through the door, stopping short at the sight of us. "Oh no..." He wraps his hands over his head. "What happened?"

Morgan hurries in, breathless. "Is everything okay?"

"We were just talking," I say, holding back tears. "And he collapsed."

"What was the conversation about?" Nibs kneels beside me.

"A painting Peter gave me."

"Where is it?"

"It slid under the chaise."

Morgan bends to retrieve it. "Nibs, you better see this." She holds it toward him, and he strokes his jaw, examining it.

"Let's get him to bed," he says, rising.

"What do you see?" I ask. "Is it the painting?"

"Don't worry, everything's okay," Morgan says.

"You sure about that? Because Johnny just dropped for no reason. Tell me what's going on."

John stirs, his eyes fluttering open. "*Hey...*" He sits, rubbing his neck.

"Blast it, Johnny!" Tears spill as I wrap my arms around him. "What happened?"

"I haven't the faintest idea." He strokes my back. "A touch under the weather, I suppose."

"Is that the truth?" I pull back, searching his face. "Because it sure seems like you're all hiding something from me."

I glance at Morgan and Nibs. I could swear they look guilty—but of what?

"I'm okay." John grips my shoulders.

"Morgan, help John to his room," Nibs directs.

"Of course." She guides him to his feet, and they shuffle toward the door, John rubbing his head.

Once alone, Nibs shuts the door and flops onto the couch with a sigh. "What a mess."

"I agree." I sit beside him, arms crossed. "So, tell me, what's going on?"

"Trust me," he says. "If I could, I would."

"This is positively mad!" I slap my hands to my knees and stand. "First, Jan says we can't be friends, and now this. What the devil is going on in this house?"

He doesn't get irate or match my energy; instead, he walks to me, resting a hand on my shoulder. "Let this go. It'll do you no good to dwell on unanswered questions."

"Is this because I'm getting married? 'Bye-bye, Wendy, exit's that way'."

"You have so much potential, but if you don't get out of this town, it affects more than just you."

An icy chill shoots through me. "What are you talking about? What happened to the Nibs who told me this place wasn't so bad? Now you're trying to get me out."

His lip twitches, and he glides to the bar. Uncorking a bottle of whiskey, he pours a glass. "It's like this…" He takes a long swig. "As queen, you can ensure a better life for all those you love. But without you—" A shadow crosses his face. "Last stop, Winter Woods."

I sit, stiff. "So now you want me to free everyone from this place?"

"Why not?"

"I don't know." My voice wavers. "I hadn't even considered it. Guess that's what Jan meant… Blimey." I rub a hand over my face. "This should have been my idea, shouldn't it?"

I peer up as he lowers himself onto the chaise, elbows on his knees. "It's easy to overlook the good we're able to do. Trust me, I know." He raises his glass to me. "Maybe this is your moment. The moment you finally comprehend what you're capable of. And it's more than being arm candy for King James."

I lean against the back of the couch, staring out the window. The neighbors are on their porch, waving goodbye to guests as they stroll down the snowy street. The group sways together, some singing, some laughing—all of them equally merry and bright.

"So, what happens?" I ask, chin resting on my hands. "I marry James, then what? Ask him to free you all? That's my plan?"

"Time will reveal it. But your purpose is far greater than you've allowed yourself to consider. It's quite unfair, though. We're not given the full road map, and because of this, we're bound for a dozen regrettable choices."

"It's certainly an idea, relocate everyone. And here I was, making every choice to satisfy myself."

He stands, a bittersweet smile on his lips. "You're not as selfish as you think. And when the time comes, I'm confident you'll make the right choice."

He moves to the door, then looks back. "Merry Christmas, kid."

I nod slowly. "Merry Christmas, Nibs."

He slips out, leaving the door slightly ajar, so I walk to it, and as I draw near, hear Morgan ask. "How did it go?"

The hallway is empty as I step out and peer around the corner into the parlor. The two of them are on the couch, Nibs staring into his glass, contemplative.

"She's like a sister to me," he says. "It's bloody torture to push her away."

"I know." Morgan rubs his back. "But it's not pushing, it's releasing. This is the best, for everyone. Especially her. We must see the big picture, and not get caught up in emotions."

"Damn Peter and his feelings. Why couldn't he just walk away? He's going to screw everything up."

"I get it's frustrating, but imagine if you were in his shoes. The last time I saw him, he was a half-drunk mess, desperate for another way."

"Yeah, well, there isn't another way, so he needs to trust us." He rests onto her lap with a groan. "Wake me up when it's over."

She brushes a hand through his hair. "And when it is, you and I won't get these moments anymore."

"That's not helping."

"What I mean is, don't rush through life. We have gifts today, we won't tomorrow."

He presses up and cups her face. "Then know this. I love you, Morgan Gwyn. Right here, right now. And if a tomorrow comes when we're no longer together, none of that's going to change."

"Poetically said." She leans in and kisses him, his arms wrapping around her, pulling her down.

Turning away, I wander into my room and pick up Peter's gift from the couch. I carry it with me as I curl into bed, holding it close. Gazing at his face, those green eyes twist something deep in my chest. How can a few strokes of paint affect me this way? It's like he's taunting me. Yet it's always like this with him... he forever gets the last word.

"Someone's lost in thought." Henley slides a lunch tray beside mine.

"Hey." My hand drifts up in a partial wave.

"What's got you?" He lifts a string of green grapes and pops one into his mouth.

I exhale, all the pent-up confusion swirling around my mind. "An odd encounter on Christmas. A few, actually. But you first. How was your holiday?"

"Oh, it was nice enough. Father surprised Mother with a grand piano, Antony and Julia are expecting, and though Warren and I felt a bit useless by comparison, I'm looking forward to being an uncle."

"How nice. I'm pleased for your family. But I pity the child, being raised in this place."

"I'll be sure to convey the message to my sister." He frowns.

"Sorry... That wasn't kind. It's just one of those days."

"And what type is that?"

"Oh, you know, the pitiful kind that would have Margaret working double time to cheer me up."

His shoulder presses into mine. "Well, I'm not Margaret, but I know the face she'd make." He crosses his eyes, looking ridiculous. "Okay, now spill it."

I giggle and wrap my arm around his, resting my head against his shoulder. "That works surprisingly well. *Okay*. The day itself was lovely. James joined us for the first time, and everything was great. No... It's what happened *after* that's weighing on me."

"And what happened?" He lifts his mug for a sip.

"If I tell you, promise it stays between us."

"Of course. Shall we spit-shake on it?" He holds his hand to his mouth.

"Gross." I tilt my head up at him, eyes narrowing. "It started with Jan. She's upset about my engagement, mainly because I'm moving. Said she didn't want to continue our friendship. Claims this'll hurt less."

"That's rough. Do you think she meant it? Jan is a bit... high-strung."

"For now, yes. Then she gave me a gift from Peter. I didn't tell you, but he moved out a week ago. No goodbye. Just left while I was asleep. The gift was a painting of a group of us. John came by later and... fainted when he saw it."

He pulls back, forcing me upright. "John fainted? Over a painting?"

"Yeah. Nibs and Morgan came in and all but affirmed it. Though they wouldn't say why."

"You're joking."

"Not at all. Nibs was stressed to say the least. Told me I should marry and make it my mission to 'get them out of here'. The whole thing was strange."

"I'm not following. What does marriage have to do with that?"

I lean forward, lowering my voice. "James is going to be the next king."

"He's what?" His brows lift. "Wendy, are you saying you're about to be—"

I nod slowly. "The next queen. Seems doable when you think of it that way."

"My gosh, I feel special just sitting next to you." He tilts his head, studying me. "My best friend, queen of Neverland. Wow."

"Let's not spread that around, shall we." I roll my eyes. "Back to the topic at hand."

He grins. "Sorry. Well, that's a lot of pressure for Nibs to put on you."

"What choice does he have?" I bite into a grape, the tangy sweetness flooding my mouth. "Truthfully, I've only thought about getting myself out. Seems pathetic now, but you remember our conversations. Margaret talking me off a ledge?"

"I could never pretend to know what you and she had gone through," he says thoughtfully. "Losing your past the way you did. But I expect everything you've endured is part of the process. Who would I be if I woke up one day without my past? Don't beat yourself up over this."

"You're sweet. And maybe you're right. Everyone else seems to have figured themselves out, but not me. Or maybe I never let myself. I don't know... anyway, enough about me."

He taps a finger against his chin. "Since we're trading secrets, might I share one with you?"

"Of course. Anything to get my mind off this." I pretend to spit in my hand. "Spit shake?"

He chuckles, a flush creeping up his cheeks. "I'm in love with Grace."

"My Grace?"

"Yeah. She's pining for David and way out of my league. But look at you and James. I didn't expect to love again, but she's stirred something in me, and it just... happened."

"Oh, Henley. I'm so pleased for you!" I squeeze his hand.

"Don't celebrate just yet. I'm not the man she's doe-eyed over. I'm just the one she talks to about that man."

"Until she marries him—" I poke his chest. "She's fair game."

"Hey, you two," Grace says, plopping her bag down, her timing impeccable. "What are we talking about?"

"Our holidays," I say, a knowing look passing between Henley and me. "How was yours?"

"Swell. David spent it with us, and Father's really taken to him. Auntie too. But before I forget…" She claps her hands. "I have the *best* news! Father announced we're having a ball in four weeks! Isn't that fantastic?"

"A ball? That's terrific," I exclaim. "So soon, though? How will you manage?"

"It was a Christmas surprise. Auntie's been planning it for months without telling me. No idea how she kept it a secret. We've had small gatherings, but this is my first *real* ball. I'm over the moon!"

"Oh, no, four weeks?" My excitement fades. "James will be gone at least seven."

"Say it isn't so!" She grips my hand. "Can't he come back early? He must be there."

"Afraid not, and I can't contact him at sea. It's okay, we'll have our time. For now, Henley, what say you and I go together?"

"Me? I don't see why not. But what about you, Grace? Who will you go with?"

"David asked me outright." She bites into her apple. "This'll be a dream!"

"Yeah, a dream." Henley crushes a grape between his fingers.

"You know," I say. "Tiger Lily's been pestering me about wedding plans. I can't decide anything. Maybe with your help, I could. Want to come by later?"

"Are you serious?" Grace lights up. "Of course we'll help—right, Henley?"

He gazes at me, thoughtful. "Sure. What could be better?"

"What could be better?" I echo, offering a cheeky grin.

❄ ❄ ❄

As classes end and Kit drives us back to the house, we are greeted by a sullen-faced Tiger Lily upon entering.

"What's going on?" She throws up her hands. "We agreed you would pick a dress today."

"Yes, we did, and they've come to help." I cross the room to the waist-high radio and flip the switch. The dial glows amber, and after the usual crackle, Fred Astaire's voice floats out.

"So, you're telling me, Kit, and—Henley, right?" Tiger Lily glares at them. "You're going to plan her wedding?"

"I'm just the driver." Kit plops onto the couch. "But I'd say the more the merrier."

"Don't worry," I assure her. "It'll work fine."

"Well then, here's the wedding dress catalogue. Have at it." She tosses it to Henley, who catches it and stares down at the cover, uncertain.

"Alright, well, come here and we'll get started." I sit and look at Kit. "Since you're not participating, how about you rustle up some coffee for everyone?"

"I said I'm a driver, not a waiter." He tips his hat low and leans back.

"We'll get it together." Tiger Lily snags the hat from his head. "You start looking. We'll be back, come on, *driver*."

He stands, shoving his hands into his pockets. "Didn't realize Cap put you in charge. Maybe we can talk about a raise while we're out gathering coffee."

As they slip from the room, I call out, "Thank you!"

Grace and Henley settle on either side of me, and the three of us lean close as I flip open the catalogue and we begin perusing the endless selection of gowns. When Kit and Tiger Lily return with a tray of cookies and coffee, Tiger Lily squeezes Henley's shoulder. "Go on and play cards with Kit; I'll take over."

"Yes, come along, boy," Kit urges, pulling out a deck of cards and slapping it onto the table.

"If I must." Henley hops up and joins him.

"Cigar?" Kit offers, fishing two from his coat. "Snagged these beauties off Cap."

"Why not?" Henley takes one and sniffs it.

Once they're lit, the two lean back in their chairs, puffing contentedly as they dive into a round of Gin Rummy. Meanwhile, Tiger Lily, Grace, and I sift through pages of dresses until, finally, we choose the one, the moment earning applause from the girls.

The dress is made of silk crepe, tailored in a sleek silhouette, with Chantilly floral lace across the arms and bodice. Tiny crystals are embroidered throughout the lace, resulting in a glorious gown I cannot wait to wear on the day I leave this town for good.

"We have to celebrate!" Grace declares. "Dinner's on me."

"Oh, Grace, you don't have to; it's just a dress," I say.

"It's *the* most important dress you'll ever wear." She rises, hand outstretched. "No excuses. And everyone's coming."

"A free meal is a free meal." Kit slaps down his final card. "I'm in."

"Oh, well—fine. Why not?" I concede, taking her hand.

We squeeze into the sedan, and Kit drives us to Will's Bakehouse. Over plates of veal marsala and crisp potato croquettes, Grace raises her glass of cognac and toasts, "To dreams fulfilled!"

We clink our glasses. "To dreams fulfilled!"

A few days later, on New Year's Eve, Grace invites us to a private dinner party at the Gilmour, a glitzy nightclub bathed in candlelight and champagne-fueled revelry. We sip cocktails and savor hors d'oeuvres, dancing the night away to the lively tunes of the jazz band on the brightly lit stage. As midnight nears, we gather on the balcony watching a stunning display of fireworks. The mirage of colors culminates in a final, dazzling explosion at the stroke of twelve. And all around us, couples kiss, friends link arms, and voices lift in song:

"Should old acquaintance be forgot
And never brought to mind?"
Should old acquaintance be forgot,

And days of auld lang syne?

In a moment of courage, Henley slips an arm around Grace, and she leans into him, singing heartily:

"For auld lang syne, my dear,
For auld lang syne,
We'll take a cup of kindness yet,
For auld lang syne."

And then—he kisses her. Maybe it's the spirit of the moment, maybe a few too many drinks, but she giggles, wraps her hands around his neck, and kisses him back.

Kit and I watch, slightly stunned.

"Well." Kit turns to Tiger Lily. "How about it?"

"Don't be ridiculous." She grips the railing, overlooking the snowy streets flooded with celebration.

His brows narrow, and he grabs my arm, pulling me into him, kissing with an unexpected ferocity. "Don't tell Cap..." He winks.

Tiger Lily's eyes flash, and she storms inside, vanishing into the glittering crowd.

"Serves her right," he mutters. "The princess thinks she's too good for the prince."

"You certainly showed her." I wipe my lips and loop my arm through his. "Let's not do that again, though, okay, pal?"

He swallows hard, offering an impish grin. And we head inside.

Fortunately, the choices made by both men carry no lasting consequences, and by Monday, we're all back together, lounging in my quarters after classes. This easy rhythm continues for weeks. Evening hangouts, impromptu dinners in town, occasional nights at the theater, and dancing our weekends away at the Gilmour—Kit and I returning home at dawn, humming, twirling, and covering our mouths to stifle tipsy laughter.

For the first time in my brief life, I'm happy.

Though we're still planning my wedding, thoughts of life beyond the gates have quieted. For once, I'm simply, contentedly—living in the moment.

Chapter 13

"You haven't asked her!" Grace exclaims. "The dance is tomorrow night."

"Wendy, will you please tell her?" Kit sighs, massaging his forehead. "She rejected me, Grace, on New Year's Eve."

"Don't remind me." I press two fingers to my eyelids.

"You say that because you liked it." He glances over his shoulder with a sly grin. "If Cap finds out I've stolen your heart, I'll be walking the plank."

"Returning to the topic at hand," Grace interrupts, cheeks flushed—likely recalling her own New Year's kiss. "You *do* want to go with her, don't you?"

"Of course I do." He drums his fingers on the steering wheel.

"Then do it." I urge. "She just left. Go to her."

"You know what? You gals are right. I'm going to do it."

"Good for you!" Grace cheers.

But instead of leaping from the car, he presses on the gas and pulls away. Grace and I exchange glances and settle back as he drives downtown. He parks in front of Mullin's General Store and turns toward us. "I'll be right back."

He hops out, disappearing into the store.

"Gone mad, hasn't he?" I muse.

A few minutes later, he bounds down the stairs clutching a sizeable bouquet of roses.

"Or maybe... not mad at all." My eyebrow raises.

Back at Tiger Lily's cottage, he pulls to the curb and parks. "Wish me luck."

"Good luck!" We chime together.

He slips from the car and approaches the front door, hand raised to knock—then freezes. Spinning around, he faces us, and we wave him back. He bobs his head, shakes out his arms, and prepares himself once more. As he turns around, Tiger Lily appears on the porch, head tilted. We giggle, watching as he offers the bouquet, and she takes it. They converse briefly, and then, without ceremony, he turns to go, his face somber as she enters the house and closes the door.

"Well?" Grace asks as he settles in. "Did she say no?"

"Did she say no?" He shoots her a look. "Doll, no woman in her right mind would say no to me."

"I'd say no." I snort.

"Exactly." He reaches back, patting my hand. "Key words: *right mind*."

"Well, congratulations!" Grace chuckles. "Now, we're all paired up for the ball."

Overnight, I barely sleep, my mind spinning with thoughts of the dance. It's a shame James couldn't join me, but even so, this is my first and I'm delighted for it. Come morning, I lay my gown on the bed and head out, counting down the minutes.

At the academy, the girls are abuzz with excitement. And when classes finally end for the day, Grace and I stroll through the halls, surrounded by a horde of others, chattering enthusiastically.

"My dress arrived from a city called Paris!" Gwendylon boasts, dabbing powder onto her nose with a compact mirror.

"Where's Paris?" I ask.

"How should I know?" She shrugs, as if it's a silly question.

"Well, I'm going with Gregory Wilkins. Can you imagine?" Cynthia Evans says gleefully, her face glowing.

"Gregory?" Gwendylon snaps her compact shut. "How did *you* manage that? Let me guess, your father *bought* him for the night."

A few girls giggle at the jab.

"Of course not." Cynthia wrinkles her nose, arms folded. "I don't need Daddy's money to succeed, like you. No, we were invited to his home, and he asked me himself."

Gwendylon's eyes narrow, but before she can respond, Lila cuts in. "What about you, Wendy? Who are you going with?"

"My fiancé's out of town," I say. "So, I'll be attending with Henley."

"The dancing assistant?" Annabeth peers up from her magazine.

"Yup, the same. We're good friends."

The girls glance at one another, uncertain. I suppose to them this equates going with '*the help*'.

"And what about you, Grace?" Lila asks. "Who's your date?"

"David, of course." Grace tucks a strand of hair behind her ear, cheeks pink.

"He sounds dreamy." Cynthia sighs. "What if he proposes tonight?"

"Phooey," Grace says. "Obviously, he won't propose—at least, I don't *think* he would." Her ears turn scarlet. "Oh, seriously! Now you've got me thinking nonsense too." She grabs my arm. "Come on, Wendy, let's go."

We walk to the cars and I hug her goodbye, before slipping in beside Kit.

"You ready?" he asks.

"Most definitely."

At home, we part ways to prepare, and after a shower and dressing, we reconvene in my room. Kit wears an elegant black tuxedo. And I've slipped into an icy blue, off-the-shoulder satin gown with layers upon layers of gossamer tulle. My ethereal dress is covered in sparkles, spreading across the fabric like tiny snowflakes glowing in the moonlight.

"I feel like Cinderella off to the ball." I twirl, the skirts flowing outward from a cinched waist.

"No idea who she is." Kit steps beside me and holds out his tie. "But you look lovely."

"And you look very handsome." I take the tie, looping it around his neck and maneuvering it into place. "You may just get the kiss you've been waiting for."

"You're sweet, doll, but I've got my eye on someone else."

"You ought to take that act on the road, see how far it gets you." I tighten the knot and step back. "There. Not bad, if I say so myself."

A knock sounds at the door.

"Mr. Williams," Kit declares, swinging open the door. "Please come on in. The lady of the hour is ready."

Henley steps in, wearing a sharp blue suit and tie.

"Well, my goodness, dear Wendy." He takes my hand. "You look beautiful!"

"May I offer similar compliments?" I brush a hand over the front of his suit. "You're quite dashing. That color suits you."

"Indeed, it does." Kit runs a comb through Henley's hair. "I'm sure young Grace won't be able to resist you."

"You *told* him?" Henley glares.

"I didn't tell him anything!"

"Oh, come now, friend." Kit chuckles, throwing an arm around him. "It's obvious to anyone with eyes. But don't worry. Your secret's safe with me. I might even help your cause... maybe sabotage this David fella a bit."

"Now, now, Kit," I say, "let's not go overboard. I'm sure Henley can manage on his own. Anyway, you'll have your hands full with your own date. Speaking of which, shall we go pick her up?"

"We should." He agrees, opening the door. Henley offers me his arm, and we step out into the evening.

Arriving at Tiger Lily's cottage, Kit stares into the mirror longer than usual. "Okay, here goes." He releases a breath, straightens his jacket, and steps from the car.

At her door, he knocks, and a moment later, she appears in a soft peach gown with a swooping neckline and off-the-shoulder sheer sleeves. The bodice shimmers with swirling beads in a feathery pattern, and a sparkling diamond pendant rests in the center of her forehead.

"Wow..." I whisper.

Draping a thick wool shawl over her shoulders, Kit guides her to the car, where he opens the door and she slips inside.

"Good evening," she says, through trembling lips, while arranging the poofy skirts.

"You look beautiful," I say.

"Positively smashing," Henley adds.

"Thank you! Grace kindly gifted me this dress."

"Of course she did," Henley murmurs.

Leaning back, my mind drifts as the car speeds toward Neverpeak Hills, the world slipping past in a haze of color. Starkey Manor is nestled at the end of a long drive, lined with glittering trees guiding the way. As we round the last corner, the house appears, a towering stone mansion, wide enough to house three of my own home, side by side. Lofty windows span its length, casting warm, yellow light onto the guests and across the snow-blanketed lawn.

Staring is enough to overwhelm me.

Kit parks the car, then hands the keys to an attendant, and takes Tiger Lily's arm. Henley loops his arm through mine, and together we follow the throng of guests up the steps, beneath towering columns wrapped in frosted evergreen garland. As we pass through the grand double doors, our shoes click against the cream-colored floor. A footman greets us with a polite nod, takes our coats, and gestures toward our hosts. Mr. Starkey and Ms. Diana stand at the base of a sweeping staircase, its dark red runner complementing the scenic oil paintings lining the walls.

"Good evening, Wendy." Ms. Diana takes my hand. "My, you look lovely tonight."

"Thank you, ma'am. As do you." I offer a slight curtsey.

"Wendy," Mr. Starkey's mouth lifts in a gentle curve. "Wonderful to see you again. And you must be Mr. Williams." He clasps Henley's hand between his. "My Grace has spoken highly of you. Of you all. I'm pleased to have you join us this evening."

"We are grateful to be here," I say.

"Speaking of Grace, where is she?" Henley peers around.

"She's preparing for the first dance," Mr. Starkey replies.

"And she asked me to tell you that she and David will join you after," Ms. Diana adds. "She's eager to see you four."

"Well, the ballroom awaits." Mr. Starkey gestures toward the mahogany archway. "Enjoy."

We thank them and step into the room, rosy with candlelight and fragrant with exotic perfumes. I breathe in, gazing at the vaulted ceiling, where glittering chandeliers frame a mural resembling a golden afternoon. Along the walls, floor-to-ceiling windows are draped in crimson velvet, the curtains spilling elegantly onto the polished floor.

As we sweep across the room, I catch my reflection in a tall, oval mirror set against gilded panels.

I must be dreaming.

"This house is incredible." I strain my neck to take it all in.

"Can this rightly be called a house?" Henley says. "More like a fortress with some pretty décor."

"Hardly." I giggle. "But to think of Grace living here."

"And soon, you shall join the club." He nudges me. "A palace, I imagine, is even grander."

A young footman in white gloves approaches, carrying a silver tray. "Champagne?"

We each take a glass and raise it to one another before drinking.

"I've never seen so many beautiful people in one room." Tiger Lily pulls her arms close.

"And yet, none compares to you." Kit purses his lips, staring up.

Tiger Lily beams and steals a glance his way, a softness in her I'm not used to seeing.

"I can relate, Tiger Lily," I say, sipping the bubbly drink. "It's easy to feel rather plain amongst such opulence."

"Nonsense. After tonight, you'll both leave with a few marriage proposals." Henley teases.

"Indeed," Kit agrees. "Cap might just have competition."

"Well, you boys certainly know how to charm a lady." I pinch Henley's cheek, and he grins like a child.

"Ladies and gentlemen!" Mr. Starkey's voice booms across the ballroom, and a hush fills the space. He stands near the raised dais, where an orchestra is positioned, instruments ready.

"My family is honored to welcome each and every one of you this evening," he says. "And now it's my pleasure to announce... the first dance."

We drift to the edge of the room alongside the other guests as a doorway opens beside the orchestra, and two figures appear. Grace—radiant in a soft pink gown, and crowned with a sparkling tiara—glides forward with her hand clutching her partner. *David*.

A gentleman shifts in front of me, obscuring my view, and I step back, sighing. The music swells, and I press onto my toes, craning my neck for a better view. Grace and David glide onto the dance floor, holding onto one another, their movements gentle and delicate.

"I don't want to see this." Henley shakes his head.

He steps away, and I take his place. Grace looks at David, glowing with affection, and though I'm pleased for her, I'm torn for Henley's sake. Spotting me, Grace's face lights up, and she whispers something into David's ear. He turns, searching the crowd until his eyes find mine. My breath catches, and I reach for Henley, clutching at air. That face... those unmistakable green eyes.

There is no David. It's Peter.

Chapter 14

"Whoa now." Henley slips an arm around my waist, holding me upright. "What just happened?" He guides me to a side table.

"It's Peter," I whisper.

"What are you talking about?"

"David is Peter. Peter is David. *Look*!" My voice breaks, and I point toward the floor.

"There's no way..." He stands, tilting his head to get a better view, and once he does, sinks into the chair. "He lied to her?"

"It doesn't make any sense." I glance at the sea of dancers, filling the floor.

"Are you okay?" He grips my wrist. "You nearly collapsed."

"It shocked me. It feels so long since I saw him last."

"Hey, you two," Kit calls as he and Tiger Lily pass by. "Why the long faces? Come on!"

"You'll see." Henley offers a hand, guiding me up. "Well, let's not waste the night away."

"I suppose not." I hold onto him as the orchestra starts to play *Fascination*. "Look at that, it's our song."

"Sure is!" He beams at me as we begin to move. "Perhaps Ms. Diana will assist us, ensure our footing is just right."

For this moment, I block out the world, letting the melody carry me. Shock or not, I've waited eagerly for this night, and I won't let one disturbance ruin it for me. Then, that disturbance comes into view, blinking once—then twice—as if he isn't quite sure I'm real. I dig my nails into Henley's shoulder, the music far away.

"It's okay." Henley glances behind us, spinning me around, and pulling us away from Grace and Peter.

But 'okay' is not how I feel. Peter has been a thread woven through my life, steadying me in ways I barely noticed. And now, he's near enough to touch, yet far enough to miss. Still, it's as if something beneath me has shifted.

When the song ends, we clap, though my thoughts remain distant.

"Would you despise me if I went to her?" Henley asks.

"The heart wants what it wants. Go on. Steal her heart."

He kisses my cheek. "Peter's mighty stiff competition, but I shall try."

He releases me and strides away, pressing through the crowd until he stands behind her. Peter spots him first and turns her toward him. She steps closer, her gaze steady, as she listens to him speak. After a moment, she nods, then glances back at Peter before Henley glides an arm around her, and they sail away.

I make for the edge of the dance floor, but just as I'm about to step off, a hand grips my shoulder. "Not leaving yet, are you?"

My body tenses. I turn back to Peter, his body close, his gaze fixed on me.

"I was. You may have noticed my partner is currently... preoccupied."

"What a shame." He shakes his head. "I'll just have to step in then, won't I?"

His features soften as he laces his fingers through mine and settles his other hand over my shoulder. As the violin strings pulse, my heart trembles, leaving me light-headed as I fall into step with him, the music sweet and stirring.

"Well, *hello*," he says, voice smoother than the wine I've drunk to forget him.

"Hello."

"Heavens, Wendy. You look divine."

"Oh well, thank you." Heat rises up my neck. "You don't look so bad yourself."

And he doesn't. Not bad at all...

"Marvelous." He offers a crooked smile. "Goal achieved."

He loosens his hold, and an ache sweeps over me as he extends an arm. My body twirls, skirts floating, the world fading into a blur of light. For a heartbeat, we're nearly apart, then his grip tightens, drawing me back in, skirts fanning as my body melts into his embrace, our faces hovering inches apart. We move as one, his eyes never leaving mine.

The music waves, stringed instruments quivering, flutes rising, piano intensifying. Each note flows into the next until it peaks and holds. He spins me one final time, pulling me close, my lips parting as the melody weaves around us, as if to bind us together.

Yet, in that final note, as the instruments exhale their last breath, the sound like a shiver on a cold night—I freeze.

"Excuse me." I lift my skirts and hurry from the room, mind racing as I navigate the winding passageways in search of an exit. When I spot a door leading outside, I press through, breathing in the chilly night air that cools the fire burning within me.

This is ridiculous; it was just a dance.

I take in my surroundings, forcing myself to calm. A pale stone pathway stretches ahead, lined with flickering lanterns on either side. In the distance, a greenhouse twinkles, smoke curling gently from its chimney. Wrapping my arms tightly around myself, I follow the path to the glass-paneled structure and step in, greeted by a rush of warm air.

Inside, rows of leafy green plants rest atop rich mahogany tables. At the center, a stout wood-burning stove casts an orange glow throughout the room. Delicate scents rise from the vibrant ruby-red and peach fuchsias trailing over the edges of their baskets, swaying along the walkway. Against the back wall, a white wicker love seat with a pale green cushion catches my eye.

I stroll toward it, the wood stove crackling softly behind me. As I settle, moonlight streams through the glass panes above, illuminating my dress and causing it to shimmer like stardust.

A soft tick, tick, tick draws my attention—the faint murmur of pipes expanding along the walls, as if the room itself were stirring in its sleep.

"*Wendy...*" Peter steps out of the shadows. "Can we talk?"

I nod, and he settles beside me. "I'm sorry about that."

A wave of nervous energy washes over me. "You want to tell me what's going on, *David?*"

"Your name and mine were scribbled on a piece of paper in James' office." He shifts closer, his face outlined in the silver glow of moonlight. "I intended to tell you that night, but when you returned engaged, I couldn't do it. You were happy. Had the one thing you always longed for. So, David is my middle name, and I decided to try it out. Don't ask me why."

"I saw your paper. So it's true, then. We existed before all of this. That vision of you and I, it was real. Tell me your full name."

"Peter Pan."

"That suits you." A grin creeps onto my face.

"As does yours—*Wendy Moira Angela Darling.*"

My smile fades, the name leaving me uneasy. It's a reminder of that face in the mirror. The one begging to be set free. The one I replaced when I woke up. "Tell me, did you know Grace and I were friends?"

"Yes. Impossible not to. She talks about you all the time."

"And what?" I rub my arms. "You pretended not to know me?"

"What do you want, Wendy? You're getting married. There's no room for me in your life now."

"And do I get any say in this?" I press forward, wandering toward a table lined with colorful, spiny plants. Running my fingers along their prickly edges, I say, "You decided there was no space for you, not me—and that wasn't fair."

A searing pain cuts into my palm, and I yank it back; a glint of red seeps through the glove.

"What's wrong?" He's off the couch in an instant, taking my hand.

"Nothing. It was the plant, it cut me, but I'm fine."

"This is fine to you?" He slips the glove off, revealing a bloody gash lining my palm. "Come here."

He guides me back to the loveseat, then strides to a sink tucked in the corner. Lifting a glass pitcher, he fills it with water. "This'll be cold."

I lean on one elbow, watching him. "You certainly know your way around the place."

"I do indeed." He settles beside me, the pitcher on his lap. "Hand, please."

I hesitate, reluctant.

"Would you prefer James do this? I'll fetch him."

"He's not here." I offer my hand, and he dips it into the freezing water. "Oh, that is cold!" I breathe out.

"Maybe don't pet plants like they're puppies, darling." He lifts my hand, dabbing it dry with his sleeve. Lifting a handkerchief from his chest pocket, he uses it to bandage the wound, tying it snug. "Not professional, but it'll hold. So where is your fiancé tonight?"

"Away on a trip." I hold up the bloodstained glove. "It was a nice pair."

"How about I buy you another?" He takes it from me and tosses it into the wood stove, the fire blazing a little brighter. "Now look—it's like we're blood brothers." He holds out his hand, smeared in red.

"I do believe that requires both of our blood to count." I drip water onto his palm and rub it clean. "With James away, Henley is my date or was."

"Lucky bastard." He offers a wry smile.

"Hardly. He's far more taken with another."

"And is that person my date? He did notably cut in on her and me."

"I'm not permitted to speak of such things." I rest my arm along the wicker edge. "You and she are close, though, yes?"

"Maybe." He matches my stance. "What's it matter to you?"

"It doesn't. If you've found love, I'm pleased for you."

"Glad to hear it." He drums his fingers against the seat. "Well, let's get back. They're probably wondering about us."

I press a hand to his chest, holding him still.

"Wait. I have a few questions first."

He waves me on. "Ask away."

"What in the world was that cryptic painting about? And did I really see you at *Rêveur Éveillé* on Christmas Eve, or was it my imagination? And..." I pause, my chest tightening. "Why did you leave without saying goodbye?"

"Did you require a goodbye?"

"Did you assume our impromptu dance was enough?"

He lets out a breathy laugh. "For a second there, I thought I might've dreamt that."

"Do you often dream about me and you dancing?"

"Well, you're a firecracker tonight." He rises and walks to the stove, hands outstretched to the heat. "Look, I'm sorry I left without a word. My behavior was uncalled for that night. Thought it was best I let you be."

"I understand, but it hurt to learn you were gone without a word. Thought I did something wrong."

"Never." His tone eases as he turns back toward me. "You could never. Haven't you learned that by now?"

I give a small nod, my voice quieter. "What about the painting then? John fainted when he saw it. Nibs and Morgan acted as if it were unsafe. Why?"

"What do I know?" He shrugs. "You saw it. It's just a picture. A keepsake for when you leave this place. What harm could that be?"

"I don't know. But I think you do. And that's why you painted it."

He holds my gaze a long moment, something in his expression strained, then shrugs again and kicks at the ground. "As to your last question, yes. You saw me at the restaurant. Grace and I shared a meal before the Christmas Eve service."

"And you didn't want to say hello?"

"No. I didn't."

A dull ache settles in me. As if sensing it, he adds, "You were with James. I figured I'd interrupted enough of your meals. Now, have I answered to your satisfaction?"

"Not at all." I lift myself, flattening my dress. "But I think you knew that."

I step past him, and he follows me out of the greenhouse, leaving behind the toasty warmth for a mind-numbing chill.

"Lovely day for a stroll, isn't it?" He slips off his outer coat.

"We've had worse walks, haven't we?" My teeth chatter as an uncontrollable tremor runs through me.

"Yes, but I wasn't so capable then, was I?" He drapes the coat over my shoulders and draws me into his side, his nearness leaving me as frazzled as our dance.

"Henley's in love with Grace," I blurt.

"Is he now?"

"Yes." I swallow hard as we walk. "And if you're in love with her, just be mindful of his feelings."

"Oh, I see." He stops and turns to me. "So no kissing in front of him, is that it?"

"Well, I don't—"

"No flaunting our feelings? Or perhaps you tell me exactly what I can do, so I don't hurt him by daring to be with the woman he loves."

"I've angered you." I look down, the chill cutting through my dainty heels.

"No, Bird. Didn't I say you're incapable of angering me?"

"And yet, I clearly have." I lift my chin.

"Why are you engaged to James?"

"*What?*" The question catches me off guard. "Why would you ask that?"

"Do you love him?" He steps closer, hand wrapping around my arm, thumb brushing lightly over the fabric. His touch stirs something I wish it didn't. "Does his touch captivate you—or is he still just your way out?"

Fury blooms at the accusation, and I shove him away. "You have no right to say that to me!"

"You're right." He steps back, jaw set. "Forget I said anything."

I slip the coat from my shoulders and press it back into his arms. "Thank you for this."

I walk the rest of the way shivering, unwilling to take another step by his side. As we enter the home, the space between us widens. Nearing the ballroom, I spot Grace pacing in the entryway.

"Hey, are you okay?" I ask.

"Where did you go?" Her eyes narrow.

Peter wanders in behind, and she looks between us. "What's going on?"

"Gracie, there's a lot we need to talk about." Peter strides past me and takes her hand. "Can we go somewhere private?"

"No!" she cracks. "Do you two know each other, David?"

"We do." He looks my way briefly. "My name is Peter. Wendy and I lived in the Children's Home together. I'm sorry I wasn't fully honest."

"*Okay.*" Her face pales as she drops into a chair. "So, what is true about you?"

"Everything was true. I just left some things out."

"Somethings?" Her eyebrows shoot up. "No, you left out everything! She told me the truth right away. No deception at all. But you, how can I trust anything you say?"

Henley enters with drinks in hand and passes one to Grace. "Am I interrupting something?"

"Tell me, Henley," Grace says coolly. "Do you also know, David?"

He glances at Peter. "I do."

Kit and Tiger Lily stroll in, laughing together. "Peter!" Kit pulls him into a hug. "I thought it was you. Looking good, friend."

Grace downs her drink and slams the empty glass on a side table. "Excuse me." She lifts her skirts and disappears through the doorway.

"Did I say something?" Kit's eyes widen.

"It would seem so." Tiger Lily turns to Peter. "You're David, I presume?"

He nods, glancing between our group.

"What the hell, man!" Henley slams him against the wall; Peter's head hits hard. I wince.

"Whoa, now." Kit plants a hand on Henley' chest. "None of that."

"Why not?" Henley grits his teeth. "He's a bloody coward!"

"It's not like that." Peter's eyes darken as he adjusts his shirt. "It wasn't meant to hurt her."

"Hey." I tug Henley's arm, knowing this will only end in regret. "Let's take a break."

"Yeah, whatever." He shoves Kit and me aside.

As I follow him through the archway, I glance back at Peter, rubbing his head, still frowning after us.

Henley guides me to the dance floor and pulls me close, rougher than usual.

"Why does it seem like this goes beyond his deception?" I wrap my arms around his neck, the melody far too sweet for the intensity in him.

"Because it does. I've had a problem with him for a while now."

"But why? You and Peter were once good friends."

"Until Margaret's death, yes. But when I should have been with her in those final moments, he was."

"Oh, come on." I step back. "You can't hate him for that. "

"Can't I?" I've never seen him so angry. "How long did he sit with you once she was back again? All that time wasted, when he could have fetched me, given me that final moment."

"Oh Henley." He folds into me, and I hold him, uncaring how we appear to those around. "I wish more than anything she could have told you she loved you herself. But please, know this. Peter was in as much shock as I. Had it not been for Morgan, I would have sat by the fire all night."

He closes his eyes. "I know. Still, I need someone to blame. Because the ice certainly isn't going to apologize for ripping her away from me."

I guide his chin up, my voice tight. "Then blame me. Not him. She wanted to leave, and I said no. If anyone's to blame it's me."

"You know I'd never. Could never." He exhales heavily, and wipes at his eyes. "So I guess that means I'll have to forgive him at some point, huh?"

"Yes. It does."

"I could consider forgiving him for Margaret, but then..." His voice tightens. "There he is, stealing Grace. All the joy in the world is within my reach, and he's blocking the way."

I sigh. Knowing nothing I say will fix this. Only time has the potential to ease his hurt. "Let's take a break."

"Good idea."

I lead him to where Tiger Lily and Kit relax at a side table, a deck of cards between them.

"Take a seat, buddy." Kit pats the chair beside him. "Tell us your tale of woe."

Henley sinks into the seat, and I give his shoulder a reassuring squeeze. "You just relax and I'll find a new partner. Perhaps one of those sullen-faced boys in the corner."

"Are you sure?" His look is pitiful.

"Yes. And maybe you'll feel better if you tell them everything."

"I believe you're right." He folds me into another hug. "Thanks, old girl."

✳ ✳ ✳

I thread my way through the crowd of men and women, some engaged in conversation, while others fan themselves, likely listening to a bit of gossip. A group nearby cackles loudly, their faces flushed and their multiple glasses empty. As I arrive at the drink table, I find the champagne arranged in a multi-tiered tower, making me hesitant to take one for fear of toppling the rest.

"A beautiful lady like yourself shouldn't be fetching her own drink," A man murmurs beside me. "Where's your date, lovely?"

"He's playing cards." I glance up and tip my head. "Chas?"

"Wendy! Now it makes sense why you seemed familiar." He scans the room. "Where's James?"

"He's on a trip. I'm here with a friend."

"Oh?" He looks me over, slow and deliberate. "Well, he's missing out. You look dazzling, darling."

"Thank you. And where's your date? Surely you've got five or six young women waiting on you."

"I'm wounded." He presses a hand to his heart. "I may be a ladies' man, but only because I haven't met the right one. Surely this makes me redeemable?"

"As long as the right woman thinks so."

"But of course. You're devoted to the superior man. That makes the rest of us useless, doesn't it?"

"Certainly not." I take a sip.

"In that case..." He bows low. "Madam, may I have the next dance?"

I stare, hesitant.

"Unless, of course, you'd prefer to watch your date shuffle cards all night?" He quirks an eyebrow.

"No, I certainly don't." I hold up my hands. "Alright good sir, you may."

I take his arm and we coast onto the floor, swept away by a lively waltz. Song after song, we spin and twirl until I'm dizzy and giggling with delight. It's a needed respite after the tension between Peter and Henley.

Despite the odd first impression, Chas is quite refreshing to be around. He isn't ridiculous or rude, and there's a quiet respect in the way he carries himself.

As our legs begin to tire, he guides me to the room beside the orchestra where Grace and Peter emerged earlier.

"Welcome to the Back Room." He gestures around as we enter the dimly lit lounge.

Couples linger at a pale marble bar, sipping drinks under a line of low-hanging glass lamps. At the center of the room, men crowd around a table, clutching cards and cigars, the air thick with smoke. At the back, a fire crackles beside a sweeping half-moon couch, where Mr. Starkey reclines with an arm draped around a young woman who bears a striking resemblance to Canary from the diner.

"What can I get for you, honey?" A young man asks behind the bar—his smile as slick as his hair.

"You pick for us, Chas."

"Let's go with something sweet," he says. "We'll take two Pink Ladies."

"Gotcha. And a couple of extra cherries for the lady." The bartender winks at me, casually tossing a crisp white towel over his shoulder.

"So, you must recognize a few faces around here, yeah?" Chas asks.

"I do." I glance around. "That's Mr. Foggerty—my friend John works for him. William from the Bakehouse—we frequent there often. Oh, and Mr. Mullins from the grocers. And tell me, is that Canary beside Mr. Starkey?"

"Sure is. She's kind of his lady of the night."

"You're teasing!"

"Not at all. Does it shock you?"

"Yes, it does. She's always been friendly, like a proper lady."

"Well, I never implied she wasn't. I'd assume that's why Gentleman likes her."

"Ciao, Wendy!"

Cecco and Jill stroll over. Cecco wears a bold turquoise suit, oddly similar to the curtains in my bedroom. Jill wears a red dress, a few sizes too small.

"Hello," I greet them both. "It's lovely to see you here."

"Darling..." Jill pinches my cheek. "As always, the image of perfection."

"Senza dubbio!" Cecco says, with his usual dramatic flair. "And where's Signore James?"

"He's out of town."

"I see." Jill surveys Chas with a glint in her eye. "That didn't stop you, though, did it?"

"Now, now, Jill, go on with you and leave us be." Chas waves them off.

"Certainly, and when the little one's gone to bed, come find me." She blows a kiss. "Enjoy your night, Wendy, darling."

"Buonanotte, tesoro." Cecco kisses both my cheeks.

"And to you," I say as they flitter away.

Lifting our drinks, Chas guides me to the couch in the back.

"Do my eyes deceive me, or is Chas Turley with Captain James' fiancée?" Mr. Starkey says.

"It's the man's fault for leaving her alone." Chas hands me my drink. Out of an abundance of nerves, I take a long sip, earning a few raised brows.

"Ms. Wendy, you'd best watch your back with this rake," Canary says, pursing her lips.

"You see how they attack me unprovoked?" Chas protests.

"Yes, that's you, Chas. Innocent." Canary laughs, her finger twirling around a strand of Mr. Starkey's hair.

"Anyway." He leans closer, voice low. "That's Black Gilmour playing poker with Alan Herb, our esteemed mayor. Cookson, he's the Chief Constable, as well as Wibbles, the deputy. Then we've got Alf Mason, our town clerk, currently snogging the young maiden."

He pauses, leering darkly. "And that fella there, leaning against the window, staring at you? That's Noodler, bit unsavory. Unfortunate for us, we all frequent his pub, so he remains part of the circle."

Noodler has greasy black hair, which obscures half his face. The sight of him, coupled with the memory of Juke mentioning their friendship, sends a shudder through me.

"So, you're all close friends, then?"

"Yeah... we're mates. But the truth is, it's the captain. He brought us together. Encouraged the loyalty."

He lifts his glass high and calls out, "To the Captain!"

All around, men and women raise their glasses and cheer, "Hear, hear!"

"Every soul here is loyal to him. And once he's on the throne, with you by his side, you too will have our swords."

"Devoted friends are a true blessing, and my fiancé appears extraordinarily blessed."

"Cheers to that."

We clink glasses.

Before long, others gather around the couch, and a game of charades begins. It's not like the version I'm used to from home. Though humorous at times, it's also vulgar, the men acting out things I don't fully understand, nor wish to. After it mercifully wraps up, Smee—clearly intoxicated, stands and begins reciting a selection of poetry, prompting the others to throw things until he yells at them angrily.

"Ye wouldn't be carryin' on like that if the Cap'n were here, no sir!"

Next, Canary takes the floor with a risqué dance that leaves me staring at the detailing on the carpet while the men clap and whistle.

Out of the corner of my eye, someone enters the room and strolls to the bar. Peter. He speaks briefly with the bartender, then turns, leaning against the counter—gaze fixed on Canary. I glance between her dancing and Peter's expression.

Does this really attract him?

When she finishes, she bows low, then shoots me a look. "Now, your turn, love."

"What?" My neck burns. "Oh no, no. Thank you." I wave my hand, brushing away the foolish notion.

"Surely you must have a hidden talent somewhere in there," Chas prompts.

I chew my lip, catching Peter's stare—his expression insufferably amused.

"Come, come, dear." Mr. Starkey raises his glass. "Grace says you play piano. Go take a seat and play us something to soothe our savage souls."

"Okay, fine." I concede. *I can't believe I'm doing this.*

I swallow the last of my drink and wander to the grand piano. Lifting the lid, I let my fingers glide across the ivory keys. Maybe it's the alcohol, but a calm settles over me as I sit and press down, a hush falling over the room.

"Down in the valley, the valley so low,
Hang your head over, hear the winds blow.
Hear the winds blow, dear, hear the winds blow.
Hang your head over, hear the winds blow.

My fingers dance along the keys, eyes closed, voice tender.

Writing this letter, containing three lines,
Answer my question, "Will you be mine?"
"Will you be mine, dear, will you be mine?"
Answer my question, "Will you be mine?"

I gaze around. Some stare with soft grins, lifting cigarettes to their lips, while others lean on their elbows, quietly attentive. Peter strolls idly to the wall opposite me and rests against it, drink in hand, sipping slowly as he watches.

Roses love sunshine, violets love dew,
Angels in heaven know I love you;
Know I love you, dear, know I love you,
Angels in heaven know I love you.

My voice trembles slightly. I should look away.

If you don't love me, love whom you please,
Throw your arms round me, give my heart ease.
Give my heart ease, dear, give my heart ease.

The final words come out quiet.

Throw your arms round me, give my heart ease.

I rise, and offer a wobbly curtsey, the room erupting in drunken applause and whistles.

"Darling, you are a treasure," Chas calls out, clapping enthusiastically.

"When the old man gets tiresome," Noodler says from a nearby chair, "you come find me."

I wrinkle my nose in disgust, which garners cackles from his friends. Replacing me at the piano, Cecco launches into a jazzy tune, crooning loudly.

I collapse beside Chas, breathless, and he holds a cigarette to me. "Here, my darling. You were lovely."

I frown at it.

"It's quite fashionable, I assure you."

"Of course." I lift it to my lips, and take a puff.

I glance at Peter and hold the cigarette to him, beckoning. He stares for a moment, then joins me.

"Thought it was a yucky habit?"

My mouth tilts teasingly, and he takes it from me.

"Can't say I imagined you performing for this pack of animals, but you've just about captured every heart."

I look at Chas, caught in a conversation with Mr. Starkey, then turn back.

"You seemed quite attentive," I say. "Though not nearly as much as Canary's dance. Perhaps I do one of my own."

"Funny. You'll be over my shoulder before you get halfway through it."

"You wouldn't dare."

"Oh, but I would." He offers the cigarette back, but instead of taking it, I lean forward, my lips brushing his fingers as I inhale. Pulling away, I exhale slowly, the smoke lingering between us.

He presses his forehead to mine. "James wouldn't want you here. As you once so politely told me—*you're drunk*. And I promise you; these men are not trustworthy friends."

"Is James here? No. Where's Grace, anyway? Did you two kiss and make up yet?"

"No. She doesn't want to talk or see me right now."

"This party's tame, Starkey," Noodler growls, pulling our attention.

"Oh, now, now, this is my daughter's first ball." Mr. Starkey holds a pipe to his mouth. "Be glad you were invited at all, you scoundrel."

"If Juke were here." Noodler crosses his arms. "We'd be having a proper time, always had a few ladies on his shoulders."

My breath catches at the mention of Juke.

"Got to wonder what old Bill's up to these days," Chas says, reclining.

"Wendy would probably know." Mr. Starkey replies. "Where is Juke these days, dearest?"

My nails dig into Peter's arm.

"Steady now," he murmurs.

"Why would I know what Juke's up to?" My brows wrinkle.

"Well, he's about to be your brother-in-law." Chas chuckles. "Figured your fiancé might've mentioned something."

"What are you talking about?" I'm struggling to keep my voice steady.

"I'm sorry." Chas straightens, suddenly serious. "You didn't know? Juke and James are brothers."

I say nothing, the silence deafening as I stare at him, desperate to make sense of his words. Peter lets out a sharp, stifled breath, and I glance down—blood pooling where my fingernails dig into his skin.

My mouth parts, but before I can speak, Noodler's laugh cuts through the quiet like a blade.

"Captain's in trouble, ain't he?"

Chapter 15

There's blood on my fingertips. The room spins, and a wave of nausea washes over me. The surrounding noises blur—the piano, once melodious, now screeches. I push off the couch. "I need some air," I manage. "Excuse me."

"Want me to join you?" Chas presses up.

"No! No, thank you." I stumble toward a side door and push through. My stomach churns as I hurry to the edge of the patio, bending over as the alcohol rises in my throat. An invisible hand slips around my hair, guiding it over my shoulder as I retch. My body angrily expels the bad choices I've made tonight.

Once emptied, I stagger backward, dizzy, and my body presses into heat. I don't need to see his face, just the weight of his arms around me and the immediate relief to tell me who it is.

"All better?" Peter whispers in my ear, dabbing my lips with a handkerchief.

"No. And I doubt I'll ever be..."

I tilt my head at him, sensing he carries the same weight as me. "Thank you. I should feel embarrassed, shouldn't I?"

"Don't you dare." A smile creeps onto his face. "Come sit with me."

He steadies me as we step to the house, and I collapse, body sweating.

"I'm sorry," I whisper, resting my head back, delicate snowflakes swirling around us. "It's just... Juke's going to be my brother-in-law."

"It explains why he wasn't concerned about James' retaliation, huh?"

"He'll be at family dinners. Holidays." I shudder. "How will I ever face him again?"

"You won't." His muscles tense. "If James loves you at all, he wouldn't dare bring him near you."

"Why do you think he didn't tell me?"

"You'll have to ask him. But I can think of a few reasons a man might not want to admit kinship with Juke."

"James will be back soon, and then I'll have to broach the topic."

He folds his hands, and I catch sight of thin, angry, red cuts covering the top of his wrist, my nails having sliced straight through.

"I'm so sorry." I lift his hand onto my lap. "I made a mess of my night."

"It's okay." His fingers squeeze mine. "I once told you we're a bad combination, and it sure seems to be true. First your hand, and now mine."

"Yeah? And what do they both have in common? *Me*." I pull a laced lavender handkerchief from my pocket, pressing it gently against his wrist as fresh droplets of blood stain the cloth. "You're much safer without me."

"I'm certain you're right." He offers a knowing look. "But I'll still take my chances."

Lifting the material, I stare at the spots of red, then untie his handkerchief from my hand, letting it slip away as I press my injured palm over his wrist.

"What are you doing?"

"Blood brothers." I shrug.

His eyes lock onto mine, a rush flooding my chest. He exhales a slow laugh, and I can't help but giggle as I let him go.

"Oh well," I say shaking off the lightness, "so much for a magical night. Do you remember when Margaret and I planned that ridiculous ball at the house?"

"Sure do. Henley nearly passed out from nerves, like it was some official event we were attending."

"Life wasn't perfect, but looking back now, there's a sweetness about it I've begun to miss." I tilt my head to him. "I'm sorry he flipped out tonight."

"I can't say you didn't warn me."

"He's hurt. Says you're always stealing moments that should've been his—with Margaret at the end, and now Grace."

"He should know I'd give him those moments with Margaret if I could."

"He knows. But just understand—you've got competition for the girl you love."

"Trust me, Wendy Darling. I'm well aware." He runs a hand down his face.

"And I'm sorry, because it wasn't right to ask you to be mindful of him. Whatever is between you and Grace—"

The wind bites at my skin causing me to twist toward him. He strips off his jacket again and drapes it over my shoulders, pulling me close. The chill eases as his warmth spreads.

"You were saying?"

I lift my gaze—my eyes settling on his mouth.

"Wendy?"

"Yes?" My voice is too high.

"You were saying something about my relationship with Grace?"

"Oh... yeah. Just that one must..." I trail off as his fingers brush my cheek, pressing aside a stray hair. "...She'll have to accept it."

"She?" He squints.

"I mean Henley. He'll have to accept it."

The door swings open, and Grace and Kit peer out. Peter straightens and I instinctively press away.

"There you are!" Grace exclaims.

"You're a mess, woman," Kit shakes his head. "Well, come on, let's get you home."

"Always a pleasure to see you, too."

"Of course it is, doll." He helps me to my feet. "Henley and Lily are already in the car, so we'll slip around the side, ensure none of the good folks in there see you like this."

"Goodnight, Peter." I steal a glance at him, but he keeps his focus on the dark horizon.

"Night, Bird," he murmurs, not quite looking my way.

"Thanks for coming, Wendy." Grace hugs me. "I'll see you soon, okay?"

I give a half-hearted wave and follow Kit to the car. Henley is asleep, and Tiger Lily greets me warmly, full of questions I'm not particularly eager to answer. As we drive away, the lights of the mansion fade behind us, like a fairytale without its happy ending.

A week passes. Grace isn't herself for most of it and declines our usual hangouts. I want to know what happened between her and Peter after the ball, but I don't press. Henley is unfortunately miserable company—with Kit, Tiger Lily, and me tiptoeing around his bad moods all week.

I can't pretend I'm overjoyed myself. The news of James and Juke's kinship has weighed heavily on me. That James used Juke to attack Peter unnerves me—his own brother, doing his bidding. Once, I could believe James was blind to Juke's flaws. But not anymore. He knew precisely who Juke was, and as Peter said, let the animal loose in our house for years.

Friday night, we head to the Gilmour, but it lacks its usual sparkle. After returning late and getting very little sleep, I stare at the ceiling, the noise in my mind unyielding. Fluffing my pillow, I flip over, trying to rest until sunshine streams through the slits in my turquoise curtains, urging me out of bed, exhausted. My head aches as I glide into the slippers beside my bed and pull on my robe.

In my tired state, I stumble past my usual routines, not caring how I look in the least. Shuffling out of my room, I enter the dining room, where the conversation abruptly stops.

"I didn't sleep well." I hold up a hand. "So, unless you have coffee, please don't bother me." I glance at Slightly. "I'm talking to you. Whatever you're about to say, don't."

He puckers his lips and pretends to zip them.

"I've got you covered right here. Fresh cup of coffee for the lady," a voice says, and my body stiffens as I meet Peter's amused face at the far end of the room. "Good morning, sunshine."

My stomach twists. Is it too late to return to my room and never show my face again?

"You feeling okay, Wendy?" Grace asks from beside Peter.

I blink slowly, gazing in her direction, passing over Nibs, who's biting back laughter.

"I'm fine, thank you." I swallow the scream rising in my throat. "Didn't realize we had guests this morning. What brings you both here?"

"Isn't it wonderful?" Nibs gestures to the chair beside him. "The prodigal's returned. Now, come, sit, and I'll grab you a plate of delicious breakfast. Grace is right, by the way; you look terrible."

I drop into the chair and glare at him. "Thanks, always so supportive."

"You know it, sweetheart." He pats my shoulder and slips into the kitchen.

I attempt, rather poorly, to comb my fingers through my messy hair, knowing full well it's a lost cause.

"So." I eye the pair. "A bit surprised to see you both."

"Just visiting with the old crew." Peter presses a steaming mug of coffee into my hands. "Drink up."

"Thanks..." I lift it and take a reviving sip. "I apologize for my appearance, didn't expect company."

"I don't know what you mean." He holds another mug to his lips.

"You tease."

"Never," he mouths.

"I'm sorry," Grace says. "You didn't expect us. But don't worry, I look far worse on any given morning, and it usually takes two staff to prepare this."

Peter's hand slides over Grace's, and something tugs inside me—a desire to put some space between them.

Nibs returns and sets a heaping plate in front of me. "Dig in."

My nose wrinkles as I survey the gooey eggs and overcooked bacon. "Whose day was it to cook?"

"That'd be a Nibbler special." He grips my shoulders a bit too tight. "We're down one cook without you, princess. So don't complain. In your absence, I'm expected to chip in. Anyway, if you think those are bad, you should see what the others got, nearly inedible."

"Inedible is a stretch," Slightly says, shaking his head.

"Burned trash is more like it," Tootles adds with a chuckle.

Nibs rolls his eyes. "Aren't they pleased with themselves? I'll ensure Morgan schedules you both for tomorrow's breakfast."

Both their smiles fade as they consider what that means.

"Yeah, who's laughing now," Nibs mutters.

I grin and turn back to my food, pressing the fork around to see if any of the meal is safe for consumption. I try a minuscule bite of flapjack, but only to appease Nibs.

"Atta girl. Now these dishes won't wash themselves. Excuse me." He gathers the empty plates and disappears back to the kitchen.

"Wendy," Grace says. "I'm truly sorry for how I've acted all week. You can imagine, it's been... confusing."

"Don't worry about it. You both appear to have worked through things."

"Yes, you could say that," Peter says, gazing at Grace.

"Just took a few *long* conversations." She smiles at him.

"Grace!" John peeks in. "I'm ready for you, come on."

"What are you ready for?" I lift a piece of burnt bacon, rotating it in search of the edible part.

"Board game orientation," John says smartly. "Join us when you're finished eating, okay?"

Grace touches Peter's shoulder, possessively, and a leer creeps onto my face before I can stop it.

"See you soon," she says.

"Sure thing." His gaze follows her as she leaves.

"Well..." I push the plate aside, giving up. "You're both chummy."

"Indeed we are."

I hold the coffee close and breathe in the rich aroma, wishing it were something stronger.

Slightly and Tootles rise, and wink as they pass by, arms full of paper-work for their business.

"How's your hand?" Peter asks.

"Better than my heart." I hold it to him.

He takes it, turning it over gently, finger grazing the faded red line. "Healed well."

"And yours?" I pull his over. Four faded pink lines spread across his wrist. "It'll get there. And if you're lucky, you won't have my claw marks on you forever."

"That would surely ruin me."

I laugh and release his hand.

"So, when's James coming home?"

"Three more weeks. He's left for longer, but somehow this one feels like a lifetime."

"You miss him a lot?"

"I should say yes, but—I don't know anymore. At first, I counted the days. But then, it sounds awful, but I started to exist without him. For too long, I existed *because* of him. Like he held all the hope and joy in the world, and I'd only possess it once he gave it to me."

"Maybe I'm naïve," Peter says. "But I think love shouldn't be about existing because of someone. It should be about existing with them. You know? Sharing your own joys with that person."

"You're not wrong. There's another bit of purpose to he and I marrying, though."

"And what's that?"

"To save you." I lean forward. "Become queen and free you from this place."

His expression sharpens. "Why would you say that?"

"Because I can. Wouldn't you want that?"

"You marrying James to free me?" He chuckles coolly. "No, I wouldn't."

"Well, it's not the only reason. Just... a benefit."

Pressing back from the table, he straightens. "This town isn't ideal, but it's not the prison you think it is." He taps his temple. "But this is."

He turns and strides out of the room, leaving me alone, his words lingering, stirring something I can't quite understand.

Returning to my room, I close the door, and rest against it for a long moment. I drag myself through the motions—hair, dressing, make-up—before returning to find everyone gathered, including the Keepers. The sight fills me with an unexpected ache for times gone by, and somehow, a longing for what's right in front of me.

I relax beside Maimie, and she wraps her arms around me. "Isn't this wonderful?" she says. "We're all together again."

"Yes... perfect."

And it is, isn't it? I swallow the emotion, fighting to release itself. Why am I only now seeing what's been here all along? I've let myself pass through life faster than the sedan tearing down Main Street. But what am I running toward?

Freedom. Escape. Warmth.

Yet I'll be leaving them behind to attain it. And what if Nibs is wrong and there's no rescuing them? Then, I'll be free—while the only family I've ever known stays locked away.

In one corner, sprawled on the floor, John talks animatedly while Grace, Peter, Michael, the Twins, Slightly, and Tootles listen. A board game lies between them, and he directs their moves like a conductor.

JaneAnn and Hannah are curled up in chairs, lost in the worlds of their books. On the couch, Morgan, Agnes, and Elizabeth chat, their knitting needles as fast as the flow of their conversation, and by the fire, Llewelyn and Nibs stand together conversing.

Maimie tells me about life. The latest lessons in the classroom. The choir at church. A bit of gossip about the sweet-faced boy and the nasty so-and-so girl who's garnered his attention. I listen, enjoying her tales knowing I won't have them soon.

Once the board game wraps up, John continues directing by rallying everyone for a round of Hats. One by one, teams take turns, putting on amusing routines: Morgan and Nibs, John and Slightly, Michael and Maimie, Grace and Peter, and it concludes with Jack and Agnes.

Jack plays a violinist afraid of strings, running around crying, "*I must warn you... I'm allergic to scandal!*"

Agnes is a nurse who faints at the sight of blood, exclaiming in a singsong voice, "*She danced straight into the fireplace!*" before dramatically swooning.

Their skit involves a suspicious parcel arriving. At first, I laugh along humored, but Agnes' repeated fainting unsettles me as the memory of John collapsing on Christmas Day springs to mind.

I slip away to the porch while they finish the performance, but soon the door swings open, and Maimie informs me we're walking to the Diner for lunch. Following the rest, I bundle up warm, and we begin our stroll through the snowy streets toward town. My heart is heavy, though I can't understand why.

Gazing behind him, Nibs catches my eye and jogs to my side. "What's got you down? Was it Peter and Grace seeing your hair a mess? Don't worry, you wear it like a style."

"I'm fine."

"You're not, so tell me." He nudges me with his elbow.

"I'm fine."

"*No*, you're not." He pauses, brows pinched. "And you're usually honest with me so—"

"Mind if I join you two?" Grace appears at my side.

Nibs blinks, clearly minding the interruption. "Actually, we're just—"

"Finished," I complete the sentence, disregarding his attempts at a heart-to-heart. "It's fine. What's up?"

"You and I *will* finish this later," he mumbles, then marches back to Morgan.

"So... how are you?" Grace asks.

"Goodness, everyone wants to know how I am. Why do I feel like that's not why you're here, though?"

She grasps my arm, and we stop. "I need to ask you something. And please be completely honest with me."

"Okay..." Her tone leaves me uneasy. "What's going on?"

"Is there anything between you and Peter?" She twists a strand of pale hair around her finger. "I know you were unaware that he and David were the same, so any encouragement was in ignorance. But what about now? Do you still approve? Because you're my best friend, and I would never want to hurt you."

I'm caught off guard by her question. What is between Peter and me? And do I approve of them? I glance at him, gazing over his shoulder at us, and a knot forms in my stomach. Grace waits, fingers drumming at her side, yet words fail me, and I'm not sure why. But I know what I ought to say.

"No. What could possibly be between us?" The words sound hollow. "I'm engaged to James. And yes, I was surprised to learn he was David, but I'm happy for you. Do you love him?"

"I don't know." She reddens. "But we're open to finding out."

"Then do so with my blessing." I hug her too tightly.

We walk on and soon the Diner comes into view, and I'm relieved to escape further conversation. Inside, my nose perks at the scent of brewing coffee and sizzling bacon. We come here often, so the boys are already shoving a few tables together before settling in and grabbing menus.

"Long time no see," Canary chirps behind me.

I spin to find her standing close, grinning from ear to ear.

"Hello again," I reply warmly.

"When are you coming by to see us? You left an impression on Chas, and that's not easy to do."

"Really?" I purse my lips. "He seems easy to please, as long as you're a woman. What makes me different?"

"Likely because you're off-limits." She chuckles wickedly.

"Well, I'm sure I'll be by once James returns."

"Why wait? Come by tomorrow night. It'd be nice to have another female around who's not Jill."

"Maybe I will."

I slip into a seat beside JaneAnn, and Canary heads off to take orders.

JaneAnn looks around, avoiding my gaze. She hasn't spoken to me since Christmas. At first, I found opportunities to smile, say a friendly word, but after enough rejections, I gave up. She meant it; we're no longer friends. Still, we're forced together now.

"Hey," I say, gazing at the menu.

She turns and studies me. "Hi."

"How are you?"

Great, now I'm the one asking that question.

"Is there something you needed?" Her expression is blank.

"I've thought about what you said." I drop the menu. "And I want you to know, I'm going to get you out of here. I swear it."

Her eyes narrow. "It's not your job to save us."

"But you were right." I lean in. "I was abandoning you, and I'm sorry. I stopped caring about anything except escaping this place. But that's changed, and I wanted you to know."

"Is that what you want?" She taps her fingers against the table. "To be our savior? Marry James, become his queen, and save all the poor little orphans? This is Nibs' idea, isn't it?"

"Yes, but I agree. He's right. Why must you and Peter act like it's an insult?"

"Because it *is*?" She runs a hand through her hair and huffs. "There's only one reason to marry someone. And I question if you even know what that is."

"What can I get for you ladies?" Canary cuts in cheerfully.

Using the opportunity to end the conversation, JaneAnn turns away and begins talking with Elizabeth. I exhale, fingers clenching. What does she want from me? Five years of friendship—gone. For what? Even when I try to show care, she won't take it.

Fine. She can have it her way.

We eat. Or rather, they eat. I pick at my food, glancing around, everyone appearing content but me. I can't even fake a smile. So, I don't. I swallow tasteless bites of burger until I shove it aside, half-eaten.

Maybe I should visit James' friends, spend time elsewhere. I just need to get through these final weeks and leave this place behind. Yet something nags at me... A fear of giving up James, because maybe JaneAnn is right. Maybe I'm not marrying for the right reason. I glance up at the spot I've avoided all meal. Peter's sitting with Grace, an arm draped casually around her, feeding her pieces of muffin. She giggles and he chuckles, dabbing her lips with a napkin.

It feel sick.

Eventually, they slip out the door, and then Nibs announces it's time to go. We say our goodbyes to Canary and slog outside, as Alexander and Jack finish some ridiculous story from their latest woodworking escapade with Slightly and Tootles.

"Looks like we're missing two, Grace and Peter aren't here." John looks around. "Let me go tell them we're leaving."

"I'll go," I offer. "They stepped out for air earlier. Be right back."

At the stairwell, I follow a pair of footprints curving around the side of the building. Just ahead, muffled laughter drifts through the air. But when I round the corner into a narrow alley, I stop short. Peter's body is pressed against Grace's, pinning her to the brick wall. His lips are on hers, and her fingers tangle in his golden hair.

I should leave. Walk away. But I don't. I just *stare*—wishing I could blink it away. *Go*, I will myself. But my foot catches on a bin, it teeters, and crashes over with a thunderous boom. I freeze as Peter's head jerks toward me and Grace angles to the side, running a hand across her mouth.

"Wendy?" she says.

I brace against the wall, my stomach twisting. "The group's leaving," is all I manage.

They stare at me, and I at them.

Then I turn and walk away, slow and steady, until I'm out of sight—then I run, as fast as my legs will carry me.

Chapter 16

"Another?" the young bartender asks, brow lifted.

"Yes, please," I say, my head heavy after two glasses of wine. The bartender makes a throaty sound and knocks against the bar. "Chas? A minute."

Chas glances up from his cards, looking between the two of us. "Uh, yeah? Just a second."

I sigh and fix my eyes on the young man, waiting. In the background, the radio hums softly with Gene Austin's velvety voice:

"Oh ain't she sweet
Well see her walking down that street
Well I ask you very confidentially
Ain't she sweet?"

I hum along, fingers dancing along the bar top to the piano, fast and soulful. Chas throws down a card and glides to my side. "What's up?" He presses his hands against the counter.

"He doesn't want to give me my drink," I say.

"Ma'am, it's only—you be Captain James' woman." He turns to Chas. "She's already had two, sir."

"Give it to her," Chas replies. "But maybe we call it a night after this."

He looks at me, and I hold up my hands. "Yeah, sure."

The bartender pushes another glass toward me, and I take it to the couch, collapsing without grace, the drink splattering lightly on my dress.

"What's going on?" Chas kneels beside me, his stare searching. "You've been here all week, and every night you drink a bit more and seem a lot less happy for it. What am I supposed to do with you?"

"I'm trying not to think, and this is the time of day I have the privilege to do so."

"But why? What's got you like this?"

I chuckle coolly. "Like you care what a woman thinks. No—" I poke his chest. "You care what a woman wears, or better yet... doesn't."

"You insult me." He sits and pulls out a cigarette. "Did you know James and I grew up together?"

"Yeah, he told me."

"Well, when everything went down five years ago, James hit a real low point. But I swore I'd be the kind of friend he'd always been to me. With him away, I consider it a duty to make sure you're looked after."

"You're a good friend, Chas."

"I may not always understand every choice he makes, but he's a brother for life so with that said, try not to hurt him, okay?"

"Me hurt him? He's the one who lied about Juke being his brother! Please."

I squeeze his leg and drift to the piano, drink in hand. It's Friday, and I've successfully avoided my life this week, skipped out on Madam Esme's, and dodged Grace at every turn—though unbeknownst to her, I spend every night in her home. But so has she. She and Peter. I saw them slip through the long hallway, talking, laughing, disappearing behind a closed door.

I hate myself for caring. Even Henley behaved better than me. But I've lied, said I was sick, wanted to be left alone. Canary's been kind enough to pick me up after her shift and bring me here, to Starkey Manor, where we've spent our nights doing all the things Reverend Andrew would advise against.

But I don't care. For once, I just *don't* care. And there's something in *not* caring that keeps me coming back, night after night, drinking until I care even less.

I press down on the keys, and the song finds me. As the chorus builds, I sing a little unhinged.

Though goodbye means the birth of a teardrop
Hello means the birth of a smile
And the smile will erase the tear blighting trace
When we meet in the after awhile
Smile the while you kiss me sad adieu
When the clouds roll by I'll come to you
Then the skies will seem more blue
Down in Lover's Lane, my dearie

I'm playing too hard, singing too loud, emotion too thick—because dammit, Peter's face is in my mind again. His mouth against hers. It stokes a fire through me, and I close my eyes, letting the final words pour out like wildfire.

Wedding bells will ring so merrily
Ev'ry tear will be a memory
So wait and pray each night for me
Till we meet again

I'm breathing hard. Terrified of the thoughts forming. I rub my fore-head. It's burning.

Chas rests a hand on my shoulder. "Let's get you home."

"I'm fine! I could use a few minutes alone."

I push away, grab my drink, and turn to go. Everyone watches me pass, but no one speaks. They know better. I exit the Back Room, the world spinning at the edges. I'm only a shadow as I click across the ballroom floor.

"That was quite the performance." His voice echoes across the empty room.

I stop, nostrils flaring.

"Grace said you haven't been to class all week. So I did a little thinking and, for some reason, landed on you and Chas back here at the ball. Turns out I know you pretty well."

"What do you want, Peter? A medal?" I stare at him, the chandelier's dim gleam casting shadows across his face.

"Something isn't right about you." He steps closer. "I think it has something to do with Grace and me."

"You're insufferable!"

"What the hell did I do wrong?" He throws his arms out.

"You know Henley's in love with her!"

"And you said he'd have to accept it. Or were those just words?"

"Fine." I cross my arms. "Then good luck."

I start to turn, but he catches my arm.

"What is wrong with you?" His jaw tenses. "As miserable as you can be, this isn't like you. Drinking every night?"

"You've been watching me?" My voice wavers.

"Someone had to. You do remember these are Juke's friends, right? And you remember what he was about to do before I stopped him."

The memory leaves me stiff.

His shoulders deflate, and he reaches toward my lace-covered arm. Hesitant, he taps it lightly before his hand settles there, eyes soft with concern. "What do you want from me?"

I want to scream. Tell him to never touch Grace again, never look at her, never think of her. But he seems happier with her than I've ever seen him. I'm the one who's insufferable. Because why shouldn't they be together? And why should I care? Especially when I wear a diamond ring from a man who loves me deeply?

"*Wendy?*" He edges closer, analyzing me.

"I just... need some air." A lump fills my throat, the emotion threatening to spill.

"I think you need to call it a night." He steadies me.

"I can manage." I take a shaky breath, an odd lightness washing over me as a cold sweat breaks out across my forehead.

"You're shaking. Let's sit."

"No!" I try to move, but my legs hold no feeling. I reach out, breath coming in short gasps, eyelids fluttering. "I'm fine," I murmur—just before stepping out, the world dissolving like silk, wrapping me tight, pulling me down where everything fades away.

I blink back the darkness, and when the world reappears, it's Grace's face I see, apprehensive.

"Can you hear me?" she asks as though from some faraway place.

I nod, neck stiff, a band of pain throbbing across my forehead.

"You fainted. Are you okay?"

Another nod. I turn my head. Peter sits across from me, hands folded beneath his chin. Behind him, Chas leans against the wall, watchful. I push myself up, and Grace guides me to a sitting position. I'm on her couch, in what appears to be a private sitting room.

"What happened?" I ask, my voice raspy.

She glances at Peter. "He said you were talking, started slurring your words, and fainted. I was reading in here when he and Chas brought you in."

"Oh. I'm sorry."

"It's okay. How are you feeling now?"

"Fine." I stagger to my feet, but my legs wobble and give way. Peter catches me before I hit the ground.

"You shouldn't go anywhere yet," he says, a faintness creeping over me as his hands wrap around my waist, his touch almost too much to bear.

"No, I want to go now—Chas." I look to him, and he straightens.

"No," Peter cuts in. "I'll bring you home."

"I *want* Chas to!"

He leans in, voice low. "Let me take you. I don't trust him with you alone like this."

"I'll be fine," I insist, heart hammering. "Chas, if you'd be so kind?"

"You know it, doll."

He crosses the room and after an uncomfortable pause, Peter releases me, allowing Chas to lift me into his arms.

"Don't worry." Chas grins widely. "I'll carry her right to bed. She won't have to lift a finger."

Peter's lips press into a hard line, and he glares at me, but I ignore him.

"Thank you for your help," I say. "I'll see you Monday, Grace."

"Of course..." She casts a cautious glance at Peter. "Let me walk you out."

I turn away from Peter, choosing the ceiling instead. Soon, I'm in Chas' car, and the hum of the engine roars, soothing my rattled nerves. When we arrive home, Nibs meets us at the door, having received a call from Grace. After a whispery exchange, Nibs says goodnight to Chas and closes the door.

The moment we're alone, he turns toward me, and without thought, I book it to my room, unwilling to explain anything. I want the night to end, along with everything that happened during it.

❄ ❄ ❄

When I wake, the sun's in my eyes; the blinds are thrown open, and the sweet scent of a muffin curls into my nose, twisting my stomach until I groan and roll over. A pair of legs comes into view—Nibs perched on a chair he's dragged close to the bed, watching me. On the bedside table, a tray of breakfast waits, and just the sight of it makes my stomach lurch all over again.

"Good morning," he says. "I wanted to ensure you didn't run away like you have for the last week. You and I are going to talk."

"Leave me alone..."

"No. And you're not leaving this room until I feel confident you haven't lost your mind."

I glare at him through low lids, massaging my temple.

"Yeah, three glasses of alcohol will do that." He crosses his arms. "Does it feel good? Cause I sure hope it hurts real bad."

"This has to be a crime, breaking into a woman's private apartment, holding her hostage."

"And you're welcome to fetch a bobby once we're done here." He chuckles.

I reach for the iced water. "What do you want?"

"Why, Wendy?" He hands me the glass and leans forward. "Faking sick all week, sneaking out at night. And last night? Chas said you downed multiple glasses of wine and were acting erratically before collapsing. You know I just want to make sure you're okay."

"Yeah sure." I lift the cool glass and drain it in one long gulp. "Thing is, I haven't wanted to talk. I don't need questions or expectations."

"Does Peter's return have anything to do with this?"

"Does it?" My frown deepens. "Maybe. I've chosen not to think about it."

"But why?" He splits the muffin, handing me half.

"James is my choice." I stare at the muffin. "He'll free us all. Peter, he doesn't see things the way you and I do."

"Then keep your distance, focus on your goals. I don't understand why this has you messed up?"

I push the muffin back into his hand. "Me neither. He's just tugging at something in me that's destined to ruin everything."

"Then don't let him. I love the kid, but you're right—he'll keep all of us trapped here. You love James, you're marrying him. Don't let Peter distract you."

I nod slowly. "How did you know you loved Morgan?"

"Oh gee, a hundred ways. What do you want to know specifically?"

"I don't know. Just tell me how you knew?"

"Okay. Well, her very presence had me confused and sure all at once. She understood me like no one else. And with her, I didn't have to protect myself, or hide anything. It was her presence. It pulled at me. And I wanted to be better because of it. Not because she asked, but because I would do anything for her."

"Oh," I murmur, overwhelmed by the depth of it all.

"What about you? Does James make you better?"

"He does." I think of the promise I made to be worthy of him. Yet was that because of my love, or his? "Anyway, you've given me lots to think about. For now, at least, I think the self-destruction is over."

"Good." He pats my shoulder and stands. "It better be. And, as I said, just focus; don't let Peter get to you anymore. Soon you'll leave here and he'll be but a memory."

Lifting the tray, he walks out, leaving me staring at the wall. He's right, soon Peter will be nothing more than a memory. Yet there's nothing liberating in the thought. It only leaves me feeling strangely hollow.

❋ ❋ ❋

As the weekend ends and Monday looms, my spirit maintains a quiet apprehension about the future. Yet for a moment, in Van Lori's classroom, I find solace.

My fingers press against the cool ivory keys, a symphony of emotions flooding through me with each note—the secrets, the losses, and the unknowns. The sound rises from deep within the wooden frame, escaping as a melody infinitely greater than my words could express. Eyes closed, the music becomes my voice, reflecting the chaos within.

As my fingers lift after the final chords, I glance at Theo Van Lori, surveying me, hands clasped to his chest.

"Only he who knows longing, knows what I suffer," he recites softly. *"Alone and cut off from all joy, I look into the firmament, in that direction. Ah. He who loves and knows me, is far away. I am reeling, my innards are burning. Only he who knows longing, knows what I suffer."*

His lips press tight, a knowing look on his face. "That is: *None but the Lonely Heart,* by Johann Wolfgang von Goethe, and your performance rightly brought his poem to mind."

"He speaks from the heart." I close the piano lid and spin to face him. "So, how did I do? Not too rusty after a week away?"

"Not at all." He rubs his chin thoughtfully. "Your classmates have been taught since childhood, and some play well. But greatness comes from the depths of your soul. In my experience, it's born from emotions so boundless our bodies can't contain them."

"You sound like you speak from experience."

"I do." He meanders to the window, leaning against the ledge, scanning the outdoors. "Was it not Tennyson who said, *'It is better to have loved and lost than never to have loved at all.'* Though at times I question his logic."

"What happened?"

"My dream was to play on the world's stage; hers wasn't so grand. We could never quite align our desires. Now, I've achieved my goal, even dined at the king's table, and taught his children piano. Yet, staring at her photo, I can't help but wonder what if? Such a question can turn a man mad, so in those moments, I bury it and play."

"I, too, have multiple desires." I pull my sweater tighter. "Like you, they don't seem to align."

"It's an unfair part of life, and there's no perfect answer. The key is to determine what matters most and why. You must always know why. Then you choose. Maybe you're wrong, or maybe you're right. Either way, you'll rest easier knowing the reason you chose what you did."

"Thank you, Mr. Van Lori." I lift up, tossing my bag over my shoulder. "Ms. Diana says, our job is to prepare for the future, not worry about the past. I suppose it goes along with your wisdom."

"Yes, that is sage counsel. Well, off you go, wouldn't want you to be late for Ms. Diana."

"See you." I wave.

"Oh, and Wendy."

"Yeah?" I glance back at him.

"Glad you're feeling better."

My lip twitches at the corner. "Me too."

I exit the classroom and stroll through the hallway; distant echoes of my song linger alongside the poem.

Ah. He who loves and knows me, is far away. I am reeling, my innards are burning. Only he who knows longing knows what I suffer.

Rounding the corner, I enter the dance studio, where Peter reclines against the wall, book to his nose. *Only he who knows longing knows what I suffer.* I set my bag aside and lean against the doorframe.

"What are you reading?" I ask.

He glances up, warmth in his gaze. "*Sentimental Tommy.*"

"Read a line to me." I sit beside him, letting my arm brush against his.

"Okay… '*Tommy was beginning to discover that it is not what we do, but what we are, that makes us great.*'"

"Well, do any of us know who we are? Guess that means it's hopeless for us, huh?"

"How do you manage being so optimistic all the time?"

"I tell you, it's hard being me." I sigh melodramatically.

"So then." He closes the book and fixes me with a look. "Are you okay?"

"Probably not, but that's not new. In truth, I'm no good left to myself. As you witnessed, I do stupid things, so I figured it's better to keep busy than sit alone with my thoughts."

Footsteps echo from the hallway and Ms. Diana enters the studio. "I'm so sorry, I'm late."

"It's no trouble."

"Grace and Henley were quite beside themselves without you here." She takes a deep breath. "Peter, Grace is waiting for you in the foyer."

"Certainly. Never keep a lady waiting." He shoves the book into his bag. "See you around, Bird."

"See you."

As he approaches the doorway, Henley appears around the corner, and for a brief moment, they face each other.

"Hello," Peter says, with a nod.

"Hello," Henley replies stiffly, then pushes past, plopping into the corner chair as Peter disappears into the hallway.

"Hey." I wander over to him. "Long time no see."

"Yeah? You all better?" He glowers at me. "You've got some nerve abandoning me all last week."

"Forgive me?"

"What choice do I have?" He tugs me into a hug. "You're the only girl who'll put up with me."

"I'm sorry. I promise it won't happen again."

"Alright." Ms. Diana says, turning on a record. "Henley, take a break. She and I are going to work on posture today. Now come, come, Wendy." She claps.

I get in line beside her and face the mirror while she demonstrates the movements. Over the duration of my time in her class, she's expected precision in my technique, often leaving me exhausted and my muscles aching from the repetition.

"Lengthen your neck—keep your shoulders relaxed," she directs, and I follow her guidance. "Eyes up, we're dancing, not napping. Good, press through the toes, not the knees. Perfect."

I am her marionette, moving in accordance with every pull of the string. Each correction she speaks lifts, tucks, and tightens some part of me until she falls silent, nodding with each movement, and when the song ends, we begin again. To what end do I learn these things? I don't know anymore.

All around, I'm tired. Weary of weakness having its hold on me. Tired of needing my circumstances to change before I can smile.

I gaze at my reflection in the mirror... Pearl earrings. A white ribbon holding my hair in a neat bun. Pale face. Red cheeks. Long lashes meant to allure. Outwardly, I'm exactly what Madam Esme would call "right." Yet inside, I'm a jumbled mess. But I'm going to fix that. I'll gather the pieces, put them in order, and figure myself out. James returns in twelve days. And I have faith that when he does—everything will make sense again.

At least, this is what I'm going to tell myself to keep from falling apart again.

Chapter 17

Nestled on a plush, sunlit couch, I gaze lazily at the greenery above my head, humming to melodies that resonate from the record player beside me. It's Saturday afternoon, and Grace invited our group to her greenhouse for a leisurely lunch filled with lounging, finger foods, and staff flitting about, ensuring we're always at peak comfort.

Over the past couple of weeks, our little circle has found its way back to one another. I'd taken their companionship for granted, but no longer. After a humble apology to Kit and Tiger Lily for ignoring them the week prior, we agreed to a meetup at Grace's home.

The first night was uncomfortable due to Henley's feelings for Peter, which he made no effort to hide. But by the second night, forced by Kit, the two sat by the fire in Grace's sitting room, engaged in quiet conversation for hours. Whatever was said worked, and gradually, Henley's intensity lifted until their laughter filled the space.

I didn't ask what was said. I was simply grateful for Henley to smile again. From there, we found a rhythm. Setting aside all talk of relationships, we spent time as friends, and it's been more healing than I could have imagined. There have been quiet nights by the fire, playing cards.

Dinners at Will's Bakehouse, our old haunt. Skating on the creek near Grace's house and even the occasional evening at the Home, enjoying the charming chaos lingering there.

Thankfully, Peter and I also found a moment to lay aside the discomfort between us. One afternoon while skating, we managed a minute alone, and I posed the question simmering since the night I fainted.

"What exactly did you see when you found me in the Back Room those nights?"

He bit back a smile. "Do you really want to know?"

"Yes." My face was already burning from the memories.

"Well... I was lucky enough to catch your exotic dance."

"Stop." I covered my eyes, groaning. "Canary dared me."

"Was definitely tempted to fulfill my promise of carrying you out, but figured I'd let you be. And it wasn't altogether bad. I quite enjoyed it."

I slapped his arm. "Hush."

He laughed and rubbed his chin. "Okay, what else? Oh yeah—your confrontation with Noodler, that was something. Lots of colorful language. Bea would have given you quite the talking to if she'd heard."

"He deserved it. Tried cheating at poker."

"And you were not having it. Other than that, you were cozied up a bit too close to Chas one evening. And then, of course, your song. But that's about all. Are you satisfied?"

"Not at all, I'm horrified. Please don't tell Grace about my behavior."

"It's our secret. She still thinks you're an innocent little angel."

"But not you." I slipped in front of him, skating backward. "Not anymore."

"My opinion of you is caught somewhere between saint who can do no wrong and feisty little minx who's a menace to all men."

"Indeed? And which do you imagine is closer to the truth?"

He analyzed me as we glided along, and for a moment under his gaze, I felt as if I were floating.

"A menace to all men," he said, giving the end of my braid a playful tug before speeding ahead.

"All men?" I called after him, pushing faster to keep up.

He tipped his head back toward me, amusement curling through his voice. "Every single one."

Now, a week later, despite my usual confusion, something in these final moments has left me at peace. I know I'll be okay.

Sitting together in the greenhouse, Tiger Lily rests into Kit, the two of them giggling over some shared secret. Grace is tucked up rather cozily beside Henley, telling him a story from class this week. He's terribly taken with her, and I wonder if she even notices. That leaves Peter and me. He's propped against the loveseat I'm sprawled across, our faces side by side as we play a conversation game.

"Am I a person?" I ask.

"A type."

"A type... a woman?"

"Male and female."

"Both? Golly... okay, where do I live?"

"In many homes, most often in the parlor."

I pause a moment, then exclaim, "A radio!"

"Indeed." He chuckles. "You're too quick. I'll have to try a harder one next time."

I smile, and he returns it, something soft budding inside me.

"So..." He folds his hands beneath his chin. "Tomorrow's the big day, isn't it?"

"Yeah—can't quite believe it. He wrote to me last week, overjoyed. He couldn't wait to be back."

"And what about you?" He inclines toward me. "Are *you* overjoyed?"

Before I can answer, Grace claps her hands. "Time for some ice-skating! It's far too nice a day to be cooped up in here."

A young man and woman carry in our gear, and relieved to escape the question, I grab my skates, strap them on, and head outside, where the sunshine kisses our cheeks as we step onto the frozen creek and glide away from shore. Tiger Lily, still getting the hang of it, remains close to Kit, her fingers holding tightly to him. I've started to wonder if she's better at this than she lets on and just uses it as an excuse to stay wrapped around him.

Pressing ahead, Grace, Peter, Henley, and I move on, picking up speed, the wind lifting our hair—a thrilling sense of escape.

"So, James should return any day, right?" Grace twirls nearby.

"He is." I wish people would stop asking this question. "I was telling Peter, he sent a letter last week, and if all goes well, he'll be here tomorrow."

"And are you over the moon to see him?" she asks.

"Of course. Though I fear it's been so long I've nearly forgotten what he looks like."

"We can help you with that," Henley offers. "Thick, wavy black hair, blue eyes, nice beard."

"Usually wears a neat captain's uniform," Peter adds.

"Speaking of which, where does a fella get one of those?" Henley spreads his arms, examining his navy-blue coat.

"First, you'll need the boat," Peter says. "Now, come on Williams. Let's see how you are on the ice."

"I don't think you want to do this." Henley grins, rubbing his hands together. "Crying in front of the ladies isn't a good look."

"Oh, my boy." Peter stretches, cracking his knuckles. "You'll have to tell me how it feels after I beat you."

"Ms. Starkey, if you'd be so kind." Henley touches the ice beside Peter.

"Certainly." Grace giggles. "Three, two, one—go!"

They speed away, wind whipping through their hair, shoving each other as they disappear down the creek.

"Come on." I loop my arm through Grace's, and we glide forward. "So.... how are you? You and Peter doing well?"

"Maybe."

"Maybe? What do you mean?"

Kit and Tiger Lily swoosh past us, her arms outstretched. "This doesn't seem safe," she yells.

"You're doing great," I call back.

"Wendy." Grace stops, serious. "I need to talk to you. When Peter and I began... whatever it was, it wasn't pure for me."

"What does that even mean—*pure?*"

"You asked if I loved him, and I said I was willing to find out. But when you caught us kissing, it wasn't love. It was curiosity. I was attracted to him, but... I built him into something he wasn't. It didn't take long to realize we weren't a good fit. And then, I found I was already drawn to another."

I don't say it, but I'm not sure if I can bear it if she says any name other than Henley's. "Dare I ask who?"

She keeps her gaze forward. "I've started doodling Grace Williams on all my papers. I'm going to tell him today."

"Oh! Grace." I throw my arms around her, overwhelmed with relief and happiness. "I'm so pleased for you both! It's not easy to see someone hopelessly in love, yet not get the desire of their heart."

"Speaking of which..." She places a hand on her hip. "You lied to me, Wendy, and don't deny it. You said there was nothing between you and him, yet when you caught us kissing, it wasn't shock on your face, it was heartbreak."

I stare at her, body tensing. "Don't go there, Grace. I'm engaged."

"And? You're going to tell me you're madly in love with James? You can't even plan your wedding with any genuine excitement. Yet every time you're near Peter, you melt. And I feel pretty confident you just about hated me when you caught us together."

She's chipping away at the thoughts I've kept safely locked away, and it angers me. I'm painfully aware of how Peter makes me feel. It goes beyond anything I've ever felt with James—and that only unsettles me more.

"Hey." She takes my arm. "Tell me, what's on your mind? Don't stuff it away or hide it. Just let it out. No more pretending."

"You don't understand." The words spill out. "He ruins everything. I'll never leave this town, nor will any of my friends. Everything is figured out, the plans in motion, and if I even consider him, it's all gone, burned up in some uncontrollable blaze. The problem is..."

The words catch in my throat, the confession long overdue.

"I think I actually want him to ruin everything."

Grace's shoulders deflate. "Oh, Wendy..."

Tiger Lily's shriek echoes in the distance as she tumbles backward, dragging Kit with her. There's a crashing thud as they hit the ice, and she bursts into laughter, shoving him off.

"It's okay." He stands, chuckling. "We're okay."

I nod to them, and we start again.

"Let's take a break," Grace says, her voice pacifying.

But as we continue skating, something grabs my attention—a spider-web of cracks fanning out beneath the ice, stretching from where they fell, crawling straight for us. I'm quick and throw out an arm, stopping Grace as a sound like snapping twigs echoes underfoot.

"Don't move," I whisper, the hairs on my neck rising.

"What do we do?" She squints at the ground.

I sense what's coming seconds before the thunderous crack and yell, "Run!"

I lunge forward as the ring around Grace shatters, and she plunges into the icy water below.

"Grace!" I cry out, as her body resurfaces for a breathless moment. Her screams split the air—then silence, as the current tears her under.

"No!" I drop to my knees, helpless.

Kit and Tiger Lily race our way, eyes wide with terror. And far off, Henley's roar echoes across the ice as he and Peter hurtle toward us. But they're too far. I'm not brave by any means, but there's no time, and Grace's only hope is me. Facing Peter and Henley, I meet their eyes for a split second before rising on shaking legs, sucking in a final life-giving breath—and diving through the jagged hole into the blackness below.

The water slams against me like a sledgehammer, and my chest seizes. I've felt cold my entire life, but this is unfathomable—beyond comprehension. I momentarily forget why I'm here as a profound pain envelops me, like a thousand needles piercing my skin.

The current tugs at me, and I'm doing all I can to stay in place. Then something grabs my leg, a hand. *Grace.*

Shadows gather above us, and someone dives in, entering our world. This is my chance, the reason I'm here. I grip Grace's arm, tugging her forward, shoving her into the shadowy arms awaiting her. She's caught and disappears above. I would cheer if I could, but now it's my turn.

Mustering the last of my strength, I push forward just as Henley appears, his thick hair floating around his ashen face. He's calm as we take in the other. For a moment, I imagine I'm Margaret and we're about to turn back time. She's going to live. He's going to rescue me. Our fingers shimmer as we extend them, yet the ferocious current batters my numb body, and when his hands have nearly grasped mine, my muscles yield. I'm torn away, my face masked by the bubbles rushing out of my mouth.

The water around his body explodes as he lunges forward, but it's too late. We're yanked apart, my body set adrift. The light of salvation fades into the distance. My lungs are bursting, and try as I might to fight, my limbs are useless, the feeling in them fading fast. This is it. There's no escape or rescue. I knew the risk, yet I couldn't help myself. Of course, I couldn't. The world fades behind closed lids, and I picture Grace and Henley, wrapped in one another's arms—the consolation prize for my damning sacrifice.

The pain dulls, my mind clouding, and I drift along, the water becoming oddly comforting, even while sucking away my existence. Fear of death is distant, as I embrace it like an old friend. I can already sense the warmth of the world beyond, wrapping around me, pulling me deeper. Somehow, I'm content. No more choices, no more ruining my life or anyone else's.

Fate has decided for me.

Yet as I await the end, my mind fractures and I see him: Peter, young and wild, his green eyes sharp and curious. He's by my bed. Is this a dream? A memory?

"What's your name?" he asks.

Beside him, floats a Faery. She's lovely, with blonde hair, a green dress, and piercing blue eyes. She examines me with a scowl.

"Wendy Moira Angela Darling," I answer, my voice small, childlike. "What's your name?"

Light flickers, and I'm back in the creek, squinting at the shadowy sheet of ice above.

"Peter Pan," he says, "and this is Tinker Bell."

Glass shatters in the distance, but *I'm back in bed, propped on my knees. "Where do you come from?"*

Shouts echo from a faraway place, *and he points to the window. "Second to the right, and straight on till morning."*

The darkness collapses around us, Peter fading as he whispers, "Come with me!"

"To where?"

"Neverland..."

The word echoes, then bursts to life around me. A vibrant emerald lagoon glistens, and mermaids perch on rocks, combing their colorful hair. Pink flamingos soar gracefully across a twilight sky. Then gradually, Peter's painting comes to life, taking shape with its intertwined branches resonating with the joyous laughter of children. It's a Neverland I've never seen before, and it's glorious!

The cocoon around me dissolves into light, along with the warmth and safety it provides. The world slams back into view, and I lurch forward as hands grab hold of me, their touch like fire to my flesh. I can't cry. I'm sucking in air, desperate to breathe again—but it's incomplete, agonizing, and I feel as though I'm being cut apart. Peter's above me, dripping wet, eyes blazing. I try to speak, yet there's no sound. My lips cannot move. The noise around me is piercing.

I've lost all control, as my body spasms violently. I cough, water clawing up my throat like razor blades, and a weak sound escapes. He gathers me into his arms, his touch scorching as darkness engulfs my vision, and all goes silent.

"Where the hell is everyone?" His voice echoes far away.

"They've gone to Grace!" someone shouts.

I'm laid down, and I twist, clawing at the frozen garments clinging to me. It hurts so much I could scream—but there's no air.

"What are you doing? Are you mad?" someone gasps.

"Hang on, Bird." The world spins as Peter tears at my clothes. "Stop staring, dammit, and help," he barks.

Multiple hands fumble at my clothes, but they stick like plaster on a wound.

"Are you sure about this?"

"Strip down to your shorts," Peter orders.

"What?" It's Kit... "Why?"

"She can't reheat alone. Come on! This isn't the time for modesty."

"Peter—I-I. You do it!"

There's silence before Peter mutters, "Fine. Then get out!"

I grip the air, shoulders quaking as my vision flickers. Peter's beside me, lifting a blanket over us, pulling me against his chest. Heat penetrates through me, his skin baking against my own, and it isn't comforting; it's agony. The camiknicker clinging to my frame melts like ice before a flame. His arms tighten.

"Breathe with me," he directs, inhaling and exhaling. His chest guides my own with every rise and fall. A shudder shoots through my legs, and I cling to him, fingers clawing at his back. Every bit of ice in my veins melts while his body stokes the fire within me.

It's torture.

Minutes turn to hours, and waves crash over me. Occasionally, the world goes silent until the tremors return, and coughing turns to gagging. Through it all, he remains constant—the anchor guiding me back to life.

The trembling gradually subsides, first in my legs, then in my arms, until my jaw relaxes and I can breathe again. My fingers grip his neck, the pulse soothing, then sleep finds me. It isn't sweet, it's heavy and thick, wrapping around me, pulling me under. And though there's no peace in it, it's safe and healing.

✳ ✳ ✳

I wake to a light shining on my face.

"Good, good," someone says, then clicks it off.

It's Doctor Smith, scribbling notes on a pad. Everything is hazy, but beneath me, there's a wealth of warmth, and I know it's Peter.

"How long was she under?" the doctor asks in a low voice.

"I can't be sure, it all happened so fast," Peter replies, his words blending with the rhythm of his heartbeat. "Could have been a few minutes."

"That's significant." Doc Smith pulls the blanket off my back and presses something cold against the skin. "This might feel a bit chilly, darling. I'm checking for fluid in the lungs. Breathing is shallow, but thankfully, it's clear. Has she coughed much? Vomited?"

"Yeah. Early on. Just a bit of water."

"That's good, especially after being submerged for so long. I'll be honest—she's downright lucky to be alive. A little more water in the lungs and... well, she wouldn't be here. Okay, quick listen from the front."

The stethoscope slips under my arm and presses against my chest.

"Perfect, I don't want to separate you both." His face hovers above, brows furrowed in concentration. "Good."

He pulls the blanket back over us and takes my hand, pressing on my nails. "Ms. Wendy, can you flex your fingers for me?"

With slow determination, I curl them forward.

"Well, we won't be winning any wrist-wrestling matches just yet, but we'll get there." He smiles, satisfied. "Before I go, let me applaud your efforts, son. I couldn't have done it better myself. You saved her, no doubt."

Peter holds me closer. "Is there anything more I should do?"

"No, time is the real healer. So, give her that. Regression is always possible in such delicate situations. I'll come by in the morning. But if anything changes, don't hesitate to call. Coughing fits, fever, anything at all."

"Thanks, Doc."

The door clicks shut, and a gentle silence envelops us, broken only by the crackling of the fire and the pounding of our hearts. I fold into the darkness, drifting into a deep, rejuvenating sleep, pure and peaceful, until images flash through my mind: my fists pounding against the ice, crying to be freed.

I awaken with a gasp.

"Bad dream?" Peter asks, placing a book aside.

"Yes."

My tears pool against his skin, and he gently guides a finger along my cheek, wiping them away. I grip his hand like a lifeline as images of the accident flash. "What happened?"

"Henley and I were on our way back when we heard screaming. We saw Grace in the water, and then in a flash, you were on your feet, diving in. It was horrific. I meant to dive in after you, but Henley physically stopped me, insistent he would go."

He's silent for a long moment. "I let him and I shouldn't have. But I didn't want to steal another moment from him. I'm sorry. I knew I was far more capable, but I thought he needed this. A chance to heal after Margaret."

"I had a similar thought when he dove in."

"For a second, I thought it would be simple. Grace surfaced almost immediately, and then we waited for you to follow. But that didn't happen. Instead, Henley tore against our grasp, and we nearly lost him. That's when I knew you were gone."

"He was close."

"I would have broken free."

"And then you would have died with me." I trace the veins of his arm, gliding my fingers into the hollow of his elbow and over the rise of his muscle, firm beneath my touch. He watches me, and it's like I've lost my breath again. He's not all strength. No—he's just enough, enough to break through ice and rip me from my grave and bring me back to life.

"Call me an idiot, but I'd rather die by your side than visit your grave alone."

His statement startles me, and for a moment, a new pain appears as I ache to close the space between us. I think we share the same thought as he cups my chin, and I press closer.

But as though something passes over him, he hesitates. "I should get you something to eat."

"But I'm not hungry."

"I know. You won't be for a while. But it'll help your recovery."

He inches to the edge of the bed, but I cling to him. "Where are you going?"

"To get your food. I'll be right back, I promise."

Though I don't want to, I let him go. And the moment his body leaves mine, I'm flooded with a sense of loss like he's taken my lungs with him.

He pulls on a shirt and stares down. "You going to be okay?"

"I'll manage."

I hold the blankets to my face as he steps out. Minutes pass, and the wind slams against the window. I cover my ears, muscles tense, images flashing across my vision.

"Hey." Peter's voice breaks through, and he gently shakes me. I blink, sweat lining my forehead. "You're holding your breath. Stop!"

I gasp, senses returning, and he kneels beside the bed, frowning.

"I'm barely aware I'm doing it," I say.

"Well, your body's bound to fall in line soon enough, stubborn as you are."

He exhales and rests his head beside mine, his presence a salve.

But then—behind him, the door slams open, and we jolt upright, the stillness shattered as a figure rushes past, stopping short at the sight of us.

It's James.

Chapter 18

James gazes between Peter and me, a torrent of emotion swirling in my chest because he doesn't belong here. He's invading an intimate moment, made worse by the accusation in his glare. But then a glance at the ring on my finger, and reality crashes in.

"They said you nearly drowned." His voice is strained.

I nod.

"I should go." Peter rises. "Try to get some of this in her. It'll help."

"Peter, I was told she'd be dead if it weren't for you. So, once again, I owe you my thanks for rescuing her." He extends a hand.

Peter hesitates, then shakes it.

He turns to me, no words, only a long, unreadable stare, before walking through the door and closing it—not loud, nor dramatic, yet it shakes something loose in me all the same.

James doesn't rush over. And I know, he senses the space between us, far greater than the distance between our bodies.

"What can I do?" he asks.

"Pass me that robe, please." I gesture to the chair where the staff left a silky, sky-blue robe for me.

"Of course." He lifts it and holds it out. "May I?"

"Yes."

A chill passes over me as he wraps it around and then ties it, an attempt at intimacy. Settling beside me, he stares, his expression as unreadable as Peter's. Is it grief? Regret? Heartbreak?

"I'm sorry I wasn't here!" There's a quiver in his chin. "It's like anytime you need me, I'm nowhere to be found."

"Don't be sorry. I told you to go."

He tugs me into his arms, and though he's safe, it's not his safety I desire anymore. I ease away, and he lifts the tray Peter brought.

"Will you eat something?"

"I'll try. But I'm sorry this isn't the homecoming you expected."

"Nonsense. You're the homecoming I expected, and here you are."

"I'm likely a wreck." I comb my fingers through my hair. "Drowning probably doesn't suit my complexion."

His face softens, and he cups my chin. "You're always beautiful to me. I love you."

He kisses me, but I feel nothing. I feel nothing... The understanding slices through me, cold as the ice that bound me.

"Maybe tell me about your trip." I lean against the pillow, body taut, as the realization strikes—without meaning to, I let Peter tug at that hidden thing inside me, the thing destined to ruin everything, until it surfaced.

"You don't need that right now." He offers me a piece of warm, buttery bread.

"Go ahead." I take the slice; it's a sweet, hearty aroma that's achingly familiar after everything. "I'll listen while you talk."

"This isn't what I want, but okay." He begins, recounting his journey as I alternate between sips of tea and bites of bread. And though I've always been drawn to his faraway worlds, what's awakened around me here in this place feels far more alluring, something I never imagined possible.

"You okay?" He asks, brushing a finger across my cheek.

"Yes. Just tired. Mind if I rest?"

"Of course." He hesitates. Perhaps hoping for an invitation to stay. When it doesn't come, he lifts the tray. "I'll check on you later."

"It's good to see you, James."

A muscle twitches in his jaw as he pauses in the doorway. I sound like a guest visiting for tea, not his beloved. The look on his face before he closes the door brings tears to my eyes. What have I done? Why did I ever let him leave? But would it have made any difference had he stayed?

I lie back and reach for Peter's wool sweater, forgotten on the side table. Clutching it to my chest, I know, truly, there was nothing James could've done to change any of this. A heaviness pulls me under as I drift, but the dreams aren't sweet; they're dark, cold, and isolating. It's a world I long to flee from, yet the waking world... it holds no better escape.

Someone knocks at the door, and I wake, frazzled. "Come in."

"Good afternoon," Doctor Smith says, entering with Ms. Diana. "Mind if I come in for a quick check-up?"

"Sure." I knead two fingers into my stiff neck.

"Hello, Wendy," Ms. Diana says as she sits beside me, her gaze soft with affection. "How are you feeling?"

"As you'd imagine. Thank you for letting me stay and recover."

"You stay as long as you need. My brother had to leave for work, but he sends his regards and insists you get extra attention."

"He's very kind. Thank you."

The doctor approaches, lifting his stethoscope. "Are we ready?"

Ms. Diana gives my back a gentle rub and stands. "I'll let him work. See you soon, dear."

She slips into the hall as he begins a familiar examination. When he's finishing, there's another knock at the door.

"Come on in," I call.

Henley steps in, hair disheveled and clothes wrinkled. "I'm sorry to interrupt. I'll come back later."

"Nope, just finishing up." Doc Smith waves him over. "She needs some company, so you come here, and we'll swap."

Henley shuffles to the bed and flops down, dark circles under his eyes. "How is she, Doc?"

"Well, son, she's coming along. Give it a week, and I imagine all three of you will be right as rain."

"I'm relieved to hear it." He takes my hand in his.

Doc Smith lifts his black bag and heads for the door. "I'll be back tomorrow, and I expect more food, more liquids, and plenty of rest. Doctor's orders."

"I'll try," I reply. "But restful sleep is hard to come by."

"It'll be that way for a bit. I'll leave a sleep tonic with the staff, might help."

"That would be wonderful. Thank you."

He slips out, and I turn to Henley. "You look as exhausted as I feel."

"I am," he admits. "But I had to see you. Can I convince you to join us in the lounge? Everyone wants to see you."

"I'm not much for visiting. Look at me."

"Fine." He walks to the dresser and picks up a hairbrush. "I shall make you respectable." He steps behind me and runs the bristles through my thick hair. "Now you have no excuse."

"I still go under protest."

"Protest noted." He takes my arm and guides me up, my legs unsteady. It's slow going, but we enter the hall, and sounds of conversation echo out of the sitting room.

"Before we join them," he says, "You must know how broken I am over what happened. It was my fault. Peter was about to jump in when I shoved him, and went instead. I'm ashamed of myself."

"I didn't die." I press his hand to my heart. "It's beating. We did our best, and sometimes that's all we've got. He and I both understood why you wanted to be the one."

"But you're not Margaret, are you?" He smiles, though it's layered with emotion.

"No, I'm not. But I can't deny Margaret was on my mind too. Is Grace okay?"

"Yes. Tiger Lily and I got her back to the house and..." He lets out a breathy laugh. "She said she loves me. I was so shocked, I kissed her outright. Probably the least romantic moment in all of history, but who cares."

"She told me before the accident." I hug him. "I'm so happy for you. Truly."

He holds me close, then kisses my forehead and guides me into the sitting room. The chatter stops, silence settling as everyone turns toward us. A fire blazes at the center, flanked by two couches, with Tiger Lily and Kit on one, and Grace and James on the other.

"Wendy!" Grace runs to me, wrapping me in her arms. "You're my angel."

Relief floods through me to see her safe. We're all safe. She pulls back, a look of understanding passing between us after everything.

"Come and sit." She leads me to the couch where James waits.

"Hello again." I ease down beside him.

"Did you rest well?" he asks.

"As well as can be expected."

Henley sinks into a plush chair, Grace reclining on his lap. A reminder or what a couple in love looks like.

"Peter! Won't you come join us?" Grace says.

I glance over and find him tucked into a corner chair by the bay window, a book in hand.

"Thank you, but I'm comfortable," he says.

"Sure, you are." She shoots me a pointed look.

"It's a relief to see you up again," Tiger Lily says. "We've all been so worried."

My ears warm at her concern. "You're sweet. Doc Smith said I'm on the mend, so all is well."

"I hope so," she says, though I can sense the tension in her, and in everyone else. They look at me with a quiet unease. Maybe because I'm like a dead woman walking. From what I overheard Peter tell Doctor Smith, I should have died. They thought I did. I thought I did. And yet... here I am.

"So," James says, "they've been telling me all about the fun you've had while I was away. I can't deny, I'm a bit jealous. The theater, nights at the Gilmour, a ball."

"Yes. Quite the time."

Yet those days seem distant now.

"He didn't believe me about Chas Turley," Grace pipes up. "Said there was no way you two were spending time together. I said you certainly were. You even sang the boys a song, and had them all googly-eyed."

"I can't imagine." James grins. "Tell me, darling, how did that happen?"

"We met at the ball. He asked if I'd like to dance. And after that, we spent many nights together in the Back Room. I met all your friends, in fact."

The memory of Chas mentioning Juke and James' relationship hits, forming a knot in my chest.

"Oh, well, I hope they were on their best behavior. They're a rowdy bunch at their best."

"They behaved as expected. Chas told me about Bill."

His face drops. "Bill?"

"Yes, Bill. Mr. Starkey seemed to think I'd know where he was, seeing how we're soon to be family."

The room grows quiet.

James clears his throat. "Maybe we can talk in private."

"You know." Grace slaps her knees and pulls Henley up with her. "I could use a bite to eat. How about we all migrate to the kitchen and see what Cook's got for us?"

Kit and Tiger Lily agree and follow her, but Henley lingers.

"I'm okay," I say. "See you soon."

"Alright. Holler if you need me." He narrows his eyes at James and disappears into the hall.

James turns to speak—but catches sight of Peter. "I think they're serving up something to eat. Perhaps you're hungry."

Peter glances over but shakes his head.

"We could use a moment alone," James says, jaw tight. "If you'd be so kind." He gestures toward the hallway.

"No!" I hold up a hand. "Peter was with me when Chas explained how Juke's your brother. And since he beat Peter, at your bidding, I'd say he deserves to hear anything you've got to say."

"Fine. If that's how you need it." He exhales. "He's Thomas' son, my step-brother. But it's no secret we're not close. He was getting into trouble in the Capital, so Father asked me to take him in. He hoped Winter Woods would have a calming effect."

"So basically, a place to get him out of their hair?"

"Yeah. I figured he was strong, capable, and useful in protecting the home. I was wrong—about all of it, and I'll never forgive myself for that." He regards Peter. "I'm sorry. I was wrong to ever assume you didn't have her best interest at heart."

Peter looks between us and nods slowly, then lifts the book and leans back.

"So, when was I to find out he and I were to become family?" I ask

"Is there ever a good time to tell your fiancée that the man who attacked her is your brother? I guess I naively hoped we'd avoid it altogether."

"Come now, James." My voice sharpens. "Don't be daft. You can't always escape a reality you don't like. I've made peace with the mess I am. You should do the same with yours. Juke is your brother. I deserve to know. Not find out through Chas."

"If I could go back and do it differently, I would, but I can't. All I can ask is that you forgive me."

"I can forgive you. But I can't help but wonder, what else you're not telling me?"

"Nothing." His eyes widen. "I swear it."

"Okay... I want to trust your word." I inhale deeply and release, knowing nothing will be okay. Everything's about to change. "Can you please take me to the kitchen?"

As we turn to leave, I glance once more at Peter, focused on his book. He behaves as if none of this concerns him, and part of me wishes that were true.

It's late in the evening, and the seven of us sit together in the sitting room. The Shadow blares from the radio, a welcome distraction after the day I've had. I lean into James' arms, but there's no denying the chasm between us. And it won't close, will it? We won't find our way back to each other.

My thoughts drift to Peter, seated by the fire, lost in the flickering flames. What's behind that faraway gaze? Hours spent with him replay in my mind, holding me captive even as I remain wrapped in James' embrace.

How much longer can I pretend?

Exhaustion finally claims me, and I excuse myself, James guiding me to my room. He says goodnight and leaves with a pained expression lingering on his face. I hurt for him. I do. It's not his fault I'm so indifferent. He returned the same man. But me? I'm a different woman now, and it's going to break him.

"Good evening, Ms. Wendy," a young woman says as I shut the door behind me. "I'm Ava, your lady's maid. I've finished changing your sheets, and there's a bath drawn. I can assist you, if you'd like."

"I'm not so sure about a bath." I ease onto the edge of the bed.

"I understand. I can stay with you, if it'll help." She gently pulls the curtains closed for the evening. "And perhaps think of it this way, you're washing away the whole experience. A kind of cleansing."

The thought of returning to the water leaves me numb. I can't avoid it forever, though, can I?

"Okay, it's probably for the best. And you can stay."

"Wonderful." She offers her arm. "Then come along."

We saunter into the bathroom, and I slip off my robe and camiknicker. The bubbles look inviting, and the steam beckons. This is different. I step in, cautiously sinking until the heat envelops my body. The sensation of water grips me, dragging me back into the nightmare. I tense, ready to get out, but Ava lifts my hair, gently washing as she sings.

Her voice is soft, soothing. The tension dissolves. I focus on the words as she continues, allowing my mind a reprieve from the endless storm within. When I'm clean and the water cools, she helps me out and into bed, dressing me in a floor-length cream-colored satin nightgown. I gaze into the fire, ready to sleep, almost.

"Where's Peter's room?" I ask.

She perches on the edge of the bed, gliding the brush through my hair. "His room is next to yours; he insisted on being close."

"Really?" I dip my head, a small spark of warmth touching my mouth.

"Yes. But you must know he cares for you deeply. I was there during the earliest hours, when you were at your worst." She pauses. "He could have left, but he stayed, attentive to your every need. I won't pretend I wasn't impressed."

"It's hard to recall it all. But I know you're right. Thank you."

"Shall I stay a bit longer?" She places the brush on the side table. "Do a bit of knitting on the rocker while you fall asleep?"

"Oh, no, I'll manage, go on and get some rest."

"Okay, miss. Goodnight."

She closes the door, and I lie back, eager for sleep to embrace me, but it doesn't. Instead, sounds of the night—an owl, the rustling wind, the house softly settling—capture my attention, returning me to a state of restlessness. Frustration mounts until I kick off the blankets and hop from bed. I cannot rest, and though I should stop, ignore dangerous impulses, my need transcends mere desire; it's primal.

I open the door. The hallway is silent, and I step out, creeping to the door beside mine. I try the handle—unlocked, so I push it open and peek inside.

The light from the fireplace casts long shadows over the room, leaving everything swathed in a flickering golden glow. Closing the door softly behind me, I lean against it, contemplating my next move. The bed lies straight ahead, a four-poster, but Peter's not in it. I glance around and realize he's the shadow beside the fireplace, resting on his back, one arm above his head, the other on his chest.

Nibs said to put distance between us. Focus on my goals. But in Peter's presence, none of it matters. I sigh and walk toward him, my footsteps silent.

Goodbye world beyond the gate. Goodbye, dreams of sunlit meadows. Barefoot strolls through hot sand...

I'm beside him, he's stretched across a blanket, asleep, his chest rising and falling gently.

Blast you, Peter...

I bend and gaze at him; he's like a painting. I shouldn't, but I hold my hand to his skin, gliding my fingers across the ridge of his collarbone, the feeling velvety smooth. How long have I suppressed this desire, insisting the world beyond mattered more?

Without warning, his hand closes around mine, his eyes lifting to meet my own. "Have you been drinking?"

"No." My voice is calm. "I couldn't sleep."

"And you thought I could help with that?" He pushes up onto his elbows, releasing my hand.

"Yes."

"You've been through a lot," he says slowly. "But you're not yourself right now, and I'm not your fiancé."

"I know..."

The instinct returns, primal and undeniable. I hold out my hand, the ring glistening in the firelight. "Take it."

"What?" He straightens. "What are you saying?"

"Take it off. Please."

He hesitates, studying me, then gently takes my hand and lifts it, pressing his mouth to the skin before sliding the ring down my finger until it falls free.

I move to him, aware there's no turning back, and rest into the crook of his neck. His scent, rich vanilla and lavender, floods my senses. He swallows hard, his breath intensifying. For once, there's no doubt in my mind; only longing.

His fingers thread through my hair. "It's damp."

"I bathed." My lips brush his ear.

"You're confused, Wendy." A shudder runs through him. "Those hours together were... intimate, yes, but this isn't what you want."

"You are what I want." I kiss along his neck.

"Just know I tried to stop you." His voice breaks at the edges. "Your happiness... it lies elsewhere."

His eyes close as my fingers dig into his hair, my forehead pressed to his. "No, it doesn't. It's right here. Now kiss me."

His breath is ragged as he grips my face and pulls me to himself. Our lips meet with the force of everything we've tried to pretend isn't there. Yet it is. Undeniably.

After endless moments of denying my heart, I realize with startling clarity that this desire existed long before I ever knew it.

His fingers slip around my neck as I melt into his kiss, surrendering completely. His mouth moves against mine with a tenderness I can scarcely bear. Weaving my hands through his thick, golden hair, the strands glide against them like silk. I pull back and stare at him, the words spilling out unguarded.

"I love you."

He says nothing, only tilts toward me, as if memorizing my face. Then his lips brush mine, soft at first, then again. His mouth lingers at my bottom lip, slow and tentative, then drifts to my top. When he finally covers both, fuller and deeper, he stays there, and the ache in my chest blossoms like a flower under the sun.

Time ceases as he holds me close, the world dissolving as only he and I remain, no words, just a hungry embrace that will never be satiated. His lips are irresistible—soft, honeyed. His hands trail the length of my arms and up my back, the fire blazing brighter between us than in the hearth.

When we part, our foreheads rest together, a light in him as his thumb strokes my chin, and he kisses my nose. Sinking back, he cradles me to his chest, holding tight, as if he'll never let go. And that's okay, because I don't want him to.

Not ever.

We don't speak; there will be plenty of time for words tomorrow. Instead, he exhales softly, and I lean in, leaving light kisses along his cheek, down the nape of his neck, and one final lingering kiss on his lips before resting my head against him. Without meaning to, I drift into a sweet, dreamless sleep.

No tonic required.

Chapter 19

Sunshine pours through the window, warming the room. A lively group of birds flutters around the sill, chirping cheerfully to one another. What could they be discussing? I stretch, easing the stiffness from my body, and sit. I'm back in my room. Peter must have brought me here while I slept.

The door opens, and I glance over, expecting him, but it's Ava.

"Good morning," she chirps. "I came in earlier, but you were asleep. I apologize. I forgot to give you the sleep tonic Doctor Smith left. Did you rest well despite my forgetfulness?"

"I did," I say, the sensation of Peter's kiss lingering. "Better than I have in a while."

"Oh, good. I'm so glad to hear it. Now." She holds out a yellow day dress. "Ms. Grace sent this for you. Would you like to try it on? She made it clear that you shouldn't be pressured. Wear whatever is most comfortable."

"I'll dress." I chuckle. "I'm anxious for the day ahead."

"Well, the missus will be glad for it." She lifts my nightgown over my head. "She's terribly concerned about you."

She settles my brassiere in place, and I pull on my camiknickers. "She can put her worries to rest," I say, waving away the girdle. "I've never felt better in my life."

She helps me into the yellow day dress and a pair of wool stockings, then brushes out my hair, clipping it back.

"Can you help me to the mirror?" I ask. "I'd like to ensure I look my best."

She guides me to the standing mirror, and my chest tightens at the sight in the glass. James' engagement ring glints on my finger once more.

"You look like sunshine," she says. "The captain will be mighty pleased; he's been so concerned."

Why would Peter return it? I take Ava's hand, and she leads me out of the room, my spirit unsettled as we arrive in the kitchen.

"Good morning." James rises from his place at the table and practically sprints to my side. "I can take her from here."

"Certainly." Ava curtsies and slips away.

"Good morning," I say, glancing past him to the table where Kit, Tiger Lily, Grace, and Henley enjoy breakfast. No Peter... He doesn't regret what happened, does he?

I sit by James, and the others are quick to greet me.

"The dress is marvelous on you." Grace squeezes my shoulder.

"Indeed. You appear much recovered," Henley adds.

"I am." I take a bite of oatmeal. "How are you both?"

"Much better." Grace rests her head against Henley's arm, and he grins at me.

"Wendy, would you care for some coffee?" Tiger Lily offers.

"Yes, please. Thank you."

"We thought a board game might be nice today. Something to pass the time?" She fills a mug for me. "Will you join us?"

I take a long sip. "I'm not going anywhere just yet, so I suppose so."

Stretching his arm across my chair, James rubs my back while he and Kit discuss wedding details. My fingers tap against the mug, each word he speaks twisting like a knife in my gut.

"Have you seen Peter today?" I whisper to Grace.

"Yes... Um." Her eyes dart at James as she reaches into her pocket and presses something onto my lap. "He asked me to give this to you."

A prickle of unease crawls over me as I gaze at the envelope. "He's not here?"

"No. But I imagine the letter explains it all."

I push away from the table, and James stands with me.

"No," I say quickly. "I'll be back. Just need a minute alone. Excuse me."

A footman stands in the hallway as I step out.

"Sir, can you guide me to the front door?"

"Miss?" He walks to my side.

"I have a letter I'd like to read in private. Please, just to the porch."

"Of course." He bows and takes my arm, walking me to the entrance, where he provides a warm shawl and a pair of slip-on shoes.

"Are you sure about this, miss?" He peeks outside. "The chill won't be good for you in recovery. My sister went for a cold bath like you and was ordered to stay inside for weeks."

"I appreciate the concern, but I'll be fine." I step onto the windy porch.

"Well, alright, miss. But here." He hands me a golden handbell. "I'll wait right in here. Ring when you're ready."

He bows and closes the heavy door, leaving me alone on the porch. The wind rips at my shawl while gray clouds swirl overhead. I take a breath, but there's nothing refreshing about it as it scrapes down my throat like nails.

I rip open the envelope and lift out the letter, Peter's handwriting across it.

Wendy Darling,

I can already see your face, red with rage, because here I am, leaving while you sleep again. I couldn't stay. You have a wedding to plan, a future beyond this town, and I'm only holding you back.

Forgive me for distracting you. On your wedding day, please, get out of here and do what you have to. You were right. This place is a prison. Run and don't look back.

Fly high, Bird.

Peter

The letter slips through my fingers. *He's left me...*

"Well, hello there, I didn't expect to find you outside." I look up as Nibs approaches. "Something the matter?"

"What are you doing here?" I tuck the letter back into the envelope.

"Grace called yesterday, told us what happened." He sits beside me. "I thought we agreed, no being a hero?"

"That was about Juke. And had I not jumped in, Grace would have died."

"And had Peter not jumped in, you'd be dead."

Hearing his name sends a shudder through me.

"Whoa now—" He slips an arm around me. "What's that for?"

"Peter left."

"Yeah. He came by this morning."

"So you know where he went?"

He's silent for a minute. "I do, but he asked me to keep it to myself."

"Nibs." My body shivers as the wind whips past us. "If Morgan left without a word. Wouldn't you want to find her?"

"That's different." He rubs a hand across his face. "You need to forget him and focus on your marriage."

"Blast it, Nibs!" I stand, voice cracking. "Don't you understand? I'm not in love with James. If I'm being honest, I was using him to escape this town. I love Peter. And I'm ready to put those dreams away for him."

"Even if I tell you where he's gone, it's useless."

"Not to me." I kneel and grip his hands. *"Please."*

He looks away, jaw tight. "I shouldn't, but... it's as I said. It's useless to know. Because—"

He hesitates.

"Because *what?*" My grip tightens.

"Because he's no longer in Winter Woods."

The words slam into me, leaving me breathless. "*What?*"

"I know." He nods slowly. "I'm sorry."

"No." I collapse backward, mind spinning. "You're lying! No one leaves here, Nibs. That's impossible."

He moves to my side, holding me upright. "I swear to you, Wendy, this is no lie."

"But there's no way out except—" Then it hits me. "*James*... The look on his face when he saw us yesterday." I'm already cold, but now there's ice in my veins. "He's done this, hasn't he?" I grip his arm, voice rising with emotion. "He freed Peter, so I wouldn't leave him."

"You don't know that, don't assume anything."

"But I do." My teeth break through the skin of my lip, blood pooling in my mouth. "I'd have been better beneath the ice."

"Stop that!" He guides me to my feet. "You've had a shock; I get it. But this isn't the time to give up."

I reach for the bell and shake it, and after a moment, the footman peeks out. "Ma'am, you ready?"

"Yes. Please take me to my room." I hold out a hand, which he takes and guides me forward, my footing unsteady.

"Sir, if you'd follow me," the footman says, holding me secure. "I can let Miss Starkey know you're here."

"No, thank you," Nibs gives me a hard stare. "I'm leaving. But here—" He reaches inside his coat and holds out a pair of blue satin gloves. "Said he promised you a pair."

I take them, fingers trembling as I gaze at the material. The footman guides me back into the house, through the silent hallway, until we reach my room.

Stepping inside, I thank him and close the door, locking it. I stare at the gloves and blink once, and then the dam breaks, tears spilling unhindered. Clawing at the yellow dress, I tear it off and fling it into the corner. I crawl into bed, burrowing beneath the thick blankets, tears soaking the pillow as I cling to the gloves.

✳ ✳ ✳

Time passes. There's a knock—a distant voice—just a blur, then silence. Morning turns to afternoon. Another knock, firmer this time, voice resolute. I ignore it. By dark I hear him again, and it brings fresh tears to my eyes.

"Wendy, I wish you'd let me in," James says. "It's killing me to stay away."

Silence.

"Wendy? *Please.* Just let me know you're okay, at least."

Part of me longs to open the door, let him in to hold me while I cry. But how could I? How could I receive his comfort over Peter? I cannot, so I remain soundless, numb.

By evening, Ava is by my side. "Doctor Smith was by earlier." She caresses my hair. "Everyone is concerned about you. Is there anything I can do, miss?"

"No, Ava. I want to be alone."

"You're hurting. Is it physical?"

"No."

"I understand." She presses a finger against my chest. "It's the heart. Is this about Peter leaving us?"

"I love him. You must think me horrid, but I can't help it."

"Some might," she says thoughtfully. "But I believe one cannot help whom their heart desires."

"I imagine you're right," I mumble.

"My dear." She glides her hands through my hair. "I will say a prayer for your heart tonight and pray come morning, an answer will appear."

"Thank you, Ava..."

"Before I leave." She hands me a cup. "It's a bit of sleep powder from the doctor."

I drink the bitter medicine and hand it back, resting onto the pillow.

"Rest well," she whispers, slipping away.

I wrap myself in the silky sheets, and with the tonic's help, sleep finds me.

I'm at the academy, it's a day like any other, and Madam Esme prattles on as I stare out the window, listless. Beside me, JaneAnn reclines, feet on the desk, reading while Hannah braids her hair.

"You're next," JaneAnn says, flipping the page.

"What?" I ask.

"She said you're next," Hannah replies. "Are you ready?"

I shake my head. "Ready for what?"

She points ahead, and when I look, I'm in front of a mirror, my reflection smiling back. I lift a hand, but the reflection only tilts her head, strangely disconnected. And then, it hits me, she's a child. I press my palm to the glass, drawn toward her, but a hand snakes over her mouth and drags her backward. As she disappears into darkness, something hooks into me as well, yanking me through the glass, and I stumble into the space beyond.

I shoot upright, alert, and John sits beside the bed.

"Johnny? What the devil are you doing here?"

It's morning, and John reclines on a chair with a tray of food and drink.

"Good morning to you, too," he says. "I brought breakfast. A bit of toast, some berries, and a warm smile. Wasn't that kind of me?"

"How did you even get in here?" I hold the blanket closer.

"I saw myself in. They said you refused to see anyone, so I found the key and came to bother you."

"Hand me that robe."

"Sure thing." He grabs the robe off the dresser and tosses it. "So, I've heard troubling stories, had to come see for myself."

I pull the robe on and tie it snug. "And what have you heard?"

"You nearly died in the river." He places the tray on my lap. "Eat up."

"That's true."

"Okay." He adjusts his collar. "And how do you fare?"

"The doctor said I was improving and should recover soon. What else?"

"You're being a stubborn ass and not permitting anyone in?"

"Two for two." Hungry for the first time in days, I lift the toast and take a bite.

"Why?" He crosses his arms. "What's prompted this behavior?"

I stare at the tray, thoughts blurring.

"Hey." He leans toward me. "Tell me."

"John?" A voice says from the doorway, and I spin around to see JaneAnn standing there. "Hey, you found her!"

"Is the whole home here?" I ask.

"Obviously not." She closes the door and locks it. "There, now no one will bother us."

"Gee, almost like before either of you entered." I sip my tea.

"So, have you discovered why she's hiding in here?" JaneAnn sits on the bed.

"We're almost there," John answers.

"Are we?" I gaze between them both.

"This is about Peter, isn't it?" she asks.

I drop my gaze, and she chuckles. "Bingo. So, what's happened?"

I pop a berry in my mouth. "She doesn't talk to me for months," I say, "but now expects answers."

"Is Jan right?" John asks. "Is this about Peter?"

"You won't let up, will you?" I shake my head. "Fine..."

I don't know why I'm doing it, but I tell them about the absolute mess I've made of myself recently. Yet they don't judge me when I confess what occurred between Peter and me that night. No, instead, Jan beams mischievously.

"So, let's get this straight," she says. "You told him you loved him, and then he somehow leaves town by morning?"

"Pretty much. He left me this note." I hold out the letter, and John takes it, reading before passing it to JaneAnn.

"So now what?" he asks.

"I don't know. Marrying James remains the only way out, yet how can I do it under the circumstances?"

"Did you see the words scribbled at the bottom of the envelope?" JaneAnn extends the letter to me.

"What are you talking about?" I rip it open, and read a few familiar lines:

Writing this letter, containing three lines,
Answer my question, "Will you be mine?"
"Will you be mine, dear, will you be mine,"
Answer my question, "Will you be mine?"

"What does it say?" John asks.

"It's words I sang at the ball." I press the envelope to my chest and smile. "He's telling me something." The room is suddenly brighter.

"Explain."

"He knows my heart, and knew I was giving up leaving for *him*. I suppose when James offered him a way out, he took it. Not for himself, but for me. I can't believe I'm saying this, but... I'm going to continue the engagement."

"But not marry him?" John straightens.

"I know it's cruel, but if I break it off now, what good does that serve me? Either way, it ends. The way I see it, this gives me a chance to find Peter on the other side of all this."

"Sounds like you're postponing the news until a more convenient time," JaneAnn says. "Nothing wrong with that."

"I don't know." John shakes his head. "Sounds awfully risky. Can you honestly pretend until the wedding?"

Peter appears in my thoughts. His gaze locked on me moments before our lips touched for the first time.

"Yes, Johnny. I'm very confident I can do just about anything under the circumstances."

"Well, I'm all for it." JaneAnn touches my shoulder. "You were starting to lose me there, hitching yourself to the rat."

"Now, now, Jan," John chuckles. "Let's not get carried away. Wendy's plenty motivated as is."

"Sure, Johnny." She rolls her eyes. "So, how long till the wedding?"

"Too long," I finally say. "But I promise you, when the time comes, I'll be ready."

Part Three

The Emerging

Chapter 20

For a brief moment, while Peter held me close, I felt better, worthier. But now, thirty-nine days have passed since he vanished, and with him, any goodness I may have once possessed. For weeks, I've been living a lie, a horrible, despicable one. I finished my program at the academy, knowing full well I'll never need the skills. Still, I imagine Peter and me drinking tea, pinkies raised, finally able to laugh about this madness. And it's thoughts like this that comfort me during these long, agonizing weeks.

The hardest part is the betrayal I feel every time James and I kiss. Gone are the days of shivers and giggles; now it leaves me sick. Not because of who James is, but because of who I am, and the twisted choice I made to lead him on only to break his heart.

As I stare into the mirror, it strikes me: tomorrow I leave Winter Woods. But first, I must soldier through the engagement dinner at Grace's home. Jan insists I'm making the right choice, that I must remain strong, but regardless, I'm awash in nerves. I'm breaking James' heart, abandoning my only family. The guilt is suffocating. Yet John reminds me: I am not their savior. If I sacrifice everything for them, how could they ever be truly happy? So, I'm saying goodbye, knowing full well it means leaving them to the darkness and cold.

Nibs may just curse my name till the day he dies.

I gaze around the room. My are bags are packed, my trunk filled, and some of the furniture already sent to the palace. I still can't believe it's over. I slip into the sky-blue dress from my birthday, secure the necklace from Llewelyn, adjust my golden band, and tuck Peter's note into my pocket. My hair is pinned, makeup subtle, and with a final steadying breath, I step to the door, ready for my final masquerade.

James paces in the hallway, but when he sees me, he straightens. "I must be dreaming."

I offer a tight-lipped smile. "Let's enjoy this final night, shall we?"

He leans close and kisses me, a gentleness in him that I ache to embrace. My heart belongs elsewhere, but that doesn't erase all of the years James kept me afloat. I can only hope that one day he'll see what a wretched match I would have been, and find someone who would gladly give up the world for him.

Still, I miss the simplicity of life before Margaret's death, before Peter took over all my thoughts, before security no longer became the goal. A time when I dreamed big, but lived small.

We join Kit and Tiger Lily in the car, driving away from the home, emotion rising with every mile. Downtown blurs past the window, and as we near Starkey Manor, I wonder if I can truly see this through. I have no choice, I know that. But still, this may be the most agonizing night of my life.

My fingers drum against the glass, and James presses a warm hand to my leg. "Tomorrow will be the best day of our lives," he whispers.

While he's all smiles, acid creeps up my throat. When the manor finally comes into view, I don't wait for Kit to get the door, but push it open myself, sucking in the bitter night air.

As Kit steps around, he offers me an odd look. "You okay, doll?"

"Yeah." I avoid his gaze.

James takes my arm, and together we ascend the stairs, past the marble pillars, into the candle-lit entryway. Heat creeps up my neck with memory—all the moments that unraveled me. Unbecoming everything I told myself I had to be.

This isn't just a home. It's where all the magic began.

We enter the ballroom, and I quiet the tremble in my fingers as the guests rise and applaud. James guides me through the crowd, and I wave to a delighted bunch from the home, then another from the chapel, including Reverend Andrew and sweet Bea. Oh, the guilt that fills me every time I see them, aware I must be the worst of all God's children.

We continue, and I catch kisses from Chas, nod to a cheerful Smee, and meet Rose's wistful gaze. JaneAnn and John offer knowing looks, spurring me on.

The girls from Madam Esme's visibly swoon over James, prompting a chuckle from him as he pulls me close, and I roll my eyes. But then, his grip tightens painfully, and I glance around, confused. Standing before us are two unfamiliar figures—his parents, I assume. But they aren't the source of his tension. No, it's the man beside them, staring at me like I'm a treat he means to devour. It's Juke. I swallow the dread, unwilling to cower.

"Father, Mother." James hugs them both. "What an unexpected surprise!"

"We couldn't rightly miss your engagement party," his mother replies, looking me over. "You must be Wendy."

"Yes." I take her outstretched hand. "It's a pleasure to meet you, ma'am."

"The pleasures all ours. My son speaks highly of you, and I can see why. It does a mother good to see her child so happy."

"Child?" James scoffs. "Now, now, Mother, I'm not exactly your little boy any longer."

"Nonsense." She grips his chin affectionately. "You will always be my little boy."

"Well, if you two are done bickering." Thomas turns to me. "I'd like to meet our new daughter-in-law."

"Hello, sir." I curtsey.

"Oh, none of that." He chuckles and pulls me into a warm hug. "Tomorrow we'll be family."

The word *family* nearly undoes me, until his mother adds, "Wendy, I imagine you know our other son, Juke." She gestures to him.

"Yes, of course," I reply. "We're acquainted."

"We sure are. Wendy and I were good friends." Juke leers. "And I dearly look forward to getting reacquainted."

James takes a step forward, and I grip his arm, squeezing. He gazes at me, and I whisper, "I'm okay. Ignore him."

His nostrils flare, but he nods. Amongst all the lies I'm caught in, this statement is true—I *am* okay. Facing Juke isn't what I envisioned, but my feet remain steady, despite his clear desire to see me crumble.

"If everyone is ready," Mr. Starkey mercifully announces, "let's fill our bellies."

He waves us over to a table where Grace, Henley, Canary, Ms. Diana, and Theo Van Lori are already seated. Grace hugs me, gushing over the thrill of the night, and then we sit. While eating, I observe Mr. Starkey and Henley laughing heartily. If anything has brought me joy this season, it's seeing Henley happy after years of heartache. As I've been torn between guilt and longing, he and Grace remain blissfully in love. I wonder if she'll soon be celebrating her own engagement? Pity I won't be there to witness it, though.

"I'll miss you in my classroom," Theo says, pulling me from my thoughts. "I'm losing a favored student and friend."

"Oh, I'll miss our visits too," I say, blowing on a spoonful of steamy stew.

"In the future, I hope we find one another again." He holds his glass out as the server refills it with wine.

"I hope so. But it's hard to say where I'll be after all of this."

"Are you... nervous about what's to come?"

"My marriage?" I arch a brow. "Why should that cause me nerves?"

"Long before Winter Woods, before the curse," he gestures around, "before all of *this*, you had dreams far beyond..." his gaze slides to James, engrossed in conversation with Henley and Mr. Starkey, "a loveless marriage."

A chill washes over me. There's no hint of deception or humor in his words. "What are you saying?" I whisper.

"I know you, Wendy Darling." His eyes betray the depth of emotion in him.

"But how?" I'm fighting the urge to raise my voice, lest the others hear. "Why haven't you said anything?"

"There's more at play than you understand. But the memories, they haunt me." He presses a hand to his mouth, thoughtful. "You once called me Uncle Theo. And I remember you begging your father to let you taste heartache, just so you could play as I do. We laughed and he said, 'Just a wee bit, little one,' because he would have given you the world."

Tears prick hot and sudden. I take his hand. "Tell me who he was."

"I cannot say, I'm truly sorry." Regret etches the lines of his face. "I wish I could, pretending has been harder than you know. But your story isn't mine to tell. Just know this—soon, you shall understand the world, and the world shall understand you."

"That's it? That's all I get?" My voice cracks. "Where did I live? Who was my family? Please, tell me something!"

He shakes his head and the sorrow in it nearly undoes me. "I cannot. Believe me, if I were able to, it would already be yours."

"That's not enough!" The words burst out as I shove back my chair. The legs scrape loudly; James' head turns at once.

"Everything okay, darling?" he asks, calmly.

"Perfectly fine," I answer too quickly, blinking away the tears. "Just need to powder my nose. If you'll excuse me."

James is on his feet in an instant, catching my arm. "You're not okay. What happened?"

I meet his eyes, chest heaving. "It's okay. Just a bit overwhelmed by tonight. Forgive me, I just need a moment alone."

"Let's get out of here," he murmurs. "I knew seeing Juke would be upsetting. I'm so sorry. I swear I had no idea they'd bring him."

"It's okay. You're sweet." I lift my hand to his face. "I'll be back, just a few minutes. Okay?"

He stares a long moment before conceding. "Okay. I'm here. Just call for me and I'll be there."

I turn and walk slowly from the room, but once out, break into a sprint. There's someone who holds all the answers, yet refuses to give me even one. I hurry through the house until I find the door—*his* door—and slip inside.

It's dark, a chill in the air. Flickers from our night shimmer through my memory as I cross to the bed, recalling his sleeping form stretched on the floor. I lie sideways on the mattress, curling in on myself, releasing all I've choked back, wishing more than anything that Peter were here to hold me.

The door creaks open, and I press up, strands of matted hair clinging to my wet cheeks. Someone enters and flips on the light, a soft glow filling the room.

"Llewelyn?" I whisper as he closes the door.

"*I saw you leave*," he signs, sauntering to the bed and settling beside me.

"I'm sorry." I swallow hard. "I don't know what to say."

Tears rush back, unbidden, and I'm in his arms before I know it. Words have never been our language; this is. An understanding that goes beyond words. Once I've cried myself clean, though, the confession spills out.

"I'm not marrying James tomorrow."

He doesn't move, so I continue, "I love... I love Peter. I didn't realize it for so long, but when I did, it was too late, and he left."

I inhale shakily. "James doesn't know, of course; only JaneAnn and John do. For months, I've lied—let him believe in us, and used him as I always have. I'm not a good person, nor have I earned this deception. But I can't marry him, and I have to get out to find Peter."

A smile slowly spreads across his face. "*Okay*," he signs.

"Okay?" I echo. "You don't think I'm the worst?"

"*Never. I saw it all along.*" He takes my hand and rises, guiding me up. "*Come spend one final night with those who love you.*"

"There's nowhere I'd rather be."

I consider mentioning Theo's confession, but what's the point? He won't tell me anything, and with me leaving in the morning, any opportunity for pressing him is gone. Somehow, I must find him again someday and make him tell me everything he knows.

For now, though, I find my heart is not lost in the past, but firmly anchored in the present. "Thank you for always loving me."

He kisses my forehead, and we enter the hallway, the soft strains of music drifting toward us.

"*Beautiful dreamer, wake unto me...*" A singer croons softly.

Of course.

As we step into the ballroom, Bea sweeps to my side, looping an arm around me. "May I steal our girl for a moment, Llewelyn?"

He bows, winks, and disappears into the crowd.

We circle the edge of the dancers and slip into the dimly lit Back Room. It's empty save for the cozy crackle of the fire, so we wander to the half-moon couch and sit. It's odd to be here again after everything.

"I've known you for many years," she says, settling in. "And I'd like to think we've shared a trusting relationship. Am I right?"

I never confided as freely with Bea as I did with Margaret, but she always had a way of easing my tangled thoughts into the open.

"Wendy?" Her blue eyes sparkle as she looks at me. "Something's been troubling you for a long while now, and my usual prompts haven't worked. Sometimes the burden eases when shared."

First Llewelyn and now her. John was right to be concerned. I can't hide the truth well at all. They see straight through me.

I tell her everything, her presence all the assurance I need that she's safe. When I finish, I lean back, expectant.

She taps her fingers lightly against the arm of the couch, then asks, "And you thought Andrew and I would judge you for your choices?"

"When you ask it now, I know it sounds silly. You've never before."

"And we weren't going to start. Did you know Andrew and I volunteered to come here?"

"Heaven's sake, why?"

"Because some are broken, living with little, and life can seem bleak. Andrew and I live to share the Savior's love. As he often says, 'our job is to bring joy to the joyless and hope to the hopeless.' Simple as that."

"But what do you get out of it?"

"A great deal. Purpose can be found anywhere, darling. Even in a place like this. I imagine this world felt quite confining to our Lord—bound by human constraints. A tremendous challenge, I'm sure. But He embraced it with joy, for us, so we could have hope too." She leans in, earnestness in her tone. "Now, I want you to go home tonight and talk to your Father. Okay?"

"Bea, I have no father."

"Of course you do. We all do. And though the great prowler would love you to believe He's far from reach, that isn't so. You may hold no memory of your earthly father, but this much I know: a parent's love is boundless. It doesn't swell when you are good; or wither when you falter. No, a true parent loves at all times. And so it is with our Heavenly Father. So, go home and talk to Him. Pour out your heart to Him. You *will* leave here tomorrow, but that alone won't bring you lasting peace. Faith, hope and love, they are wonderous things, but they aren't attainable without Him."

She rises, smoothing her dress. "Now, I've talked your ear off long enough. Before I go, Andrew wanted you to have this." She offers a small-sized Good Book, and I take it.

"Thank you, I've never had my own."

"Well, now you do. I love you, lass, and I'll surely miss you."

I tuck the tiny volume into the side pocket of my gown and return to the ballroom. Llewelyn stands at the edge of the dance floor.

"A final dance?" I say to him.

"I wouldn't miss it," he signs.

We glide forward, and he sweeps me into his arms, holding me close, his face tender and affectionate. We sway and spin, my hands outstretched, as childlike giggles rise up in me.

"I love you." I kiss his cheek.

He touches the pendant at my neck. *"My love goes with you."*

I rest against his chest, on the edge of tears again. But I won't cry. Not now. This is a moment I'll surely return to many times when I'm homesick. As I gaze around the room, I spot James, laughing as he twirls his mother around, wearing a look I've never seen. I'm glad for it, knowing what's to come.

The countdown is nearly over, and soon, I'll be free.

And yet...

I can't pretend this place is what I once believed. Perhaps Peter was right, the prison was in my mind. And perhaps Bea is right as well: maybe there is a purpose far greater than my escape.

I filled myself with doubts, fears, and unfulfilled desires. The bar was set so high I could never truly reach it. Now, as dreams slip into reality, ironically enough, I find my heart breaking to say goodbye. I'll never forget where I came from, nor do I wish to. Once, I was ready to let these people fade—shadows at the start of life. But now, I see it clearly: they are my foundation, and I wouldn't exist without them.

The little book in my pocket weighs against my side, and I think of what Bea said. They weren't forced here like the rest of us. They chose it. And yet, they have immeasurable joy. For the first time, I wonder if I might embrace the hope she speaks of, and find a joy no circumstance can remove.

❋ ❋ ❋

The remainder of the night slips away like a breeze. And then—I'm on the porch, and James faces me. "Tomorrow begins our forever." His hand brushes against my cheek.

Say something... anything.

"Thank you." Is what slips out. "If it weren't for you, I'd have been lost long ago. But since the beginning, you were hope for me. And for that, I love you."

He doesn't lean in for a kiss this time, but holds me to himself. *This is it—time to say goodbye.* Yet it hurts more than expected. So I give myself one last lie and share it with him. "I'll see you tomorrow."

"Goodnight, beloved," he says softly, then turns, vanishing into the night and out of my life.

As I step inside, I don't linger for conversations but hurry to my room. Trepidation coils in my spirit as I undress and pull on my nightgown before slipping into bed. I hold open the tiny book Bea gave and let my finger follow the little black letters.

"Therefore, you now have sorrow, but I will see you again, and your heart will rejoice, and your joy no one will take from you."

The words seem alive under my touch, and for the first time, something in me shifts, like a weight lifting, as I continue reading.

Chapter 21

My hand presses to the glass. Robin's perched on the windowsill, singing sweetly, and I know this'll be my final song from him.

"It's happening, Margaret," I whisper. "You said it would. I only wish you were here."

A lump forms in my throat, the familiar ache of missing her. I take a shaky breath and release.

It's time.

Opening the bedroom door, I find Tiger Lily and Grace busily preparing my bags while Morgan stands by the window, quietly surveying my wedding gown. Today might once have been a joyous occasion, but now I wonder where I'll be by nightfall. The uncertainty is unnerving.

Oh, James, you deserved so much better.

In many ways, I told him so. But he chose to trust me, to hold out faith. And now, that faith will be crushed. He'll be humiliated as he waits for me at the end of the aisle. I will never emerge, never walk toward him clad in white. It'll be a beautiful dream burned to ash. I left a letter on my desk so he knows I'm okay, and I'm sorry. But that's all I trust to leave behind.

"You ready?" Tiger Lily asks, resting a hand on my shoulder.

I glance from Grace to Morgan. "There's no time like the present," I say.

"Indeed. Let's do this." Grace claps her hands together, her enthusiasm far greater than my own.

The dress is perfection. And I can't help swelling with emotion as I gaze into the mirror, an image of beauty and elegance. For the first time, I imagine I could have been a good queen, done something worthy. But that's not what I'm going to do, so it's worthless to consider.

"Are you nervous?" Tiger Lily asks, slipping the heels onto my feet.

"Hard to find the words."

"It's going to be okay," she whispers. "I promise."

I squeeze her hand and sit as Morgan applies my makeup, her eyes brimming with tears the entire time. When she finishes, she kisses me on the cheek and lets Grace take over, carefully arranging my hair with the white veil, while inserting baby breath along the edges.

I did what Bea encouraged me to do last night and had a long, overdue talk with God. I thought it would feel strange—talking into the air, confessing and then weeping, asking for the forgiveness and strength I desperately need. But it didn't. Somehow, it was exactly as she said, like speaking to a father who could never be ashamed to call me his own.

Though I hold no memory of my parents, I imagine their love would feel much like the warmth and acceptance I felt. So, though unease tugs at me as I step into the unknown, there's also an unexplainable assurance pressing me forward, giving me the courage to go and not look back.

When they're done, I step in front of the mirror, one final time, and the three of them admire my reflection. Then the door opens, and before stepping out, I take one last look around the room. My little world, about to shatter wide open for the first time in my life. Never again will I see this fragile sanctuary. How many nights did I spend here, longing to be set free like the birds, whispering prayers that James might one day carry me away? And now, when that dream was to come true, I've gone and changed the course.

I step into the hallway where Kit and Henley await us. Henley approaches, lips pressed tight.

"Look at you." He takes my hands. "Absolutely lovely."

"The last thing Margaret said was she knew I'd leave someday. Told me to be patient." My eyes sting as the world blurs. "But leaving here feels like leaving her... like losing the presence that's been with me all these years."

He pulls me close. "She's never far away. You know this. She's right here—" He presses a hand against his heart. "For both of us."

"Yes," I sniff. "I love you."

"And I love you. I'm proud of you. And I know, were she here today, she'd say the same."

"Alright, doll." Kit steps closer. "Time to go."

I look at Morgan, suddenly aware of how quiet it is. "Where's everyone else?"

"They left earlier. You'll see them at the church."

"Oh..." My heart drops. "I wasn't aware of the change. When was it decided?"

"Last night. Is that a problem?"

"No." The weight in my chest grows heavier. I didn't say goodbye, and now I suppose I never will.

"Cheer up." She hugs me. "You'll see them soon. But you'd better get going. Big day ahead of you."

"You're not coming with us?" My voice cracks.

"I'll join you soon."

"Oh. Okay.... well, my goodness. How can I begin to thank you for everything?"

"You're acting like this is goodbye. Save your goodbyes for later. I love you. Go on."

"And I you." I breathe in, the floodgates ready to burst.

"Now don't start crying or we'll have to redo your makeup," Grace says as she guides a soft fur shawl onto my shoulders.

"I can't help it," I say, lips quivering, and glance into the dining room, echoes of the past flashing through my mind. All of us kids gathered around the tables, conversations loud, laughter lingering through time. I take a few steps forward, fingers trailing along the smooth wooden surface of the table. The classroom door stands open, an aching silence within that's nearly unbearable.

Days turned to years in this home, all spent trying to put myself together, while making sense of our limited world. I push through the swinging door into the kitchen, recalling the many moments around the circular table—morning tea with Jan and Mams and late-night cocoa and board games with John and Michael. A dance with Peter, a cry with Morgan, or giggling over Nibs' antics. I glance out the window. There's no smoke rising from Llewelyn's chimney today. It's dark. I didn't value the moments while they were happening, and now... I desperately wish I could go back and hold each one a little tighter than I did the first time.

I could enter every room, cry for times gone by, but it's too painful. So, I take one last look around and walk from the cozy cream kitchen to the front door, where the others wait for me. As I step through, I know: I'm leaving the Home, the only place I've ever known, and stepping into an unknown that, at this moment, feels far more daunting than anything I've faced before.

Kit speaks with a uniformed guard, handing him a slip of paper. The guard scans it. "I'll be back momentarily."

"Certainly." Kit leans back. "We'll be out of here shortly; there's a process before allowing anyone in or out."

"Are you excited?" Grace asks, seated between Henley and me.

"I think I'm the only one in this car who's never experienced the world outside of Winter Woods," I say.

Henley frowns. "How awful."

"But that all changes today," Grace says brightly.

"Yes, everything changes today." I lean against the window; gaze fixed on the tall wrought-iron gate.

"It's taking a while, isn't it?" Tiger Lily strains her neck to take in the elevated guardhouse.

"This is perfectly normal." Kit takes her hand, his thumb brushing gently across her skin.

What if the guard returns and says, I've been found out; my plan leaked. But no, how could it? Llewelyn wouldn't betray me. Nor John or JaneAnn.

The guard returns. "Alright, sir." He hands Kit the slip. "You are all set. Have a good day, and good luck on your wedding, ma'am."

"Thank you." I fold my hands, swallowing the nerves.

The guard raises his hand, twirling his fingers, signaling someone inside the guardhouse. A low rumble follows as the gate opens—perhaps it's a single button that has kept me locked away my entire life. I glance at Henley, radiant with joy. We're both from Neverwood Valley. Neither of us has left since we arrived. Kit catches my eye in the rearview mirror, then presses on the gas, slowly driving beneath the massive gate, and—just like that, we're out.

I can barely believe it as the car speeds on, and Winter Woods fades into the distance. Staring out the window, I'm spellbound, as a world I've only imagined blurs past.

"Ladies and gents," Kit announces, slowing the car, "you're free to open your windows and take in a glorious breath of air that won't freeze your lungs."

I wrap my fingers around the handle and crank—it's foreign but delightful. In Winter Woods, you don't roll down windows; you close them tightly. Now, though, the glass disappears, and I brace for the blast of cold, but it never comes. Instead, a satiny warmth washes over me, as all around, snow melts, and wildflowers peek through, basking in the golden sunlight streaming through the canopy of trees.

Sprigs of vibrant green grass emerge. Soon, there's no snow left anywhere, only lush grass spreading far and wide. I lean through the window, and Grace stares.

"Uh, what are you doing?"

"Hold my legs," I say.

She promptly does, and I spread my arms, the sun baking my cheeks, as I breathe in the fresh floral scent from nearby lilac bushes. Kit slaps the side of the car, hooting loudly, and Henley follows my lead, reclining on the edge of the window, leaving poor Grace to cling tightly to us. Wind whips through Henley's hair as he lets out a shout, and I join him—screaming into the glorious world beyond.

"What is happening?" Grace laughs, breathless as she lets go. "You've both lost your minds!"

This is what I once knew, the girl I used to be. I envision her breaking free from me and soaring into the air, twisting around in pure delight. Yet, she's still trapped within. And I promise her, silently, I'll make her proud.

Driving along, calm settles in the car, and I gaze at the passing scenery, mesmerized by the beauty. I have to leave soon. It's now or never, before we draw any closer to James. Yet the thought of breaking away from my dearest friends cuts deep. The idea of going it alone threatens to paralyze me in my seat, but the hope of Peter somewhere out there presses me on.

"Could we stop for a moment?" I ask.

"Sure," Kit says, "Everything okay?"

"Just nerves. I could use a breath of air. I feel a little queasy."

"Alright, I know a spot. Hang on." He accelerates, and Henley and I sit back. Ten minutes pass before the car veers off the main road onto a bumpy dirt path. There's a sense we're getting hopelessly lost, taking one turn after another, zig-zagging deeper into the forest, the road far behind.

"You sure we need to go so far in?" I ask, body slamming into the door as the car coasts over a hole.

"Don't worry, nearly there."

The path disappears entirely, and he brings the car to a stop. "Okay, have at it. If you need some privacy, go around the corner of the hedge."

"Thanks." I step out. The ground is firm beneath my shoes. They all watch me as I go to close the door. "Be back soon."

"Perhaps I come along to assist." Grace inches out.

"No!" I clear my throat, not meaning to alarm, though her wide eyes say I clearly have. "I'll be okay."

She nods, and I shut the door, taking one final glance at the four, as I edge backward, whispering a goodbye. When I'm far enough away, I turn and race to the bushes Kit pointed out. But as I round the corner, I stop, heart in my throat. I'm facing a towering, ancient oak. Peter's oak, the one he painted. It's real, and there's no question in my mind that he knew this.

Fingers trembling, I step closer, knowing this isn't a coincidence; I've been led here. But why?

"Wendy," Kit says softly behind me.

I turn. There's no one around. "Kit?"

"I'm here." His voice echoes all around.

"Where are you?" I spin. "Why can't I see you?"

"We know what you're doing.

A quiver runs through me. "Yeah?" I tilt my neck, searching. "And what is that? What am I doing?"

"You're running to find Peter." His voice is suddenly close—right beside me. "But it's okay... we're not going to the wedding."

I whirl around; Kit isn't Kit anymore. I stumble backward. "What are you?" I shriek.

He approaches, body the size of my hand, wings fluttering. "Do you remember me?"

I search his face, and yes, I've seen it in this form before. "It was you! You were the faerie who saved Peter."

"Yes. That vision was my own memory. My name is Kit, and I'm from Elphame, and I'm a prince. Tiger Lily and I came here to rescue you and the others."

"I don't understand. Why would you do that?"

"Wendy." He flies closer. "You are the daughter of Neverland's last true king."

I stare, then let out a breath of disbelief. "That isn't funny Kit."

"It's not. Nor is it a joke."

My legs carry me back a step, his words leaving me faint. "I just—I don't understand."

"It'll take time to set in, but for now, I can help with that. I can break the curse. I can return your memories."

The words knock the air from my lungs. "You can return my memories? But how?"

"You saw me do it before. *Think.*"

I close my eyes, and Peter's on the floor, bloody. My hands wrap around his forehead, a golden light streaming out, then he wakes screaming.

"All the way back in the warehouse? Peter knew everything?"

"He did. But he couldn't tell you. None of them could."

"Who's them?"

Kit waves his arms, growing in size. "Look behind you."

I turn hesitantly, and one by one—John, JaneAnn, Michael, Maimie, and lastly, Nibs—emerge from an opening in the oak. Seeing them here, in this place, I can't make sense of it. Something in their demeanor, in their faces, they're changed.

"You're the last one," Tiger Lily says.

I look at her, standing by Kit, just as Grace and Henley join them. I'm surrounded, like a cornered animal.

"Is this true?" I ask John.

"You saw the signs."

"The fainting? You and Peter..."

"Yes," JaneAnn says. "Blast, it's been painful not telling you. It's why I couldn't be around you anymore. Seeing you so confidently deceived. I would have blurted it out sooner or later had I not put space between us. I hope you understand."

"What were you waiting for?" I throw up my arms, surveying the group. "That was *months* ago."

"Your wedding," Nibs answers. "It's what I said, if you didn't leave, none of us would. But because of your wedding, we were all driven out of town. The perfect escape."

My emotions rise. Anger and hurt. All these months of confusion while each one of them knew exactly who I was. "So you used me?"

"Call it what you want—I call it a plan, and it worked bloody well," Nibs says.

I step closer, barely holding back my fury. "You knew how torn I was. You could have eased my misery. I would never have turned on you."

His jaw quivers. "It was a chance I refused to take. Not just for me, but for you. And Peter couldn't either."

"So what happens next?" I turn, gesturing at them all. "The curse breaks, and my younger self returns with a vengeance?"

"You and she aren't so different." John steps closer. "Don't let fear of the unknown hold you back. Not now."

If only Peter were here to guide me through this, but he's not. "I can't think straight." I shade my face; the sun too bright, too hot.

"Wendy?" Michael says, eyes glistening. "Please, do it. If not for yourself, then for us."

"Michael's right." John rests a hand on his shoulder. "We love you, but hell, we sure miss our sister."

I'm drowning in white fabric as I let myself fall, my legs giving way. *John and Michael are my brothers?*

"Look." Kit kneels beside me, voice gentle. "I can't break this on my own. Your will stands between me and the curse. Only you can open the way."

No one speaks. They just stare, waiting, hoping. It's not that I don't want this, I *do*. It's knowing who I've become will be altered, my whole existence trampled by whoever I used to be.

Yet Peter... Do I want to face all of him with only half of me?

I rip a handful of grass from the ground, crushing it between my fingers. "Okay... I'll do it."

Relief washes over their faces, and I understand now, no one felt assured of my choice till this moment.

"I can't tell you what'll happen," Kit says. "It looks different for everyone. Just, be strong and don't turn back. No matter what."

"I understand."

John and Michael each take a hand, and I look between them as Kit reaches for me. My heart pounds as his fingers draw near.

I whisper a prayer for strength and then—my mind is engulfed in an all-consuming darkness. I gasp, the pain agonizing as it rips across my forehead, tightening with each passing second. My prayer intensifies, begging for it to end, unable to bear the paralyzing pressure any longer—but like a veil lifting, a brilliant light bursts through, sweeping away all sense of time and existence.

Chapter 22

Her shoes shimmer a dazzling blue. "How are you here?"

The world around me holds no time, no sensation. I'm not dreaming, nor am I awake. I'm unsure where I am—yet I recognize the other person. She's me. The one I saw in the dream.

"Hey." She claps her hands, the sound echoing through the emptiness. "Why are you here? Do you understand me?"

"Yes." I glance around, trying to make sense of this place.

"Well, good." She crosses her arms, circling me, each step clicking sharply. "So, clearly we know each other. No introductions needed."

"I wouldn't assume so." Something about her makes me uneasy.

"Still here you are, what a mystery." She folds her arms, head tilted. "How old are you?"

"Fourteen." There's a hint of superiority in her tone. "What about you?"

"Nineteen... So, you're me before the curse?"

"I am. Ripped from my mind and shoved far beneath the surface. You showed up, took over everything."

"But how can you exist? If I'm you, then you're me. I don't understand."

"Don't ask me. You're the adult here. So, spill it, why are you here? What happened?"

"The curse broke. Have you been watching all these years?"

"Time is different here. It's as if everything happened yesterday and years ago simultaneously. On occasion, I catch glimpses of the world. Mostly, it's observing you making a mess of our life. You do realize James is the reason we're here, right?"

"I was under the impression we didn't meet him till after the curse."

"Funny." She laughs coolly. "We knew him very well. He cursed us."

My heart isn't truly racing—after all, this must be in my mind. Yet the pounding fills my ears nonetheless. "How do you know he's responsible?"

"Because he looked me dead in the eyes and said he was sorry. Then he watched that winged demon curse us. He knew everything."

I collapse to my knees, staring into the white void. "But... why?"

"I don't know the why." She sits beside me. "Father trusted Thomas, as we trusted James. But in the end, they betrayed us."

"And did you love him?"

Her face twists. "I'd like to think not, but he was handsome and kind. A friend I valued being around. Until that day."

"Here I've spent months wrapped in guilt, believing I was betraying him."

"You weren't the first. And he certainly deserves it."

An archway materializes before us, glistening with iridescent light.

"This is for us," I murmur. "Are you ready to go?"

She looks from me to the exit and back again. "You want us to go through that? Where's it taking us?"

"The world, I imagine. We'll wake as one. Don't you want that?"

"Not really. I'd prefer you stay and let me take over, start back where things left off."

"Well, that's not an option, is it?"

"No." She glares at me. "I don't like it, though."

"Can't say I like it any better."

She extends her hand, and together we rise. This girl is young, full of spirit, and I fear I'll extinguish it by merging into one; we're so different, but time cannot be reversed. She must become me, and I must embrace her.

"Tell me," she says. "How did you break the curse?"

"It just happened. My friend is Fae, and he broke it. Now, are you ready to get out of here?"

"Guess I don't have a choice." She gazes around. "Thought it was my one wish, but now that it's here, I find I'm rather uncertain."

"Perhaps you and I aren't so different." I smile at her, a protective fondness filling me for this younger part of myself. "Come on, we'll do it together."

Her hand in mine, there's a firmness in her grip. We step forward and enter the archway. Light scatters, breaks, and bends—a rainbow of colors wrapping around us. Our hands fuse, gazes locked as we merge.

She looks terrified.

"It's okay!" I call above the roar. "We're going to figure this out together."

She closes her eyes in surrender. And an explosion sends a tremor through me as everything dissolves.

I blink. Grass beneath me. Oxygen in my lungs. I'm alive!

Rising, my legs wobble, but I'm whole, puzzle assembled. The group watches. John's on his knees, lips parted, expectant.

"Johnny, you've grown so big," I say—but it's not me. It's her. No... it's *us*. Our lives are merging. Her memories haven't taken root, but flutter around my mind like butterflies.

John laughs, tears springing into his eyes. He runs to me, slamming onto his knees, pulling me into his strong embrace. Michael follows, tackling us as I giggle, wrapping him into my arms. She—I, am elated, heart bursting.

"You're you again?" Michael asks.

"I am."

Flashing into my mind, *Michael's nestled in my arms, a baby. He's in the carriage and I'm pushing him around, singing lullabies to calm him. We're picnicking in the field of wildflowers behind our cottage. John and I are racing, while Michael toddles behind, brown bear in hand.*

Releasing a scream, we leap into the air, plunging deep into the lake's depths. A smile appears as my face breaks the surface, sweet, soft, Mother. A hand wraps around me, lifting me high, tossing me with a deep booming laugh. I glimpse his wide grin as I hit the water, Father.

I blink and I'm on the ground again.

"I can't believe we're all back." John wipes his face. "We're really together again."

Glancing around, each face now holds a name, an identity beyond the Home.

JaneAnn Hodgeson: daughter of the Lord Chamberlain.

Maimie Mannering: daughter of the Lord High Treasurer.

And there's Nibs. He, the Twins, Slightly, and Tootles: royal wards of my parents.

Though not with us, Agnes and Elizabeth Thomas are sisters. Of course they are—daughters of the High Steward.

Hannah Ansel, she and Margaret were also sisters. Daughters of the Earl Marshal.

An ache swells in my chest, *Margaret*. The recollection that she was always my closest friend, cursed or not.

Her words resurface. *"You'll get out of here someday. I'm sure of it."*

"But how can you be?"

"Because I saw it. We were in pink..."

An image springs to mind. Margaret and I, young, facing one another in lush pink gowns, ready for our first ball.

She remembered. At the very end, she was reclaiming our lost past. My heart is fuller, knowing her world was wider, more vibrant before it was over.

"Let's get you inside." Kit pulls me from my thoughts, guiding me to my feet. "Things tend to get messy as the memories return."

"Okay." I agree.

Seven hollow trees encircle the great oak, each serving as a separate entrance to the underground home below. I follow the others, slipping through a narrow slit into one of the trunks, where a damp, earthy scent wraps around me.

It's surprisingly spacious, a tall cavern carved by time and decay. Perching above the opening in the ground, I release myself. Flashes of younger selves flicker past my vision, their screams trailing me as I descend deeper into the heart of the earth. Then, as though I'm flying, I burst through the narrow passage and hit the ground.

I rise slowly, taking in the spacious room nestled beneath a ceiling of thick, tangled roots. Along one wall stretches a long wooden table, where the ghosts of young children, dressed in earthen garb, bleed into reality. They look like wild animals—faces smudged with dirt, hair jutting in every direction, yet their smiles are grand, their voices loud, boisterous, and endearingly innocent. I shake my head to clear the vision; the memory more than I can bear.

At the center of the space, a blazing fire bathes everything in a soft, golden glow. Decorating the walls are spears, bows, and arrows, with skins of the beasts hunted long ago displayed nearby. In one corner, makeshift beds, crafted from leaves, sticks, and grass-woven blankets, complete the cozy atmosphere.

Kit wasn't wrong; the memories don't stop as they roll in like storm clouds on the horizon. *The summers we spent here as children, running through the forest, staging imaginary battles against pirates, water fights in Kidd Creek, and exhausted naps on sandy shores under the warm sunshine. These moments collide in my mind, vivid and colorful. We were together, immersed in the freedom of youth, and nothing could ever hold us back.*

❄ ❄ ❄

A dull ache presses against my forehead. I'm lying in bed while the others sit around the table, engrossed in a lively conversation. My gaze drifts to the ceiling, tracing the intricate, braided patterns of intertwined roots.

"You fainted," John says.

I tilt my head to where he sits, one leg propped over the other, book in hand.

"Was it something about this place?" He licks his finger and flips the page.

"All those summers spent here."

"Naturally. Maybe now you can appreciate why I reacted to Peter's painting the way I did."

"Why did he do it?"

"To wake you, of course. He wasn't supposed to, though. Kit woke him, then Nibs, followed by Jan and me. Before your engagement, we debated plans to get out. Like Kit flying us out, but Tahreek had Anathema watching for just that. We could have tried, but everyone agreed it was too big a risk. Were we to get caught, there's no telling what they would do. So, with your engagement looming, we agreed it was the safest plan. Peter and Jan disagreed. Both felt you deserved the truth about James."

"I understand why Nibs was so heated with him Christmas night."

"None of us expected you to regain a memory in the underground," he pauses as JaneAnn slips to my side, pressing a mug of tea into my hands.

"Sorry to interrupt," she says, "Kit wanted you to have this; he said it'll help the process."

"Thank you." I take a sip, it's sweet and mellow with the slightest bit of citrus.

Her face softens with a nod and she heads back to the table.

"Anyway," John continues, "I suppose he hoped with just enough pressure, the crack would break."

"Tell me about James. I don't yet remember what happened. Kit said our father was a king?"

"Yes. Father was Grand Duke to King Charles. And when the king's health failed, and no heir was named, the court followed Charles' wish, crowning Father as King of Neverland."

"Gosh..."

"Indeed. Thomas was a trusted friend, and this relationship led Father to appoint him as Chancellor. But he wasn't aware that Thomas was a royalist. In Thomas' view, Father stole the crown from Charles' rightful heir."

"But I thought Charles had no heir?"

"That was the story. Yet before taking the throne, Charles fell in love with a stage actress, Eleanor, also known as 'Nell' Gwyn. They had two children."

"Gwyn?" A memory stirs—Nibs whispering, *I love you, Morgan Gwyn.* I breathe in sharply. "Johnny... is Morgan the daughter of King Charles?"

He nods slowly. "And not just Morgan. She has a brother. Do you dare guess the lost prince Thomas destroyed everything to restore?"

I press a hand to my chest, the pieces locking into place. "You're not saying... James and Morgan were the King's children?"

A slow smile spreads across his face but before he can answer, Grace exclaims, "Time to eat!"

"Would you look at that, got to run," John says, rising.

"No wait." I push forward. "Do not walk away. Answer my question!"

He chuckles and joins the group gathering at the table. I shake my head. James and Morgan... royalty?

Then it hits me—they're not the only ones, are they?

I step out of bed and move toward the table, gazing at John and Michael. My brothers. Both princes. Kit flutters past and grows, settling at the head of the table. Also a prince.

Grace pats the spot beside her as I draw near, and sit. This new information hurts my brain. My family was royalty, but James was by blood.

"You okay?" Grace hands me a sandwich.

"You have no idea." I take a bite.

She swallows and shakes her head. "Consider this. I've just discovered that the man I thought I was in love with isn't who he who said he was. Then I find out he was one of the cursed. And then he tells me my best friend is actually the lost princess."

"Okay," I concede. "Maybe you do have an idea."

"Yeah, I really do."

John scooches to my side. "Well, you haven't keeled over yet, that's progress."

"I'm not happy with you." I purse my lips.

"Oh, come on." He laughs. "I moved here just to finish the story. Okay?"

"Fine. Continue."

He leans onto his elbows. "As the story goes, Eleanor married Thomas Blood, and he set out to restore James to the throne."

"Hang on, Blood?"

"Yes, like, '*Beware, Blood*'. The warning you saw underground, refers to Thomas. He and a group of renegade pixies, the Anathema, led by Prince Tahreek, sought the dust hidden in Winter Woods."

"The entrance to the underground village disappeared."

"Yeah, Kit did that. He had to ensure you didn't return and regain more memories."

I glance down at my hands. "Dare I ask... do you know anything about our parents' whereabouts?"

"Unfortunately, no." He taps a finger against the table. "Kit believes some officials may be held on an island near Silver Mist, but the Anathema have it surrounded. Like in Winter Woods, no one in or out except a select few."

"So, what happens next?" I pick at the sandwich, losing my appetite.

"Kit and Tiger Lily risked everything to rescue us. This is our kingdom. We either fight for it, or we best stay hidden."

"And Peter? You know I have to find him."

"He's living in Elphame. If you're able, we'll leave at first light."

"Carry me if you must, but I'm going."

He chuckles and rubs my back. "Then tomorrow, you'll see him."

By bedtime, everyone insists I take the bed, though I protest. Their reasoning isn't reassuring. According to them, I'm about to have a hell of a night, and I'll need all the comfort I can get.

Sinking into the pillow, I let my thoughts wander. Over the next few hours, I slip in and out of consciousness, memories washing over me, pulling me under, then releasing me. It's both wondrous and torture, each memory shifting reality.

Father's coronation springs to mind. The procession from the palace to the Grand Abbey. Citizens lined the streets, shouting, "God save the King!"

The ceremony comes alive: the Coronation Oath, the crimson robe, the holy oil, and the choir's ghostly song. The golden crown placed on his head. Me, elated—running into his arms, spinning through the air. The carriage ride back to the palace, John, Michael, and I waving to the sea of smiling faces that reached out to us. Flowers tossed, kisses blown, and heads bowed low with hats in hand. The day ended with fireworks lighting up our balcony while the citizens cheered below.

These memories leave me wistful. Others cut without mercy.

Recollections of James unravel me: *He was sweet and shy. We shared our hopes and dreams. Then Thomas attacked, and James swore he was sorry, vowed to protect me, and said he had a plan, and then stood by while the faerie broke my mind.*

Part of me is angry. Hurt. Betrayed. But another part still aches for him. Because I'm confident his love wasn't a lie.

Morning arrives, and I'm exhausted. My head throbs. I don't fully understand James, but after everything I've learned, it's clear he's torn. He isn't the person Thomas wants him to be.

And maybe... that makes him useful.

He must know what happened to my parents. Once I'm reunited with Peter, I need to find him. He owes me answers. If he truly loves me the way he claims, *he* might be the key to restoring Neverland.

As the day begins, everyone allows me to drift in and out without questions or expectations. We eat a cold breakfast of muffins Morgan sent along and apples picked from outside. It's not much, but it's enough. Kit insists we'll be dining at the Palace by evening.

The Faery Palace, to be exact.

The words sound strange. The world within Winter Woods appeared ordinary. Yet we were the odd ones.

Magic is real and not just in a storybook.

As we prepare to leave the Oak, I squint at Kit, fluttering nearby in his faerie form. Catching my eye, he approaches until we're face to face.

"Want to take a walk?" he asks.

"Why not."

He flits to the rope ladder, and I tail him, climbing until my head breaks through into open air. For a moment, I can't breathe. The sky above is brilliant blue, with birds soaring and singing as though this day is as ordinary as any other. The few clouds are wispy and not filled with thick snow ready to bury us beneath it.

"Come on!" Kit calls, flying towards the woods.

I pull myself through the opening and onto solid ground, relishing the tufts of grass brushing between my fingers. *Real* grass.

I stand and draw in a breath, sharp and crisp, but not frigid. It tastes of living things: the damp moss clinging to the bark of tall, willowing trees, the mushrooms nestling beneath their twisted roots, and wild-flowers—not cut and shipped in, nor sheltered in a greenhouse, but blooming freely along the path ahead.

This is magic.

I wander away from the old oak where Kit hovers, waiting at the edge of the wood. Entering together, it's exquisite. A butterfly flutters past—wings a vibrant orange and black. Bees hum busily around a cluster of blue bells, dipping in and out, busy with breakfast.

"I figure you must have some questions," Kit says, growing in size and resting against a tree.

"I do." I settle on a rock across from him. "So you can just shrink and fly around, or become human at will?"

"Yes. Though I'm not truly human, no matter the appearance I take. If anything, one might say *you* look Fae."

"Funny." My fingers tap restlessly against my knees. "But to fly, you have to be that way? Tiny and all?"

"Not exactly. It's a choice. When we fly, we're exerting more energy; it's easier to do in that size."

"This is a lot to take in. You're a faerie, some kind of dashing prince, and I'm a lost princess. Also, how could you possibly have given me your memory of finding Peter?"

"Quite simple really. I slipped in that night and passed the memory to you with a touch to your forehead."

"You were in my bedroom?"

"Funny, isn't it?"

"Oh, absolutely hysterical... And John said you hid the entrance to the underground Winter Woods. But tell me, how is it still so... alive?"

"Both versions of Winter Woods have magic in their veins. They don't die, unless destroyed."

A rustling along the path draws our attention as Tiger Lily glides toward us. "Am I interrupting?"

"No, please, join us," I say.

She sits by me on the rock and looks between us as I ask, "I'd really like to know how you both came to be in Winter Woods."

"My people have kept watch over Neverland for centuries," Kit answers. "We never got involved in human affairs, until your father came along. His service to King Charles caught our attention."

"What was the service?"

"Your family came from another world, far beyond the sea. The ship that brought you here was the *Jolly Roger*."

"James' ship?"

"Yes. He stole it after Thomas seized control. But before that, under your father, it was a bridge between two worlds. He ferried people and goods, modernizing Neverland."

"My father did all that?" I blink, absorbing the revelation.

"He did. But such a change doesn't go unnoticed. Travelers have always found their way to Neverland, but this—this was different."

"It's been five years since my father's kingdom fell. Why help now?"

"After the invasion of Winter Woods, Father learned from the pixie king, Gilberto, that his son Tahreek acted alone. The problem was, he was now cut off from something we call Aether Dew dust.

"This rare substance exists in three known places. A glade in pixie Parlour, an ancient cave under Elphame, and various locations within the Neverpeak Mountains. The dew crystallizes into luminous mineral veins, and the Fae and Pixies mine it."

"So, why did Tahreek leave home if he had access to the dust?"

"Tahreek craved black magic—*curses*. Gentleman Starkey's business focused on harvesting the dust for the Anathema. Father and Lord Malori prepared for war, but the elders forbade it."

"Not sure I like your elders much," I mutter.

"Father felt like you. It wasn't until years later when a scout overheard James express his plan to marry you, that Father decided to act. Though Neverland is one realm, it's divided among nations: the pixies, the fae, and the humans, including your Father's kingdom, and the Piccaninny. Father sent me to the Piccaninny Tribe for help, where I met Tiger Lily."

Tiger Lily nods, tone gentle. "My mother Lilium and brother Lean Wolf vanished with your family. We searched for years, but stopped after losing too many scouts. When Kit asked for help, Father refused him. The risk was too great.

"But you were my friend, so I joined him. We journeyed to Silver Mist, where he secured our work with James. Our first night in Winter Woods was the night Peter got hurt. I saw Juke drag him into the warehouse and sent Kit after him. And that was the beginning."

"Goodness," I say, astounded by the tangle of our lives. "Here I thought we were alone, but you were out here doing all this for us. Thank you."

"Our families were like kin." Tiger Lily places her hand over mine. "And there's nothing I wouldn't do for family."

The edges of my vision darken, another memory tugging me down like a current. "Here we go again," I mumble, swaying as I tumble forward.

We were two princesses, bound like sisters.

Her father, Chief Little Big Panther, was dear to mine. Her mother, Lilium, just as beloved by my mother.

Lean Wolf taught my brothers and me to track prey and let the arrow fly.

We came from different worlds, but were united by what mattered: family. Our families visited often, always with open hands and hearts.

The day of the curse, Lean Wolf and Lilium were visiting. I don't know what happened—only that I never saw them again.

When I come to, the world is sharper, more in focus. Tiger Lily watches me, expectant.

"Yes." I steady my breath. "It's all there again."

Relief brightens her face, and she pulls me into a tight embrace. The memories swirl around me, familiar, slipping back into place, one by one, where they've always belonged.

Chapter 23

We're on our way to Elphame—home of the faeries. By nightfall, I hope to be in Peter's embrace again, and yet, something nags at me. A seed of doubt tugging at my thoughts. Did I read too much into everything? Surely not... he wrote the lyrics and kissed me, *many, many times.*

Grace has a line perfectly encapsulating the confusion we feel with the opposite sex: "*Men...*"

I suppose they're not so different from us. We all have our ways, those maddening differences. Still, was I just a snog to satisfy Peter's sense of masculinity? A moment of warmth on a cold night? Am I assuming too much from the song lyrics?

We hike through Never Wood, a vast forest stretching from the edge of Winter Woods to the borders of Elphame. Like its underground twin, Elphame can't be accessed through normal means. It's hidden, accessible through a gateway that shrinks you to proper size—Fae or not. At the front, Kit leads the way with Tiger Lily at his side. Behind them, Michael and Maimie, John and JaneAnn, Grace and Henley, and finally Nibs and I trail the group.

We've walked for over an hour, and Nibs has barely spoken two words to me, so I eventually ask, "What's on your mind?"

"Nothing really," he says, stepping over roots jutting out from the ground in all directions.

"You thinking about Morgan?"

"I'm always thinking about Morgan."

For the first time, I understand him.

When Nibs told me how he knew he loved Morgan, I couldn't relate it to what I had with James. I didn't think about James constantly. I thought about what James could give me, what he could secure for my future.

Looking back, it's horribly shameful.

But with Peter... it's different. He rarely leaves my thoughts and with him, I have to be willing to let go of certainty, and place my faith in something real.

"You'll see her again," I say, gazing toward the Neverpeak Mountains. I can't see them, but they're there, same as always, and those we love are still within their borders, likely confused, feeling abandoned. My heart aches for them. "We both just have to have a little faith right now."

"You're right. But while you and I were trapped in that town, she could have left at any time. I worry James will harm her for helping us."

"He won't harm his own sister."

"You sure?" His voice sharpens. "Because he hurt the girl he supposedly loved. Why not his sister?"

A lump forms in my throat, because he's right. "I can't guarantee anything. But he spoke about her, and trust me, he loves her. He doesn't view himself as a villain; he sees his actions as necessary, for his family, for her."

"Yeah... maybe." He chews his lip. "But tell me, Kit said you were running away."

"Yes." I brush aside a branch, lime green buds growing along its edges. "For a long time, I planned to leave and find Peter as soon as I was out."

He exhales. "I'm sorry, kid. I knew how you both felt, and tried to suppress it. I feared your relationship would keep us all stuck in that town."

"If I'm honest, you weren't wrong. The day he left, I was ready to break things off with James and stay with him. Ironically enough, I made the same plan you did, use my wedding as an excuse to escape. But now that I'm on my way to Peter, I fear I may have read too much into everything."

"Nonsense. Why do you think he drank himself silly the night of your engagement?" He nudges my shoulder with a grin. "After you left, Jan and Peter insisted we bring you into the plan that night, but the rest of us thought it was too much pressure. And if it failed, we'd all be stuck."

"And people did see through me at the end. You were right."

"No, I wasn't. You did it. You convinced James and here we all are now. Because of you."

"Tell me, was it James who sent Peter away at the end?"

He glances at me, almost amused. "No. Peter left by choice. For you. He didn't intend to leave, but after your... visit that night. He felt he had no choice."

"But how could he just leave? It doesn't make sense."

He wraps an arm around me and draws me close. "Oh, you'll know soon enough."

We settle in for lunch beneath a canopy of chestnut trees, sunlight streaming through the glossy emerald leaves. I look around at my friends—safe, happy, and free. This is far beyond anything I ever dared hope for.

Grace rests on Henley's lap, enjoying a leftover sandwich. Kit and Tiger Lily sit high above on a thick branch, overlooking the forest. John stretches his arms wide, elation lighting his face as he shares some grand story, Michael clutches his stomach, laughing along. Nibs and I find a spot at the edge, enjoying the quiet.

Lifting the tiny Good Book from my pocket, I show it to Nibs and tell him about my conversation with Bea. Then I mention the night after Juke's attack, and how Morgan read it to comfort me.

"I never understood what she saw in me," he says, leaning back on his elbows. "Do you remember when we met her before all this?"

I think back, a flicker of Morgan in a small town, a street glowing with lights and dancing, and the way she gazed at Nibs as if he were the whole world. "Of course... odd to have forgotten."

"It's like, she chose me. She knew what was coming, and the only thing she could do was stay close, though I never knew it. Not till everything came back. I've been a fool for a long time; it's hard to feel worthy of her now."

"The night she read to me, it was all about people full of faith throughout history. And what struck me was how many failed, over and over. Yet one choice, one step of faith, and they were remembered for it. We both lost our way, but... maybe we give our past too much credit. You know? Maybe yesterday is powerless to control tomorrow, and what matters is who we choose to be today."

He gives me a long look, one eyebrow quirked. "What was *that*?"

"What's what?"

"I'm just not used to hearing you talk like this. You know, from mistress to James to... whatever this is. I'm going to have to get used to whoever you are today."

I grin and nudge my shoulder into his. "Yeah, me too..."

When we begin again, the group hums with anticipation, ready for our journey to come to an end. We hike until the trail grows wild and the forest dense. Soon, a familiar gateway emerges from the undergrowth, and Kit lifts a hand to halt us.

"Alright, friends, here we go. You're about to cross through what's been nick-named the *metamorphosis mist*. It'll allow you to cross into Elphame. It won't hurt, but may feel odd. Michael, want to lead the way?"

Michael nods eagerly and steps through the doorway, vanishing from sight.

Maimie lets out a startled scream, but Tiger Lily places a calming hand on her shoulder. "It's okay. Come on, we'll go together."

They step through and disappear as well. The rest of us follow, one after the other. It's just as it was with Peter in the cave. Goosebumps rise along my arms, light swirling around my fingers. The others hold out their hands, fascinated, laughter bubbling up. Then slipping my arm through Nibs', we exchange a knowing look and move forward.

When we reach the other side, we step out onto a ledge overlooking not an underground world, but a breathtaking, sunlit expanse. Rolling green hills stretch to the horizon, dotted with sparkling lakes and a waterfall cascading in the distance. Nearby, a palace rises in elegant grandeur, nestled beside a quaint village similar to the one in Winter Woods, but here, everything is bathed in rainbow sunlight.

"There's a stairway over here," Kit calls, floating ahead.

A rugged, wooden stairwell winds along the mountainside, and we glide down until our feet touch the valley floor.

"Welcome to Elphame, home of the Fae," Kit declares.

It's far more beautiful than anything I've ever seen. Before us lies a red brick road leading straight to the palace. I pause to breathe. Peter must be close now. My heart urges me to run, but I won't. I'll remain calm and composed.

Our walk winds through a charming village, where bustling shops echo murmurs of conversations, and a bakery spills the aroma of fresh bread and warm pastries. Pale stone paths stretch from the town's center toward quaint homes dotting the countryside, where winged figures flit to and fro about the day.

As we pass a sweet shop, its front windows display an array of colorful delights, and a group of Fae children with shimmering, iridescent wings flutter out, mouths dropping open at the sight of us.

"Hello there, kids," Kit chirps as he sails past.

A dusty brown-haired Fae boy zips away into the bakery, and soon a group of curious villagers fly outside, watching us, whispering to one another.

"They're not accustomed to wingless humans," Kit explains.

We continue, passing a schoolhouse and a library, smoke drifting from their chimneys leaving the faint scent of burnt oak and old ash in the air. We marvel at the sight of so many winged beings. It's hard to grasp, this entire world has existed all along, hidden from sight. As we approach the palace, the mahogany doors swing open, and a man emerges, long flowing blue robe, and golden hair curling around a crown.

"Kit!" he cries, flying toward us.

"Father!" Kit meets him midair, folding into his embrace.

"When the scouts said you were returning, I could barely believe it." Tears rim the King's eyes.

Turning to us, he extends a hand to me. "Welcome, dear. I'm King Clarion, and you are all most welcome in Elphame. My wife, Queen Florabelle, will be along shortly. For now, come inside—eat and share of your wonderous journey."

We follow him beneath an archway of wooden vines and onto white marble floors veined with silver and gold. The entryway is vast, flooded with pure light streaming through a glass ceiling high above. Enormous paintings stretch from floor to ceiling, their colors not shadowy or bold like those of Starkey Manor, but pale, and wispy. The home's grandeur is different from those in Neverpeak Hills—less austere, and somehow even more magnificent.

He leads us through a hallway lined with open windows, overlooking the nearby gardens. On the other side, we step into a circular chamber with a ceiling of woven branches, latticed like lace. A table carved from rosewood sits, piled high with a generous feast, its edges etched in delicate, swirling patterns.

"Please, take a seat and enjoy." The king pulls out a chair. "I'm sure you're all hungry after a long trek."

As we sit, my gaze wanders around the chamber. A thick, green vine snakes along the walls, dotted with pale bulbs gleaming softly. Beneath it hang woven tapestries, each capturing the four seasons in breathtaking detail—sparkling snow, spring's vibrant blossoms, summer's rich golden sun, and autumn's glorious blaze of crimson, amber, and honeyed leaves.

Though my younger self lived through all of these seasons, a split still lingers within me, where the knitting hasn't quite drawn together, and the seams of my two lives haven't yet pulled taut. The dominant part of me, the one who's spent a lifetime in endless winter, stares on in quiet awe.

Seated at the table's head, King Clarion beckons us to enjoy and eat to our heart's content. I reach for a piece of chicken from the tray in front of me and take a bite. The meat is tender and juicy, rich with buttery herbs. The others dig in too—stuffed mushrooms, thick slices of buttery bread with jam, hearty root stew, grilled fish glazed with fragrant oil, a bowl of wild grain rice. To wash it all down: sparkling berry wine—sweet and crisp.

For a moment, savoring each delectable bite, my mind quiets. I'm safe, and nothing else matters. Across the room, a woman enters, her light-yellow hair frames a gentle face, and a silver crown rests on her head.

"Ah, my dear." King Clarion rises to take her hand. "Your son has fulfilled his quest. These are the royal children of King George, and their companions."

Queen Florabelle hurries around the table to Kit, and he rises to meet her, flinging his arms around her neck. John and I share a look, a mutual hope to share a moment like this with our parents soon.

"Mother, I've missed you," Kit says, pulling back.

"You have no idea." She dabs at her cheeks with a handkerchief. "Your father can tell you how many nights I stared at the valley, praying for your return. When he told me the scouts brought word of your arrival, I screamed with delight.

"Oh, bless, look at you all." She beams at us. "What a delight to have you here. And know, should you desire a new home, look no further."

"Indeed," King Clarion agrees. "We understand there's no certainty about the future. But you are welcome in Elphame. When Peter arrived, he told us about the terrible things you endured. We decided then we would gladly make space for you here."

"Where is Peter?" I ask, gripping my goblet.

"He's at the lake with Tinker Bell," Queen Florabelle says. "They were always inseparable, so of course, at his return, she was over the moon."

Inseparable? Tinker Bell...I know her. She was with Peter when we met. Darkness creeps in, and I grip Nibs' arm. He turns to me, a crease forming between his eyes. "What's wrong?"

"It's happening again."

His hand glides around me, as the memory hits—intensity greater than any before.

He's different—unlike anyone I've ever met. His name is Peter Pan.

I lie on my back, hands tucked behind my head, while he floats high above me, legs crossed, playing his pan flute, lost in the song. He's clothed in green, leafy garments woven from the trees themselves. Wild and carefree, unlike the rest of us. Around me, the creatures hum along with him, birds chirping from branches, and insects clicking in rhythm along the forest floor.

"Come down from there, Peter," I call.

He flips around, folding his hands beneath his chin. "What'd you say, Bird?"

"I said, come here. I'm useless lying around."

"You useless?" He chortles. "No, Wendy. You are more useful than Slightly, Tootles, and the Twins combined!"

He's slender and wiry as he swoops down, lifting me into his arms, and shooting skyward, past the tree tops, above the clouds. I cling to him tightly; yet there's no fear. He's my wings, and in his arms, I'm unafraid.

* * *

Peter can fly.

I wake on a silver chaise, facing an open balcony where sheer curtains flutter in the breeze. My head aches. The memory of Peter and me flying together is more than I can handle. I press my fingers to my temple and exhale.

What other hidden secrets have yet to surface?

"Oh, good, you're awake!" John glides in, berry wine sloshing in his goblet.

"We need to talk." I push myself upright. "Come sit."

"Sure..." He plops down beside me, wine splashing onto his clothes. "Whoops." He chuckles, dabbing the liquid with his sleeve.

"I'm glad to see you so happy."

"Aren't you?" He gestures grandly toward the balcony, sending more wine over the rim. "This place is heaven, and we've been let in."

"Johnny, it's incredible here, yes. But look." I guide his face to mine. "Were you aware Peter could fly?"

"Yeah, of course. Did you just remember that?"

I sink back into the cushions. "Yeah... I didn't know till now. Why didn't you tell me?"

He lifts a shoulder and sips from the goblet. "It's not my place to interrupt your journey. Though I shared some things yesterday, I find it better to learn on your terms." He leans in. "So, what was the memory?"

"He was floating in the air, carefree, playing his pan flute. I called to him, and he swooped over and flew me into the sky. It was amazing. But how's that possible? How can he fly?"

"Hmm." He licks his lips. "I think that's a conversation you need to have with him yourself."

My lids lower. "You know, though, don't you?"

He rises, shaking his head with a grin. "I won't say a word. Go find him. Ask him yourself." He turns to the door. "See you, sis."

I watch him vanish through the doorway, my pulse quickening. Why does this feel so much like James? The man I thought I knew is suddenly a mystery. I only pray Tinker Bell isn't more than a friend.

Pressing forward, I take shaky steps into the hallway. Pale stone walls glow softly, light spilling from veiled crevices to reveal statues of Fae—some adults, some children. In other alcoves, gemstones glisten, lit from beneath, casting rich hues of violet, teal, and magenta. I lean close to examine one of the stones when the sound of my friends reaches my ears. I turn and follow it until an open door appears, and there they are.

I enter the room, where Maimie hops onto a plush bed, stretching out contentedly, and Tiger Lily leans against the balcony door, staring out at the scenery. JaneAnn and Grace huddle beside a line of dresses hung against the wall, pressing the material between their fingers, chatting quietly.

The room has a gentle curve, with five beds arranged along the circular wall, each draped in lush lavender comforters and piled high with frilly pillows. At the center of the room, a pale round table holds a silver tray of fruits, nuts, and chocolates, with an enormous bouquet of sunflowers beside it. The walls are painted in the same dusty purple, with delicate white trim edging the ceiling, a quiet echo of the snowflakes we came to know so well in Winter Woods.

"Wendy." JaneAnn strides to my side. "You're awake! Come in, look at this room. It's ours, at least while we're here."

"And how long will that be for?" I ask.

"As long as we need." Tiger Lily inclines her head to me.

"How about we get refreshed and *you* go find your man." Grace lifts a dusky periwinkle gown off the rack and holds it out to me.

I step closer, taking it into my hands. My fingers trail over the golden ivy rising from the waist, curving along the bodice before fading into the low-cut, off-the-shoulder neckline. Sheer fabric waterfalls loosely down the arms, and the skirt shimmers with layers of soft, flowing tulle, cascading into a pool at the hem.

"He doesn't even know I'm here yet," I say, staring out the window. "What's to say he'll even care?"

"You're kidding me, right?" Grace shakes her head. "Of course he'll be glad to see you. He's mad about you!"

"Is he? Well then, who's this *Tinker Bell* the queen mentioned? *Inseparable*, she said." I plop onto the bed, clutching the dress to my chest.

"Don't worry." JaneAnn settles beside me. "She's probably just a friend."

"I don't know about that. She's in my first memory of meeting him."

"So? Look, you're overthinking this." She places a hand on my lap. "I get it. You've been under a lot of pressure these past months."

"I'm not crazy, if that's what you're implying."

I purse my lips and rise, walking to where Tiger Lily stands at the balcony door. The view is glorious. Rolling green hills, the waterfall plunging in the distance, mist rising like smoke from the valley below. Storybook cottages are scattered across the landscape, so many that they seem to litter the land as far as the eye can see.

"She doesn't think you're crazy," Tiger Lily says quietly. "Only—we've all been holding onto secrets. And maybe now's the time for all of us to rest, reset... and let go."

"Yeah, and you've all certainly held secrets, haven't you?" I glance around at their faces, all uneasy. I cross my arms, a sigh slipping out as I suddenly feel like a petulant child. "Don't mind me. I'm just overwhelmed. Does anyone mind if I take a bath?"

"Not at all." Tiger Lily says. "Go on."

I head to the bathroom attached to our quarters. A large porcelain tub waits inside—empty, but beckoning. I slip out of my blue dress, stained with mud from the hike. Our group was too large for the car, and there were concerns about driving on the road. So, my trunks were stashed in the treehouse, and I swapped my wedding dress for this simpler one.

Perched on the edge of the tub, I spin the handle until hot water streams out. Once filled, I press in, no longer anxious, no longer holding my breath. Soaking in the rose water, my body floats weightless, and I blow bubbles off my hand.

Peter can fly.

My memories seem jumbled. There are recollections of Peter being a ward of King Charlie when my family arrived. However, that doesn't make sense in light of what I saw in the river. This memory is different. We met Peter, and then, while serving at the local Children's Home with our mother, we met Nibs, Slightly, Tootles, and the Twins.

Mother insisted they come home with us, and Father made them royal wards alongside Peter. Before long, we were a rowdy tribe, painting our faces like warriors, roaming the countryside, Peter flying ahead, crowing as he beat his chest.

The darkness doesn't close in this time. No. The memories settle in, like a story before bed. I loved those boys, all of them. For a long time, I was the only girl, and they honored me for it.

Childhood was a treasure.

It dawns on me. I'm doing something I never believed possible: *remembering.* I envied James' ability to tell of his childhood, yet here I am. So many moments once locked away, now trickling out.

The fury my younger self carried is melting, softened by who I've become. I thought I was nothing all these years—an empty shell, picked clean. But now, it's as though the girl I was and the woman I've become have found peace together. And truly, nothing feels more right, more whole, than knowing exactly who I am.

I am Wendy Moira Angela Darling.
Daughter of King George and Queen Mary.
Sister to John and Michael.
Friend to many...and hopeful lover to one.

Chapter 24

JaneAnn moves beside me, dazzling in an emerald-and-silver lace gown, its cinched waist hugging with each graceful step. A crown of baby rosebuds rests atop her silky black hair, like flecks of starlight scattered across the night sky.

We stroll down the moonlit steps of a spiral stairwell, descending toward the palace's banquet hall, where an ethereal tune drifts through the air. A cool breeze sweeps in from an open window as we pass, refreshing against my skin, still warm from the bath. I'm clothed in the dusty periwinkle gown Grace offered, and I carry an unspoken suspicion that Fae clothing molds to the wearer, as the fabric slipped on as though it remembered me.

Heavy timber doors, veiled in ivy, stand ajar as we approach and step through. Candlelight flickers softly across our faces, casting gentle shadows. Moss-covered stone walls enclose the room, with roots curling up from the ground. It's like entering an enchanted forest, the floor wonderfully smooth beneath us, glimmering like a starlit lake.

Rosy lanterns dangle from the ceiling, entwined with flowering vines. Below, a polished stone table glints with streaked crystal, heaped full of silver dishes piled high with every imaginable delight: roasted meats, steaming vegetable stews, sugar-berry jams, and dark breads slathered with melted cheeses and herbs. Bowls of spiced wine and cider remain mysteriously full, even as countless guests dip their goblets, filling them to the brim.

An orchestra of Fae gathers in the corner, robed in shimmering, flowing garments. They play golden harps, silver flutes, delicate lyres, and drums crafted from the earth. Other Fae dance together in slow, graceful circles, their arms linked, and their long hair drifting behind them like silk caught in a breeze. I catch sight of Grace and Henley among them, her face beaming with delight.

Gathered around an aged wooden table, enjoying plates piled with food, are Nibs, John, Michael, Maimie, and Kit. They're lively, laughing, and conversing loudly, a bit out of place amongst this quiet group of Fae, but altogether heartwarming to witness.

Tiger Lily glides across the floor, waves to us, and takes a seat beside Kit. She's wrapped in a long, flowing white gown sprinkled with delicate purple flowers. The boys, too, are dressed up with loose, cream-colored pants and shirts; they look almost civilized, but the mischief in their eyes gives them away.

"Can you believe this?" JaneAnn asks.

"No. I'm certain this is all a dream and we're sure to wake soon."

My palms tap against my side as I gaze around, searching.

Where is he?

"Are you hungry?" she asks.

I exhale—no sign of him anywhere. *I don't understand.*

"Hello?" JaneAnn nudges me. "Where have you gone?"

"Sorry. I thought I might see him here."

"Oh. I see. Hey, it's okay." She tugs me close. "He's sure to show up soon."

"Yes, I'd imagine so. Go on, join everyone. I'm going to get some air."

"You sure? I can stay with you."

"No. I'll be back."

I slip past her and make my way toward an archway opening to the night. The sounds of the hall fade behind me as I step onto a shadowy balcony, where a cool breeze washes over me, refreshing but not cold. Below, the village lies bathed in moonlight, the Fae with their wings, twinkle like the fireflies that once danced through the palace garden when I was child.

Stars gleam high above, and then one shoots across the sky, followed by another.

But no... they're not stars. They're people! Two figures, silhouetted by the moon. They drift through the air, and for some reason, I'm confident it's them.

Their echoes of laughter draw near, and I glance down. I'm directly beneath a shaft of light pouring from a window above. My heart races—I don't want to be seen. I slip into a corner, cloaked in shadows, my fingers finding the golden bracelet on my wrist. Something grips my chest; this is my mother's, a gift passed down from hers. I never took it off. Even after the curse, I couldn't let it go.

"I can't believe you pushed me," Peter's voice drifts closer, the familiar tone sending a shiver through me.

He's really here!

"Oh, darling, you are funny," replies a sultry voice. A woman. *Tinker Bell.*

They float onto the balcony, Peter touching down with ease, guiding Tinker Bell to her feet. She's stunning—dressed in a short, leafy green dress that hugs her curves. Her golden hair is swept into a bun, and her eyes are vibrant like a clear blue sky.

"Looks like there's a party going on," Peter says, smoothing his clothes, the same forest green from my memory. "Wonder what's up."

"Who knows? We skipped breakfast, so we probably missed the invitation. But I don't care, today was worth it."

Something twists in my gut. There's a look in her eyes as she gazes at him.

"That cliff was pretty high. Not sure I agree," he answers.

She laughs, shoving him lightly. "You could've stopped yourself. It was a choice to free-fall."

"Sometimes it's fun to remember being a plain old human." He runs a hand through his hair, and *oh*, how I ache to cross the space between us, to throw myself into him. "No flying, Just plummeting to your imminent doom."

"Well." She glances to the hall. "Shall we go and join the party? I smell roasted duck."

"Certainly. Lead the way." He gestures with mock grandeur.

She moves beneath the archway, and he's about to follow when the bracelet slips from my hand and hits the floor.

Clink!

He freezes and turns, eyes scanning the shadows. Though the darkness conceals me, he walks over and crouches, lifting the bracelet into a beam of moonlight. For a long moment, he stares at it, then gradually his expression softens as his hand drifts into the shadows, fingers closing around my leg—cool and firm.

I tremble, back pressed against the railing, hands gripping it tightly, as his fingers explore upward, tenderly caressing my skin with a lingering squeeze.

"Heaven help me," he whispers, rising slowly, fingertips brushing my arms, curling around my neck. "Dammit, Bird, you don't understand how I've missed you!" His mouth presses to mine, possessive yet gentle, and something inside me melts.

He guides me backward into the light, eyes widening as the shadows lift.

"Hi Peter."

"The night you got engaged to James was bloody painful." His voice is tight. "But nothing compared to leaving you behind."

"I loved you then." I glide my finger along his jaw. "But now, even more..."

He releases a faint chuckle. "In case there's any doubt, there's not one single soul I'd rather spend my life with than you. I love you, Wendy. And it took everything in me not to say it aloud every second my lips touched yours."

"There's no doubt." I wrap my arms around his neck, and as our lips meet, the sensation is like a dream come true after months of longing. Our bodies press together—explosions of heat in my chest.

"Come with me," he murmurs.

"To where?"

"You'll see." He lifts me effortlessly, arms tight as we shoot skyward into the glittering night.

I hold him close, hiding against his chest, the world flashing by in a blur until we settle at the top of the waterfall, my feet touching the ground gratefully. The wind whips through my hair, not harsh, but temperate, and he watches me, radiant, as he guides me to a soft bed of grass, pressing me down against the cool earth. The stars dot the sky brightly above him, and yet his face glows brighter.

"I couldn't share you yet." He leans in, brushing his lips over mine, thumb tracing my cheek. Energy pulses through me as his mouth trails down my chin, onto my neck.

"Will you be mine, love?" he asks, a light smirk touching the corner of his mouth.

"Yours, and yours alone," I whisper, nuzzling his nose.

He grabs me with a grin, flips me, and cradles me in the crook of his arm. I walk my fingers across his chest, tugging at the strings of his shirt, loosening them, before I press my palm to his heart—pounding like a drumbeat beneath my hand.

I look into his face, and our mouths meet again, the rush euphoric. He's oxygen to my lungs, and I breathe him in like I've been suffocating for years. Like two pieces of a puzzle, there's something in him that perfectly matches me, and I can't tear myself away.

I don't want to.

I'd stay pressed to him forever as the world turns, through sunrises and sunsets, thunderclaps, and rainstorms. There's a sense, pure and true, that a lifetime of longing has been bottled up inside me. And I haven't known belonging like this. So here, in his arms, there's no question, no hesitation. *I'm home.*

He rolls onto his side, gazing at me as he lifts my arm, his lips trailing along it. "I love you," he murmurs.

He takes my other arm, kissing tenderly down my wrist. "I love you," he repeats. Guiding our hands together, he presses his mouth to the tips of each of my fingers, his eyes never leaving mine. "I love you," he breathes after each one.

Then, holding my other hand to his chest, he whispers, "It beats for you." Leaning in, our noses brush and he adds, "Have I told you, I love you?"

I laugh, my neck burning, and he lies beside me, one leg draped over mine, stroking my hair.

After a long silence, I whisper, "You can fly..."

"Is that okay?" he asks, hand stilling.

"Of course. But how can you do it?"

He exhales heavily. "I don't exactly know how it happened."

"How's that possible?" I push up.

His face grows somber. "I was six years old. And, much like what happened in the Children's Home, I woke with no memory of who I was. Tinker Bell found me and helped me recover.

"We spent years together, traveling the world, living in Elphame. It's said that when a faerie gives up their essence, it grants the human certain abilities. That's the only logical explanation for how I can fly. But who gave it—and why—I still don't know."

"Once is enough, but twice?" I shake my head. "It's downright cruel! Did you ever ask King Clarion about it?"

"There was no need. Tink did her best to find out what happened, but found no answers. I accepted my fate and made the best of things. But look, you don't owe me anything. I wish I could have told you this long ago, but I was forbidden. If you want to walk away, I'll understand."

"No!" I exclaim, louder than I mean to. "You're mad if you think I'm leaving."

He beams, and I lean forward, folding into him as he wraps his arms around me, holding tight. "I'm yours," I say, "and that's never changing. But tell me, being part Fae, what else can I expect?"

"A Fae's aging slows at some point in adulthood. They remain youthful for a long time. Lifetimes, really. My love, nothing about me will be normal. But I'll never send you away. Still, you must know what you're getting into. I'm not fully Fae, nor am I rightly human anymore."

"And I don't care. Whatever you are, I'll be with you till my final breath."

His brows draw together. "That better not be for a long, long time."

"You think I'm going to run away, but you're the one who will be young and handsome while I grow old and gray. Are you certain you want that? I fear I'll quickly hold you back."

"You're beautiful, but it's not about that. Who you are inside doesn't change. So, though my body may not, my heart will grow old with you."

I grin up at him. "I love you. Now, I could ask a million more questions, but I've barely eaten today. Can we go back? I'm starving."

"Only if I can stare dreamily at you while you do."

"Deal."

He scoops me up, and we're back in the air before I know it, soaring toward the palace.

"Everyone knows I'm madly in love with you," I say into his ear.

"Do they now? Well, then, they won't be shocked when I kiss you all night. Because now that I've begun, I don't think I can stop."

"My brothers might have something to say about it, but I don't mind."

"Oh, right, bother it. Forgot you have brothers. Guess we'll have to sneak off while no one's looking."

"I like the sound of that."

We land on the balcony, and he releases me. "Before I forget." He pulls the bracelet from his pocket and clasps it around my wrist. "Perfect."

He holds out a hand, and I take it, our fingers intertwining. We enter the banquet hall, and our friends all turn toward us. Peter offers a half-wave, then cups my face, bending me backward, kissing. They erupt with playful cheers, causing the Fae to look on in confusion. I'm red-faced as he pulls away, wrinkling his nose sweetly.

"Just the once," he says.

Then I see her—Tinker Bell. Watching us. Her lids low. A chill creeps through me.

She's not going to make this easy for us.

Chapter 25

Sunshine is glorious. I relish its warmth, spilling across my bed. The smile fixed on my face has been there since last night, and I doubt it's going anywhere.

I throw off my blankets and stand, arms stretched wide.

I'm in love and I don't care who knows it!

Grace sits up in her bed, rubbing the sleep from her eyes. "Glad to see you so happy again."

"I don't know what you're talking about." I purse my lips, staring at the ceiling.

"She's talking about you and Peter wrapped around each other all night long!" Maimie calls from the table.

"Oh, that." I giggle. "Though my life lengthens by the day, I don't think I've ever been this happy before."

"I understand the feeling well," Grace says. "There's having a crush and then there's being foolishly in love. Welcome to the club. It's divine, isn't it?"

"I'm never leaving." I wink and hop from bed, wandering to the table where Maimie and Tiger Lily drink tea and eat glazed tarts.

"What about you, Lil?" I grip her shoulders. "Are you in the club too?"

She sips her tea. "And who would I be in the club with?"

"Golly, you're all slow this morning!" Maimie exclaims. "Kit, obviously."

Tiger Lily lifts an arm, indifferent, "Have any of you noticed there are a few key differences between the two of us. One being he's Fae and I'm a human."

"And Peter's half-Fae or something. But we're going to make it work." I walk to the dress rack, lift a silvery-blue one off, and hold it against my body.

"Has he shown any interest beyond the dance? Oh, and being around you every spare moment he can." Grace teases.

"He wants me to stay with him," Tiger Lily says, her jaw set.

I lift the nightgown over my head. "And?"

"My father lost my mother and brother," she replies. "How could I abandon him, too?"

JaneAnn steps out of the bathroom, robed, with a towel wrapped around her head. "When Wendy was muddled by guilt and ready to sacrifice everything for us, I had to remind her if someone loves you, they want you to pursue what you want too."

"Yeah," I add, fixing the day dress around myself. "John would say, if I denied my heart's desire for him, how could he be happy knowing that? If you walk away from Kit, someday, your father will know what you gave up. And then how will he feel?"

Tiger Lily breathes in slowly. "You're both right. But it's easier said than done."

I squeeze her hand. "Give it time, an answer often appears when you least expect it."

"With that said." Tiger Lily's eyes gleam. "I second Grace's sentiment. Seeing you and Peter last night, after everything that's happened, it was a needed win."

"Speaking of which, I think I'll go and find my dreamboat." I twirl and press my chin to my shoulder, posing.

JaneAnn pushes me to the door, laughing. "Go on, love bug."

I blow kisses and slip away. As I approach the stairwell, a voice calls behind me. "Someone's cheerful this morning."

I tilt my head back as Henley jogs to my side, smirking.

"Good morning, old boy," I say. "Settling in alright?"

He bumps his arm against mine. "I'm certainly comfortable. Never stayed in a palace before. But who knows, this might be home now. Wouldn't that be something."

"What about your family? They're still in Winter Woods."

We slip down the stairwell and head toward the dining room.

"Yeah." He frowns, head bobbing. "I left quite the note. Hopefully they'll understand. But Grace and I decided together. We could stay behind and wish you luck, but in the end, we figured you weren't about to have all the fun without us."

We step into the dining area, sunlight streaming through the lattice ceiling above.

"I'm glad you both did." I pluck a strawberry from the sideboard and bite down. "Still can't believe I was about to run off into the forest on my own."

He tosses an apple into the air and catches it, taking a bite. "Me neither. What were you intending to do for food, or shelter, or well, anything? Goodness girl. Please ask for help next time."

I giggle, shaking my head at myself. I'd read survival books, yes, but they were for frozen tundras, not this. "Is it silly to say I had a whole lot of faith?"

"Ridiculous. You also have a whole lot of friends, who would have happily helped—had we not already had a plan, of course."

"And what about your plan." I lean against the table. "When exactly did you learn the truth about me and the others?"

"The night Peter and I worked things out. He told me everything. It was torture not spilling the beans every time we talked."

"Well, I suppose we both kept secrets. But let's agree here and now, no more." I hold out my pinky.

He hooks his around mine. "No more secrets. Pinky promise."

A red-headed faerie flies in, setting down a tray of steaming sausages and bacon.

"I'd best go find Peter," I say.

"And I'd best get a pile of bacon before your brothers come down and eat it all." He grabs a plate and piles it with meat, pastries, and fruit.

I ask the faerie where Peter is, and she tells me he's working in the fields. I thank her and follow the directions she gives.

Wandering along a dirt path, I take in the golden wheat swaying in the breeze under a bright, clear sky. Up ahead, a group of workers cut the tall stacks, and one of them is Peter.

He's shirtless, sweat glistening on his chest, muscles flexing with every swipe of the machete. I pause to admire him, but he spots me and grins, rubbing his forehead with a handkerchief.

I approach, avoiding the others, and call out, "Good morning!"

"Indeed," he replies, gaze soft. "It's a splendid morning, isn't it?"

"Agreed." Heat surges through me. "Are you ready for some break-fast?"

"With you? Absolutely. Give me a minute to put away my stuff, and I'll join you."

He strolls back to the field, and I watch him wistfully, ready to tackle him with kisses.

"You understand this infatuation is temporary, don't you?" Tinker Bell flutters to my side, her voice low and laced with disdain.

"Is it really?" I glare at her out of the corner of my eye. "Well, I guess I'd better value every moment we get, huh?"

She tilts her head, eyes narrowed. "He's part Fae, he doesn't belong with your type."

I suck my teeth. "I'm not in a competition with you. You may have been with him at the beginning, but I'll be there at the end. And I'm not afraid of losing what we've built."

"I'm being kind—offering a bit of fair warning." Her tone remains cool. "Understand this. While you live a brief human existence, he and I will be together long after you've turned to ash."

Peter walks toward us, his lips pressed tight as his gaze moves between the two of us. "Ladies." He takes my hand.

"Enjoy your day," Tinker Bell chirps sweetly, then takes flight.

Good riddance.

"You look beautiful." He kisses my cheek. "Did you both have a nice talk?"

"Lovely chat. What a charming faerie. So, do you often work with the Fae?" I ask, attempting to clear away Tinker Bell's damning words.

"I do, ever since I arrived. I couldn't bear to sit around moping, so Marin handed me a machete and said 'Get to work'. A man needs to sweat a little, feel accomplished, you know?"

"Oh yeah... I can't go to sleep at night until I've sweated just a bit."

"Well, I can certainly help you with that." He licks his lips, snapping playfully at my waist.

"Stop it!" I laugh, hopping away—but he catches my arm, pulling me in and kissing with an unrestrained hunger. He's all heat, and I'm dissolving into his embrace when a voice calls out.

"You two *really* need to get a room."

We pull apart. Peter's hand still cups my chin. It's Kit, swooping toward us.

"And you *really* need to avert your gaze." Peter takes my hand and guides me to the palace. We enter together and join the others seated around the long white table.

"Good morning," King Clarion greets.

"Good morning!" I glide into the seat beside Michael, Peter's hand still holding tightly to mine.

"Hey sis." Michael hugs me. "Isn't this great?"

"It sure is. Did you have fun last night?"

"I did, but," he leans closer, whispering, "Do you think we'll get to see Mother and Father soon?"

My heart sinks, and I glance at Peter, who's listening in, and he forces an encouraging smile.

"I sure hope so, Michael," I say. "Our job is to keep the faith, because they're out there somewhere—I can feel it."

"Me too." He beams and takes a bite of toast. "I spent a lot of time at the Chapel after the curse broke. It felt safe there, and I would just pray and pray for them...and for you."

The thought of Michael, grown and carrying such strength, touches me. "Thank you for that, truly. And look, one prayer answered. So let's hope for the best."

"You know I am."

While we enjoy a scrumptious breakfast, a plan forms to hike to the lake and spend the day lounging lazily in the sunshine. After the chaos of the past few days, this is a needed break.

When the meal ends, we separate to our rooms, change, and head outside. Walking along the dirt path as a group, we stroll past the wheat fields, and toward the waterfall. A line of Fae staff flies ahead, carrying large packs of gear and food at Queen Florabelle's request.

At the lake's edge, the staff flit about, setting up silk canopies that catch the sunlight as they flutter in the breeze. Blankets are spread across the lush grass, layered with embroidered cushions and trays of fruits, nuts, and cheeses. A small table stands to the side, holding pitchers of iced heather blossom and linden flower tea, alongside lavender lemonade.

The boys run straight for the water, tossing off their shirts and diving into the sapphire-blue lake. When they resurface, they splash us, laughing, until we flee to the canopy, collapsing onto the blankets, hands on our chests, breathless and giggling.

"This is heaven." Grace sighs.

"And to think we've been dreaming about this for years." I clutch her hand.

"Dreams do come true, don't they?" She gives mine a squeeze.

"So, with Wendy's memory returned, can we finally talk about life before Winter Woods?" Maimie asks, lying on her stomach.

"She's been dying to talk about it," JaneAnn adds. "I'm truly shocked she never gave the whole plan away."

"Mams did great," I say. "I never suspected a thing."

And so, we talk—not about the weights and worries, but as girls, as friends. We share our pasts and the quiet secrets in our hearts, most of it whispered, the kind of things we'd never want the boys to overhear.

When the boys finally climb out of the water, they join us with mischievous grins. Henley is the first to sneak up on Grace, her lids shut, and he slides his wet body over hers, ignoring her fierce screams of protest. The more she shoves, the more he kisses and sniggers until she surrenders to his embrace.

John unwisely shimmies beside JaneAnn, but she's up in a flash, chasing him back into the lake, where she dives after him, dunking his head under the water. Kit wraps his arms around Tiger Lily, whispering into her ear while she blushes.

Peter doesn't tackle me. No, he leans over my head, fingers gliding down my nose as I stare up at him, droplets of water dripping off his hair.

"Hey, you..." he says.

"You look scrumptious," I whisper, reaching around his head and kissing his upside-down lips—smooth and wet.

Tilting my head, I notice Nibs reclining alone beside the lake, staring at the waterfall. "He's breaking my heart," I say.

Peter looks over and nods. "Yeah. I know how he feels."

"Want to try to cheer him with me?"

"Why not?" He helps me up, and we saunter over, sitting on either side of Nibs.

"What are you thinking about?" I rest my head against his arm.

"How much I miss the snow."

"Oh yeah, me too," I say. "Give me a frozen creek any day. I do so well with those."

"Not funny." Peter shakes his head.

"It was a little funny," Nibs offers. "So, here we are. Nighttime escapades in the frozen hellscape, exploring underground towns, and now reclining beside waterfalls, baking in the heat..."

"And we're not done yet," I say. "She'll be with us soon enough."

"Oh, don't start worrying about me, kid. I'm okay. I accept this, though you might see me moping around, kicking dirt."

"Just know you're not alone," Peter says. "Seriously. We're here for you, mushy hugs and tears and all."

Nibs chuckles. "I've never doubted either of your friendships." Standing, he pats our heads. "Look at you—finally together. Stop worrying about ole Nibs. You two go kiss or something. I'm off to try whatever that flowery tea is. Perhaps it's got a magical Fae ingredient to lift my spirits."

Alone again, Peter shifts closer. "So, I'm sorry. I haven't even asked you how your transition's going."

"Surprisingly well. The first day was constant, but it's slowed down. My dreams feel like mirrors to the past, moments sorting themselves out. But there's something I keep wondering, something that doesn't make sense."

"And what's that?"

"When did you and I meet?"

"We met when you came to the palace with your family."

"Wrong. We met *twice*: once at my home, and again at the palace. When I nearly drowned, I had a vision—you and Tinker Bell at my bedside, I was just a child."

"How odd..." He rubs his chin. "What do you remember about her?"

"Nothing else. Only the brief memory." I stare at him, unease curling in my chest. "Peter... why did we meet twice? You weren't younger than six the first time, so it can't be that you forgot."

"I don't know. But I spoke to Tink about you, and she acted like she didn't know who you were."

"She... Well, I don't think she likes me very much. I sensed it right away."

"Oh, no." He wraps an arm around me. "Who couldn't help but love you?"

"She told me that when I die, you and she will remain. *Together*. Do you consider that polite conversation?"

"You must have misunderstood her. Or misread her intentions."

"You think I assumed the worst about her? Is that it?" My tone betrays my agitation, yet he doesn't seem to notice.

"She and I have been close since my first memories." He lifts a stone and tosses it into the water, where it skips across the surface, a line of ripples in its wake. "I trust her, completely." He glides a finger along my chin. "And so should you."

"I would've said the same about James, once."

"It's different. She was my closest companion. Kept me going when I had nothing."

"Sounds familiar. The day I woke in the Home, I thought I was meeting James for the first time. But time and memory have shown otherwise. I can't assume why Tinker Bell would lie, but I suspect she knows more than she lets on. What happened, anyway? Why did you leave her?"

He thinks for a moment. "A couple of years passed, and I met Charlie at sea. He took to me, and I to him. He invited me back to the palace, made me a ward. Looking back, I believe he was just missing his son, and I helped fill the void. Look—I've accepted things as they are. I wish you would, too. There's no need to dig up the past. Let it rest."

"I can't accept that." I shake my head. "Two separate meetings, and you don't remember one? And Tinker Bell, who *was* there, pretends she's never seen me? Something's not right. And I'm not willing to let the past sleep."

I rise and slip away before he can stop me, rejoining the group lounging on blankets, sipping tea, and nibbling on snacks. Settling between Jan and John, I stare into my lap as stories are passed around. Eventually, Peter returns and sits across from me, eyes narrowed in thought, squinting my way. When someone suggests a swim, the group rises one by one, wandering to the lake and diving in.

"I'm sorry," Peter says.

"For what? You're defending what you believe." I keep my eyes set on the waterfall.

"Can you blame me?" He scoots to my side. "But your smile is gone, and I'm the one who took it. What can I say to bring it back?"

I meet his gaze. "Let me speak with King Clarion. Kit broke the curse that kept our memories hidden. Maybe there's a reason for this puzzle in my mind. And maybe there's more to your past than you've learned."

"Okay. If it'll set your heart at ease."

"Maybe I'm wrong. If so, I'll accept it. And avoid your feisty friend at all costs."

He takes my hands, guiding me to my feet. "This one time, and this one time only, you are wrong. There's nothing to dig up. But I swear, all the other times, you are perfectly and justifiably right."

We walk to the water, but as we near, I hover at the edge, a prickle of fear tightening in my chest—reminders of the darkness and cold as I suffocated beneath the ice. I glance at the waterfall, mist rising into a rainbow. A few vanish behind it, diving in and out like fish.

"It's okay," Peter says. "Take your time. Or we don't have to swim at all."

"No. This is my challenge to face." I swallow hard. "Look at Grace and Henley, they're not controlled by fear."

He holds me close. "The last time I saw you before all this was the day after the accident. You shook like a leaf in my arms, and even though I held you close, I longed for you in a way I'd never before."

We step into the water, and it climbs along our bodies.

"When did you first know you loved me?" I ask, seeking a distraction from the tension filling me as water inches higher.

"Would you scoff at me if I said always?"

I look at him, a soft innocence in his gaze. "No, I wouldn't."

"I was drawn to you from the moment you arrived at the palace with your family. I didn't understand love, not the way I do now. But I wanted to be around you, close to you... know you. And when we woke up in the Home, after the curse, that feeling lingered. But everything was different then. There was a smallness about me I had to overcome. And you were so taken with James, I knew it was hopeless."

"I'm sorry," I murmur, as the water laps at my waist and he floats me forward, cradling me in his lap. "I did what seemed right at the time. Though I see now I was very much mistaken."

"We all behaved instinctively during these years. It's all we knew. I'll confess, it was I who broke your kiss with James that night. Nearly broke my knuckles on the railing."

"I suspected as much... but never for such a reason. Thought you just liked driving me crazy. And to be fair, when I saw you and Grace in the alleyway, I felt the same."

He exhales against my skin, pressing his face into the curve of my neck. "What you saw was foolishness. I was miserable because of you. And no one but Jan would consider waking you. So I was forced to sit by while you walked toward a wedding to the man who ruined us."

"We both made mistakes, but we're here now, together." I look down at the water. "Okay... I think I'm ready. Will you come with me?"

"Always." He smiles.

We dive in, and I float downward, muscles remembering the way. I'd once loved the world beneath the surface, and even now, memories come back to me. While I whirl around, fish dart past, their scales flashing silver as they slip in and out of sunken logs draped in water moss. Ribbons of eelgrass thread through my fingers like silk as we glide past, and in all of this, Peter remains by my side, watchful.

I push forward into a curtain of bubbles where the waterfall crashes above and the roar is muffled to a soft rumble. Light dances wildly on the surface, reminding me of sunlight through ice.

I'll never forget the experience, but that's okay. I don't have to flee from it anymore. In fact, it's time to embrace it—the curse, the losses, the heartbreak. I wouldn't be who I am without them. I can't change the past; I can only accept it. What's done is done.

Through the turquoise shimmer, James comes to mind.

He needs to hear this.

No matter the mistakes of our pasts, our choices still have the power to change the future. He can fix things, and it's up to me to see that he does. It might be time to consider a visit to my former fiancé.

Chapter 26

Life is a dream; one I never wish to wake from. For two blissful weeks, I drift alongside the man I adore, little thought besides how happy I am. It's heaven, the way he looks at me as if I'm the sunbeam that puts the glow on his face.

We travel across Elphame as he shows me the sights. Some days are spent with our friends, hiking, roaming the countryside, or joining in village activities. Other times, we pack a lunch and escape to some private spot, lying beneath the hot sun, half-kissing, half-talking about all we stored away these long months apart.

Occasionally, Tinker Bell accompanies us when we're with the group. When she does, I find myself unsure where I belong. She's often chatting about days gone by that I can't relate to. Tales of teasing mermaids in the Lagoon, or their travels to the farthest reaches of Neverland, seeing sights I can barely imagine.

Now, while our group explores the underground caverns where the Fae mine the Aether Dew Dust, I've just about had enough of trailing behind them like a proper gooseberry, listening with nothing to contribute. The two fly ahead through the long, dark tunnel, where the walls glisten with moisture, and the air is thick and damp. Occasionally, a glittering seam runs along the stone where the Aether Dew waits to be harvested, and I glide my finger over its bright teal shimmer, mesmerized.

Gravel crunches beneath my boots, and the distant clang of pickaxes rings out like a steady drumbeat. Flickering lanterns cast long shadows across the path as I squint, taking it all in while hurrying to keep up with Peter, until we arrive at a vast, toothy chasm stretching before us.

I stumble back, nearly pitching headfirst, while Peter and Tinker Bell glide ahead with ease, seemingly forgetting I exist at all. Tilting my head, I watch them disappear.

"He's just distracted." JaneAnn appears at my side, staring down into the blackness below.

"Yeah. It's easy to be, with her talking non-stop in his ear."

"Come on." She guides me away from the edge. "Let's follow some walking folk, a bit safer."

"I don't mind him having female friends. He has you and Grace, but you two aren't openly swooning over him. At least Grace isn't anymore. But Tinker Bell's different. Early on, she said something to me... and I couldn't take it as anything other than a threat."

"A threat? Well, do tell." She loops her arm through mine as we follow the others down a different path, one Kit announces has a bridge.

"She said his 'infatuation' with me was temporary, and that while I'll die after a brief existence, they will live a long life together."

"Okay? So why's he wasting his time with her? She sounds like a real knock."

"He assumes I misunderstood her. They're bonded after years of friendship. But there's something else that makes me wonder about her. I have two separate memories of meeting Peter. One with Tinker Bell and one without. He only remembers one, and the version with her doesn't connect to anything else. It's how I felt when I got the memory in the underground Winter Woods, out of place, with no real explanation."

"So, have you asked her about it?"

"No, I haven't. Peter said he'd be okay if I spoke to King Clarion, but I never did. And I wouldn't trust Tinker Bell's word either. There's something off about her. I know I should pursue this, but I fear learning something that'll alter the way he sees her. He defended her so fiercely. And I know from James, it's a painful thing to discover the truth about someone you trust.

"You're kind to consider such a thing. If it were me, I'd have knocked her between the eyes after saying those awful things. If she's hiding something, the same as James did, Peter needs to know. You're not doing him any favors by sparing his feelings."

"I know, you're right. But these weeks together have been a break from all the heartache of life in Winter Woods. I just know the moment I explore this, it'll all come crashing down."

The group halts as a worker, in a soot-smudged tunic, greets Kit with a wide smile, then beckons us onward. He promises we can all try our hand at mining. The boys eagerly grab what appear to be enchanted pickaxes, each with a pulsing sparkle along its wooden handle. Poe, the Fae miner, waves us over. "This way," he says as John and Michael shower him with questions.

Our footsteps echo softly as JaneAnn and I fall behind the others, close enough not to lose sight of them.

"Listen," she says, tone low. "Blissful ignorance seems nice on the surface. But one day you'll realize you've closed your eyes to avoid seeing the truth. Did you regain your past only to leave something undone? Talk to the king. Maybe you'll find out it's nothing at all."

I clutch my ruby cloak tighter, the damp air sending a chill through me. "You're right, I know. But here I am, at a crossroad again. No easy answer, but both paths mean someone gets hurt."

"You think too much, sis." She bumps her hip lightly against mine. "Sometimes you've got to make choices, and who cares about the consequences."

"You sound like Margaret now."

Her mouth quirks. "I take that as a compliment."

Margaret was always determined to enjoy life first, regret later. While I was forever trying to live in a tomorrow that didn't exist, planning for a life that was never mine. How different the path might have looked with her by my side. It's unlikely she would have ever allowed me to get engaged without ensuring the love came first.

We continue forward until we arrive at a work site, where we spend the next hour taking turns, everyone eager to find our own bit of Aether Dew. It doesn't take long to confirm the axes are enchanted as they slice through the rock, as easily as Christmas pudding. Despite the boys' determination, it's Maimie who lets out a delighted scream when she's the first to stumble upon it. Poe, amused, promises to see that she receives a bagful from the vein.

Once we've seen all there is to see, we thank Poe and return to the surface. Peter and Tinker Bell never showed again, and I can't help but wonder where they vanished to. Part of me struggles against jealousy—that he didn't notice I was gone, didn't come looking for me. But, as he said, he had to watch James and me for years. I suppose I have no right to get upset by their friendship. I trust him and know he means well. But, Jan's right. I will speak with King Clarion and hope that whatever I learn won't bring Peter further pain.

"I'm going to place my hands around your forehead," King Clarion says. "If something's missing, I'll see it. Okay?"

"Yes." I shake my hands, the nerves getting to me.

It's dusk, and I sit in his office, having requested a moment of his time after returning from our outing. His fingers settle against my skin, cool and assuring, and a gentle heat pulses through them.

"Bring the memory to mind," he instructs.

I close my eyes and let it surface: Peter by my bedside, Tinker Bell aglow at his shoulder, her wings a blur of light: his outstretched hand, the open window, the promise of stars.

He pulls back and steps away, nose wrinkled.

"What's wrong?"

"It's as you feared, someone tampered with it. The memory was hidden—and not only that one, but many others as well. Like a long stretch of darkness around that time."

"Oh..." I let out an unsteady breath. "Would my near-death experience have the power to bring it back?"

"Oh yes. Death breaks every curse. But most aren't around to appreciate it. You almost died, so your mind began breaking through."

The door slams open, and I swing around as Peter marches in. "There you are! Been searching everywhere for you." He looks between King Clarion and me. "What's going on?"

"I'm here about the memories we discussed."

"What?" He strolls to my side. "But you did that weeks ago? I assumed nothing came of it."

"No." I shrink a little. "I worried the truth might hurt you, so I avoided it."

"Look." He bends and takes my hands. "What happened today was inexcusable. I'm a jerk, a huge one. But please, don't let jealousy lead you to accusation."

"You're wrong!" I stiffen and pull my hands away. "This has nothing to do with jealousy."

"Peter," King Clarion interrupts. "Before this goes any further, you should know, Wendy's suspicion was right. Someone hid her memories. And if hers, it's only logical, yours too."

Peter rises and faces him. "And do you suspect Tinker Bell?"

"The 'who' is unknown, but I'm sure we can figure it out."

A long silence follows as Peter crosses to the wall-length window, gazing out over the courtyard. At last, he turns, eyes locking with mine. "Fine, check me."

King Clarion steps behind him. "Are you sure?"

"No, but let's get it over with."

Peter doesn't block out the world; instead, he stares at me, jaw clenched, as the king places his hands around his forehead. I'm sick as one-minute passes, then another and Peter's defenses slowly slip as the king's fingers vibrate and he begins to grunt.

He finally pulls away, panting

"What is it?" I ask, gripping the sides of the chair.

The king stumbles to his high-backed chair and collapses into it. "Would you hand me my drink, please?"

"Of course." I retrieve the glass and place it in his hand. "Tell us what happened?"

He turns to Peter. "Tell me about your childhood."

"Which part?" Peter mumbles. "I woke at six with no memory of who I was. Spent the first couple of years with Tink, then moved to the palace where I became a royal ward to King Charlie."

"You have no memory before six years old?" King Clarion takes a slow sip. "Why am I just learning this?"

"Tink tried to figure out what happened, but determined it was useless. So, I moved on. As a kid, it wasn't something I dwelled on."

King Clarion drums his fingers against the armrest. "Peter... I don't even know how to begin explaining what's been done to you. And I fear the knowledge is enough to break you."

My stomach twists. "Clarion, what did you see?"

"I'd best get Tinker Bell," he says. "She'll need to explain it. Excuse me."

He hurries from the room, and the silence is heavy. I stare at Peter, lost in thought. I'm unsure whether to approach him or give space. What could the king have possibly discovered? I'm already regretting opening this door, especially if Clarion's right, and the truth could shatter him.

I sit on the couch just as the door swings open and Clarion reenters, with Tinker Bell at his side. She gazes at me through narrowed slits, but softens when she spots Peter.

"What's going on, Uncle?"

"Sit, please." He motions to the chair. His gaze darting to Peter, standing stiff by the window. "Niece, I've learned something you must explain."

"Oh?"

"Yes. But first..." He looks between Peter and me. "This isn't known by many, but Tink's father, Dash, is my brother. Long ago, he befriended Tahreek, with whom he shared a fixation on dark magic. The invasion of Winter Woods was led by Dash, and it is almost certain that he was the one who cursed you.

"Tinker Bell's older sister, Periwinkle, fled Elphame because Dash intended to give her in marriage to Tahreek. After looking into your mind, Peter, I know it was she who gave you her Fae essence."

"What?" Peter blinks. "When I was a child?"

"This is the difficult part." He rubs his neck. "Tinker Bell, go on, tell him."

Her eyes dart around the room. "Okay... Peri was close to you after your mother's death. So, when she became sick, it was an easy choice to give you her Fae essence."

"And is that how I lost my memories? Getting the essence as a kid?"

"No..." Tinker Bell's face goes ashen, mouth trembling. "Peter, you weren't a child when it happened."

"I'm not following." His brows lower, a small smile forming. "I could fly since my first memories."

"You were—" She bites her lip, hesitant. "Uncle, I can't! Please. You tell him."

"Go on," King Clarion shakes his head, voice hollow. "Do it, Tink. He deserves to know, and you were there when it happened."

She turns back to Peter. "You weren't a child! You were a man, already thirty years old."

His smile vanishes. "What the hell are you talking about, Tink?"

"I ran from home to find Peri, and in the process, I found you. When she gave you her essence, it brought us closer. I was so much younger than you, but I couldn't help falling in love."

She wraps her arms tightly around herself. "Father—he found me, demanded I leave, but I refused. It was my fault. He took you, and he and Tahreek changed you."

Tears stream down her cheeks. "I searched for you everywhere. And then he came—he dropped you at my feet as if you were nothing. My mind couldn't make sense of the child lying before me, but the leer on his face said it all. He said, *'Now you will never possess him,'* and promised that if I told anyone what he'd done, he'd return and you would never wake again. Then he flew away, and I've never seen him since."

Peter's utterly still—a statue made of stone, except for the twitch in his jaw.

"Son," King Clarion says. "When they changed you, your past went with it. While we might recover fragments, it will never be whole again. I'm terribly sorry."

"What happened to the other memories?" I ask, my voice steadier than I feel.

"Tell her, Tink," he replies. "I can't say for certain that it was you, but I'm very confident it was."

"Why do this to me, Uncle?" Her nostrils flare. "Yes, I took them, and I'm not sorry! You were a nuisance. All I wanted was to go home, but Peter refused—because of you. Then your family moved to Neverland. So, I ended it. I hid the memories: from you, your brothers, Peter, and those Lost Boys.

"Still, he disappeared two years later, and I didn't see him again until he came strutting back weeks ago. It took my breath away seeing the man I once knew."

I trace my bottom lip, back and forth, understanding the fracture Clarion feared. I'd feared what I would unearth, but this is far worse than I could have imagined. There's no recovering the man Tink speaks of. He's gone. Peter has to live with this knowledge.

"I could use some air," Peter finally says, standing. "Please excuse me."

I watch him go, then rise to follow.

"Give him some time," King Clarion says gently.

"We shouldn't have told him." I gaze after Peter. "He was right. Sometimes the past is best left to rest."

Towering trees encircle the clearing where I sit at a table formed from interwoven roots rising from the earth, ancient, fashioned by time itself. Twelve wooden chairs surround the circular table, occupied by the six Elders of Elphame and King Clarion. John, Michael, Nibs, Peter, and I sit among them. This sacred place, nestled deep within the forest, is called the *Lucus Seniorum*—the Grove of Elders. At the center of the table, four glowing symbols are etched into the wood: a snowflake, a raindrop, a flower petal, and a leaf.

King Clarion convened the council to address Dash and Tinker Bell's actions. As the elders introduced themselves, two names stood out: Lympia Griffiths and Lord Malori, both hailing from Winter Woods. I almost nudged Peter, a reminder of our past adventures, but the hollow look in his eyes pulled me back to the present. Kit had to track him down after he disappeared, and from what I heard, practically dragged him to the meeting.

"We are grateful for your time," Lord Malori says, his voice soft, expression serene. His long, flowing silver hair frames a face both youthful and ancient. This is the agelessness Peter spoke of about the Fae.

"Words can't describe how deeply we are grieved by the actions of two of our own," Lord Malori continues. "Be assured, both will be held accountable. But before you leave this place, we will do what we can to return what was taken."

Peter exhales, his gaze drifting upward where the trees meet the violet sky. He won't be fully restored, and he knows it. John, Michael, and Nibs were stunned when I gathered them at the King's request. No one expected to learn that we were still missing something vital, a piece of our story.

"Now." Lord Malori raises his hands. "If you are ready, we will begin."

King Clarion steps to my side. Lord Malori moves beside Nibs. Lady Lympia stands with Michael, Lady Clare joins John, and the remaining two Elders—Lord McLaurin and Lord Myron—stand beside Peter.

Michael glances from John to me, uneasy, and I rest a hand on his, offering a reassuring smile.

"Ready," Lord Malori says. At his word, each Elder raises their hands to our heads. "*Release.*"

Light blinds me—the memories restoring.

We lived at Number 14, Bloomsbury, in London, England. Father was a banker. We had a happy home until the night Peter Pan appeared on the windowsill of our nursery. He spoke to me; he had been listening to my bedtime stories. He invited me to Neverland. With Tinker Bell and my brothers, I followed him. Using a sprinkle of Aether dust, we flew out the window and into the midnight sky.

We had a marvelous adventure, returning a few days later to our terribly upset parents. They locked the window, hoping to keep us safe. That week, Mother visited the local Children's Home, as she did every Friday. During the visit, we told our story to Nibs, Slightly, Tootles, and the Twins. They were enchanted. We promised that the next time Peter Pan came, they'd come too.

Sure enough, a month later he returned, and at my request, we brought the boys along. Peter called them the Lost Boys—for they were lost in the world, without anyone to love them. That adventure lasted a bliss-ful month. When we returned, our parents were heartbroken, having thought they'd lost us forever. They begged us to stay, but we insisted we could not, though we promised to always return.

Father kept watch at the nursery window for many nights. Yet, when Peter came again, he was asleep, and we tiptoed past, flying out the window once more. But this time, when we returned, our parents were ready. They proposed a plan: if we must go away, let them come too. Let us all go to Neverland. Tinker Bell had a fit, her tiny body blazing red like a flame, but Peter hushed her, agreeing.

Father sold the house and purchased the Jolly Roger. He packed what little we owned aboard, and before setting sail, I begged him to allow the Lost Boys to come with us. At first, he refused. But Mother, with her soft heart, persuaded him. And so, we all sailed away, Peter guiding the way to Neverland.

My vision clears, and I blink, surveying the darkening sky.

That must've been when Tinker Bell hid the memories. There'd always been a haze around that time, but I assumed it was normal. We can't hold onto every moment.

"Well, I believe your minds are in order," King Clarion says, patting my shoulder.

"Thank you," I reply. "We are forever grateful."

Nibs, John, and Michael murmur in agreement.

"Certainly." Lord Malori's gaze lingers on Peter, rigid as a board. "If you need anything else, don't hesitate to ask."

"Well, come on, let's get back." John heads toward the lantern-lit path winding through the woods.

"Where's Nana, do you suppose?" Michael jogs to my side.

Nana—our nurse dog. That sweet girl.

"I'm sure she's still at the palace." John presses his glasses up his nose.

"Yeah, carrying medicine to Thomas before bed," I say.

"Good ole, Nana." Nibs chuckles. "I'm sure she's causing a ruckus."

"I hope so." Michael shoves his hands into his pockets, kicking at the ground. "And I hope she still knows me."

"Of course, she will." John pats his back. "She'd never forget her charges, especially the one who put up the biggest fuss at night."

I glance behind, Peter's settled on a rock, head in his hands. "You all go on ahead. I'm going to check on him."

"Sure thing." John offers a reassuring tilt of his head. "We'll see you back at the palace."

I slip back along the path to where Peter rests and kneel beside him. "Talk to me," I say.

He looks at me, expression blank.

"I'm so sorry." I grip his hand. "I shouldn't have pushed my suspicion."

"I was young; it was easy to start over." His teeth clench. "But I wasn't young, was I? How am I expected to put myself together again?"

"We had to start over once, and we did. You and I found each other in that place of confusion. It won't be easy. But please don't let this break you."

He turns away, hand slipping from mine. "You should go."

"Why?" I stand and straighten, chest tightening.

"Because this changes everything. I don't know who I am anymore, and it hurts far worse having you stare down at me expectantly. So, please, just go." He gestures toward the woods. "I need to make sense of myself again."

"Of course... whatever you need."

I lift my skirts and move away slowly, hoping he'll call me back. Each step is torture, knowing he won't let me carry this burden with him. We spent so long apart, forced to do life alone, and now, when we finally have each other, he won't let me in.

I turn, unable to hold it in any longer, and crash into the forest, tears blinding me as I run. My shoes dig into the soft mud, the world flashing past in a blur until—*smash*.

I'm on the ground. Kit stands over me. "Whoa, now." He helps me up. "What's happened? Couldn't Father fix the memories?"

"He did. It's all back. But I've ruined Peter's life by forcing Tinker Bell to tell the truth!"

"Ah, I see." He offers a sympathetic nod. "There's no right or wrong here, not when discussing what my uncle did to him. It'll take time, but he'll recover. Don't beat yourself up over it."

"Maybe you're right, but I can't stay here."

Moonlight paints the forest a pale blue. I hold my hand under a silver beam, aware of what I must do next. "Take me to Silver Mist."

"I'm sorry, what?" He steps back, tilting his head to survey me. "Did you just ask me to take you to the home of the one and only Thomas Blood?"

"I must see James. He's our best hope for restoring things. *Please*. I've done enough damage, let me do something right."

"Wendy, it's getting dark, and my father would never approve. Neither would the Elders. And what would Peter say? Me taking you to your former fiancé?"

"I doubt he'd care even. We'll slip away, use the darkness as our cover. If James is at the palace, the night is my best chance. Everyone will be settling down. No one will expect visitors."

"I don't know. This feels like walking into a trap."

"Friend." I grip his shoulders. "You took a step of faith once, when no one else would. Please, take it once more. It may be the last required."

His face twists. "Hang it all, okay."

"Thank you!" I throw my arms around him, joy and anxiety flooding through me. "You won't regret this. I'm certain this is the next step."

"If this leads to finding Tiger Lily's family, too, I have no choice."

"Let's go and do that and bring everyone home."

He bends, and I hop onto his back. Then we're off—soaring into the sky, climbing through the clouds toward the mountain where we first entered Elphame.

When we land, I gaze out at the valley, so many I love are just ahead. The stars twinkle above, each one watching over them until I return. I don't know what's about to happen, only that I *must* go.

Kit presses on my back and guides me into the Metamorphosis Mist. It's jarring to step out on the other side. I've been altered for so long; my body feels foreign in its normal size.

He pulls out a small bag and loosens the string.

"You ready to fly?" he asks, lifting a pinch of the golden dust.

"Sounds pretty good right now."

"Okay, Wendy Darling." He cups his hand to his mouth. "*Fly!*"

He blows, the dust swirling from his palm, cloaking me in shimmering light.

"What do I do again?" I hold out my arms. "It's been so long, I've forgotten."

"Think of a happy thought, anyone will do. Something to make your heart soar."

"Oh, Kit..." I frown. "I can't. I'm miserable. How can I possibly think happy thoughts?"

"Think about your parents."

And just like that, my feet lift off the ground, a smile spreading across my face. "Oh my..."

"Come on. You've got this!" He flits ahead.

I inhale and release, focusing on their faces.

Mother—a lovely lady with her sweet, mocking mouth. And just one kiss, perfectly conspicuous in the right-hand corner. It wasn't for anyone to get—it was hers alone.

I rise higher.

Father—how he'd sit with us in a circle on the nursery floor, solemnly counting the pennies from our money boxes, always sure they tallied. Then he'd fix his tie and tell us about stocks and shares, like he was admitting us into a very grown-up secret.

Neverland lies far below. I'm flying, overcome by the wonder of it all. I now understand why Peter used to crow; for how could anyone remain silent when the wind is at your back and the birds at your side?

"Is that the best you've got?" Kit calls.

I press forward, shooting ahead, twirling upward, my hair streaming behind. The moon hangs high above, and for a moment, it feels close enough to touch. We fly for some time until a village appears, cottage lights glittering like the frost beneath the street lamps in Winter Woods.

"We're nearly there, it's up ahead," he says.

And indeed—there it is, silhouetted in moonlight: the palace. *My home.*

Chapter 27

I t's my old balcony. The one where I used to stretch out blankets and lie beneath the stars with my brothers. Where Tiger Lily and I held tea parties in our finest clothes, serving our dolls with an elegant, ladylike flair.

"This is Tiva, it means dance," Tiger Lily said, holding out her doll, the memory fresh as if it happened only yesterday. "I love dancing."

"This is Jane," I replied. "Would you like to hold her?"

She nodded readily, and we swapped dolls.

Tiva was made of soft brown fabric, while Jane was pale porcelain. Unlike Jane, Tiva was full of vibrant colors—her leather dress covered in red and blue beads that formed beautiful patterns, just like the clothes Tiger Lily wore.

Her hair was lifelike, with two delicate black braids framing her face. She and Tiger Lily could have been twins.

"Would you like to trade?" Tiger Lily asked, holding Jane to her chest. "I've never had a doll like her before, and I think she's the loveliest in the world."

"Yes, let's," I said, eager to keep Tiva.

I lifted her higher, gazing at her affectionately. She was the most wonderful doll I'd ever owned, and I knew I'd never love another the way I loved her.

Seems those memories aren't long ago, while another part of me feels like it's been a lifetime.

My old room glows brightly, and the balcony door stands slightly ajar for air as I hover nearby, drawn to it. And yet, as James comes into view, I remember—it isn't mine anymore. I cover my mouth. He'd been to my room many times in the past. He *knew* this was mine, and yet... he chose it for himself.

"What do we do now?" Kit asks.

"I go to him, and we talk. You'd best stay back. Be ready, just in case."

"Okay, call me if *anything* happens."

I float closer. He whispers, "Wendy."

"Yes?" I turn.

"Remember—he's not to be trusted."

"I'm not so sure about that..."

I don't hesitate and fly to the balcony, landing softly. Breathing deeply, the memories stir, aching to rise, but not now. Later. I peer into the room. James lifts off his shirt and tosses it onto a chair, stretching before sitting on the edge of the bed and tugging off one boot, then the other. My fingers touch the glass, emotion swelling within.

He yawns and disappears into the bathroom. It's now or never. I press open the door and step inside.

An old painting of the seaside still hangs over the bed; my name signed in the corner. On the bedside table is a photograph, black and white faces, young and bright. Chas, Morgan, Smee, Rose and James. Arms wrapped around each other; Rose tucked beneath James' arm. This is James before I knew him. Someone before all the chaos and deception.

I pause.

My own face stares back at me. It's a sketch of me on the bedside table; one Peter drew and gave as a gift. Just another reminder of the false hope I gave James.

I exhale and look away, halting as I face the shelves.

My shelves.

Lined with all my childhood treasures. He never moved them. Never touched them. They're exactly as I left them that fateful day.

I step closer, heart in my throat. There's Tiva, right in the center, surrounded by my other dolls. My needle and thread basket. And the acorn, the blasted thing, I never could understand why it mattered.

But now, I do.

It was a gift from Peter on the first night. I offered him a kiss, and instead of giving one, he simply held out his hand, expectant. The memory brings a smile to my face. So, I gave him my thimble off my nightstand, and in return, he gave me that acorn. Peter's kiss, one I could never give away.

Glass smashes behind me, and I twist around.

James stares at me, hand still suspended in the air as the cup lies shattered on the floor. "*Wendy?*" He breathes the word out like a forgotten promise.

"Yes..."

He sprints over, lifting me off my feet and into his arms, body trembling. "What happened?"

I'm fighting back tears, but I can't break.

He pulls away, swallowing hard. "Where have you been? You're note. Why did you leave?"

His fingers squeeze mine, and I gaze up into the face I once longed for.

"I know what you did to me," I whisper.

His face pales, just like Tinker Bell's earlier tonight. He releases my hand and steps back. "What did you say?"

"You cursed me." My knees shake, but I try to steady them. "You're the reason I lost my memory."

His lips part, and he presses onto the bed. "How do you know?"

I clear my throat. "Kit—he's Fae. He broke the curse. For me. For Nibs. For my brothers."

"If you remember, then you know I had no choice. I *had* to do it to save you. Thomas would've seen you dead. All of you."

"We always have a choice." I sit beside him, searching his face. "You could've told my father the truth. Gotten his help. Things could have been different."

His resolve hardens. "I did what I had to. This is *my* kingdom, and I'm the rightful heir to the throne. Do you know that?"

"I do. But you can't do this. I know you, James. You didn't want any of this, you said so yourself. This was duty, not desire."

"No." He shakes his head. stands and paces. "My father was ashamed of me. Tried to erase us. We weren't good enough. His own children, shameful creatures, born out of wedlock. Thomas though, he saw my value. He was willing to fight for us."

"But at what cost?" I rise and touch his arm, remembering how natural this once was. "You say you love me, but you took *everything*." My voice thickens with grief. "You betrayed me."

He looks away, fists clenched. "It wasn't meant to be this way. You weren't supposed to know anything. I was going to save you—return to you to your kingdom. We could have been happy."

What can I say to reach him?

"James, I'm begging you." I step closer, masking my nerves with a strength I don't quite possess. "Don't let Thomas win. He's destroyed Neverland, but together, we can stop the madness."

"Why should I?" He looks up, a chill piercing through his dark gaze. "If I sacrifice for you, I lose everything."

I stare, unable to respond. And then he wraps a hand around my neck and kisses me. But this isn't like the others. The sweetness is gone. What's left is raw. Desperate. Fueled by everything broken between us.

He pulls back, waiting for me to say something, anything. "I'm sorry," is all I choke out. "I wish I had more, but I don't."

"Then tell me." His tone drops low. "Why the hell should I do anything for you."

"Do it for Charlie," a voice says.

We pull apart, and Peter stands by the balcony door, watching. James steps in front of me, clutching my hand. "What did you say?"

"Do it for your father's sake," Peter repeats, jaw tight.

"Excuse me?" James snaps. "What do you know about him? How dare you even speak his name?"

"He was my brother..."

The revelation hangs in the air, leaving James and me speechless.

"He's your what?" I finally say.

Peter looks at me, unwavering. "Charlie was my younger brother. And I'm the reason for this whole mess."

"I don't understand—how?" James asks.

"I was next in line for the throne." Peter stares at the floor. "Dash and Tahreek... they changed me. I was a man, and they took it away."

"Took it away?" James repeats. "What does that even mean?"

"It means I went from a man of thirty to a child with no past. This forced Charlie to take my place. Tahreek was never a friend. He enjoys watching the world burn and took advantage of Thomas' unwavering loyalty to my father."

"You're insane; you know that, right?" James says, his fingers still gripping mine. I stay still.

"I certainly feel it," Peter says blankly. "If only it were true. Charlie wasn't ashamed of you; he loved you, your mother, and Morgan. Right or wrong, he wanted what was best for you."

This is it.

Peter's found the words to break through, the only ones that matter: James' true father. But as hope blossoms anew, something shifts in James as he looks from Peter to me.

"Why are you here, Peter?" His brows lower.

"Because..." Peter hesitates, glancing at me, and for a split second, I'm back in Starkey Manor, three glasses of wine about to pull me into oblivion. Yet Peter stands before me, his presence overwhelming. The need I felt then tears through me now—to fall into his embrace, to be held, protected, safe.

"Because *she's* here?" James interrupts my thoughts, looking at me, his stare piercing. "He's here for you, isn't he?"

"This isn't important." I shake my head.

"No. It's *very* important." He steps away from me. "I knew it. I *knew* it, even that day. I told myself I was imagining things. But I wasn't, was I?" His finger points my direction. "You weren't just leaving me on our wedding day, were you? No, you went to him."

I shrink under his scrutiny, the words barely a whisper. "I'm sorry."

"And here I was, ready to kiss your feet again. Tell me, how long did you know it was he you loved?"

I hug myself, quivering. Peter steps closer, face twisted with emotion. "What do you want me to say?" I mumble.

"The truth, dammit!" His voice reverberates around the room. "Tell me the truth for once."

"I knew when you returned from the trip," I admit, the weight of my lies crashing around me.

"Like an idiot, I trusted you both." His voice cracks as he looks at Peter. "And the irony, that you're my kin. Well, I'm done living with my head in the sand. Let's deal with this, shall we?"

He strides to his bedside table, reaches down, and in a flash, unsheathes a sword, pressing the blade into my back. I inhale sharply as the cool iron digs into my skin.

"Don't do this," Peter says slowly, drawing a thin sword from the scabbard at his waist.

"Oh, you came ready to battle, did you?" James chuckles darkly. "Good form. Now, the truth is revealed. My father was never the enemy—it was *you*, all along... *Uncle*. I propose a duel. Winner takes the kingdom."

"I don't want the kingdom!" Peter lunges for me, but I arch my back, gasping as the blade cuts deeper, stopping him. "Please stop!" he pleads, "keep your kingdom. I just want her."

"That's all I wanted too!" James yells. "But you took her from me."

"Don't lie to yourself." Peter shoots back. "Days before the curse, I told Rose that Wendy thought the world of you. I was jealous, angry, because you could have had anything. But this." He gestures around. "This is hers! And you stole it."

"No more." James presses the blade harder. My eyes clench shut as it slices through the material and into my skin, warm blood trickling down my back. "Fight or leave."

"Fine," Peter growls, "You have a deal. Now get that thing away from her!"

"Wonderful, stand up, Wendy," James commands, and I rise slowly, his weapon still poised. "Walk around the bed, and stand over here."

I obey, never breaking Peter's gaze. Once I'm close enough, James grabs my arm and shoves me against the wall hard.

"Are you hoping I die?" His mouth is inches from mine.

"No." I search his face. "Because you don't have to do this."

"My uncle understands, doesn't he?" He glances over his shoulder. "This is how real men work out their differences. No apologies, no talking, we fight until I feel the tip of my blade cut through his heart."

He grips his sword, catching sight of the blood on the tip—my blood. His lips press tight, cheeks paling as he looks between me and the blade. But he doesn't relent. He turns and stalks toward Peter, sword raised.

Peter chews his lip, gripping his own. I'm barely breathing as they begin to circle. Then, James swings, and their swords collide, steel on steel, the sound paralyzing me.

James stumbles back, grinning. "It's the cockiness. That's what I hate most about you. So did Juke. And honestly, who could fault him?"

Peter slams his blade into James'. "I'm not cocky—I'm confident. Something you wouldn't understand, groveling at Thomas' feet."

James presses forward, but Peter meets him, wrist flipping effortlessly, parrying each blow. They move slowly around the room, stalking, striking, defending. Sweat clings to my skin as I watch, wishing I could shut this out, but I dare not look away.

"I'm not your enemy, James. These men, they're the ones who ruined us."

"Well, for all their crimes, none of them stole the woman I loved," James grunts, exhaustion creeping into his voice as he leans against an easy chair.

"You're right, and I don't blame you for hating me." Peter's voice remains steady as he straightens. "But I didn't force her hand. She has her own mind."

"Oh, I know. Just as I know the feel of her skin, and the taste of her kiss." James grins. "You may have stolen her, but I had her first."

With stunning speed, they clash again. Peter lunges—James ducks. James thrusts—Peter blocks. Then James unleashes a flurry of strikes, one after the next, but Peter, almost cornered against the balcony door, turns them all aside, one hand tucked behind his back, and barely a sweat broken.

Infuriated, James throws aside the sword, drawing a dagger instead. In one swift motion, he ducks beneath Peter's swing and lunges at his side; dagger raised to strike.

A cry bursts from my throat, *"Peter!"*

Time slows. The blade's glint drawing near to his ribs. Peter's gaze snaps to mine—then he spins. *Slice.*

The dagger and James' hand fall to the floor with a sickening thud.

My throat tightens as James' scream pierces the air, his legs buckling, clutching the bloody stump.

Peter is at my side in an instant, yanking me into his arms, his whole-body trembling. "I'm so sorry." He breathes into my hair. "I love you."

"I thought he'd kill you!" I sob, clinging to him, shuddering. He pulls back and kisses me, wild, desperate, his skin damp from exertion. I cup his face, losing myself to his embrace, the world fading away... until my lids lift and I meet James' gaze. His face contorted with agony. He hasn't just lost a hand; he's watching the woman he loves collapse into another man's arms.

A seed of guilt takes root inside me, and a flash of memory fills my mind. James and I snuggled close on Christmas, the cool air rushing past on the sleigh as the bells rang softly, and the sky exploded with twilight colors.

"I don't intend to be a lonely bride," I murmured.

"Perfect," he whispered, nuzzling his nose against mine. "Because I intend to be an adoring husband."

Oh James...

I stiffen as Kit bursts into the room and rushes to James' side. He doesn't ask questions, only closes his hands over the bleeding stump. His palms blaze with light, and skin materializes, closing the wound. James is sheet white but nods to him.

"We have to go." Kit looks at Peter and me. "They know we're here. Dash held me back, but he flew off to get help. Come on, now! Sorry, Cap, that's the best I can do."

Peter steers me around the blood-soaked floor, where James stares at what's left of his arm, dazed.

"Hop on." Peter bends.

I lift my foot to move, but something's wrong. My body won't budge. I open my mouth to speak, but no sound comes. Then, a flash of movement, and a faerie appears in my vision, eyes darker than ink, and he vanishes.

"Wendy?" Peter turns just as James' remaining hand snakes around my neck and yanks me backward. The door bursts open, and guards swarm around us. I can't scream. I'm trapped inside my body.

Peter freezes, lips parting in shock as Kit throws an arm around him and pulls him toward the balcony. "We have to go!"

"No!" I want to scream, but I have no voice.

The guards raise their bows, and arrows fly as Peter and Kit vanish over the edge of the balcony. My lids grow heavy as fear pulses through me. But something greater overcomes me, and the world fades to black.

※ ※ ※

My hands won't budge. Neither will my legs. Nothing physically binds me, yet I'm imprisoned on a bed.

"You're awake," Thomas says warmly, seated on a stool beside the bed. "Welcome back."

I find my voice, though my throat aches. "Where am I?"

"Oh, this is the servant's quarters." He glances around the small room, sparsely furnished with a bed, chair, and mirrored dresser. Cobwebs line the corners, and the window is dusty, like no one's been here for a long time. "But we'll provide better arrangements soon. I need to get your agreement first."

"Agreement? About what? Why am I here? Why am I *bound*?"

"Don't worry," he assures. "It's only until I'm certain we're on the same page. Then you may go free."

"And what's the catch?"

He leans forward, calm and measured. "James is... stubborn to say the least. I have one purpose—to put my stepson on the throne. We were so close. However, you had other ideas, which threw a wrench in my plan. Now, on your own accord, you've returned, and I'm given a second chance. James won't become king unless you become queen. Are you catching my drift?"

My chest constricts. "You're saying you need me to marry him?"

"That's a good guess." He wags a finger, pressing back in his chair, one leg resting on the other. "Yeah, this appears to be my only option. So, what might persuade a young woman, in love with another, to marry him instead?"

A light snarl tugs at my lips. "Is this where you threaten me?"

"Only if necessary. If there were any other way, I'd gladly take it. But as it stands, James doesn't appreciate the call on his life the way his mother and I do. So, here's how this goes: if you want to leave, I'll set you free this very hour. Walk away, live your life. But." He pauses with a frown. "I will be forced to invade Elphame. And there's a little island not far from here where your mother resides, I'll be forced to clear house there too."

My stomach drops. "My mother's alive? And Father, too?"

"You have to understand, your father was a beloved ruler. I couldn't have him posing a threat to the throne. So, yes, your mother is alive and well, but no, I'm sorry, your father is no longer."

The world grows dimmer at his words. "Father is dead?"

A heavy sob rises in my chest, but I force it down, refusing to cry in front of him.

"I know this can't be easy to hear. And trust me, I feel your loss keenly. Death is not something I take lightly. I respected your father, but the Kingdom must come first.

"Now, what I *can* promise is this: after you and James are married, your mother and brothers will come home. And as queen, you'll wield the same power and influence I've used to protect Neverland. So, isn't all of that worth it? The requirement is simple: marry James. Do what you once intended to do."

"There's no way you could invade Elphame."

"Unfortunately, I do have the power. Unfortunate because I'm forced to yield it. King Clarion's brother, Dash, knows a thing or two about the kingdom he grew up in as a prince. Also, I have the Anathema at my disposal for such moments. Prince Tahreek—he's bloodthirsty. Where I do such things for a purpose far greater than you or me, he sees it as an entertainment of sorts. I don't approve, but it comes in useful in such situations."

"I need time to think."

"No, I'm sorry. There's no time to waste. And honestly, nothing to consider. You will either accept or you won't."

I can't turn away, can't hide my face. Marry James? Lose Peter? But mother would be free. Do I even have a choice? He's ensured I don't. His role is clear, secure the throne for James, no matter the cost.

"Are you truly incapable of seeing the moral dilemma in this?" I ask. "I don't love James, and clearly, he doesn't want the throne."

He shakes his head. "I can appreciate your way of thinking. A young woman, on the cusp of adulthood. I once saw life through a rosy lens, too. You think I'm selfish for wanting what's best for Neverland, while you lie there wanting what's best for you alone. Tell me, child... who's really in the wrong here?"

If I could move, I'd rub my face vigorously, try to scrub away all this confusion—but I can't. Time isn't my friend today. I can't marry James, I just can't... Yet as I gaze at Thomas, I know after everything that's happened, nothing will stop him, certainly not me. I'd rather James had thrust his sword through me than have to say yes and lose Peter. But for my family, for their lives, I must.

"Okay," I mutter. "I'll marry him."

"Wonderful!" He claps his hands, beaming widely. "I assumed you'd see sense, and I'm glad you have, for I would hate to attack an innocent people. Now, I won't make you wait long. My wife has been tasked with getting a new wedding plan in motion for the day after tomorrow. We kept everything from the original wedding, so it shouldn't be too difficult. The only thing we're missing is your dress. You wouldn't know where it is, would you?"

"I do, but not how to get there or even describe its location."

"I see. Well, no worries, Nell had a seamstress begin fixing a new one up with your measurements."

My mind drifts to the wedding gown stashed beneath the earth in the oak. In truth, I wouldn't wish to wear it again. It would hurt too much, seeing how I was set free in that gown. To be forced back into it only to lose myself, that would be the cruelest twist of all.

"Okay." He slaps his hands to his knees, rising. "I think I feel confident we're on the same page. Dash, go ahead and lift the bind."

My eyes widen as Dash, the faerie who took away Peter's life once, comes into view. Something vile fills me. A desire I've never felt before, to see someone dead. How James or Thomas can work with this despicable creature is beyond me.

"Too bad." Dash leers down at me. "Was hoping for an excuse to visit my brother, family reunion of sorts."

He waves his hands. There's no lights or sparks, just a quiet shift, and I can move again. I sit and stretch, flexing my fingers. I could grab him now and squeeze, harder and harder, until—*pop*.

But I don't, and he flits away. "Now what?" I grunt.

"One of our lady's maids will guide you to your room. Get a good night's rest and I'll see you in the morning," Thomas says.

I push off the bed, legs stiff, and shuffle to the door.

"Wendy."

"Yes?" I glance back.

"No need for tears or sadness. I know how emotional young women tend to be. But consider the good you're doing. And I'll ensure your family and friends are at the reception. That's something worth smiling over, now isn't it?"

"Sure is." I swing open the door.

A young woman straightens as I exit the room and looks me over.

"Rosetta, right?" I ask, recalling her face. "Your mother worked in the kitchen."

"Yes, my lady." She curtseys; cheeks pink. "If you'll follow me."

She leads me to the servants' stairwell, cool and quiet, scented faintly by the chamomile tea that must have passed through not long ago.

"I used to play on these steps," I say, the memory rising. "Was always eager for your mother's delicious blueberry scones."

"Yes, my lady," she replies softly.

"How is your mother?"

She clears her throat. "I wouldn't know. I haven't seen her since you all disappeared."

I stop and touch her arm. "Did many vanish that day?"

"Yes, my lady. When the pirate captain Worley attacked, he took many with him."

"Did you see him? Worley?"

"No, but Sir Thomas told us the stories of what occurred that tragic day."

She continues up the stairs, and I follow. I see now, Worley isn't real, is he? No, he's a cover story to maintain Thomas as an innocent. Tahreek is the type who'd gladly become the villain, but not Thomas. No, he's the hero of his own story, thus the made-up pirate front.

And looking at the bigger picture, it's clear: the mere threat of Tahreek and Worley was enough to lock the citizens away without a fight. Instead of realizing they were being imprisoned, they believed they were being protected. Why? Because sometimes a lie is more comfortable than the truth, just as it was with Peter's past.

"I'm so sorry for your loss," I finally say. "When I'm queen, I promise I'll find her."

She meets my gaze, moonlight pouring through the stairwell window, bathing her body in silver. "Thank you. Twould be a great kindness."

"It would be my pleasure."

And it would. If I have to lose the man I love, then at least I can return Neverland to its proper order. If James loves me even a little, he'll give me that much.

As we exit the stairwell onto the family floor, I stare wistfully at the maroon carpet glowing under the crystal sconces running the length of the creamy walls. We ran these halls as children, despite the desperate pleas of the old butler, Bernard. I can almost hear our laughter echoing through time—the ghost of us rushing past.

Rosetta and I walk on, passing by the door to my old room. A shiver of unease creeps through me at the memory of tonight's events. I fix my attention on the gold-framed paintings as we continue, all of which my mother chose soon after we arrived.

The old wall hangings were lifeless, she'd said. If this were to be our home, it ought to look it. With my memory restored, I now know these paintings are of our home beyond the sea, a tall clock tower overlooking a sleeping city, a street lined with quaint houses, and yes, there it is—number 14, Bloomsbury.

"Here's your room," Rosetta says, pulling me back. Part of me longs to take the paintings with me, to go back in my mind to that time in my life. But I will never go back; time doesn't work that way, so what's the use in wishing?

She slips a key from her apron pocket, turns it in the lock, and pushes the door open. It creaks softly, revealing a low-lit room inside.

"This will be yours until the wedding."

"Thank you." I step inside, and she shuts the door behind. The lock clicks, sharp and final. Despite what Thomas said, it's clear I'm not trusted, and likely won't be until vows have been spoken. The gravity of it all sinks in as I turn and take in the room. I'm imprisoned in my own home, forced to marry James, and... my father was sacrificed for what Thomas considers 'the greater good.'

Oh, the irony.

Once, marriage to James meant my freedom, at the cost of others. Now, it means captivity, for *their* freedom. But for them, I'll do it. In the same way, Bea, Andrew, and Morgan gave their lives for us. Sacrifice is the greatest kind of love, and it's the path I choose. Yet to lose myself and the two men I've loved most in my life in one night...

I sink to my knees and let the tears spill.

It seems only moments ago Kit asked what made me happiest, and Father came to mind. He was so alive in my memory, and now that is the only place he will ever live. The emotion I hid from Thomas, I allow to surface. I will give myself this one night to break, and thereafter, I will be strong, for all those I love.

So I weep, uncaring who hears my wails as I release them. At times, my fists dig into the floor, slamming again and again, and I relish the pain sharper than my heartache. When I'm finally emptied—wrung out to the point of exhaustion, I rise unsteady and take a step forward.

Though the walls are consoling with lavender, the room spins, cold and unfamiliar. I aim shakily for the canopy bed, with its cream, gray, and plum linens. Did mother choose these? Before dropping into bed, I note the floor-to-ceiling curtains and walk over, guiding them open. A balcony lies beyond the glass, so I grip the knob and turn. It won't budge.

Oh, please, just one breath of cool air.

But it's secure, so I step away, resigned. I need the madness to end, if only for the night. Walking to the bed, I strip off my clothes and pull on the nightgown left for me, then crawl into bed. Will pleasant dreams find me tonight, or just more of the same nightmare I've found myself in?

Chapter 28

The sun beams cheerily through the windows. Where are the rain-clouds? The thunderclaps? Why isn't creation mourning for me? No, *not* mourning. *Raging*.

I push back the satiny sheets and stretch, not at all ready for the day ahead. Somehow, I'm back to the day before my wedding.

Again.

Only this time, there's no running. I must face what's coming, rebel against my instinct to fear.

Why God? Why is this happening to me? What greater purpose could be in such misery?

The lock turns, and the door creaks open. James enters, face drawn, blue eyes bloodshot. I glance at his right arm, hidden beneath a dress.

"Good morning." He closes the door behind him.

I clutch the sheets to my neck, watching.

"This dress is for you. It was your mother's." He tosses it to me, revealing an iron hook fastened to the stump of his arm.

My hand flies to my mouth, stifling a scream.

He glares, nostrils flaring. "Get dressed. I'll walk you to breakfast."

I take the dress. "Why do you have that thing on you?"

"Thomas called it a gift. Said there's nothing like a king who strikes fear into the heart of his people." He shrugs. "I don't care, as long as it's covered."

I step from the bed, lifting the nightgown over my head, only the slip remaining. I turn away from him, acutely aware of the thin cut along my back—his doing.

"I'm sorry," he mumbles.

"Are you?"

He steps closer, features crumpling as he reaches out and brushes the marred skin. There's nothing romantic in his touch; it's him coming face to face with the reality of his actions. He lifts his other arm, staring at the iron hook, lips pressed tight.

"I'll wait at the door." He turns and strides away.

I lift my mother's gown, a pale pink dress with delicate frills at the neckline. It's lovely. Pulling it over my head, it falls neatly into place, a perfect fit. The last time I saw her, I stood in her shadow, now, we'd stand face to face.

I step into my shoes, still caked with mud from the forest run.

Oh, what must Peter and Kit be thinking? This is no one's fault but my own. *I* insisted that Kit bring me. *I* was going to save Neverland. Instead, I ruined myself. Before the tears return, I shove them down and approach James.

"Okay. I'm ready." I take his arm, the one with a hand.

He guides me through the hallway to the stairwell. With every step, a memory flickers—Margaret chattering at my side, Mother humming, Father's deep laughter, Peter cheekily swooping me into his arms and flying us out of the home. My brothers' pounding footsteps before breakfast.

"Do you remember the New Year's Ball?" I ask.

"You wore a pink dress, similar to this one," he says. "You were beautiful."

"Did you know that was my first ball?"

"No. Nor would I have guessed with the way you danced."

The echo of music seems to drift in the air—ghosts of lively conversations, the tapping of shoes on hardwood.

"I'll be dancing until dawn," Margaret said, her skirts swaying.

"Unlikely your mother will allow that." Peter chuckled, that easy charm he wore so well.

I can almost see the four of us, walking ahead, vanishing into the hallway, the night young, free—but not for long.

Now the music is long gone, the laughter with it... and Margaret. All of it faded long ago.

"I wish I had gone with Peter," I murmur.

"Then why did you say yes to me?"

"Because I was a foolish little girl. And when I saw him that night... I longed to be the one on his arm. But now I never will be."

We reach the first floor. Around the corner lies the dining room. Meals there were never quiet, nor was there ever enough chairs.

We weren't like most royalty. Mother would be deep in conversation with us girls, while Father balanced trays alongside the staff, never one to sit back and be served. My brothers and the other boys would earn the occasional look from Mother as their wild behavior slowly improved over the years.

And then there was Peter, back when he was younger, ill-mannered—floating over the table just to bring me another biscuit.

Bernard would nearly faint, while Father, red-faced from holding back laughter, would offer a shaky correction: just because one can fly everywhere, doesn't mean one should.

I miss it all so much it aches.

James stares down, then lifts my hands and studies the bruises left from last night's weeping.

"I heard you," he says. "Do you hate me so much?"

"I've lost Peter," my voice is stony, "and Thomas told me about my father's death."

"Oh." He exhales, shoulders falling. "I see..."

He leads me beneath the archway into the oval dining room. I know it by heart, white walls adorned with gold stenciling, five tall windows draped in sky-blue and gold. The chestnut table remains unchanged by time, with its thick, cushioned chairs. Along the edge of the table are the notches from Peter and John's butter-knife fight.

The one-time Mother did lose her temper.

"Wendy?" a voice says.

I look up. Morgan stands beside the table.

"Morgan!" I cry, rushing into her arms. She holds me tightly, thinner and paler.

"Are you okay?" I whisper.

"Yes, I'm okay." She wipes my tears, laughing through her own.

"What about the others—Llewelyn?"

"Last I saw, they were okay too. Everyone misses you all terribly. I explained what I could. But you know."

"I do."

"Now, now, girls," Thomas barks from the head of the table, newspaper in hand. "That's enough. Sit."

I pull away, but she holds fast. "Don't get in a tizzy when you see him."

"See who?" I glance beside her, and Nibs looks up at me.

"Hey, kid." He offers a crooked grin.

A shock runs through me so hard my knees nearly buckle. I want to run to him, throw myself into his arms, but Morgan gives the slightest shake of her head. I nod and collapse into the chair James holds out for me.

"Thank you," I say mindlessly, eyes locked on Nibs. His expression mirrors my own emotion. *What's he doing here?*

"Hello, Wendy," comes a curt voice from across the table.

Eleanor 'Nell' Gwyn regards me, her lips pressed into a tight line.

"Hello," I manage, trying to make sense of the stories I've heard. This isn't only James and Morgan's mother; this is the woman Peter's brother was in love with. The woman he spurned.

Thomas folds his paper, eyes sweeping the table. "Well, what a full table we have this morning. Wendy, as you've seen, you're not our only guest. Nibs here was caught last night, lingering near the palace. Surprisingly, he had no idea how, or why, he came to be here. But I think we both know, don't we?"

He doesn't wait for an answer.

"While his associate got away, having maimed James here, he was not so lucky. Still, we've made the most of it. Haven't we, son?"

Nibs nods, head lowered.

"Yes, worked out quite well," Thomas says, clearly pleased with himself. "Morgan here has been like a love-sick puppy. Now, I've promised her they may wed just as soon as you and James do. Some fathers wouldn't be so permissive, but I have no qualms with love, as my Nell here could tell you."

"Quite right, dear," Nell says, with a forced smile.

"But, just in case Morgan or this young gentleman gets any ideas that would tempt you to break our agreement," he goes on, tone sharpening, "I've made sure they understand exactly what's at stake. But enough of that unpleasantness. Let's turn to better things. Nell tell James and Wendy what's on the agenda today."

"Certainly, dear." Nell lifts her teacup, blowing away the steam. "Cook has kindly put together a few wedding dishes you may choose from. We'll also visit the palace chapel, and the ceremony itself will be intimate, just a handful of guests. The celebration, which your family may attend, will take place in the grand ballroom. The florist is currently preparing both locations with his staff. I used all of your original plans, so this should be to your liking."

"Yes, ma'am." I lift my mug of coffee and sip.

"And my seamstress is finishing a dress. She'll arrive later today for your fitting."

"Can hardly wait," I reply, flatly.

James exhales heavily. "Enough wedding talk. Let's eat."

***

When the meal ends, we stand and James grips my arm to leave, but I tear away, sprinting straight into Nibs' arms, a sob rising up as he cradles my head.

"*It's okay,* " he whispers, "*we'll be okay.*"

A pair of strong hands clamp around my waist and yank me away like a rag doll. Before Nibs can react, a soldier plants a hand on his shoulder.

"What the hell are you doing?" James shouts striding to the soldier holding me secure.

With his one hand, James shoves the man away. "Get out of here!"

"Now, James," Thomas says mildly, "the men are following my orders. I'd like to keep some space between these two. She's got things to do. Make sense?"

James glares at him. "They touch her again; this hook will be in their neck. Understood?"

Thomas barks a laugh. "Of course! Look at you, taking charge. That hook may just be a blessing in disguise."

James doesn't respond, only presses on my back, and guides me away.

The day is a whirlwind—one stop after the next. James and I are guided around, first tasting all sorts of dishes and desserts, then surveying the tastefully decorated chapel and grand ballroom. The return of so many memories nearly has me faint again, but I soldier through it.

When it finally comes time for the dress fitting, I'm exhausted, and James is sent away. We kept things cordial all day, pretending this marriage isn't happening at knife-point. Yet the tension simmers, as we both know this isn't real. And this makes it doubly painful. For me, because I don't wish to marry him, and for him, because at one time, I did.

After he's gone, Nell ushers me into a chamber and introduces me to Marlene, a pleasant, middle-aged lady with pins stuck across her collar and frizzy black hair twisted into a messy bun.

"You go on, Nell. I'll get her all set and call you back for the big reveal," Marlene says brightly.

"Whatever you say," Nell replies, gliding out and leaving me alone with the bubbly seamstress.

Thankfully, Marlene doesn't bombard me with questions. Instead, she chatters cheerfully about her life, which focuses on her ten grandchildren and four beautiful daughters. It's a welcome distraction from my own miserable thoughts, which creep in every time I catch glimpses of myself in the white gown.

After forty minutes, she steps back, satisfied. "It's lovely. Master James will be most pleased when he sees you tomorrow."

"I'm sure he will." I gaze at myself in the three large mirrors surrounding us.

"Well, let's fix this." She pins a veil into my hair and gently drapes it over my face. "There. Now I'll go collect Miss Eleanor. Be back in a tick."

She slips from the room, closing the door behind her. I sigh, waiting for them to return so I can pretend I'm pleased. The door creaks open again, and I turn, expecting Nell. But instead, a soot-faced young man steps in, clothed in black. A cap is pulled low over his eyes, and he heaves a heavy sack of supplies over his shoulder.

"Scuse me, miss, but I was told you was 'avin a bit o' chimney bother in 'ere?"

"Oh, um... I suppose?" I say, uneasy as I stand like a statue on the pedestal. "Go ahead and check."

"Much obliged, miss."

He strolls to the fireplace and drops his load with a thud. "Lovely day, ain't it just?"

He tips his cap, and when he looks up, green eyes sparkle beneath the brim, and I know that face, even beneath a layer of soot.

"Peter!" I lift my veil.

"Shh." He holds a finger to his lips.

I'm nearly in tears as he takes my hand and helps me lower to a seated position. I want to hold him tight, but he's covered in soot, forcing restraint.

"You look beautiful," he whispers. "But we need to go. Now."

I glance at the door as footsteps near. "I can't, Peter. I'm so sorry."

We both freeze as the steps pass by.

"I don't understand?" He shakes his head.

"I know... Thomas will invade Elphame if I don't marry James tomorrow."

"There's no way, how is that possible?"

"Dash. He's here. He's the one who bound me yesterday."

A shadow passes over his face at the name.

"Thomas also has Prince Tahreek and the Anathema. As my reward, he promises that my mother and brothers can come home. But if I don't marry James..."

"Then the opposite." He chews his lip thoughtfully. "And James is going along with this? Marrying you by force?"

"He's broken. I don't think he's thinking straight anymore. The light's gone out in him, and I can't help but feel we're the ones responsible for dousing it."

The door opens, and Peter pulls his cap low, strolling to the fireplace, spreading a white sheet across the floor.

"What in the world?" Nell cries at the sight of him. "Young man, this is not the time for such things, can't you see the maiden is in her wedding gown?"

"Right, sorry, miss," Peter says, lifting out his brush. "But if you gives me a tick, I'll be outta your 'air. Just finishin' up, I am. But you carry on, I won't be no bother."

"We will not! Now you just pack up and go."

"Can't do that, miss." He shakes his head and taps his brush against his boot, bending beside the hearth. "Master Thomas, 'e insists I get this clog cleared proper. Way it's lookin', could start a right nasty fire, it could—filthy as a coal cart, this one."

"Well, I never," Nell mutters, then turns to me. I rise, smoothing the dress, positioning the veil back in place.

"It's lovely." Her head bobs. "Just as I imagined."

"It is indeed, ma'am," I agree.

"Yes, well—I was given little time to choose, but it'll do. Now, Marlene, come see this list James put together. He wants a full wardrobe ready for her upon return from the honeymoon."

They wander to the far side of the room, their backs to us.

Peter steps closer, pretending to fiddle with his tools. "There's no way in hell I'm leaving you here again," he whispers.

"I know. But this time, we have no choice." I glance at the women, bent over the sideboard. "I love you, with all my heart. Please remember that."

He lifts his gaze to mine. "Wendy..." There's a tremor in his voice. "I want to see you in a dainty white gown... but to marry *me*, not him."

"Oh, Peter!" Warmth floods me. "I'd marry you in a heartbeat."

"Then do it. Wait for me, because I'm not giving you up."

The women begin to stroll back, and Peter hastily packs his tools.

"G'day, ladies." He bows. Then, turning to me, he tips his cap, and a silver tear streaks through his soot-covered cheek. "Miss..."

"Good day, sir," I murmur.

He swallows hard, then strides out the door, the thud echoing through me. Were I alone, I'd rip off this dress and scream until the tears flowed freely. But with both ladies staring at me, I steady my breathing and focus on my mother. My brothers. All the Fae whom I'm sparing by marrying James.

❆ ❆ ❆

"How's your tea, Wendy?" Nell asks, lifting the delicate porcelain cup to her lips. Soft pink rosebuds bloom across its surface.

Mother's tea set.

My blood boils hotter than the tea in my cup as I watch her sip. Part of me is ready to knock it from her hands, scorch through her dress, ruin this ridiculous charade we're playing. Instead, I say, "It's delicious, ma'am."

"And Morgan? You've barely touched yours," Nell says delicately.

"Just not thirsty, Mother." Morgan stares into her cup.

"So." I lift a cucumber sandwich. "How is it that you and Thomas came to be? I heard you were in love with King Charlie before him."

Morgan glances up, head tilted, while Nell chokes and sets her cup down, pressing the napkin to her lips. "Excuse me?"

I stare at her, blinking. "Just curious how your family came to be."

Her face flushes crimson.

"You were the love of Charlie's life," I continue. "So... what happened?"

Morgan's eyes dart between us, one brow lifting.

For a moment, I think Nell might slap me or storm out. But then her chest deflates. "The kingdom happened. He was obligated to step into his father's shoes. We weren't abandoned altogether. We had a lovely home by the sea that, for many years, he would visit. But when the children grew older, and I met Thomas, he thought it was inappropriate for Charlie to be around."

She clears her throat. "Charlie died within a few years of my marriage to Thomas. Does that satisfy your curiosity?"

"Sort of. Why Thomas, though? What could you possibly see in him?"

"You know nothing of Thomas." She pushes back from the table. "To some, his loyalties seem misplaced, but I understand him. Charlie was a confused young man who acted without asking questions. James belongs on the throne, and Thomas is fulfilling his duty to the king."

She turns to leave, and I call after her. "But Charlie *was* the king, and this wasn't what he wanted."

She pauses in the doorway. "Not *that* king…"

"What's she talking about?" I ask Morgan.

"I don't know." She stares after her mother. "But I've never heard her speak of my real father before."

I lift another sandwich and crush it. "Why are you even here and not in Winter Woods?"

"Thomas came for me soon after you left. Said I was no longer needed at the Home. I've been stuck here ever since. I quickly regretted not leaving with you. But someone had to stay behind." A shadow crosses her face. "Nibs said you were in Elphame?"

"Yes." I push the tea away. "Let's walk; if I'm allowed."

"I don't see why not."

We stroll through the open doors onto the wide, arched porch over-looking the gardens—lush, vibrant, and heartbreakingly unchanged. The fountain bubbles in the sun, framed by pale blue and purple hy-drangeas, Mother's favorites.

"It all looks the same," I say. "But tell me… You must've been surprised to see Nibs. What happened?"

"Just as Thomas said. He came with Peter to get you, but in all the chaos, he got caught. Thomas talked with him, then brought me in." A small smile fills her face. "I felt complete again to be near him. But I'm aware Thomas is using him to keep me in line. He knows I won't do anything reckless if Nibs could be hurt."

"Then don't worry. I don't intend to run."

We descend the warm stone steps into the sunlight, following the curved cobblestone path flanked by neatly trimmed green hedges and blooming rosebushes. Birds sweep across the sky above us, their song stirring memories of Robin.

I bend, inhaling the soft, velvety scent of the blossoms. "Mother and Father loved to garden together. They'd come out in the evenings, when the air cooled and the sun set, work side by side, talking, laughing. I'd sit on the porch with the boys, sipping sweet tea and dreaming of a love like theirs."

"And did you find a love like theirs? The note you left for James... What happened?"

"Peter happened." I sigh reflectively. "He snuck into my heart, captured me, and then disappeared. But he was waiting for me in Elphame."

"I'm so pleased to hear this." She squeezes my hand. "But why not fight then? For him?"

"He came to me today. But we can't fight, not this time. Thomas means what he says. He'll attack Elphame, and I fear the destruction that would follow. He also says my mother will be returned safely tomorrow. How can I not agree? If I resist, she dies, my brothers die, and the Fae are destroyed. No... this is my duty to Neverland. But if I must lose everything, at least I gain you as a sister."

I hug her arm, and she pulls me close. "Marriage to my brother or not, we're sisters regardless."

* * *

Dinner is a strained affair. Nell and Thomas arrive already two glasses of wine deep, and though I can't be sure, I suspect my bringing up Charlie has something to do with it.

Nell talks too loudly, firing questions at James about our upcoming honeymoon to the seaside town of Moat Brae. He answers in clipped, brief responses. There's no joy in him, only a quiet, brooding spirit.

Nibs sits beside me, and with Thomas distracted, we take the opportunity to talk.

"You doing okay?" he whispers, around a mouthful of chicken fricassee.

"I saw Peter today and explained everything." I lift my wine and take a small sip. "I'm marrying James. Then you and Morgan will marry."

He shakes his head and sets down his fork. Thomas glances our way, studying us, before turning back to Nell.

"Once, I tried convincing you this was a good idea, for everyone's sake," Nibs murmurs. "Now I'm trying to figure out how to do the opposite."

"I have to. So don't waste time trying to talk me out of it. It's not ideal, but I'll have my family back. You and Morgan, too. Be strong for me, please. If I break now, everyone suffers."

He looks at me, eyes round. "I love you, kid. My heart's breaking for you and Peter. But I'll say no more."

James slams down his whiskey glass and pushes away from the table. "Excuse me."

I watch him leave, then stand up and follow.

"James—wait," I call as he nears the stairwell.

He turns, tone sharp. "What do you want?"

I move to his side, but words falter. "I, uh..."

"That's what I thought. I'll see you tomorrow." He turns to go, but I grab his hand.

"No, wait." I breathe out the nerves. "I'm sorry. Truly sorry."

His forehead creases. "For what?"

"For using you."

"So, you admit it. Was any of it real? Or was it always you and Peter's plan?"

"No." I shake my head quickly. "Marrying you was my desire, and when you proposed, those tears were real. But, yes... at some point, Peter took hold of my heart in a different way. It went beyond the curse and all of my perfectly laid plans."

"I knew I shouldn't have left you."

"James." I hold his gaze. "It wouldn't have mattered. I care for you deeply, but not in the way that matters. At this point, I only want peace between us."

"Why apologize? Why offer an olive branch now?" His voice breaks. "You know what I did to you. I don't deserve your pity. I deserve your hatred."

"Hatred, unforgiveness, it serves nobody. You're not faultless, but you've also spent your life as a piece in everyone else's game. Your mother. Thomas. Me. The only person who never used you was your father. He did the hardest thing—he let you go."

My mind drifts back to that day, long ago. The waves lapping softly at my feet, Tahreek and Dash hovering over Peter and I, ready to take away our lives. At the time, nothing made sense. But now, the memory burns sharp and vivid.

It's James' face that lingers.

Not dominant or cruel—but broken and fearful. Regret etched every line as he shook his head, mouthing an apology.

When I woke up, he found me. I can see it all. His tenderness and calm, the need to protect me, it was all he could do to live with himself.

I take him in now: a hand missing, cut off in a fit of passion. He's real. Not like Thomas who's so detached that the people around him became nothing more than pawns.

"James." I guide his hooked hand into mine. His breath grows heavy. "God knows I've done many things wrong, so maybe I don't deserve a happy ending. But perhaps you do."

He pulls away, anger tightening his face. "No. I don't."

I watch him go, then turn and find myself facing Nell, a tremble in her lips. "Excuse me."

She slips past and disappears up the stairs.

I amble back to the dining room, and Rosetta steps around the corner, hand to her heart. "Oh, there you are! Are you finished with your meal?"

"Yeah. I'm all set."

"Okay, I was asked to return you to your room for the evening."

"Sure, let's go."

I follow her, empty of any real emotion as she locks the door behind me. I move to the easy chair, sinking into it. This night won't be an easy one; I'm certain I won't sleep a wink. Staring out the windows, I watch the clouds drift past.

I remember Michael saying he spent his waiting time after the curse broke in the Chapel, praying. And if I can't sleep, that's better than sitting and staring at nothing. My lids close and though I've spoken prayers freely many times before, this time I keep the words close to my heart. Hope seems distant, but I refuse to give up.

I'm not sure how much time passes, but when I've found a level of peace, the sky has gone dark.

Turning toward the bookshelf, I spot *Gulliver's Travels*. I rise and take it down, flipping through its worn pages. My eyes catch on a line just as a key turns in the lock. Perhaps Rosetta forgot something.

I glance up just as Juke enters, a broad grin stretched across his face, and the words I read flicker to life, so I say them aloud:

"My horror and astonishment are not to be described when I observed in this abominable animal a perfect human figure."

"My, my, Juke. How impeccably this describes you."

He closes the door and steps toward me. "I just got home, but when I heard from the footman what's been going on, I could hardly believe my ears. James' bride is here? And they're to marry tomorrow. Well, says me, I ought to go and congratulate my old friend."

He leans against the bookshelf. "Of course, I already did that the night before her wedding, didn't I? So, I guess I'm a little perplexed why we're doing this charade a second time."

"Yes, you're right. It *is* odd. But then, forced marriages usually are. The men in your family never could take 'no' for an answer, could you?"

"What do I say? I take after ole Dad."

I rise and walk past him, pushing the book back onto the shelf. "Well, maybe go and spend quality time with him, then. However, I'd appreciate it if you would leave now. I need my beauty rest for tomorrow."

"You still owe me an hour." He glides to my side, gripping my shoulders. "Last time was interrupted, remember?"

I tense as his fingers trail up the side of my neck.

"Yes, I recall Peter knocking you out cold very well."

"But he's not here, now, is he?"

"You know," I say, voice calm. "I tire of this game. Would you like to leave before it begins?"

He chuckles and presses a kiss to my neck. "Not at all."

I clench my fist and swing it backward, elbow slamming into his gut, doubling him over with a groan. Then, lifting my knee, I smash it into his chin.

"Consarn it, woman!" he cries out, clutching his jaw.

"Well, well," James says from the doorway. "Doesn't look like you need my help."

"Not at all." I eye Juke as he wipes blood off his lip, glaring between us.

"Apologies for his intrusion." James steps inside. "Oh, brother. Will you never learn? If you hadn't been an idiot tonight, you might've spared yourself a lifetime of regret. But since you're here..."

James looks up at the ceiling. "Dash, I'd like a manservant who obeys my every command."

Juke stares up as the faerie floats into view. "What are you talking about? You feeling alright, brother?"

Dash raises his hands. A yellow flame forms between them and begins drifting in Juke's direction.

"Whoa now." Juke chuckles nervously, backing away. "What's he doing?"

"You heard me." James folds his arms. "I'd like a manservant. And you'll do just fine."

Juke ducks as the light comes near, scrambling for my bed as the glow floats toward him. "Come on, James! I was always your man, doing as you bid. You going to turn on me now? I was just messing with her, I swear it."

The light shoots forward and wraps around him, binding him in yellow strands. He grunts, falling to his knees.

"Oh, sure you were. Just like when you assaulted her? Yes. You were *always* my man, weren't you?"

"Nothing wrong with taking turns." Juke growls, thrashing as the light wraps tighter. "What's happening?"

"Go to the *Jolly Roger*," James says with a flick of his hand. "Prepare her to sail by dawn."

Juke's face reddens as he struggles against the magic, but it's useless. Slowly, he rises to his feet, panting. "Let's talk, please!"

"Be silent, while you're at it," James says flatly, waving him away. "Go on now."

Juke glares at me with an accusing stare—then stumbles out the door, the light fading into him.

"Well, that was easy." James rubs his hook against his palm. "Now you and I have a long journey ahead of us. Are you ready?"

"What are you talking about?"

"There's somewhere we need to go." He gestures for me. "Come on; we haven't much time."

I follow him into the hall, Dash flying close behind, but we don't take the main staircase. Instead, he leads me down the narrow servant's stairwell. As we pass through the lower level, a few staff look up at us from their duties. One young man polishes silverware, while another, older, peers over his newspaper, a cigar between his teeth.

"Sir?" The older man calls, standing.

"We were never here," James replies.

"Yes, sir." The man sits slowly, watching us go.

Outside, a grey sedan waits, and James opens the door for me. What is he up to? I slide in, stomach in knots. He gets behind the wheel, starts the engine, and glances over his shoulder as we back out. Then we're off, driving through Silver Mist, winding past quiet shops and flickering streetlamps. Townsfolk stroll along the sidewalks, oblivious to who passes by them in the night.

"It's going to be a long drive," he says. "Might as well get comfy."

I press back into the seat and glance over at him. His gaze remains fixed on the road; mouth pressed tight.

"Will you at least tell me where you're taking me?"

He reaches behind his seat and places something soft on my lap. My white cashmere coat, the one he gave me for my birthday. I run my hand along the material. "Winter Woods?"

"Yes."

And with that, he hits the gas, and we're speeding out of town.

Toward the cold and the wind.

Toward where it all began.

Chapter 29

The gate groans open before us.

My whole life led to the moment Kit drove me away from this place, and now, I return of my own free will. I can't quite name the emotion stirring in me as we pass beneath the gate, but whatever it is, it leaves me determined.

I'm back in Winter Woods.

I left as Wendy. I return as Wendy Darling.

This steadies me. No matter what happens, I will face it as all of me, and something in that gives me strength.

I press my fingers to the glass, the chill seeping through. The car slows, then stops. James rolls down the window, and a fierce wind rushes in as he motions to the guard.

"Yes, Captain?"

"Call Smee at Will's Bakehouse," James says. "Tell him the captain needs him to gather the group at Starkey Manor. Tell him… 'the ticking has stopped.' Can you do that?"

"Of course, sir." The guard salutes. "I'll pass on your message, exactly."

"Thank you." James presses on the gas and rolls the window back up.

"What's that about?" I tug the coat tighter, shivering.

"You'll see. One stop before we head that way. This one, I think you'll like."

Once, these streets were all I knew. And it's like a dream, remembering. Nothing existed beyond Winter Woods. Now, there's all of Neverland, and even the world beyond the sea where I came from.

This place felt larger than life, and now it appears small and insignificant.

The Home comes into view, streetlights casting their glow onto the dark house. It must be nearing ten as James parks the car and shuts off the engine. He chews his lip, staring at the house. "Let's do this," he says at last.

He opens the door, and Dash soars out. Then he steps out, and I follow. My shoes aren't made for this, and sink into the snow.

"Blast it," I mutter, sloshing forward.

James watches, amused. "Wait there."

He strides over and lifts me into his arms. "It's my fault for not bringing you boots."

"It's okay." I wince. "My back's sore, just be careful."

He stills, face falling. "I'll never forgive myself for hurting you."

"Why did you do it?"

"I swear I didn't intend to hurt you—not like that. Though looking back, it sounds foolish to say. I was angry and not thinking straight. The goal wasn't to harm you, but an act to force his hand." He chuckles darkly, glancing at the hook. "What irony... that he forced mine."

An ache fills me at his words. "For what it's worth, I believe you, and I forgive you."

"I know you do." He runs a finger along my chin. "You can't help yourself."

We hold each other's gaze a long moment. Despite everything, something about him still feels like home.

I press into him, eyes slipping shut, and I can almost hear it: the sounds of children echoing from the house, girlish laughter at James' arrival. The way he'd stride in, with far more charm than is good for a young man. Morgan, standing by with quiet resolve. Nibs, quick with a joke. And me, melting, just a little, with every word he spoke.

How do I let this all go—say goodbye to the world that formed me? I gaze up at him, and the softness in his expression assures me he understands exactly what's in my heart.

He carries me around the house until we reach the shed, where smoke curls from the chimney, and warm light spills onto the lawn. A shadow passes the window, and emotion rises—Llewelyn.

James sets me down and walks to the shed door, knocking. I can't imagine what we're here for. The door opens, and Llewelyn peers out, eyebrows lifting at the sight of us. I smile wide, and he steps forward, pulling me into his embrace.

"I'm so glad to see you again," I say, tears rising.

He pulls back, studying me. "*What are you doing here?*"

"Can we talk inside?" James asks.

Llewelyn glances at him, then nods, motioning us in.

The shed is the same as always. Air rich with smells of cedar and pine. Floor carpeted with a fine layer of wood shavings and sawdust. He guides us past shelves lined with chisels, sandpaper, and jars full of screws and nails. His treasured workbench remains the same, etched and worn from the hundreds of projects he's crafted—mostly for us.

He removes his leather apron and hangs it on a hook, warming his hands over the woodstove. "*Please, go ahead,*" he signs.

"He says to go ahead," I tell James.

We sit on a squashy old sofa, blanketed with thick wool throws, as Llewelyn lifts his steaming mug from the handmade coffee table and watches us, expectant.

"Llewelyn, you're a good man, far better than I," James says, leaning forward, knees vibrating. "The time has come to let you go."

The mug slips from Llewelyn's hand, shattering against the floor. He doesn't move to clean it, doesn't kick away the shards, just stares at James.

"Yes, I know it's unexpected," James continues. "But it shouldn't be. If I had to guess, I'd say you always knew this day would come."

Llewelyn's face pinches, holding back emotion.

"James, what's going on?" I ask. "What are you talking about?"

He turns to me. "After I left you tonight, my mother came to me."

"Yeah, I saw her. She heard our conversation. Is that what this is about? Something she said?"

"She asked me if I wanted to marry you. It wasn't about love, or desire, but heart. What did I truly want? You were right when you said I've let myself be used. So much of my life has been spent trying to keep everyone happy. But it was impossible. To please one meant hurting another. Every single time."

He leans back, rubbing his chin.

"She gave me permission tonight, to say no. To say I didn't want to marry you, or become king. That I was free to be the man I know I should be, not who she and Thomas wanted."

His fingers graze a golden band around his wrist. A charm rests at its center, but I can't make out its shape. "Thomas in all his loyalty went mad. And I nearly went with him. But I was saved. And now, it's time I do the same for everyone else."

I swallow hard, afraid to blink, or breathe, afraid he'll take it all back.

"You were right, Wendy." His gaze sharpens. "I could have told your father what Thomas intended to do. But my pride held me back. A desire to prove myself worthy in a way I thought my father doubted.

"Cursing you felt like the only way. And it nearly cost me my soul. You were right; I never really wanted a crown; I just wanted my father to think I was worthy of it."

He pauses, then says the words I've prayed to hear, "It's over. You and I will not marry tomorrow."

My lips part, overcome.

"And it's time I do the one thing I ought to have done five years ago."

"And what's that?"

He looks at Llewelyn. "Go to your father for help."

I look from Llewelyn to James, head shaking. "I don't understand."

"Dash," James says. "Undo the cloaking spell."

The faerie comes into view and clasps his hands together. At first, nothing happens, but then a misty green light begins to lift off Llewelyn. I watch as Llewelyn stretches his arms, the green light dissolving into the air.

"Wendy," James says. "When Thomas took over, it was I who was in charge of your father's death."

My face screws up. "Why are you telling me this?"

"Dash, lift the final bind." His voice is heavy with emotion.

"*Verba Solvo, Vox Obscura.*" Dash's voice vibrates through the little room.

Llewelyn trembles, clutching his head. Then, drawing in a deep breath, his gaze lifts, and he looks straight at me. "*Wendy?*"

His voice... a shudder rips through me.

That voice...

An ache cracks open in my chest, a sob bursting free, and I press a hand to my mouth.

I see him—my *father*.

He rises, hesitant. "Do you know me?"

"Yes." I nod frantically, tears blinding me.

His face is alight with sorrow and joy, like rain slipping through golden sunlight. He kneels at my side, lifting a hand to my face, strong and steady, and brushes away my tears, just as he did when I was a child.

"Little one..." he breathes. "I fear this is just another dream."

I collapse into his arms, weeping. He holds me secure as I let it all go. How foolish I feel to not have known. All these years. Of course. Of course. The man who loved me best could only be my father.

"I thought you were dead," I whisper.

"And yet I never left you." He pulls back, eyeing the necklace he gave me. "I was always with you."

"I'm sorry I didn't tell you right away," James says. "Thomas believed he was dead, and this was the only way to keep it that way. I'm sorry Llewe—George, I truly am. I'm returning everything I've taken from you, and by tomorrow, all of your family will be with you again."

Father doesn't speak, just dips his head, taking it all in.

"We must go now," James presses up. "There's more to be done."

"But the children." Father glances toward the house. "I can't leave them behind."

"They'll be brought to the palace in the morning. Don't worry; they'll be safe."

Father looks to me.

"You can trust him," I say. "We'd better go."

Helping me to my feet, he takes one final look around the shed before dousing the fire. Hand in hand, we leave his workshop behind.

We follow James to the car, and I sit in the backseat, pressed close to my father's side, unwilling to let him go again. From the very beginning, Llewelyn was attentive—always watching out for me. He dried my tears, offered healing hugs, and found endless ways to make me laugh through the pain.

Never once did he let on that I belonged to him. But the truth is, he didn't need to. He was still my father, without the title or acknowledgment. He was my father because he chose to be. Every single day, in every possible way.

❋ ❋ ❋

Entering Starkey Manor, we're met by Gentleman Starkey himself—his hair disheveled, face tense.

"What's going on, James? Smee said the ticking has stopped?"

"Yes, I'll explain in a moment." James motions Father and me forward.

Starkey looks at us, then grips the wall. "Is that who I think it is?"

"Yes," James replies. "King George, in the flesh."

"Wendy?" Starkey squints at me, stumbling forward to grab my shoulders. "My daughter—where's my Grace? She left with you weeks ago."

"Kindly release my daughter," my father says, his tone calm but firm.

Starkey backs off, sweat lining his forehead. "Of course."

He looks around like he's lost in his own home.

"She's safe, sir. I promise. She's with Henley and they're happy."

This seems to comfort him as his lips lift slightly and he nods. "Oh good. Good. I want her to be happy. That's all a father wants..." He leans against the wall, winded.

"Are you okay, sir?" I step closer, and touch his arm.

"I've made many mistakes. The reckoning's here."

He turns and walks away, and we follow. A soft glow spills from the Back Room into the ballroom. James stands at the door, waiting for us. Together, we enter, facing a room full of his companions.

"Cap'n, it be good to see ye!" Smee rises, but his face twists at the flash of iron on James' arm.

A clatter nearby draws our attention—Rose beside a tipped tray, glass shattered on the floor. She stares at the hook, a crease forming along her forehead. "What happened, James?"

The room falls silent, all eyes on him.

"Yes." James holds up the hook. "This is, unfortunately, the new me. Does anyone have a problem with that?"

"Course not, Cap," says Black Gilmour, lifting his drink. "Looks mighty fine, if you ask me."

Smee shakes his head, though clearly uneasy. And James looks to Rose, still lost in the metal's gleam. "Rose?"

She shakes her head, slowly, and bends to gather the glass.

"Alright. You're wondering why I've gathered you so late," James begins, pacing in front of the bar. "We're leaving tonight. All of us."

A murmur spreads through the room.

"Silence, please," James calls. "George."

My father steps forward, glancing around.

"Bloody hell," Chas exclaims. "Is he?"

"Yes. This is King George. I'm not going to explain how he's here, only that he is. My time is done. And by tomorrow night, anyone who helped Thomas or me? You'll be done too. We have this one chance. We'll board the *Jolly Roger* and escape."

"What about our businesses, James?" Chas asks. "You expect us to drop everything and just leave?"

"That's entirely up to you. But George here will be in charge again, and despite his calm demeanor tonight, I wouldn't count on a free pass tomorrow."

"How much time do we have?" Foggerty calls from the back.

"Two hours."

The room erupts in voices—questions, complaints.

"Now look, you ungrateful bastards!" James barks, his voice sharp as his sword. "I could've left you to rot—get locked up with the rest. But you've been faithful to me, so I offer you this chance. Now… stop talking, get up, get your bloody bags, and let's go!"

"Ey!" Smee cheers, throwing up a fist. "I'm with ye, Cap'n!"

The rest agree, voices rising in a chorus of, "Eys."

"Good. Now, we can't take much. Canary, we'll need food supplies. You, Smee, and Rose—gather what you can in Alf and Robert's trucks. Anything we might need for a very long voyage."

He points across the room. "Cookson, Wibbles—gather weapons, as many as possible. Noodler, Gilmour—you're with them.

"*Signore* James," Cecco calls, waving his hand. "Che about-a *us*, eh? Che we do now, Jill and me?"

Jill nods silently, clinging to his arm.

"Uh." James frowns. "You two can help with supplies. Foggerty, Mayor Herb—destroy whatever records you can. Sorry, George," he adds with a glance, "but we've got to do what we can."

He scans the room. "Chas, Starkey—money. Don't steal it, just take what's ours. You have two hours. Then we're on the road. Let's move."

❄

Two hours later, we're in the sedan pulling away from Starkey Manor. As the car begins to move, I catch a glint of red in a second story window—Ms. Diana. I hurriedly roll down the window and lean out, uncaring about the cold. She lifts a hand to the glass, and I offer a small wave.

"You'll see her again," Father says behind me.

I settle back and raise the window again. "I know... but still."

As we pass under the gate once again, I catch sight of a line of cars and trucks trailing behind us. My father rests his head against his hand, watching the snowy world fade into the distance.

"I know how it feels," I say. "When I first left, I opened the window and screamed. Henley and I both did. Grace thought we'd lost our minds."

James gazes at me through the mirror, a small smile gathering at the corner of his mouth.

"I wish I could've seen you." Father tilts his head to mine. "But I can imagine. Oh, there's so much to talk about. Are your brothers alright?"

"They are. Happy as can be in Elphame."

"And." He leans closer, whispering. "Peter? Did you find him?"

My cheeks flush.

"He loves me too," I say. "But right now, he thinks I'm marrying James today. Thomas threatened to destroy Elphame if I didn't."

"Well then, we're going to have to do something about him now, aren't we?"

Eventually, I drift into sleep, and when I wake, we're parked at the palace docks, dawn spilling slowly across the sky. The *Jolly Roger* rests in the water, proud and majestic. Once, I dreamed of the day I'd board her, sail the seas at James' side. But now, as I step out of the car and walk to the edge of the dock, gazing upon her splendor, I know she and I have already taken the grandest journey of all.

"So," Chas says, bumping my arm, "you going to miss me?"

"Of course." I gaze at him, recalling a much younger version. "But are we going to continue our charade, like we didn't know each other before all of this?"

He exhales and shoves his hands into his pockets. "I was wondering when you might bring that up. I swear to you, I knew nothing that final night. My father kept it all a secret until we moved. I'm truly sorry."

"It's okay. What's done is done. Thomas had James convinced and James had all of you convinced. But tell me... are you much of a sea-man?"

"No, but I'd better learn fast. Dash it, I'll sure miss my restaurant. But the way your pops is staring at me, I'm sure he'd lock me up for life. So, I'd best go while I can."

"Good luck to you, Chas. Truly." I squeeze his arm. "And thanks for the fun."

He kisses my cheek. "No, my darling. Thank you."

He slips away as the others finish loading the last of the supplies, and they gather around James as the moment to board arrives.

"Well, men," James says. "Say goodbye to this place. We won't be seeing her for a long while."

"Mademoiselle." Cecco takes my hand and kisses it. "*Sei Bellissima*."

"*Sei Bellissima*, Cecco," I say, affectionately.

Jill dabs at her nose. "You really should come with us. Captain will be mighty broken without you."

"Thank you. But I belong here. This is my home. Good luck, Jill."

She turns to Cecco, who wraps an arm around her and guides her up the gangway.

Gentleman Starkey steps in front of me, Canary at his side. "See you, Wendy," she says.

I hold out my hand, and she clutches it.

"Make sure my sister finds Grace," Mr. Starkey says, shakily. "And tell Grace, I'm sorry, and I love her."

"I will," I reply, saddened she couldn't be here herself.

He guides Canary forward but pauses. "One more thing." He glances back at me. "Tell Henley, he has my blessing. The only comfort I have in this is knowing they'll be together."

"Of course. I will tell them. Goodbye, sir."

He joins the others, shoulders drooping.

"See ye, miss!" Smee calls with a gleeful wave as he totters past. "It were mighty fine knowin' ye, it truly was!"

Rose follows after, watching me, with a pained look. I feel for her loss, from the poor man's docks of Kirriemuir to Neverpeak Hills, and now into exile. I raise my hand, and she dips her head, continuing on.

James steps beside me, watching her go. "I've ruined her. Same as I did to you."

"I'll be okay. And so will she. You can make sure of it."

He wipes at his nose and nods. "Well, it's time."

"I wish you didn't have to go."

"For a moment, I saw a future with you." Emotion catches in his throat. "It was beautiful. But... at least I know you'll be happy and safe."

He wraps his arms around me, and I breathe him in, one last time. We remain for a moment, and then as he pulls away, I hold onto his arm. "James... I know he hurt you. But, are you still angry with Peter?"

His jaw tightens. "I wish him well, for your sake. But pray our paths never cross again, for I cannot say what I'd do."

He leans in and kisses me—then, he's gone, disappearing onto the ship.

The lines are cast off, pulled in by Juke, who watches me from the deck. One by one, the men and women gather around James, and he turns, facing me.

"Cap'n." Smee's voice echoes from the deck. "We're awful grateful to ye, we are."

"And know this," Chas adds, "all of us—we're your men. Through and through."

"Let's 'ear it for the Cap'n!" Smee calls, raising his voice. "For Cap'n Hook!" He gestures to James' right hand, now replaced by the hook.

James stares, unsure, as Smee guides the hook higher. One by one, the group joins in, hands clapping, feet stomping with each shout.

"*Hook! Hook! Hook!*"

A grin breaks through James' guard and he shakes his head, covering his face.

Their voices echo into the air as the *Jolly Roger* steers away, sails catching the wind. A gunshot cracks the sky—Noodler laughs, and others follow, firing into the air.

Through the revelry, James stands tall, his black hair blowing in the wind. And as the first light stretches its gleaming tendrils across the water, it sets fire to his coat, red as blood, golden buttons glimmering like stars. There's no denying—a piece of me goes with him. The part of me that saw him as the morning sun to my midnight world. Now, as the sun climbs higher, and he becomes a speck on the horizon, that part of my life sails off with the waves of the sea.

Gone, but never forgotten.

Chapter 30

Father drives the navy-blue sedan along the streets outside the palace. A few greys blend with his brown hair, but otherwise, he's much the same as he was five years ago. Can't say the same for the rest of us. Mother has been separated, unable to witness the changes time brought. If James was being honest, she'll be back soon. I run my fingers along the golden edges of her bracelet, a bit apprehensive.

Will she be the same? Was she also cursed?

"You've got that faraway look," Father says. "Care to let me in on it?"

"Thinking about mother." I study his tired face, neither of us has barely slept in a day.

"I can relate. There were times I'd imagined she was with me, in the shed, or at mealtime, smiling at me. Her loss was far more profound than even my own voice. But unlike her, I had you kids to keep me going."

"I fear what's happened to her."

"She's safe. Thomas would've disposed of the lot of us to ensure the throne for James. But James, being young, was thankfully not so hardened by time. When everything went down, he promised me she would be okay. Compromised as he is, he's been honest thus far."

"I pray you're right." I wrap my arms around my legs.

He pulls the car alongside the palace, down a winding road bordered with hedges and canopied by towering oaks. Beyond the palace lies the sea, with its glorious emerald waters sparkling under the sunbeams.

"It's as beautiful as I remember," Father says, gazing toward the water, a soft breeze ruffling his hair.

"Yeah, it was night when Kit and I came, so I—" My words are cut short as a figure bursts from the hedges and sprints into the road, unaware of the oncoming car.

"Father, watch out!"

He looks toward the road, and slams his foot down. Breaks screech, tires protest, but we skid to a stop just in time. The figure spins around, wide-eyed.

"It's Nell!" I exclaim.

Father parks the car and steps out. I follow. Nell backs away, face pale as a ghost as she gazes at him.

"You're... dead," she stammers. "This is impossible."

"Hello, Eleanor," Father says, calm as ever. "You haven't changed a bit. What's it been? Five, six years?"

"You remember?" She darts a look my way.

"Of course. We sat by one another at the Turley dinner party, don't you recall?"

"Yes. I just didn't imagine you would remember me."

"You were uneasy." Father steps closer, voice gentle, as though she were a child. "I wondered what could weigh so heavily on a person... Now I know."

"James killed you. I don't understand what's happening?"

"He never intended to kill me. He only said so to appease Thomas. Does this disappoint you?"

"No." She shakes her head. "I cried many nights. I never agreed with Thomas' methods. But..." She glances at the ground. "I was angry and willing to believe him if it meant seeing James on the throne."

"Why are you out here?" I finally ask. "What are you running from?"

"It's over." She motions to the palace. "The Fae, the Piccaninny... they've invaded. And Thomas, Dash—they're nowhere to be found. I didn't know what to do, so I ran."

Father lifts something from inside his jacket, and I can't hold back a gasp as he grips a gun in his hand.

"What?" He offers a sheepish grin. "They had a truckload of weapons, can't blame me for grabbing one when no one was looking."

"What are you going to do with it?" I ask.

"Nothing." He presses the cool steel into my palm. "I'm going to the car. She's yours, darling. Do what you think is best."

He doesn't wait for my response but walks to the car and hops in. I turn to Nell, memories of the night we met returning. "You knew what was going to happen to us?"

"Yes. And I'm so sorry." She sinks to her knees, unsteady. "In Barrie's final days, he directed Thomas to ensure the throne stayed in the family. He knew Charlie had no intention of passing the crown to James, and like himself, Charlie was sick. He knew his son wasn't long for this world. If another took the throne, Thomas was charged with returning it to the family—at any cost. And that's what he did."

I stare at the gun, then lay it on the ground and kneel beside her. "Thomas didn't meet you by chance, did he?"

"No. We had met before. When Charlie became king, he and Barrie showed up one day. It wasn't a grandfatherly visit, either. I was so wounded by Charlie, and they took advantage of it. The marriage was arranged, and Barrie promised my time was coming."

"Charlie wasn't ashamed of you. He knew he was dying, and that James would have to take the throne. He wanted better for you, a life free of the ties that bound him. He loved you."

"Losing his brother really broke him," she says. "The last time I saw him, I told him to never come back." She wipes at the tears forming in her eyes. "I wish I had said I loved him instead."

"Love's funny like that." I gaze up, and a flash of memory flickers, young Peter soaring past, hands pounding his chest, crowing like a bird. "We say things we don't mean. But love... it transcends everything, you know? Those we love, they *know* us. Even when we speak out of hurt or anger, they still see us. If Charlie loved you, he knew how you truly felt."

"I hope you're right. I want to believe you are right. Thank you. Speaking of love...where's my son?"

"He's gone, freed my father, and left on the *Jolly Roger*."

She glances toward the sea, exhaling. "I'm glad. Everything was for me. And everything I did was for him. I'm grateful he finally did something for himself."

"You spoke to him last night." I rise and offer a hand. "Whatever was said, it helped him."

"He needed me to release him, so I did." She stands and straightens, chin high. "Now what?"

"James earned you a second chance. Take this opportunity to start over, and please, don't live life on anyone's terms but your own."

"The last time I did that was when I was a young woman." A soft smile touches her lips. "Well, I am sorry things couldn't work between you and my son. I'm confident you'd have made a lovely daughter-in-law."

"And I'm confident James will find the right woman, one far better than me. Go in grace, Nell. And good luck."

She nods. "Goodbye, Wendy." And steps into the hedge, vanishing from sight. I breathe out and lift the gun. Did Father truly expect me to use this? I walk to the car, fling open the door, and get in.

"Here you go." I hand over the weapon. "I'm sorry if that wasn't what you wanted."

"No, darling." He offers a reassuring tilt of his head and presses the gun back into the jacket. "That was exactly what I wanted."

❋❋❋

The palace is silent. Eerily so.

"Where is everyone?" I look around. "Nell said the Fae and Piccaninny were here, so why does it appear deserted?"

"Indeed," Father murmurs, his boots echoing across the marble floor of the entryway.

There's a look on his face, one I can't quite place—probably because this moment is unlike any other for him.

"It was painful coming back and seeing them live here," I say. "Nell was using Mother's tea set, and James took over my old room. Not to mention Thomas."

His features pinch. "It feels like waking from a bad dream. None of it seems real anymore."

"I don't know how you did it. I would have gone mad knowing what you did."

"It wasn't all bad." He wraps an arm around me. "There was something nice about no longer carrying the weight of a kingdom on my shoulders. Becoming a nobody, working on my projects, no endless schedule to keep up with. It was like, life just froze, and I could rest.

"To some that would be a nightmare, but to me, I kind of liked it. Of course, without your mother, it was hard to ever truly be at peace, but, with you and your brothers there, I almost was."

A bark echoes through the hall, and in a flash, something white knocks me backward. A wet tongue licks my face.

"Nana!" I giggle, petting our shaggy nurse dog. "Where did you come from?"

Father bends and wraps his arms around her. Nana nuzzles her face against his.

"Nana?" Michael bursts into the hallway, John at his heels. "Wendy! You're here!"

Father looks between them and rises. Confusion and awe flicker across their faces as they take him in.

"I don't understand." John steps back.

"Johnny." I cross the space to his side. "Who do you see?"

"Llewelyn. But also..." He readjusts his glasses. "No, that's impossible." Father's gaze is set on John.

Michael looks between the two. "You're our father."

It isn't a question; it's a fact.

"I am." Father nods.

Their faces twist with disbelief—emotion flooding in as they rush into his arms. My heart overflows, for this is a dream I had given up on.

"I can't believe this." John pulls back, studying Father's face. "You're *him*."

"It was a cloaking spell," I say. "James did it to keep him alive."

"All these years, and you were there the whole time?"

"Never missed a moment." Father cups his cheek.

"We need to go," Michael says, stepping away. "Mother's coming, and she's almost here."

"Truly?" Father inspects himself, smoothing his shirt and adjusting his collar. "Well, mustn't keep her waiting."

"She'd certainly have words if you did," John says.

"James sent a messenger to the Piccaninny," Michael adds, "Word was a ship would arrive today with Mother, Lilium, and Lean Wolf aboard."

"Meanwhile," John continues as we start walking. "Peter returned yesterday with news of what Thomas planned for you. We were ready to leave when the Piccaninny messenger, Pox, arrived today."

We stroll through the dining room, food left uneaten on plates; clearly, something interrupted the meal. How strange it is, knowing I might have been there too, preparing myself to marry James.

"What about the others from the Home?" I ask. "James said they'd be brought here."

"They arrived an hour ago." John pushes open the door leading to the gardens. "Kit got to work immediately and everyone will soon be back to normal.

"As normal as Slightly and Tootles ever were." Michael smirks.

"This is amazing! Oh heavens, there's the beach." I take his hand. "Let's go find her!"

I glance back at Father and John; both dip their chins in agreement, and we sprint ahead, passing through the gardens until we reach the white fence leading to the water. A crowd gathers near the shore, and yes, a royal ship rests in the distance, smaller boats rowing to meet the land.

The gate swings open, and we're shouting, tearing down the beach, splashing into the water, scanning the line of boats, until we spot her.

She's holding onto Lilium, waving, calling our names.

JaneAnn puts a hand on my shoulder, and I grab her into a hug, laughing, pure delight written across her face. Maimie is the first to speed ahead, and soon the rest of us follow.

Passengers leap into the water, swimming to shore. All around me, people rush to their loved ones. JaneAnn dives into her father's arms. Agnes and Elizabeth wrap themselves in their parent's embrace. Hannah's parents drop to their knees, clutching her, weeping with joy and sorrow, for Hannah comes alone, without Margaret.

Father reaches Mother first, lifting her into his arms, laughing as he twirls her, then stops and bends her backward, kissing. Beside me, Nibs and Morgan join us, then the Twins, and Slightly and Tootles. They're all here. And I realize: she's not just John's, Michael's, and my mother; she belongs to all of us.

"Is that... Llewelyn?" Nibs asks. "No wait—it's George! Wait no. I'm losing my mind, aren't I?"

"You'll see." I giggle and press into him, his arm holding me close. Mother and Father stroll toward us, and the boys rush to greet them, arms flung around them, their excitement filling the air. Surprise flickers on every face at Father's reveal, but I hang back, savoring the moment.

Then Mother lifts her eyes and looks at me. There's her smile—that familiar kiss still tucked into the corner of her lips. She's still every inch a mother. Overflowing with love, and ready to pour it all out. She sweeps through the group, a vision in her pale green dress, auburn hair swept high.

We look so alike.

"You've grown into quite the lady, my dear." Tears streak her rosy cheeks.

"I can't believe you're really here!" I throw myself into her arms, and we hold each other.

Looking around, I spot Chief Big Little Panther embracing his wife, while Lean Wolf, and Tiger Lily watch. And yes... there's Rosetta with her mother.

Everything is perfect!

As we pull apart, we stroll to the shore while I pepper her with questions. She and the other officials, including Lilium and Lean Wolf, were indeed kept on an island. But James kept her informed about us, ensuring they lived comfortably. In the end, he became the broken, deeply flawed hero we all needed. Thomas thought he was pulling the strings, but in truth, James had cut them long ago.

Within the day, news of the royal family's return is met with joyous celebration throughout Silver Mist. Messengers are dispatched to every town, bearing a royal proclamation: the gates of every safe haven shall be opened, and the citizens freed—from Silver Mist to Kirriemuir, and from Moat Brae to Winter Woods. Piccaninny and Fae, alongside royal soldiers, are sent to the havens with lists compiled by Morgan of men and women loyal to Thomas. True to James' word, by nightfall, anyone who aided Thomas will be detained.

The rest of the day, the palace hums with festivity. The royal orchestra is summoned, and food and drink are laid out. By nightfall, there's dancing and singing, laughter and stories. No one is sorrowful, even where grief once lingered. The windows and doors are kept open, the wind curling softly through the rooms—sweet and soothing. I could be perfectly at rest... except Peter is nowhere to be found.

At first, I assumed he was lost in the commotion. But now I'm certain, he's gone. Slipping out to the porch overlooking the gardens, I sit on the steps, wrapped in a beam of moonlight.

"Why are you out here by yourself?" Kit asks, settling beside me.

"Where is he?"

"I was wondering when you'd ask." He exhales heavily. "He left with Father. They went to King Gilberto to get assistance bringing down the Anathema."

"And why did Peter have to be the one to go?"

"He saw you and James."

"What?" I twist around. "Saw us where?"

"On the dock. Kissing. When we arrived at the palace and found you gone, we went searching. The kiss was innocent, I'm sure, but it was enough. He said he was going to help Father and flew away. I didn't mention it because I didn't want to dampen your joy."

"I see. Dash it... I wasn't thinking. Peter's been through so much, and now I've only added to it. James was saying goodbye, that's all. What should I do now?"

"I have an offer for you." He leans closer. "After you and I left the other night, the council reached a decision. They gave Tinker Bell two options: leave Elphame, or stay and surrender her Fae essence."

"Seems extreme. What did she choose?"

"She chose to give it up. You must understand. If Fae believe they can freely mess with human lives, it won't take long before magic-kind enslave them altogether. The first step isn't small. Tinker Bell interfered with nine lives. In essence, she played God. She knew the punishment even then, yet did it regardless. Unfortunately, her father's waywardness enabled her."

"I pity her, all the same. Either path strips away a key part of who she is. And from experience, I know what a sorry place that is to be."

"Then you might struggle with what I have to say next. Father proposed that the Fae essence be given to you. The vote was unanimous. If you want it, it's yours."

My lips part, and I stare at him, waiting for the laugh that never comes. "You're serious?"

"Dead serious. Your choice to show mercy over vengeance, not only with Tink, but with James, says you're the perfect candidate. What Tinker Bell did was horrid. But maybe this is an unexpected blessing. You and Peter could live as equals." He studies me, eyes searching. "What do you say?"

"I don't know." I stand and step away. "Do I age?"

"Of course." He chuckles. "Fae age, in a decade or so, you'll notice time slows. You and Peter could share a long life together, exploring the world and seeing its wonders. Don't you want that?"

I stare at my hands, envisioning them aging, the skin wrinkling with time. Could I bear to stay as I am while everyone I love fades to dust?

Yet—Peter.

What I wouldn't do for him? Shall *he* be the one to watch *me* turn to dust? And with that thought, I know the answer.

"I'll do it."

"Really?" He rises and takes my hands. "You will?"

"Yes. I may regret this, but... I love that boy. I'll do anything for him."

"Okay... wow. Great! Uh, when would you like to have it done?"

"How about now? Everyone's distracted; no one will notice we've disappeared. Besides, if I wait, I might lose my nerve."

"Now?" He blinks, then nods. "Alright. Let's do it now. We'll need to travel to Elphame, but it won't take long."

He reaches into his pocket and lifts out his dust bag, taking a handful. "By tomorrow, you won't need this to fly."

He blows, and the dust settles onto my hot skin like a cooling breeze. "Let's go, doll."

We're just about to take off when a voice calls from behind, "Whoa now, where are you two sneaking off to?"

I turn to see Henley, Grace, and Tiger Lily trailing toward us.

I glance at Kit, who raises the bag again. "The more the merrier."

"Yeah, I'd say so. We've got a quick stop to make," I say. "Want to come with us?"

"Where to?" Grace asks.

"Elphame."

"But we just left there this morning," Tiger Lily points out.

"I know. This wasn't planned. Kit can explain on the way."

Henley tilts his head. "Are we going by car, or…?"

Kit strolls to them and blows the dust across all three. They blink, wave it away, surprised—then slowly begin to lift off the ground.

"What is happening?" Grace holds out her arms, looking around.

"You dear Grace, are about to fly," Kit answers. "Now, think of your greatest joy in life."

Henley and Grace exchange a look, then rise higher together. Tiger Lily stares down at the ground, then up at Kit. Her body begins to lift.

Kit narrows his eyes playfully. "Why are you looking at me like that?"

"No reason." She blushes.

He points to himself. "I'm not your happy thought, am I?"

She giggles and rises further. He glances at me, and I follow after her. "I think that's your answer."

We soar into the sky, past the clouds, our fingers brushing the edge of heaven. Grace spins upside down, her hair splaying toward the earth, the wind whipping through it. Henley, realizing the extent of his ability, zooms ahead, circling her, like bees around the bluebells.

"I saw Tiva in my old bedroom," I say to Tiger Lily, who flies alongside me.

"You kept her?"

"Of course. She was always my favorite."

"I still have Jane," she replies. "I'll give her to my daughter some-day—something special to pass down."

I glance at the gold bracelet on my wrist, wondering what made it special to my grandmother. Perhaps it, too, was given by a dear friend.

"If I have a daughter," I say softly, "I'll give her my doll as well. And when they're old enough, they'll play together, just as we did."

"Now we just have to have daughters." She chuckles.

Kit shoots to her side. "If everyone wants to gather around, I'll fill you in on what's next."

Grace and Henley drift closer, listening in awed silence as Kit shares about the plan. At last, we reach the mist and cross into Elphame, where he leads us to the grove of Elders.

"Will they join us?" I ask, nerves creeping in.

"No. There's not a specific place for something like this, but it felt right. I'll be back shortly with Tinker Bell. She's... detained at the moment. After though, she'll be free again."

He flutters off, leaving us in the shadowy hush of the grove.

"Shouldn't Peter be here?" Grace asks.

"He left," I say. "And honestly, it's probably better. I'd be far more anxious if he were."

"Did you tell anyone else about this?" Henley lowers himself into one of the wooden chairs.

"No. It was sudden. Kit mentioned it, and I agreed. You caught us just as we were leaving. I didn't want to lose my nerve."

Tiger Lily leans over the table, brushing her fingers over the four symbols carved in the center. All around us, glowing glyphs spark to life across the ground.

"Whoa." Henley steps back, eyes darting over the light.

I stare at the glyphs, mesmerized until it hits me—I haven't told Grace about her father. And there's no better moment than now. "Grace, could I talk with you?"

"Sure." Her brows draw together. "Is everything okay? You sound uneasy."

"Come sit." I gesture to the table. "You too, Tiger Lily, Henley."

We gather close, the three of them watching me expectantly.

"I am uneasy," I admit. "There's something I need to tell you."

"Okay." She takes Henley's hand. "I'm ready."

"Last night, James brought me to Winter Woods. As you know, he freed my father, but after that, he brought us to your home."

Her voice drops. "I think I know where this is going."

"James gathered his companions there. They packed their things and fled on the *Jolly Roger* at dawn. Your father asked me to tell you he loves you, and he's so very sorry."

Her lips tremble, eyes brimming with tears.

"He was broken about it all night. But he knew if he stayed, he'd end up in prison for his part. So he and Canary left together."

I glance at Henley. "He also wanted me to tell you he gives you his blessing. His only comfort is knowing you'll be together."

Henley nods and gathers Grace into his arms, where she weeps. My heart aches for her, but I know this is better than watching her father be locked away for life.

I think of Chas, hips swaying as he danced through his beloved restaurant. Jill and Cecco, laughing giddily at their own jokes, sipping wine, and strutting across the Back Room. Smee and Rose doting on us each time we stepped into the Bakehouse. Canary, joining us for flapjack breakfasts at the diner, leaving us breathless with giggles. And Gentleman Starkey—cigar in mouth, content in his own quiet world, full of pride for his daughter and peace in his life.

They were all tangled in the chaos, yet carried their own unique charm.

Who would I be now if I didn't have my father, Morgan, Andrew, or Bea around reminding me of truth? These steady souls who never wavered, no matter what. Without them... who would I have become?

Even the best of us can lose our way. It's frighteningly easy, one wrong choice, then another—until you hardly recognize the person staring back at you. My younger self was bitter. Had she stepped back in alone, there would have been little mercy. But I'm not who I was, and I'm forever grateful for that.

Two figures appear at the edge of the circle, and I rise, heart pounding.

"We're here," Kit announces.

Tinker Bell stands beside him, scanning the grove, her mouth drawn tight.

"Wendy." Kit gestures. "Please, come here. Tinker Bell, beside her."

She and I step toward one another, eyes locked. "You don't have to do this," I say.

"Yes, I do. I could leave, keep it all. But then I lose my family. My people. I've thought it through, and then thought it through some more. Ultimately, my uncle lent me some perspective. My father's not someone I ever wanted to emulate... and yet, I did. I'm ashamed of that. So, this—" she gestures faintly, "—this is my choice."

A wry smile touches her lips. "Who knows? Maybe someday, if I behave myself, some old Fae, nearing the end, will think I'm worth giving their gift to."

"I hope so."

"Okay," Kit interjects. "Let's begin. Tink, if you will."

Our hands find each other, fingers interlacing.

"**Trado essentiam meam,**" she begins, her voice calm and steady.

"*I surrender my essence,*" Kit translates.

"**Huic animae dignae.**"

"*To this worthy soul.*"

"**Sit ipsa digna.**"

"*May she be worthy.*"

She extends her hand to Kit, who motions for me to do the same. He holds his hands over them both, and a thin slit opens across each palm, blood seeping to the surface. Then he presses our hands together.

"**Sanguis ad sanguinem,**" he declares. "**Essentia ad essentiam. Fata ad hominem.**"

In a quiet voice, Tinker Bell echoes, *"Blood to blood, essence to essence. Fae to human."*

A pale blue flame shimmers between our joined hands, and I sense it instantly—a tingle spreading up my arm and into my body. A minute passes. The light fades, and Tinker Bell collapses backward, Kit catching her with ease.

"You good?" he asks, tenderness in his tone.

"I will be. I take it I don't have to return to confinement?"

"No. You're free. Father said he'll see that you receive dust. That should help some."

"Uncle is far kinder than he needs to be." She stares at the ground, then lifts her gaze to me. "Is Peter okay?"

"He will be, in time."

"I should've told him long ago. Please... tell him how sorry I am."

"No," I say firmly. "You can tell him yourself."

A light stirs in her. "Okay. I will. When he's ready." She turns to go, but pauses. "I'm sorry for what I said to you, and for taking your memories. I knew he'd never be mine, but still... I'm learning to be thankful he's found joy again, even if it's with another."

"I forgive you. What happened to you both was despicable. I'm sorry for the pain your father caused, and I can only pray the future is brighter without him in it."

Her palms hit the sides of her legs, and she disappears into the woods—not flying, but walking, each step silent.

"You okay?" Tiger Lily touches my arm.

"Everything feels fuzzy. Not sure if that's normal."

"Passing the Fae essence isn't a common occurrence," Kit explains. "But it does happen, usually when a Fae nears death. Like Periwinkle with Peter."

"I thought becoming a queen was grand, but gee." Grace shakes her head. "This far surpasses that."

"I don't know if I should say congrats or what." Henley pulls me into a hug.

"Goodness... what do you suppose my parents will say?"

"Let's get you home and find out." Kit lifts his dust bag once more, coating the others in shimmering gold, but not me.

Then, we're up and flying, but as we break through the mist and into the sky, I have to push away the mounting unease.

"You sure you're okay? Kit asks, drawing near.

"What exactly is about to happen to me?"

"The next twenty-four hours are a bit unpredictable as your body transitions. Truthfully, not sure what to expect."

I bob my head, continuing on, mind a whirlwind of emotions. I know what's next, and can only hope I have the strength for it.

Landing in the open courtyard beside the terrace, Grace leans against a railing. "I need a drink, come on, Lily."

Tiger Lily laughs, and they run up the stairs, disappearing into the palace where the music and laughter echo out.

"A drink sounds good." Henley slips up the stairs and through the wide-open double doors.

"Now that we're alone." I turn to Kit. "Where's Peter?"

"Why do you ask?" He shoots me a sidelong glance.

"I'm going to him, so please tell me where he is."

"First: no, you're not. Not in your condition. You're going to bed. Second: No, you're *really* not. It's dangerous, and I'd be destroyed by Father and Peter if I helped you."

"Fine." I lift into the air, lids low as I stare down at him. "I'll find them myself. Let my parents know where I've gone."

I flip around as Kit groans and follows after. "Will you stop! I'm trying to help you. Where he and Father went is no place for you."

"I don't care; I go where he goes."

"And how do you plan on finding them?"

"I don't know. But I can take an educated guess."

He floats in front of me, blocking my path. "Where?"

"Winter Woods. That's where the Aether Dew is. So, I imagine that's where Tahreek is, too."

"You're smarter than I give you credit for," he mutters. "Okay, fine, I'll take you."

"Did I hear you say we're going back to Winter Woods?" a voice asks behind us.

I spin around, and Henley watches, a knowing smile on his face. "Yeah, I saw you sneak away."

"Well then." I reach out, grabbing hold of his hand. "Looks like we're all on the same page. Let's go."

Chapter 31

Our journey to Winter Woods takes longer than expected, and as the Neverpeak Mountains loom in the distance, icy air nips at my cheeks, fatigue hitting hard. Why hadn't I grabbed a coat before we left? A shudder runs through me, the need for warmth growing by the second.

Below, the gate stands open, multiple car tracks half-coated with snow, leading away from town. Flashes of yellow flicker ahead, and I whisper a prayer that our friends escaped. How strange, to fly so easily over the high walls that once kept us in, the same walls I once dreamt of getting beyond.

And yet, here I am, soaring straight back in. Perhaps the dumbest impulse of my life.

We halt mid-air, an explosion ripping through the night, the impact twisting my insides.

"What was that?" Henley clutches my arm.

"Clean-up," Kit says. "Assuming Father got help from King Gilberto, we'll witness the end of the Anathema within the night."

"So, what's the plan?" Henley's shoulders quake from the cold.

"Get Peter and get out." I flex my fingers. "But we'd best find something warm because your lips are blue and my hands are frozen."

"We'll land near Main Street, find coats, and keep a low profile," Kit calls, shooting ahead.

Returning with James felt strange, but this—this is otherworldly. Kit begins the descent until our feet touch the snowy ground: no boots, no coats, nothing. How I could have lived here so long and still forgotten its all-consuming chill is beyond me.

I look around Fourth Avenue, once alive with glowing windows and smoking chimneys, the occasional shout of children's laughter. Now it's gone. I'm grateful they left, but somehow the stillness leaves me hollow.

The clash of Fae and Pixie echoes from a street away, sharper, nearer, giving me pause. "Do the Anathema have any real chance?"

"They have dark magic," Kit says. "But King Gilberto's pixie power plus our Fae gives us the upper hand."

"*Psst! Wendy?*" A voice calls, and we spin around. Henley nods toward a dark cottage across the street.

"It came from that direction."

"Well, of course!" I tug his hand, heart quickening. "That's Reverend Andrews' house!"

The door cracks open, and Bea peers through. "Come, come, all of you. Quick!"

We hurry inside, the living room glowing dimly from the hearth. Bea pulls me into a hug; her blonde curls tucked beneath a red scarf matching her dirt-stained apron. "We spent all day getting families out. So, why in the world have you come back?"

"We're here for Peter," I say. "He's out there, fighting with the Fae. What about you? You should be gone by now."

"You know Andrew." She sinks into her rocker, motioning for us to sit as a loud boom shakes the house. She sighs. "The man's got a heart of gold, out there now, finishing one last thing before we go."

"That's most unwise of him." Kit leans forward. "What's happening out there, it's—"

"Magic," Bea finishes. "Trust me, I know. So, if Peter's out there, surely you don't intend to join him?"

"I have to." I glide to the fire, warming my hands. "He's going to get himself killed."

"If that's the case, you're hardly dressed for the weather." She pushes up with a grunt, hand to her back as she shuffles to the closet. Flinging open the door, she rummages through a line of coats. "Donations for the poor."

She holds a navy-blue coat to my neck. "That should fit."

"Thank you." I squeeze her hand and pull it on while she finds coats for Kit and Henley.

"We knew change was coming." She hands a black coat to Henley. "Still, it's surreal having it arrive."

"You're not alone in that." I wander to the wooden shelves and pause before one of my favorite paintings, a golden lake at sunset. There's something about the laughter on the young couple's faces while splashing each other. Both are fully dressed, yet utterly carefree. There's a sense their joy was etched into the canvas, there whenever someone gazed at it. "I'm finding it hard to move on."

"Oh, well." She lifts the painting off the shelf, gazing at it fondly. "You have far grander things ahead, *princess*."

"News travels fast."

"What news is that?" She offers a cheeky grin and carries the painting to a half-filled box. "So much to do, so little time. You'd best get going, find that boy of yours."

"You and I are going to talk when all this is over," I whisper in her ear.

"I expect we will. And boy, do I have some stories to tell."

Pressing a hand to my back, she ushers us out, snow drifting gently down. I lift my collar, eager to find Peter and go home for good.

We cross the street and slip through a narrow passage toward Main Street, bins and boxes strewn from hurried departures. Before we step out, Kit holds up a hand, light exploding in front of us as full-sized Fae and Pixies streak past.

"How are we supposed to know who's who?" I shout.

"You aren't," Kit says. "You stay by my side and ignore all of this. We're here for Peter, nothing more."

A silver light spreads from him, wrapping around Henley and me.

"Stay close and you'll be fine. Leave the shielding, and I can't guarantee your safety, so please, don't."

We nod. The noise beyond deafening—pings, shrieks, the thunder of magic colliding. Most clash without weapons, sparks flying from their hands, but others hold glowing blades.

"That's Thomas' men," Kit says, leading us down the road, dodging the chaos, or 'clean up' as he rightly called it. Yet the further we walk, the thicker it gets.

"There's Father!" He motions to Will's Bakehouse, where King Clarion huddles beside Lord Malori. He hurries ahead, Henley close behind, but then someone touches my arm and I spin around.

Reverend Andrew!

"Heavens, you scared me!" I clutch my chest. "We saw Bea—you need to go back to her! It's not safe."

He glances around and pulls me into a shadowy corner. "I'm here for you."

"I don't understand."

"I had to give you something."

Glancing at Kit, he and Henley are with Clarion and Lord Malori now. "How could you even know I was coming?"

"It's a long story. But regardless, this is for you."

He draws a blade from his coat, pressing it into my hands. "An enchanted dagger. You'll understand its value soon."

I stare at it, then him. "Are you sure you're not a pixie in disguise?"

He smiles faintly. "It makes little sense, I know. But I was sent to help you."

"By God?" I whisper.

This causes him to laugh. "No, not this time. I can't explain the details, only that this person has been watching from afar."

My brows lower. Kit told me to stay close and ignore the fighting, yet Reverend Andrew, of all people, is offering a weapon meant to be used against someone.

"Who's this person, and why should I trust them?"

"I understand your hesitation. All I ask is that you trust me."

My fingers tremble, but I take the dagger. "What now?"

He shakes his head. "I've said all I can. You'll know soon enough. Remember, Psalm 23? *Though I walk through the valley of the shadow of death...*"

"I will fear no evil," I murmur.

"Yes. *For Thou art with me.* Courage and hope, child. He gave them to you long ago, and now's the time to lean on them."

"Come with me." I grip his wrist.

"I can't. It's time for Bea and me to go."

Questions race through my mind. How much do he and Bea really know? But he's already retreating, so I throw my arms around him, holding tight. "Thank you!"

"Few battles are worth fighting, but the greatest will always be for the soul. Remember that."

He squeezes my shoulder, then vanishes around the corner, just as another blast vibrates through me and I breathe out, fist clenched tight, ready to scream at someone, *anyone.* But then I see him. A cloaked figure in the street, his eyes fixed on me.

Prince Tahreek.

I knew him once, his charm, his easy smile. But that masquerade is gone. Now his gaze is icy, one finger beckoning to me. And I know, without a doubt, he's the reason Andrew gave me the dagger.

I step forward, the silver protection fading as I move away from Kit, yet neither he nor Henley has noticed, their backs remaining turned.

It's for the best.

Hovering now, I drift toward Tahreek, but he slips between two buildings facing an isolated street. *He wants me alone.*

I gaze at the dagger. Surely, this weapon signifies there's hope. *Hope and courage,* Reverend Andrew said. I press through the narrow stretch, and as I emerge on the other side, Tahreek pulls back his hood, revealing a youthful, pale face with a sharp jawline, high cheekbones, and black eyes—a face straight out of a nightmare.

He spreads his arms wide, the sleeves of his cape fanning out. "Is this a game to you?"

"Perhaps." I lift the weapon.

He lets out a bark of laughter. "A child's dagger?"

Opening his hand, a scarlet wave pulses at the blade, but nothing happens. "How odd. Where did you acquire such an item?"

"From a friend."

Though my voice remains calm, I'm about to be sick. What in the world does Reverend Andrew expect me to do next?

"Well, no matter. You won't have the chance to use it. Pity for you, you've come to me like a lamb to the slaughter."

He's right. I can't imagine any scenario ending with me gaining the upper hand.

"So," he sneers, "will you lie still while I make an end to you? Or shall I do to you what I did to the boy?"

A shudder rips through me, but I remain calm. "You assume wrongly that I'm a willing sacrifice."

At that, I shoot away, dizzy as I slip behind an abandoned car, still as a statue.

"Oh, I see," he calls out. "Little children do love games."

I peek up and he's searching, so I plop down again. I have no plan. But if I can draw him in the direction of the main street—

"There you are!" he hisses, appearing beside me, and I let out a piercing scream. But before his fingers grab hold, I dart again, heart pounding, surprised by my newfound agility. Even with my incredible speed, his power thrums behind me as I weave through the narrow lane between The Gilmour and Foggerty's Paper.

"Maybe I'll reset the boy again," he says, inching closer.

Ahead, Fae and Pixies clash, blasts of energy shooting between them. *God, let the impossible be possible!* I break into the open air and dive beneath the chaos, sparks flying around me. Through the haze, Tahreek loses sight of me. *Just like hide and seek.*

Gliding out the other side, I brace for his attack, but something captures his attention. Using the opportunity, I rise, soaring at him, dagger poised, willing myself to do what needs to be done.

End him!

Yet a voice draws my attention, and I see what stole Tahreek's focus. Peter's flying upward, one hand clamped around Thomas' neck as he spews profanities, his hands clawing at air. The sight paralyzes me. Then a blast ripples through my body, the pain wrenching a cry from my throat. Peter's head jerks sideways, eyes wide. Tahreek presses his hands to my chest and stomach, emitting a final shock wave shooting me to the ground.

Releasing Thomas, Peter swoops my way, leaving Thomas to plummet, his final scream cut short by a sickening crunch.

Peter gathers me into trembling arms. "No, no, no! What are you doing here?"

He holds my head, but I can't speak. I look at Tahreek, expecting another assault. But something is wrong. He struggles against unseen binds. Kit appears, waves of energy pulsing from his raised hands.

"Why did you do that!" Henley bends beside me, breathless. "You were supposed to stay with us!"

I offer a small smile, blinking, lids growing heavy. Peter holds me closer, heat radiating from his heaving chest. "Don't do this to me, Wendy!"

Darkness closes in. And for a moment, the world is silent. But then, *sounds of ice clinking against glass fills my ears. Nibs sits across from me, whiskey in hand. "Maybe this is your moment." He stares, intensity in his gaze. "The moment you finally comprehend what you're capable of."*

My hand begins to vibrate, a cool sensation flooding my fingers. *Is this a dream?* I squint. Snowflakes fall gently around me. Peter's forehead rests against mine, his tears wetting my skin. I tilt my neck. The dagger in my palm is glowing yellow; the power from Tahreek's attack is seeping out of me and into the weapon.

"It's leaving!" Peter grips my wrist. "What is that thing? Where did she get it?"

"I don't know," Henley says, looking to Kit.

The last of the energy drains away, and I drop the dagger as it sears my skin. Attempting to push up, Peter guides me to my feet.

"I'm okay," I rasp, taking an unsteady step forward, Peter's arm still firm around me.

"You idiots!" Tahreek snarls. "My men will swarm you like flies." He lifts his chin and releases a shriek. I press into Peter, bracing, but nothing happens.

"No one's coming," King Clarion says, stepping forward. "I've ensured our privacy. It's over, son."

Tahreek's nostrils flare. "Where's my father? You wouldn't dare touch me without his say-so."

"But that's where you're wrong. Wendy." King Clarion looks to me. "He's yours, darling. Do what you think is best."

My father's words echo: *Do what you think is best.*

With Nell, there was no question. But what about Tahreek? I twist and reach for the blade, still blazing yellow. Was it made to end his life, or to save mine? I glance at Peter, attempting to read his expression as he looks at the weapon, then me, brows drawn.

"She's afraid." Tahreek chortles. "Do the dirty work yourself, old man."

"I'm not afraid," I say coolly.

"Maybe not." He looks at Peter. "But the boy, he's been dreaming of this moment. Haven't you? Would you like to know whose idea it was to change you? To destroy everything about you?"

Peter's jaw tightens. Tahreek licks his lips, cat-like. "Do you suppose she's told you everything they did behind closed doors?"

"Silence!" Kit roars, forcing Tahreek's mouth shut, yet the corner lifts, amusement evident.

"Don't let him get to you." I whisper to Peter. "What do you want me to do?"

"This isn't my decision." He takes both of my hands. "What's in your heart?"

I pause and Reverend Andrew's words, come to mind. "The greatest battle will always be for the soul," I murmur. "There's justice, and mercy. And then, there's *rebirth*." I look Tahreek in the eyes, calm settling through me. "Clarion, will you do something for me?"

"Anything."

"Make Tahreek into an infant."

Tahreek's face twists.

I step closer, self-assured. "You will live again, as a new man, with a new purpose. And he will *never* know the wretched creature you've become."

His cheeks flush crimson, as his shoulders thrash uselessly. Death is clearly more desirable than the fate I've chosen. Clarion walks behind him, nodding slowly, placing his palms over Tahreek's head. "Son, may the man you become be grateful for the gift you've been given today."

Light swells, Tahreek's eyes meet mine, widening, mouth dropping open. Then the light engulfs him, too bright to bear, and I shield my face.

A cry cuts through the air—the cry of an infant.

When I lower my hands, a red-faced baby lies on the ground, wrapped in a thick cloth, wailing. Peter bends and lifts the child, all of us leaning forward to see what's become of Tahreek.

"Clarion, where's my son? I heard him!" A booming voice rings out. King Gilberto charges down the street, stopping before us, gaze fixed on the baby. "Where did this child come from?"

"Give him to me, Peter," I say, softly.

He passes the infant over, and I turn to Gilberto. "Sir, this is your son."

His intensity melts at my words. "He's been given a second chance," I continue. "Please, don't waste it."

Breath hitching, he takes the child into his arms. "I don't know what to say." The baby calms. "I couldn't forget this face. So many restless nights, staring at him, hoping for the man he'd become." He swallows hard. "What if he doesn't change? What if he's destined to fail again?"

"No. He's not bound to his past." Peter wraps an arm around me. "Tahreek is gone, but your son remains."

Gilberto exhales an unsteady breath and looks at me, eyes round. "When I left, my wife begged me to bring him home safe. I told her I couldn't promise that. He made his choices. But so did you. I'm in your debt."

"I have to believe there's a soul inside worth saving." I glance at the dagger in my hand.

King Clarion places an arm around the pixie king, and together they vanish into the crowd of onlookers.

It's over...

I look back at Kit, Henley, and Peter, all a bit shell-shocked. "Well," I say, releasing a shaky laugh, "that was something else."

Then a flash of red fills my vision, and, like a dream, she's there before me. Same dress as the day she died, hair fluttering in the breeze.

Margaret.

"Told you you'd get out of here," she says, her voice silvery.

My mouth goes dry as the world sways, knees buckling, and Peter catches me. "Whoa, now. What's wrong?"

She still holds the familiar sparkle in her hazel eyes, and though I know this can't be happening, it feels achingly real to me.

"What's got you, Wendy?" Henley looks around.

Tears gather and spill freely as I whisper, "*Goodbye*."

She steps closer, pressing a warm hand to my cheek, her heat radiating through me. "*Fly high*."

Turning, she fades in a burst of ruby red, and all at once, so does the world.

Chapter 32

Time no longer holds meaning as I drift in and out of consciousness. My lids lift, sunlight streams through a window, warming my face. Then darkness. A voice speaks to me. Then silence.

I blink and gaze up at the ceiling, but white blurs to black.

I'm not in pain—no, it's as though I'm not in my body at all. I'm weightless. Mother's beside me, asleep in the rocking chair, a book resting on her chest.

She vanishes.

Father appears, leaning on his elbows, speaking in low tones to John. They catch my stare and hurry to me, faces alight with hope, then they too fade, and I return to the twilight world.

My eyes flutter, and he's there. Sitting beside me. Staring.

Peter.

My heart leaps—feeling returning. His lips lift as our gazes meet, then he's gone. *Blast!*

A soft, warm voice drifts to my ears.

"Beautiful dreamer, out on the sea
Mermaids are chaunting the wild lorelie;

My fingers flex. Toes wriggle.

"Over the streamlet vapors are borne
Waiting to fade at the bright coming morn"

My eyes flash open, and I sit, gasping. "Where am I?" My pulse races.

Peter stands at the foot of my bed, caught mid-step. I'm in my old room, likely my parents doing. No doubt they're unaware what happened here. Striding to the bed, he collapses beside me. "What the hell did you do to yourself?"

I study his face. "Are you upset?"

"How could I be? You and me, endless time. Freedom beyond anything you've ever known. No, I just didn't expect it, much less to see you battling it out with my lifelong enemy."

He wraps a hand behind my neck, drawing me close, and I kiss him—desperately—his scent, his taste, all of him reviving me.

"I'm so sorry," I murmur between kisses.

"Why?" His lips trail my cheek.

"Kit told me what happened that day. It meant nothing to me, I swear it. I'm sorry."

"Don't be sorry." He rolls onto his back; fingers pressed against his eyelids. "Whether I liked seeing him kiss you or not, I get it. And seeing how he sacrificed everything for you... I can't even be angry with the guy. No, it was just everything compounding after what we learned about me."

I roll onto the pillow beside him. "I won't deny that when you sent me away, it was crushing. And then when Kit told me you left... well, I'm just thankful you're here now."

"Where else would I be? No one's loved me the way you have." He glides a finger along my chin. "I was angry, felt like an imposter in my own body. That man didn't just lose his memory like we did; he lost everything. And though I'm recalling bits of his life, Clarion is right—I'll never fully be him again."

"Whoever he was, he didn't deserve it," I say. "When the curse broke, I came face to face with my younger self. She was angry and hurt, and if I'd let her take over, she would have tortured me to no end for what was taken. Just know, whoever you are now, you're not an imposter."

"When I left with Clarion, all I wanted was revenge. It was stupid, and I'll never forgive myself for nearly getting you killed."

"Speaking of killed. Thomas—is he?"

"He's dead. I didn't mean to. But when I heard your scream, nothing else mattered."

"I'm sorry my actions led you to do that."

He presses his forehead to mine. "Thomas is dead, Tahreek's been given a fresh start, and who knows where Dash is off to. For now, I suppose we can find peace knowing two of the three will no longer hurt us."

"Agreed."

"I realized these last couple of days, watching you, I wouldn't exist if it weren't for what Tahreek and Dash did. It sounds mad, I know, but because of them, I have you. So, though I ache for the man I once was." He grips my hands. "I wouldn't trade this for anything."

"What they meant for evil, God used for good," I murmur.

"What's that?"

"A verse Morgan shared the night Juke grabbed me. It seems painstakingly true in your life."

"I suppose it does."

"So, what now? How do we move on?"

"We accept our past and embrace our future. And I know exactly how I intend to spend mine."

Time seems to slow as he lifts a ring from his pocket and takes my hand, gently slipping it on. "You're my world, Wendy. Marry me and be mine evermore?"

So many moments have brought me joy, yet none compare to this. The ring is delicate, golden vines wrapping around my finger, twining toward a gleaming blue topaz. It's beautiful, but it's not what brings me happiness.

"Didn't I already say I'd marry you in a heartbeat?"

"Are you certain?" He searches my face.

"I love you. That is my yes."

And it's true. Where my yes once relied on the freedom I'd gain because of it, this is different. Peter has already given me all I could desire—his heart. And I've given him mine. We could live in Winter Woods, a desert, or a palace, and it wouldn't matter in the least.

All that matters is him, with me. And I have this.

Lifting me into his arms, I don't know if it's he or I who is floating upward, but it doesn't matter. We rise together, our tears mingling blissfully with our kiss.

Six months ago, Peter placed a ring on my finger. And because of that, today is bound to be the most magical day of my life—the day we become one.

Grace, Tiger Lily, JaneAnn, Morgan, and Maimie all watch me, each clothed in soft green, semi-sheer gowns with short puffed sleeves and skirts lightly grazing the ground. Braided into their hair are crowns of ivy and baby breath; they look divine.

Behind them, a harp swells just beyond a lace curtain strung across a wooden archway, stretching the grassy aisle, painted with pale pink rose petals, where Peter awaits.

Morgan touches my shoulder, utmost pride in her eyes. She's lovely, a rounded belly with new life growing within. She and Nibs' secret elopement surprised us all, but nothing compared to the sheer delight from the news of their child.

"You ready?" she asks.

"I've been ready a long time." I gaze down, surveying myself one final time.

For my wedding dress, I opted for an airy, ivory gown with gentle puffed sleeves and delicate lace cinching at the waist, giving way to a flowing, floor-length satin skirt that trails behind me like mist. It captures the wonder of soaring through the clouds, far above land and sea, with Peter by my side, nothing holding us back.

It's time.

Maimie steps forward first, pressing through the lace curtain, then Morgan, Tiger Lily, and JaneAnn. Grace flashes me a grin. "See you out there."

Father's fingers tighten around mine, nerves rising as he guides me forward, the curtain parting in the center, the soft creak of chairs as the guests stand.

I can't believe this is happening.

The sensation is like stepping into a new world. Lightness overtakes me, my heart pounding—until I see him, the man who holds my heart. The man who will protect me no matter the cost, and the one person I would follow to the ends of the earth.

"I love you," Peter mouths, and the nerves dissolve, calm flooding in as I mouth back, "I love you."

Beside Peter stands Nibs, John, Michael, Kit, and Henley, each somewhere between grins and tears. How I adore these boys. I gaze around as Father guides me down the aisle, taking in the faces of so many near and dear who stand on each side of the walkway.

Tiger Lily's parents sit with Lean Wolf, and beside them King Clarion, Queen Florabelle, and the other Elphame Elders. Tinker Bell declined the invitation, though Kit said he suspected she was watching from afar.

Many from Winter Woods were invited, including some of the girls from the Academy, Madam Esme, Clara and Laurence, Henley's family, and, of course, Ms. Diana and Uncle Theo.

Then there's my dearest friends, Slightly and Tootles, teethy grins on their faces—Slightly offering a thumbs up, and Tootles pumping his fist, as though I've finally achieved something in life. Beside them are the four—Agnes and Jack, and Elizabeth holding onto Alexander. The girls stare dreamily, as though they're as caught up in the moment as I am. Hannah sits with her parents, cheeks pink with delight.

A few of James' group watches on, all of whom I insisted on attending. Gentleman Starkey, Canary, Smee, Rose, Chas, and of course, Cecco and Jill.

After these, there are the royal officials and the staff, like Rosetta and her mother. People I grew up around and now find great satisfaction in having here today.

Lastly, stand Mother and Bea, one my mother and the other a woman who made me feel like a daughter. They laugh like little girls as they dab their wet eyes, both beaming with pride. Gazing past them to the end of the aisle stands Reverend Andrew, clothed in a white robe. He catches my gaze, full of quiet pride, aware of the journey it took to get here.

Father places my hand in Peter's and kisses my cheek. "A father's love knows no bounds, but I pass you to one who may just rival that."

"Indeed, he might," I say. "I love you, Father."

He slips to my mother's side and pulls her close, the two gazing on, their faces a reflection of my own heart.

"Sweet little Bird." Peter winks. "Shall we?"

"We shall."

The ceremony is a dream as we speak our vows, and like the silver thread on my needle, weaving torn fabric into something new and beautiful, we bind our lives together as one. Magic is real—it's here, right now, in this place, where he and I have formed the most sacred trust.

Certainty may not exist in life, but love does. And truly, this is where the true magic blooms.

*　*　*

The lunch my parents host is nothing short of elaborate, and I waste no time piling my plate: smoked salmon on buttered brown bread, thick, creamy pumpkin soup, tender lamb with crisp roast edges, honey-and-thyme glazed carrots, and to finish, a slice of fruitcake, so moist it practically melts in your mouth. Champagne and fine wine flow freely, leaving everyone in an even better mood—if that's possible.

Peter and I barely notice the others as I rest my head against his shoulder, my arm snug around his, the world fading.

"I could stay in this moment forever," I murmur, pressing our fingers together.

"Food, drink, and my beautiful bride... yes, I imagine I could too."

"You're supposed to say something sappy, like, 'I could feast on your beauty forever.'"

"Nothing sappy about that." He kisses my forehead. "I adore you, and I *could* feast on your beauty forever."

"Peter!" John strolls to the table. "Lean Wolf was hoping to hear about the attack on the Anathema. Come on over when you have a minute."

"Perhaps another time," Peter says.

"No," I interject. "You go on. I'll get a refill and meet you over there. It's probably important to spend a little time with our guests. Right?"

"You sure?" He tilts his head, already rising.

"Yes, go on now." I stand and lift my glass. "Be over soon."

"Okay." He grabs me around the waist and pulls me in, kissing slow but sure.

"Dang." John groans. "I know you're married, but I'm still your brother. Have some decency."

"Sorry." Peter licks his lips, eyes glinting. "Just don't want her forgetting me again."

"That's hardly possible." I nuzzle my nose against his, while John makes a vomiting sound. Shooting my brother a look, I stroll away from the two and head to the drink table, where a young waiter pours a glass of red wine for Rose.

"Hello," I greet, holding my cup out.

"Oh—," Rose startles slightly, cheeks paling. "I didn't see you there. Hello! And congratulations."

"Thank you." I lift my cup and take a sip, the wine smooth and cool. "I was grateful Father allowed you all to return for the wedding."

"I am too." She drifts away from the table, and I follow.

"How have things been?" I ask.

She stops, gazing at the incline that leads to the water where the *Jolly Roger* rests.

"Things haven't been easy," she admits, "but it's not a day for such talk. Today's a joyous occasion. One I'm grateful to be part of."

"Don't think that way. Just because it's my wedding day doesn't mean the world ceases to exist. Are things very difficult, living at sea?"

"We manage. Yes, it's a far cry from life in the Hills, but I can't complain. What I gained in Winter Woods was a gift, so I'm grateful for what I had while it lasted."

"Walk with me." I take her arm and we stroll toward the hillside. We follow the pathway that slopes upward, rows of sugar maples bursting with fiery orange and scarlet leaves. This autumn, I can't shake the sense that it's my very first, so Peter has made it his mission to bring me to these hillsides, where we sit with steamy mugs of cider, gazing across the vibrant forests, a blanket wrapping around us.

"You and your brother have known James since you were young, isn't that right?"

"Yes." She lifts her goblet for a sip. "We were all very close."

"So, how did you end up in Winter Woods then?" I settle on a fallen log, and she sits beside me.

"James. He had it set up for us. I worked at a bakery in Kirriemuir, so when provided with the building, it made sense."

"Is he…" I exhale. "How is he?"

She looks at me, something unspoken flashing across her face. "He loved you. And that's a pain that never goes away."

"I guess I hoped it would. That he'd move on, find someone else eventually."

"Did you…" She bites down on her lip. "Did you ever love him?"

"In a way. But just not the way he deserved."

"And are you not angry with him? I mean, he took your memories?"

"There was something about him that was so…lost. It often felt like he was trying to find himself as much as I was. So, I found I could never truly feel angry with him. Not when I examined my own behavior. Desperate people behave in desperate ways."

Emotion swells, but before she can speak, Bea strolls up. "I'm sorry to interrupt."

Rose runs a hanky across her cheeks. "Please, join us."

I can't tell if this is a genuine invitation or an escape from our conversation.

"I don't understand." Bea plants a hand on her hip, looking between us. "Long faces, the both of you?"

"We're pathetic, aren't we?" Rose smiles.

"Indeed, we are." I laugh. "But there's no reason. You'll be next in line to snag some dashing young man."

"Oh, no, I'm afraid that's impossible." Rose shakes her head.

"But why? Don't you want to marry someday?"

"I did once. But those days are long gone, and I'm confident they won't be back."

Bea bends in front of us, gripping our hands. "My dears, there are great joys ahead for both of you. Just you wait and see. Now, the King has an announcement to make and would like you there."

"I can't imagine what it's about," I say as Bea helps me up. "Shall we?" I hold out my arm, and Rose loops hers through it. There's something about her I admire. A quiet resilience despite all life has thrown her way. How I wish I'd gotten to know her better.

James' group gathers at the bottom of the hill, Grace clinging to her father, offering a tearful goodbye. A sadness fills me, knowing how excited she has been to spend this day with him. She buries her face in his chest as he rests his head against her hair.

"I have a proposition," Father says, clearing his throat, Mother beside him. "It's an opportunity to stay and begin again. I've received the council's agreement."

Starkey turns, shoulders lifting as the offer sinks in. "I'll do anything to remain. Anything at all."

"I hoped so. The council will meet in the morning to discuss it with you further."

Starkey glances at Grace, and they hug tighter as Ms. Diana joins them, kissing her brother's cheek.

"You can live with me, and it'll be just like old times, little brother."

"Gladly…" He holds both close.

"Anyone else interested?" Father scans the group.

"Will Cap'n be stayin' too, if he wishes?" Smee asks.

"I'm sorry," Father answers. "If it were up to me, yes. His sacrifice saved our land. But the council could not be persuaded. They view him and Thomas as the same."

"Well, beggin' yer pardon, sir, but the Cap'n, well, he's needin' us. And I belong at his side, right where I always been. But ye, kind sir." He turns to Gentleman Starkey. "Such a gentleman, you'll be sorely missed, that's for certain!"

The others echo his sentiment.

"And I suppose with that said, we'd best head back to our floating home," Chas says.

Their group offers Starkey heartfelt farewells, with Canary lingering as the last. Tears shine in her eyes, though they don't compare to the sorrow twisting Starkey's face.

"I love you, Canary."

A look of shock passes over her features, and he tugs her forward, kissing fiercely.

"Maybe I stay?" she whispers.

"No." He sniffs, shaking his head. "This is where we must part ways. For now."

"Why do I get the sense I won't see you again?" She glides a hand along his arm. "Don't make this goodbye."

"Worry not, you *will* see me again. I promise."

She throws her arms around him, and they remain a long moment until she breaks away. She looks at Grace, lifting a strand of her hair. "Well, my wild girl, it's been fun. Don't let them hold you back too much. Okay?"

Grace wipes a tear and hugs Canary. Canary's eyes close, then she pulls away and turns not looking back.

Starkey's shoulders tremble, and Grace holds him tight.

Bea steps forward, holding out a hanky and an envelope. "Go on and take these," she says, her voice tight.

"What is it?" Starkey asks, accepting them. He flips the envelope over, reading the scrawl across the front. "Is this...?" A breathless laugh escapes him.

"Yes." Bea nods. "Go on now, enjoy."

He pulls Bea into a tight hug. "Tell Andrew wherever he's preaching Sunday, I'll be there."

"It's about time." She chuckles as he lets her go.

"Well, if you'll excuse me a moment," Starkey says, slipping away, while Grace watches on, perplexed.

"Guess it's my turn," Rose says. "Thanks for the invite. It meant a lot."

"Of course. And are you sure you won't stay? We can get you and your brother set up in Silver Mist or anywhere you want."

She stares for a long moment, then sighs. "We're bound to James, Will, and I. Though starting over sure sounds nice."

"Come on, Rosie!" Jill calls. "Don't get left behind."

"Goodbye, Wendy."

"Goodbye, Rose." I lean forward, embracing her. Though she's stiff at first, she softens and smiles as she backs away.

Joining her brother, he takes her hand, and together they head for the water.

"If Peter's ever not good to you," Chas calls as they descend the hillside. "You send for me, darling."

"I wasn't aware you had such a line of admirers," Peter whispers in my ear, wrapping his hands around my waist.

"And not just Chas," Tiger Lily adds. "Did you ever hear about when Kit kissed your wife?"

"I have not." Peter clicks his tongue, gazing at Kit. "But perhaps he and I take a walk, and discuss it further."

Kit's cheeks burn bright red. "Now, now, sweetheart." He pats Tiger Lily's hand. "You know that was purely to make you jealous. No need to get me killed."

"Surely Peter wouldn't do that today of all days, love. But I'd watch your back if I were you." She pinches his cheek playfully, and they stroll away.

"What a beautiful day this has been," Morgan says, stepping beside me with Nibs at her side.

"Beautiful is the way you look, with that baby growing bigger every day." I place a hand on her stomach.

"Perfection, isn't she?" Nibs gazes at her, beaming.

"Your child will be blessed beyond all measure." I hug her, then Nibs. "I'm so pleased for you both!"

"As am I," Peter says. "You'll have to offer us your wisdom as an old married couple soon."

"Give us another few years first." Nibs chuckles.

"Did you know I saw my brother today?" Morgan says suddenly.

"Oh?" I glance at Peter. "And how is he?"

"Well." She inclines her head. "He's changed. Nibs brought me to the ship when it docked, and we spent an hour together. He was my best friend growing up, but once Thomas took over, he wasn't the same. He'd always ensure time with me during visits, but it wasn't like it had been. Still, when I was leaving, he said he might find his way home for the holidays... meet his nephew or niece. So, there's that."

"The ship is leaving now," Peter says. "Shall we go see it off?"

"No," Morgan answers. "I've said my farewell for now. You two go on, though."

"Proud of you, kids," Nibs says, and they stroll away, joining Tiger Lily and Kit at a nearby table.

"You sure about this?" I ask, as we ascend the hill.

"Watching your former sweetheart off on our wedding day? Of course."

Arriving at the crest, he steps back. "You know, I forgot to mention something to Nibs, you go on ahead."

"What? No way." I grab his hand. "I go nowhere without you."

"I'll just be a moment." He kisses my hand. "Go on now."

"Fine. But just be a minute."

He moves back down the hill, so I turn, walking to the edge of the cliff, gazing to where a rowboat treads across the sparkling water toward the *Jolly Roger*, anchored in the bay. Those on the boat sing loudly, their drunken voices ringing through the air. Upon reaching the ship, they climb aboard, and he appears from within the Captain's Quarters. *James*.

My heart twists at the sight of his hooked hand, the metal flashing under lantern light. He welcomes the group back, stopping to talk, likely learning of Gentleman Starkey's decision. Then they slip away, and he walks to the edge, fingers gripping the ledge—wind sweeping through his coal-black hair.

My body glows in a stream of soft orange light as the sun dips low on the horizon. *Does he see me?* He removes his hat, holding it to his heart, and, without thought, I lift my hand upward.

I'm about to pull it back when his arm rises, not up but out, as though reaching for me. How I wish I could see him smile, know he's happy in life. Yet as his hand lowers and he places the hat back on his head, I know I'll never be sure of that.

The anchor rises, the white sails unfurling. The ship no longer bears the flag with the Neverland Crest. It's been replaced by a daunting black flag bearing a skull and crossbones. It rustles softly in the breeze as James strides to the wheel, spinning it away from me, away from Neverland—into that great unknown.

I turn, and Peters stands watching me. "All set?" I ask.

He steps closer as the *Jolly Roger* vanishes into the sunset. "I imagine we'll meet with him again someday."

"I don't know if I want to..." I push the emotions down.

"There you both are!" Grace exclaims, arriving with Henley.

"Taking it all in?" Henley's hand clamps on my shoulder.

"Yes." I breathe. "The first night of our new life."

We all gaze out, quiet in the golden hush.

"So, what's next?" Kit strolls up, one arm draped around Tiger Lily and the other slipping easily around Henley.

"Does the offer still stand to move to Elphame after our wedding in a couple of months?" Henley asks.

"Indeed, it does." Kit's brows raise.

"Be warned," Tiger Lily says. "He tends to appear at odd hours with an insatiable urge to ransack your cupboards for sweets. I got quite used to this at my cottage in Winter Woods."

"First: there's nothing wrong with a friendly visit. And second, you wrongly assume the sweets were my motivation."

She beams at him. "Are you implying you were there to see me?"

Kit presses a kiss to her forehead, pulling her close. "Oh, my dear, did you just realize this?"

"Well, back to your offer," Grace says. "Do we humans change at all, living in Elphame long-term?"

"Uh... well, aging does slow down. A lot," he admits.

"There are certainly worse things in life than that." Henley shrugs.

"Wendy and I discussed the offer," Peter says, glancing at me. "And we'd like to take you up on it."

"Really?" Kit steps back, mouth widening. "Okay, great! Henley, Grace, what say you? Can we get the whole gang together again?"

"We agree." Henley chuckles, and Grace nods.

Kit whoops in triumph and pulls Henley into a hug.

"So, it sounds like we'll be celebrating Wendy's birthday in Elphame, with all of you as neighbors," Peter says.

"But wait, Tiger Lily, when will you arrive?" I ask.

"Trust me, I'm working on her," Kit says. "She'll be mine by the end of the year. Guarantee it."

"Maybe I will, maybe I won't." Tiger Lily bites back a grin, the wind lifting her hair.

"You know, I've been kind to you thus far, but no more." Kit swoops forward, scooping her into his arms and leaping off the cliff's edge as she shrieks in laughter.

"Where does a guy have to go to get that ability?" Henley mutters, shaking his head.

✳ ✳ ✳

Goodbye isn't truly goodbye, and this thought kindles my heart as we say our farewells.

"Well, sis." John wags his head lightly. "Can't believe you actually got a man to marry you."

"Couldn't have done it without your help." I pinch his side and he laughs, cheeks reddening.

"I suppose I did pick you up when you were down, huh? But that's what brothers are for, right? That and threatening to knock some sense into your husband if he's ever mean to you."

"I'll be good. You have my word." Peter holds a hand to his heart.

"Well, I'm still your man, Peter." John salutes. "So, the same goes for you—if my sister ever causes trouble, which she absolutely will, you just let me know."

"Loyal to the end, aren't you, Johnny?" I say.

Michael stares at me, emotion clouding his face.

"Now, now, Michael. Don't get weepy on me." I hug him. "I'll be back soon, and I'll bring lots of gifts from faraway places."

"Are you trying to buy my happiness?"

"Only if it works," I giggle. "You take care of Mother and Father, okay?"

"I will, sis." He stands straighter. "Love you."

"And I love you." I ruffle his hair.

Maimie is beside him, quick to wrap herself around me. "I'll miss you. Hurry back."

"I'll miss you too. Keep a watch on Michael, make sure he behaves."

She throws him a cheeky grin, which earns a dramatic eyeroll.

"Don't need no girlie telling me what to do," Michael scoffs.

"And yet without me, you'd have gotten the stuffing knocked out of you—how many times?" She pokes his chest.

I glance at Peter and pull a face before moving along to Jan.

"Don't be a stranger." She cups my chin. "I know you're married and all, but now that you can fly, I expect you by for tea once in a while, fill me in on all the Fae gossip."

"I'll be there, I promise." We hug. "Especially if Mam makes the cookies."

"I'm sure I can arrange that," she says, pulling away. "And hey..." She glances between Peter and me. "You two have come a long way, haven't you? From Wendy squashing your face with her journal to this... not bad. Not bad at all."

Peter touches his cheek, reflective. "Yes, quite the distance. But I don't rule out the potential for it to occur again. Not with her."

"Me? Be a good boy and you'll have nothing to fear." I kiss the same cheek.

Mother and Father are waiting for us at the end, and we turn to them, their faces amused as they watch.

"I am so glad this is how your wedding day turned out," Father says. "For a while there, I imagined it would look quite different."

"Ey, don't remind us, sir." Peter shakes his head.

"And I thought I'd miss it altogether," Mother says. "But this is just right."

"I love you both." I throw my arms around them, childhood memories flashing through my mind—bruises and sorrows, fears and joys. They were always there, their love able to heal whatever ailed me. And now, though I'm grown, it still carries the same warmth.

"Peter," Father says. "I know you're not my own, but you've always been like a son. And now, with great pride, you are."

"Thank you, sir... *Father*." They clasp hands. "It's an honor to become your son, and if Charlie were here, he'd be mighty pleased with his choice to make you king."

"Go on now before I cry again." Father gives us a gentle push.

Peter takes my arm, guiding us to the cliff, a slight spring in his step. When we reach the edge, he turns to me. "You ready?"

"You know," I say thoughtfully, "you once said you and I were one wrong step from total tragedy. Yet here we are, ten months later, married."

"Oh darling, you are whiskey to my flame." He bites back a grin. "But I'd drink you up all the same."

"Indeed. And what's a flame without a little spark? As for your question, I can't imagine what the future holds. But knowing you'll be there... well, you make me far braver. So, yes, I welcome the great unknown."

"Then Bird, let us step into it together."

He takes my hand and holds it tight as we step off the edge and into the air, our bodies rising, graceful toward the moon. I glance back, the cliff filled with everyone watching, waving. I wave back, then turn to Peter, his eyes reflecting the starlight. The enchantment has returned to Neverland. Our dreams have come to life, and time's no longer important. For so long, all I longed for was freedom. Freedom from the walls confining me, gates locking me in, and a curse holding me back.

And truly, it wasn't the walls crumbling, or the gates opening, or even the curse breaking that mattered in the end. It was me... embracing what was right in front of my face—the girl in the mirror.

My name is Wendy.

I have found my wings, and with them, I can leap onto the wind's back, embracing its velvety warmth and...

Away I go.

WENDYBIRD

Acknowledgements

My gratitude to those who have spurred me on in this journey is hard to express, but I will attempt to do so.

First, I thank my parents, George and Carol, my first audience. You patiently listened while I read my earliest stories aloud at the young age of seven, always offering encouragement when it mattered most, laying the foundation for all that was to come.

To my brother, Joshua David: your support from my youngest days, reading my first stories, cheering me on, and reminding me of my purpose, even in the scribbling, meant the world.

To my sister, Julianne: you truly believed in me when I needed it most as a teen, celebrating my potential even when I could not see it myself.

To Nicole, my writing bestie. Whenever insecurities held me back, you helped me break through, believing in me without hesitation. To you and Austin, thank you! Your encouragement and thoughtful insights shaped this journey more than you know.

To Russell, my husband: You are my constant inspiration and joy, and I would not be writing this without your unwavering love and support. The love stories I write are so real because of you. I love you!

To my darling children, Samuel Gene, Carolanne Faith, James Thomas, and Melody Grace.

You are my daily inspiration and boundless joy. I love you all!

And lastly, I wouldn't be who I am, have the passion to write, or the ability to create were it not for my Savior, Jesus Christ. Writing would have little value for me without the desire to share faith, hope, and love with the world around.

And to you, my reader, know what an absolute honor it is for me, that you spent your time and energy on my story. It means the world to me! Thank you!

Afterword

I'm thrilled to share this story, fully inspired by the brilliance of J. M. Barrie. Every element, from the enchanting locations to the characters, draws from Barrie's remarkable life and his masterpieces *Peter Pan*, and *Peter in Kensington Garden*. Additionally, I've woven in nods to his earlier work through *Sentimental Tommy*, which played a key role in his creation of Peter Pan. I thought, how funny would it be to have Peter Pan reading about Tommy, the character who later inspired him? Just a bit of writerly silliness there.

The iconic figure of Captain Hook is deeply influenced by Barrie's own creation, including inspiration from the suspected "real life" person who James Hook is believed to have been based on. More on that below.

My heartfelt wish with this story is to honor Barrie's legacy through themes of magic, memory, faith, love, and the value of growing up and letting go while learning to embrace who you are. Thank you for embarking on this journey with me. As Barrie once beautifully said,

"Those who bring sunshine into the lives of others cannot keep it from themselves."

—J. M. Wilday

Hidden and Not-So-Hidden References in *Wendybird*.
Peter Pan Inspiration

Peter's middle name, David, comes from J.M. Barrie's brother David, who passed away young and inspired Peter Pan's character.

JaneAnn, Hannah, Agnes, Elizabeth, Alexander – named after Barrie's siblings.

Margaret and Henley - Margaret Henley was daughter to J. M. Barrie's friend, poet William Ernest Henley. She called Barrie "fwendy" before passing away at the age of five. Barrie named Wendy in her honor.

Jack – John (Jack) Llewelyn Davies

Llewelyn – Barrie became the unofficial guardian of The Llewelyn Davie boys: George, Peter, John, Michael, and Nicholas.

King Barrie – named for the King of the Peter Pan universe, J.M. Barrie himself.

Ansel surname inspiration for Hannah and Margaret – after Mary Ansell, Barrie's wife.

Hodgson, surname inspiration for JaneAnn – after Mary Hodgson, nurse to the Llewelyn Davies family.

Captain Hook Inspiration

Barrie once wrote,

"'Hook' was not his true name. To reveal who he really was would even to this date set the country in a blaze."

This line has led many to speculate Hook's character was secret royalty or noble. Historical hints suggested inspiration from Charles II. My version of James Hook in *Wendybird* draws from the theory that Hook might be Lord James Beauclerk, grandson of Charles II and Nell Gwyn.

Thomas Blood Influence.

Some 19th and early 20th century writers imagined Thomas "Colonel" Blood, the Crown-Jewel thief and Irish adventurer, kidnapped, mentored, or trained a young noble of Stuart blood—often assumed to be *James Beauclerk*.

James Gwyn in *Wendybird*

So with the story ideas flowing, I created the character of James Hook you find in Wendybird. His personality and appearance are mainly inspired from *Peter Pan*. Though I presented a younger, softer version retaining the "Gentleman Pirate concept lightly" while strongly incorporating Barrie's version with his tragic, obsessive traits and the ways he was haunted by past failures.

James' character is explored in greater depth in the following book, half captured from his POV.

Other Character Inspirations

Morgan Gwyn – originally called Canary, renamed from the list of pirates on the Jolly Roger.

Maimie Mannering and Grace – both characters from *Peter Pan in Kensington Gardens*.

Tinker Bell Films References

Winter Woods

Silver Mist – fairy character

King Clarion – taken from Queen Clarion

Periwinkle – Sister to Tinkerbell in the films.

Lord Malori – Inspired by Lord Milori, Lord of Winter Woods

James' Friends/Crew

Gentleman Starkey, William Smee, Chas Turley, Bill Jukes, Cecco, Cookson, Alf Mason, Foggerty, Noodler, Whibbles, Black Gilmour, Canary, Robert Mullins– All from the Jolly Roger crew in Barrie's book and stage play.

Additional Nods

Jill – a wink to Red-Handed Jill from the film *Peter Pan (2003)*

Lean Wolf, Tiger Lily, Chief Little Big Panther – All mentioned in the original Piccaninny Tribe in *Peter Pan*

Lilium – Latin genus name for "lilies".

Lady Clare – Picked for Rachel Clare Hurd-Wood, Wendy Darling in *Peter Pan 2003*

Lord Myron – Picked for Jeremy Robert Myron Sumpter, Peter Pan in *Peter Pan 2003*

Lord McLaurin and the bird Robin – Picked for Robin McLaurin Williams, Peter Pan in *Hook*

"The ticking has stopped." – This line was inspired by the Peter Pan novel. The ticking represented the crocodile's presence. The one who had taken Hook's hand. So it was used in this story as a nod to represent a similar idea of, "the end is nigh."

Locations

Moat Brae – Moat Brae the "birthplace of Peter Pan" Barrie credited the house and gardens as the inspiration for the magical world.

Kirriemuir – Kirriemuir Scotland, birthplace of J.M. Barrie

Dumfries- J.M. Barrie lived in Dumfries, Scotland

Number 14, Bloomsbury, in London, England – Straight from *Peter Pan*.

Solomon Caw's Pond – Taken from *Peter in Kensington Garden*

About the author

Joy M. Wilday was born and raised in Upstate New York. Writing since she first learned to spell, she spent countless hours from youth through adulthood sharing herself through stories and poetry. Blessed with an over active imagination, she would create imaginary friends, lavish stories for her stuffed animals, Barbies, and Polly Pockets. These tales were always flowing often making their way to paper, or later, the computer. The desire to write a book followed her since childhood, and now, at the age of 32, she brings that dream to life with her debut novel, *Wendybird*.

Living on the Emerald Coast of Florida with her husband Russell and their four children, they enjoy spending free time at the beach, biking, watching movies, playing video games, reading, crafting, and doting on their loveable furball cat, Mipha.

Joy is currently completing the next book in the *Second to the Right* series, continuing with James and Rose's story.

To follow and support her journey, find her on Instagram at jmwilday_author.

www.ingramcontent.com/pod-product-compliance
Lightning Source LLC
Chambersburg PA
CBHW061043310726

48969CB00004B/1064